P R

The Anatomy of Death

"Fans of Maureen Jennings's Murdoch novels will welcome Australian author Young's promising debut, inspired by an actual riot in 1910 London . . . [Young] delivers a truly surprising reveal of the murderer's identity." —*Publishers Weekly*

"Beautifully written and edited, with the historical genre handled with care . . . It was a joy to read and one I am so glad I didn't miss out on." —*Book Binge*

"A fantastically well-written historical mystery with a unique protagonist and rich period details . . . The best historical mysteries are those that manage to transport the reader to the past, envelop them in the complexity of a good mystery, and make them feel as if they know the protagonists so well that they can peek over their shoulders while collecting clues along the way. Felicity Young achieves this kind of excellence in *The Anatomy of Death*." —*Night Owl Reviews*

Berkley titles by Felicity Young

THE ANATOMY OF DEATH

ANTIDOTE TO MURDER

Antidote to Murder

Felicity Young

BERKLEY BOOKS, NEW YORK

THE BERKLEY PUBLISHING GROUP
Published by the Penguin Group
Penguin Group (USA) Inc.
375 Hudson Street, New York, New York 10014, USA

USA / Canada / UK / Ireland / Australia / New Zealand / India / South Africa / China

Penguin Books Ltd., Registered Offices: 80 Strand, London WC2R 0RL, England
For more information about the Penguin Group, visit penguin.com.

BERKLEY® is a registered trademark of Penguin Group (USA) Inc.
The "B" design is a trademark of Penguin Group (USA) Inc.

Berkley trade paperback ISBN: 978-0-425-25354-0

An application to register this book for cataloging has been submitted to the Library of Congress.

PUBLISHING HISTORY
Berkley trade paperback edition / May 2013

PRINTED IN THE UNITED STATES OF AMERICA

10 9 8 7 6 5 4 3 2 1

Cover art by Alan Ayers (Lott Reps).
Cover design by George Long.
Interior text design by Laura K. Corless.

ACKNOWLEDGMENTS

Thank you again to the usual suspects: Patricia O'Neil, Carole Sutton, and Christine Nagel. Also my talented editors, Janet Blagg, Deonie Fiford, Kate O'Donnell, and the gang from The Berkley Publishing Group. Thanks also go to my agents, Lisa Grubka and Sheila Drummond, for all of their support. The idea behind this novel may not have developed without the helpful staff at the Wellcome Library, London. Thank you, one and all!

When a doctor goes wrong he is the first of criminals. He has nerve and he has knowledge.

—SIR ARTHUR CONAN DOYLE

Prologue

I climb onto the bridge wall and sit just beyond the gaslight's beam. The iron weight of the Thames below draws me with a magnetic pull as powerful as my own impulses. How easy to jump, to fracture the murk and sink into the river's fetid embrace. Will I struggle? I like to think not, but who knows? Perhaps I will, when a reflex breath betrays me and invites the rushing waters in. I am unable to swim and the thrashing won't last long. My body will sink and rise again with none of the beauty of resurrection. Black, eyeless, and bloated, I will finally show my true form.

Big Ben strikes. Seven, eight, nine, ten. The clatter of traffic across the bridge has eased, though the heat still presses through the dark like the stink of the river in my nostrils.

I straighten my seat on the warm stone ledge and press my heels into the wall. Mortar crumbles like stale bread. I brace myself and prepare for the Gates of Hell.

"Come on, mister—t'ain't that bad."

I gasp and turn to face the voice.

"Nothin' a bit o' comfort won't fix, I reckon," another female voice chimes in. What is it to them? Is it the expensive cut of my tailcoat draped across the parapet, the sheen of my top hat sitting next to it? The bridge light shines on their painted faces. Their garish dress makes them almost identical clowns.

I glimpse the waif Jack, hanging about in the shadows. I'd given the boy a penny and told him to go home. He must have guessed my intentions and enlisted the help of these streetwalkers.

"Go away. Leave me alone," I cry, beads of sweat tickling beneath my shirt.

"Whatcha wanta do a fing like that for?" the larger whore persists, dropping a heavy hand onto my shoulder. I turn to shrug her off and find myself caught in the glare of the streetlamp.

The slighter one says, "Hey, Maisie, I know 'im—it's the doc. The geezer I been tellin' you about from the Satin Palace." She turns to the boy and cuffs him over the head, knocking his hat to the ground. "Why didn't you tell us that in the first place, you li'l rascal?" Then to her friend she says, "This is the gent what fixed me up when I worked there."

I squint at her through the unnatural light; perhaps the pinched face does hold a vague familiarity.

"Blimey," Maisie says. "We can't let a talent like that go to the river."

A shell bursts inside my head. I touch my temple and feel the throbbing scar, taste the cordite as it dissolves upon my tongue, and pray to keep the fit at bay. Please, God, not now.

"'*Now if I do that I would not, it is no more I that do it, but sin that dwelleth in me,*'" I recite. I abhor what I do, but seem unable to stop it. I slide down from the wall and stand at the large whore's side. The moment has passed.

Maisie looks puzzled; she does not know her Bible and that in itself grieves me.

A smile traces her lips. "Well, 'ooever does it do it, we're mighty grateful an' all." She links her arm through mine and I feel the heat of her flesh burning through my shirtsleeves.

The thin whore takes my other arm and with her free hand scoops up my hat and coat. "C'mon, Doc, there's nuffink a good shot o' gin and a bit o' comfort won't cure. We owe you that much at least. Get lost, scallywag."

I hear Jack's bare feet pattering into the darkness. God-forsaken boy.

"You don't owe me anything," I protest, but it is useless: the women will not take no for an answer. And neither will the Beast.

Chapter One

June 1911

It was unlike Pike to be late. Dody McCleland pulled out her fob again and frowned. She scanned the rattling traffic and was treated to a mouthful of dust and petrol fumes. Hansom cab, motor taxi, omnibus—or would he choose to walk? Not the latter, she hoped—not with that knee. Perhaps he'd been unable to find transport at all. There always seemed to be someone on strike these days. She should have sent Fletcher to pick him up in the Benz.

Dody had never experienced such a heat wave. The sun, felt more than seen, pressed invisibly upon the London streets, and the low blanket of smoke and cloud ensured that its heat stayed there, steaming like clams any foolish enough to linger in it. A fool she was not. Dody clung to her boater and was about to dash through a gap in the traffic to the shady side of the road when a hansom slid to a halt alongside her and out stepped a trim, suited figure.

Pike. He held his cane and small suitcase awkwardly in one hand and tipped his bowler with the other. "Sorry I'm late; the traffic was terrible." His northern accent, barely discernible for the most part, today sounded straight from Leeds. He turned to pay the driver.

Dody tried to hurry him up. "We'd better not dawdle. Surgeons don't like to be kept waiting."

He appeared not to have heard. For a moment he stood trancelike, watching the cab ease from the kerb to the jingle of harness and the clash of metal hooves on stone. She put a hand on his arm. "Matthew? It's going to be all right, you know. Mr. Barker performs this type of surgery almost every day."

"Of course it's going to be all right." He smiled, patted her hand, and pointed to the gate with his cane. "Shall we go in?"

They climbed the steps and passed into the hospital's front entrance. It was slightly cooler inside. Pike removed his bowler. He'd been sweating. Dark hair plastered his scalp.

Dody checked with the clerk at the desk that all was in order, then pointed towards a sweeping stone staircase. "Your ward is on the third floor, but we can take the lift, if you like."

"I can manage the stairs," he said. "In fact, I'll wager I reach the top before you."

Dody laughed, picked up her skirts, and followed at a brisk pace, allowing him to beat her by a hair's breadth.

"You held back," he said, panting. She waited with him near the lifts while he got his breath back. The odour of carbolic reached them from the ward.

"I won't be holding back for much longer. Once your knee is fixed, there'll be no stopping you. Soon you'll be leaving me for dead on that ridiculous bone-shaker of yours, or galloping off in a cloud of dust on a horse through the park—"

"I'd like to see you on a horse," he interrupted.

And I you, Chief Inspector, she thought, hoping the heat would mask her blush. How dashing he must have looked in his cavalry officer's uniform. "Off it, more like, and facedown in a soggy field. I'm not much good at riding, I'm afraid. My family were never part of that set," she said.

"I could teach you."

"You could try." She laughed. "That might be your greatest challenge yet."

The lift jolted to a halt, the metal cage clanked, and out stepped a nurse pushing an old man in a wicker wheelchair. The man had clearly been a soldier: a row of medals was pinned to his dressing gown and both his legs were amputated above the knee. Dody said good morning and the man replied with a friendly smile and a wave as the nurse wheeled him into the ward.

Dody looked at Pike. How pale he had become—was he recalling the trauma of his injury? She was visited with a sudden image of her sister Florence, ashen-faced after being force-fed at Holloway Prison. Unlike Florence, though, Pike refused to talk about his terrible experiences. This was part of the problem, she felt, and so typical of men who, like him, had fought in the South African war. He had taken a long time to agree to the operation, but it was at least a step in the right direction.

"One of your ward mates, I suppose; seems like a nice chap," she said, trying to jolly him along.

Pike said nothing.

The ward consisted of two rows of twenty beds with double doors at each end. After spending so much time at the Women's Hospital and Clinic, Dody had almost forgotten the collective odour of sick men: tobacco, urine, sweat, and Macassar hair oil. But as she gazed down the wide aisle, she could see that the ward itself was clean and orderly. Some of the men were sitting up in bed reading, with bandaged limbs propped on pillows. Others slept despite the groans of a man near the door who thrashed about in a bed with raised sides.

They stopped at the desk, where Dody made the introductions to the sister in charge. The tall, redheaded Irish woman walked them briskly down the aisle to an empty bed and took Pike's case from him. "You won't be requiring that here, Mr. Pike," she said. "Everything you need is in the locker next to the bed. Undress, change into the nightshirt, and then pass water into the bottle provided." She whisked the curtains around the bed, giving him no time to reply, let alone protest.

The man in the bed next to Pike's began to moan in his sleep. Across the aisle someone hawked and spat into the potted palm next to his bed. Pike's curtains quivered.

"Mr. Stratton," the sister admonished. "If you must expectorate, please use the cup provided."

"Sorry, Sister," the man said, wiping threads of tobacco from his pyjama jacket and lighting up a cigarette.

If Dody ever had a say in the running of a hospital, she would start with a no-smoking rule on the wards. She smiled wryly at her brief flight of fancy. What influence could she possibly have when most of the larger London hospitals wouldn't even allow female doctors to practise within their hallowed halls?

The floorboards shook under the weight of several pairs

of feet. She looked up to see Mr. Barker at the head of the ward with three younger men in his entourage. "I'll be back in a moment, Matthew," Dody said to the curtains and hurried to meet the surgeon before he began his rounds.

"Dr. McCleland," Barker said as he took her hands in both of his and vigorously pumped.

Dody smiled warmly at him. Mr. Barker had offered his support when she applied for a bone surgery internship, and it was no fault of his that she had been rejected for the course.

He leaned closer to say softly, "I'm sorry things didn't work out. I'm afraid there are too many old fuddy-duddies on the board who don't like the idea of lady surgeons."

Dody smiled again. "Thank you, but I have landed on my feet. I am working with the Home Office now as an assistant autopsy surgeon to Dr. Bernard Spilsbury."

One of the medical students failed to hold back a snigger, and even Barker looked at Dody askance. Her smile became rigid. He might be open to the idea of a female surgeon, but a female autopsy surgeon—a student of the "Beastly Science"—that was something else again.

"It's not full-time employment," Dody added to forestall any unwelcome comment, "so it means that I can still give time to the Women's Hospital and Clinic. But sir, I know you are busy, so I had better explain why I'm here. Last week you saw Chief Inspector Pike in your rooms and you booked him for a knee repair today."

It annoyed her to give in so quickly, but she had achieved her purpose and Barker seemed relieved that she had changed the subject. "Yes, I remember the man: Boer War veteran turned policeman. X-rayed his knee and found shrapnel lodged under the patella. A straightforward operation, provided the anaesthetic agrees and there are no postoperative infections."

Dody had lost count of the number of bodies she'd examined with death attributed to anaesthetic complications. It was one of the risks of the operation she had mentioned to Pike, though strangely the prospect of death by anaesthetic had not seemed to worry him. His fear seemed deeper than that. But how would she feel if something untoward happened as a result of the operation she had pushed him into having? A hollow ache formed in the pit of her stomach. Better to cast that thought to the back of her mind. Would she not advise a patient to whom she had no attachment a similar course of action? Of course she would.

"He is quite apprehensive," she said to the surgeon. "I was hoping you might be able to spend a few minutes this morning explaining again what the operation entails and putting his mind at ease. I'm afraid I don't seem to be making a very good job of it."

"You are too close to him, that's why. A no-nonsense approach is always best."

"Please don't get the wrong idea, sir. We are friends, nothing more."

Mr. Barker looked at her over his half-rim glasses. Dody felt the heat rise in her face once more and cursed the ready blush that would only confirm the argument that women were too emotional to be doctors.

"Come on then, let's go see this chap of yours," Barker said, with a sigh of impatience.

Dody bit her tongue and led him down the long ward.

The curtains were still drawn around Pike's bed. "Chief Inspector Pike, are you ready?" she called.

There was no answer.

The surgeon folded his arms.

Dody cautiously drew back the curtain's edge before ripping it fully open. The bed was neatly made; the patient nowhere to be seen.

Chapter Two

Dody drew a sharp line beneath the notes of her last Clinic patient, put them aside for filing, and picked up a clean sheet of paper. About to ring the bell on her desk to inform the nurse that she was ready for the next, she stopped her hand midair. It was all too easy to rush from one patient to the next. She needed a moment or two for herself.

Nearly six weeks had passed since Pike's disappearance from the hospital, and Dody had heard nothing from him; it was as if he had vanished with the river mists. It was fortunate, she told herself, that her work left her little time to brood. When the opportunity did present itself, as it did now, her thoughts were accompanied by a mix of frustration, helplessness . . . and something for which she had no ready word—was it loss? Yes, she was missing him. But it was not an unalloyed missing. She was angry with him, too: angry that he had not trusted her professional judgement; angry that he had left her looking like a fool in front of the surgeon and his colleagues.

Where had he gone? What was he doing and why had he not contacted her? Embarrassment, she supposed. He'd said that after the operation he was planning on visiting his daughter while he recuperated. Violet would be spending the school holidays with her grandparents—the parents of his late wife—perhaps he was there now. He'd also proposed an outing with Dody upon his return to London—a day-trip to the seaside if she could find a free day.

At least he had not taken it for granted that she would have free time. As the days went by, her thoughts were increasingly dominated by a single, strangely comforting question: even if he had made contact, apologised, and explained his behaviour, did she really have the time and inclination to take courtship with this complex man a step further?

A few weeks previously she had celebrated her thirtieth birthday with her family. Dody was now considered to be past marriageable age. Even her mother, Louise, had gently probed for her views on the subject, realising perhaps that the prospect of grandchildren from either of her daughters was becoming ever more remote. Louise managed a brave face when Dody explained that Spilsbury—the Home Office pathologist under whom she worked—had implied that more avenues might be open to her if she remained unmarried. Never could she aspire to Spilsbury's lofty heights, of course, but employment as a senior pathologist might one day be realistically attainable. A spinster's life could, in fact, be very liberating, she told Louise, and embracing it was the only way a woman could pursue a challenging career.

These reflections made her feel better and helped

strengthen her erstwhile faltering resolve. *No* was the answer to her earlier question. She had no time left for Pike, not after all this. She had spent enough hours wondering and worrying about him. Thank God they had not given more to one another, for giving more meant more to lose. Better their attachment come to an end now, before irrevocable decisions were made.

She picked up the hand bell from her desk and gave it a vigorous shake.

Dody knew what the girl wanted the moment she sat down. There was something about the way she twisted her hands, the way her eyes hunted around the shabby surgery.

"I'm not regular, Doctor," she said. "My monthlies, I mean. I need you to give me something." Her eyes rested on the corner medicine cabinet.

Dody felt the warning press of a headache and brushed a palm across her brow. The surgery was stuffy; the windows were closed against the odours of the street. A furious blue-bottle buzzed, trapped between the lowered blind and the windowpane.

She took note of the girl's distressed state, the way she smelled. She had an odour about her that had nothing to do with dirty clothes or the heat wave. It was the scent of fear.

"When did you have your courses last, Miss Craddock?" she asked gently.

"Umm, two, three months ago. Maybe."

"Might you be with child?"

Esther Craddock shook her head so vigorously a papier-mâché grape dropped from her straw hat and rolled beneath the desk. "I'm not pregnant, no, and I don't want to be, neither. You got to give me something so's I'm not."

Dody sighed. This inability to differentiate between contraception and abortion was common amongst girls such as Esther Craddock. Herbs, gin, gunpowder, washing soda—anything that caused vomiting, cramps, and contractions—had been experimented with over the years by women desperate to get rid of their unborn children. Dody had even heard of women drinking the water of boiled copper coins. Sometimes these remedies worked and sometimes the mother died also. More often than not, nothing happened at all.

"Do you use preventatives?" Dody asked.

"What?"

"French letters, sheaths?"

"You got to be joking—'ave you seen the price of 'em? Three shillings a dozen!"

"They can be washed out and reused," Dody said, fearing her advice was already too late.

"No. Don't need 'em." The girl folded her arms, turned her head towards the closed blind, and stared at it.

Dody wondered how much the girl knew about conception. Unlike the majority of her medical companions, Dody did her best to inform her young women patients about the dangers of intimacy with men. Only the previous week a fifteen-year-old had come to the Clinic fearing she had "caught a baby" through the passionate kisses of a boy. At least she had been able to reassure that misguided child, but what of all the others? Surely there would be less risk of unwanted pregnancy if they understood clearly the consequences of what they did. There really needed to be an education program.

Dody leaned down to pick up the dropped grape. The keys to the medicine cabinet on her belt tinkled and the pressure in her head rose.

Esther took the grape by its pin and rammed it back into the fruit salad arrangement of her hat. She met Dody's gaze with her own. Her face was flour white, her eyes bright and shining. "Just give me something," the girl said, balling her fists. "If you don't give me something, I'll . . . I'll . . . kill meself!"

Dody took a deep breath and tightened the light reflector around her head. "Before I can help, I have to examine you."

Ignoring the girl's sulky protests, Dody took a wooden spatula from a tray of instruments on her desk and examined her mouth, making note of a blue line on the gums near the junction of the teeth. Next, she pulled down Esther's lower eyelids and aimed her light at mucous membranes the colour of old meat. "Stomachache?"

"Touch o' colic."

Probably more than a touch, Dody thought, writing down her observations. She screwed the lid back onto her fountain pen and slowly laid it on the top of her patient's notes. "You are showing signs of plumbism, Miss Craddock—lead poisoning. Have you been exposed to lead in any form? Are you aware that lead poisoning can cause miscarriage?"

The fruit salad shuddered. "No, miss, no."

Dody proceeded cautiously. "Some women take lead deliberately to poison their unborn babies."

Over previous years lead had become an increasingly popular abortifacient, with slightly better results than the other remedies. Knowledge of its efficacy originated from the large numbers of female workers in the Midlands paint factories who found themselves suffering early miscarriage and likely passed by word of mouth from friend to friend, mother to daughter.

The girl's voice rose. "I wouldn't do nothin' like that. You shouldn't ought to be saying such terrible things!"

Dody raised her palms, "Hush now. Take off your outdoor things and climb onto the examination table. I can't be certain of anything just yet."

Esther reluctantly unpinned her hat and laid it carefully on the desk. With shaking fingers, she undid the buttons of her light summer coat and levered off her boots. As she flung her coat onto the chair, a twisted knot of fabric fell to the ground.

Esther hadn't noticed it. She lay on the examination table with her eyes screwed shut, her fingers, bare of rings, digging into the table's padding.

Dody picked the small bundle up, thinking it must be the girl's handkerchief, but discovered it was a patch of frayed muslin wrapped around some small, hard objects. She peeked beneath the fabric's folds and found they concealed a small collection of tablets.

Esther's eyes remained clamped shut. Dody slipped the bundle back into the girl's coat pocket. It would help her to treat Esther if she knew what the tablets were, but the last thing she needed now was a confrontation that might destroy the girl's tenuous trust.

Dody palpated the girl's abdomen and then her swollen breasts. There was no mistaking the diagnosis. She helped Esther rearrange her clothing and tried to encourage her back to the chair, but the girl refused to sit.

Concerned that the news might bring about a fainting fit,

Dody edged closer. "You are carrying a child of approximately three months' gestation, although I suspect you already knew that." Esther's hand flew to her mouth. It was one thing to suspect the worst, another to hear the words as truth from a stranger's lips. Dody gave her a moment to absorb the news. "Who is the father?" she asked softly. "Is he likely to support you?"

Esther lowered her head. "I'll lose me job."

"Where do you work?"

"In Bedford Square."

"You are in service?"

"Scullery maid."

Dody busied herself for a moment, giving the girl time to think. She removed the light reflector and glanced at her image in the metal disc, then tried and failed to straighten her untidy pile of mahogany hair. "Are you in love with this man?" she finally asked. "Have you plans to marry?"

"Love? What would you know about love?" Dody shot her head up to catch a sneer curling the girl's lip. "A dried-up old maid like you wouldn't even know what it's like to lay with a man, not to mention love him—though your sort are always quick to preach to those of us what does!"

It was an impulsive tirade brought about by rage and desperation, but it stung Dody nevertheless. She tried to compose herself and placed the reflector slowly back on the desk.

"I'm sorry, miss, I didn't mean that," Esther said, meek as a lamb again. Perhaps she realised that aggression would not help her cause.

"Are you still seeing this young man?" Dody knew the answer before she had asked the question. With only one afternoon off a week, courting was almost impossible for a girl of

Esther's station. The father was most likely the master or son of the house or an opportunistic delivery boy in the kitchen yard. Or it might be the case of creeping out of her window at night and supplementing her meagre wage with services provided on the street.

Esther said nothing. Dody put a hand gently on her arm. "If you are unable to obtain assistance from the man or your family, there are organisations I can put you in touch with. The Salvation Army often helps young women in your predicament, then there are the nuns at St. Luke's." *Or the workhouse.* Dody kept that thought to herself, knowing how unwelcome it would be.

Esther knocked away Dody's hand and screamed into her face, "I don't want no nuns, nor do-gooders neither. Don't you understand? You got to 'elp me!"

Dody held her ground and slapped away the hands that grasped for the keys on her belt. The girl was tall and sturdy, her work-reddened hands quick and strong. She lunged again. Dody grabbed the thick wrists and struggled to hold her back.

"'Elp me!" Esther was hysterical now, using her weight to push Dody towards the wall, desperately grasping for the keys at her waist. Dody could feel her grip on the powerful wrists failing. There was only one thing for it. She jerked her leg up and brought it down hard, slamming the heel of her boot onto the sensitive arch of the girl's foot.

The girl yelped and jumped back.

Dody took a breath. "I'm sorry, Miss Craddock," she said through gritted teeth, "but I can't do anything for you until you sit down and calm down."

The girl stared for a moment. Her pale face blossomed

with embarrassment. "I'm sorry, Doctor," she whispered as she slumped into the chair. "I don't know what come over me."

"I do. It's called blind desperation."

Dody adjusted her belt, smoothed her blouse, and willed her heartbeat to steady itself. She had two options. She could call out and have Nurse Hamilton escort the girl from the Clinic, after which Esther would doubtless continue her search for an obliging doctor. Or she could follow the recommended procedure, which was to telephone the police and have the girl arrested for attempting to procure an abortion. Either the girl would put herself at dreadful risk in the hands of an unprincipled physician or the wretched child would be born into circumstances even more reduced than they were now. To Dody, neither of these options was acceptable.

"Have you taken any other medicines for your condition?" Dody asked.

"Pills. Got 'em from the apothecary," Esther whispered. "Zimmerman's."

"What kind of pills?"

"Widow Welch's."

Widow Welch's female pills, prompt and reliable for ladies. On the back of the box in tiny writing it was written, *On no account to be taken by females desirous of becoming mothers*, a disclaimer included by the manufacturers to avoid prosecution and an irresistible lure to those desperate to abort. Laboratory analysis had shown the pills to be mostly composed of sugar, and Dody knew they would not have caused Esther's symptoms. Surely it wasn't Widow Welch's she'd seen tied in the muslin bundle?

"You took lead as well. In what form? Where did you get it from? Zimmerman's, too?" Dody asked.

Esther folded her arms and looked away.

What might this girl try next? How many girls like Esther had Dody seen on the mortuary slab, fished from the Thames as a result of suicide or bungled criminal abortion? Dody shuddered. Countless. There had to be a better way.

Dody took the keys from the belt at her waist, moved to the medicine cabinet, and took a small brown bottle from the top shelf. "I can give you something that will help with your nerves. Take the dosage as instructed and then come and see me next week when you are more clear-headed and we can discuss your options. On no account are you to take anything else, especially lead. Is that clear?"

The girl nodded.

"And this will clear up the effects of the lead poisoning." Dody uncapped her pen and reached for her prescription pad. "Have it made up by the chemist, not the apothecary," she said, tearing the paper from the pad and handing it to the girl, "and he will write the dose on the bottle."

"But, Doctor," Esther said, looking searchingly from the prescription and back to Dody, "will it make me bleed?"

The Clinic was part of a scheme devised by Dr. Elizabeth Garrett to put disused buildings to use as temporary free clinics for women of no means. Doctors and nurses prepared to work for nothing were hard to find, and all those who worked there had private incomes or other paid employment.

Dody slipped her note onto the admissions desk in front of Nurse Daphne Hamilton and held her breath as she waited for the verdict. Nurse Hamilton was one of Florence's suffragette friends; like Dody, she was from a wealthy family and devoted two days a week to the Clinic. Many of her kind treated their charity work as a game, coming and going as their whims dictated, but Dody had always been impressed with Daphne's stamina and dedication and had been encouraging the young woman to undertake an official nurse's training course. If she could persevere with the rigours of hospital-based training, Dody felt sure that Daphne Hamilton would make an excellent qualified nurse.

But birth control was a divisive subject amongst the militant suffragettes, with many against it. Dody knew that if she failed to get the support of the Clinic staff, she might as well give up now on her newly hatched idea.

When Daphne nodded with approval, Dody had to stop herself from jumping on the spot like a child. Daphne's support should have been no surprise; she had probably seen as many of the tragic results of ignorance as Dody had.

"'*A weekly lecture at the Clinic on health and hygiene,*'" Daphne read. "I take it you also mean birth control?" she added in a whisper.

Dody nodded. It was against the law to explicitly advertise, though not to discreetly provide, contraception education. "Thank you, Nurse, I'm very glad you feel that way," Dody said, slipping the draft note in her pocket with the intention of revising it once the other doctors had been consulted and a timetable clarified.

She attempted to adjust her boater by feel—the Clinic did not provide such luxuries as mirrors—and Daphne reassured her that it was on straight. Thank God Florence had not chosen the Ritz this time. Looking the way she did, she would surely be directed straight to the kitchen entrance.

"Will you sound out Dr. Wainright for me, Daphne? I

can't stay to see her today; I'm meeting Florence for lunch. But please tell her I'd like to talk to her tomorrow about a series of lectures we could give between us."

Dody glanced around the waiting room. Women of all ages, shapes, and sizes; snuffling children; and wailing babies filled the seats. Dr. Wainright was in for a busy afternoon.

"Certainly, Doctor. I'm sure she and the other doctors will be behind you, too. And say hello to Florence for me," Daphne said with a conspiratorial twinkle to her eye. "Tell her I'm looking forward to our return to the fray."

Chapter Three

The restaurant hummed with patrons who'd suspended their aquatic activities on the Serpentine for luncheon. Dody and Florence occupied a table for two by a long window. Outside, families picnicked and children hunted for minnows in the muddy water. Uniformed nannies steered cumbersome perambulators from one shady tree to the next while City men lounged on benches sans jackets and coats. It wasn't even the weekend, but all around them, well-heeled Londoners found time to relax and enjoy the hot weather.

"That poor girl—poor you, too, to be put in such a rotten position," Florence said. She drained her glass of barley water and placed it on the table with a sigh. "That apothecary—Zimmerman?—should be shot for selling sugar pills to such a vulnerable girl."

Dody agreed, to a point. "The annoying thing is that with a little education and a knowledge of the preventatives, the problem could so easily have been averted and no one would need to bother with Widow Welch's." She pushed her unfinished meal away. The fish was too fishy for her taste, the white sauce almost rancid. London was in the grip of strikes, and fresh produce and ice were in short supply. "So I've decided to start conducting education classes in the Clinic."

"Sounds like a jolly good idea to me," Florence said. "Young women must be educated not to yield in the first place. As woman is morally superior to man, it is up to her to be the stronger of the two."

"Indeed. But I hope to take my course a bit further than that and give the women some knowledge of the preventatives, too."

Florence gave Dody a determined look. "Preventatives do nothing but further loosen the slackened reins of male desire, Dody. As Christabel would say: 'Votes for women, chastity for men.' This is why we need the vote—why we need women members of parliament. A greater female say would not only temper matters of sexual morality; women's natural compassion would have a more humanising influence on every sphere of humanity, at home, our politics abroad . . ."

Although Florence and she shared many of the same convictions, Dody had no time for the violent nature of the campaign waged by her sister's Bloomsbury group and the Pankhursts or, for that matter, many of the members' narrow-minded attitudes towards birth control and morality. If Dody could have got away with closing her eyes instead of her ears, she might have been listening to a reverend mother addressing a novice. Her wealthy, beautiful sister, dressed in her lilac satin teagown and spouting ideology of the most reactionary kind, never ceased to amaze her.

Dody stifled a yawn. Florence should have been enjoying the summer season with other young ladies of her class, attending balls and fancy-dress parties, polo matches, and regattas. Instead, when not plotting, typing, or folding pamphlets in their townhouse, she was doing the same in one of the often dingy dwellings of her coconspirators. Or worse, some would say, doing what she did now: enjoying the company of her unfashionable elder sister. Most young ladies were advised to give Dody—the "Beastly Science" doctor who refused to wear a corset or allow her maid to do her hair—a wide berth. She smiled to herself; they shared a tight bond despite their differences. But enough was enough.

"Florence, please, I'm hot and I have a headache," she said. "Your principles are all very well, but they don't actually solve the problem of young women butchering themselves or being left with babies they can't care for."

Florence could not argue with that. Her face softened. "You have no appetite? Don't tell me your cholera has returned? Few families seem to have escaped it this year. Sir Anton Frobisher had it, his cook had it—the household was in turmoil for a while. Lady Harriet was at her wits' end. Remind me, I must pay her a call and see how they are getting on."

"For me it's the heat this time, I'm sure of it."

"Yes, ghastly, isn't it?" Florence used her napkin to flap at her face with unladylike vigour. "Plays havoc with the digestion. Look, Dody, I admire you for your stand, I really do, but it just doesn't sit comfortably with me."

"The practice of birth control is not illegal in this country."

"But the public advocating of it is," Florence said.

"Which is why I plan to provide verbal instruction only."

Dody paused to smile at her sister. "Besides, when have you been worried about what is legal or not?"

"Oh, you know what I mean. Surely you can understand my point of view?"

"Of course, we are both entitled to our opinions."

Florence relaxed back into her chair and returned Dody's smile. "Well, at least you have found something to throw your passions into, something that will take your mind off Pike."

Dody almost choked on the piece of bread she was nibbling. "Pike—what has he got to do with all this?"

"I take it you have still had no word?"

Dody turned back to the view.

"When I think of all the trouble you went to, to book him into that hospital," Florence went on, "arranging treatment from the best surgeon in London, and all he did was bolt. War hero indeed! You have every right to be angry."

Dody did not like to hear Pike criticised this way. She might speak against him, but it was another matter to hear him criticised by someone else. She had thought her temper recovered, but now she felt unsettled again: she could not help taking his behaviour personally. She was a rational woman—a trained scientist—yet the turmoil she had experienced since meeting him the previous year was apparently resistant to all logic.

Most of her patients held her medical knowledge in high regard and took her advice without question or compromise. But here was someone whom she herself held in high regard paying no more heed to her medical advice than he might to any High Street quack. She shook her head in an effort to send the conflicting thoughts flying; she had already resolved that she had no time for this. Let him keep his distance.

"Dody! Dody, speak to me," Florence was saying. "I'm sorry, I didn't mean to upset."

"War docs strange things to men," was all Dody could think to say.

They travelled home in the new open-topped Benz, driven by their former coachman, Fletcher. The traffic was congested and motorcars honked impatiently at the slower horse-drawn vehicles. At Hyde Park Corner there was an altercation for right of way between a whip-wielding hansom driver and a goggled motorist. A scuffle ensued and traffic ground to a standstill around Wellington Arch, until two policemen arrived on bicycles to break up the mêlée. The cabby, obviously beyond rational thought, struck one of the bobbies on the helmet, his whip, decorated with ribbons of coronation colours, flying about like a madwoman's hair.

Dody held tight to her sister's gown as Florence leaned out of the Benz to boo and hiss at the police as they led the cabby away. She wouldn't put it past Florence to leap from their motorcar and join the fracas. At last they were moving again. Dody glanced at her fob and willed Fletcher to drive faster. She needed some time at home to put the finishing touches to a research proposal she planned on presenting to Dr. Spilsbury in a few days' time.

Once they were driving peacefully again, Florence tightened the broad tie of her motoring hat and dropped her head into a novel, the pages barely stirring in the weak draught. In honour of the coronation, the suffragettes had temporarily ceased their violent protests, and with little else to occupy her mind, Florence had taken to reading novels of a popular nature. This one involved secret agents and the German threat, which Dody felt was grossly exaggerated by the press for no other purpose than to distract the population from the troubles at home. She glanced at the book's cover: *The Riddle of the Sands*—one of the better written, so she had heard. She smiled to herself. Despite her antiestablishment convictions, her sister was still a patriot at heart.

Fletcher turned from the congested Euston Road into their quiet street and dropped the sisters outside their front door before taking the car to the mews to be garaged. Home was one of a series of roomy Georgian townhouses that formed a semicircular terrace fronting Cartwright Gardens: a miniature version of Bath's Royal Crescent, Dody always liked to think.

The house and trappings were paid for by their mother with money she had inherited and which, out of respect for his wife, their father had laid no claim to—even though he was usually against money spent on what he saw as "frippery."

Dody and Florence passed between white columns standing sentry on the porch and entered the house through the colourful leadlight front door. They found themselves immediately beset by a terrible weeping and wailing.

"Good Lord," Dody said, exchanging worried glances with her sister. "What on earth is going on? Has someone died?"

There was an agitated thumping on the basement stairs and the door leading from the kitchen was flung open by their parlour maid, Annie, her face as white as her lace cap, her hair sticking out at all angles as though she had suffered an electric shock.

"Ever so sorry, misses," the girl said, "I couldn't meet you at the door—we're having a dreadful time downstairs. Cook's lost her rag and threatening to hand in her notice. She wants poor Lucy to clobber 'em with the rolling pin and Lucy's refusing, saying clobbering rats is not what a scullery maid's paid for, and I says we need to call the rat catcher—"

Florence covered her mouth with her hands. "Rats? Downstairs? In our kitchen? How revolting!"

Realising at last what must have happened, Dody shot the maid a sharp look. "Annie, I told you not to clean my study. In fact, I asked you not to go into that room at all."

"You've been keeping rats in your study?" Florence exclaimed. "Dody, how could you?"

"In preparation for some research . . ."

"I only took a little peep, miss, opened the cage door. Then one of their scaly tails brushed through my fingers and I panicked and the cage fell off the table. They must have been hungry 'cos they rushed in a mob down the stairs and headed straight for the kitchen."

Dody had difficulty maintaining a straight face. She asked Annie to fetch the cage from her study.

Florence collapsed onto the hall chair.

"Come on, I need your help," Dody said as she headed with the wire cage to the kitchen.

"You don't need me; you need the Pied Piper."

Great rats, small rats, lean rats, brawny rats, brown rats, black rats, grey rats, tawny rats they were not—they were special laboratory rats, a new line developed for scientific purposes by the Wistar Institute, and Dody had had them shipped all the way from America. They were precious and not only for their rarity. Dody found that she had become quite fond of the docile creatures with their soft white fur and beady pink eyes. Although her rats were destined for inevitable euthanasia, she could not abide the thought of their senseless clobbering with a rolling pin.

She had less trouble coaxing them back into the cage with a hunk of bread than she had settling the servants' nerves. Lucy was instructed to make Cook a strong cup of tea laced with medicinal brandy and then assist Annie with the tidying and disinfecting of the kitchen.

Florence was waiting in the hall for her return. Dody could not help herself. With a flourish, she produced a particularly robust specimen from behind her back. "Florence, meet Edward, my favourite, named after our late king."

Dody had never seen Florence mount the stairs with such speed, and she laughed for the first time in weeks.

Chapter Four

Margaretha paused as her handmaiden took hold of the edge of her veil. The piano player struck three sharp chords and out she spun, twisting her way to the edge of the splintered stage to dance seductively for the lone man in the front row, who rewarded her with a shudder and an intake of breath.

She kept her eyes on him as she danced, her remaining veils floating about and enhancing her succulent curves. It must help to have someone in the audience to focus on, the pianist supposed, although this was not the face he would imagine her choosing. Tall, gaunt, and yellow-eyed—not even Gabriel Klassen's type—this lone member of the audience must have crossed her manager's palm generously to be allowed in for the rehearsal.

Tomorrow they would rehearse with the full orchestra. Gabriel Klassen was in the shadows at the back of the hall now, writing notes, organising the publicity posters and the costumes for the sham Indian musicians. Once, apparently, at a show in Rome, the musicians had sweated so much their brown greasepaint had run and they'd arrived onstage looking like a band of lepers. The piano player smiled at the conjured image. Gabriel had better not make that mistake again—the Londoners were a tough crowd to please.

The pianist slowed the tempo. Margaretha turned her back on her lone admirer and faced him. From the corner of his eye he saw her touch her breast beneath the floating veil. Despite his knowledge that the performance was now for him, he remained focused on the music and the way the sweat stuck his white shirt uncomfortably to his body. He would give her no satisfaction. He would not take his eyes from the music. He would not play one false note.

Her handmaidens danced well, slinking to imaginary cymbals and bells. If they danced like this to a barely tuned piano in a rundown London hall, imagine how they would perform to a full orchestra at the Empire—better still, on the eagerly anticipated tour for the Army and Navy Club? He knew the thought of all those uniforms excited her: she had told him so as one of her many attempts to make him jealous.

He raised the tempo again, heard the rattle of her coin-covered brassiere. Conscious of her small breasts, she never removed her top, leaving the silver coins to enhance the mystery. She knew well the thoughts of the hungry-eyed audience, their collective anticipation, their desperate hope that this performance might prove the exception to her rule.

Margaretha glided on bare feet across the stage, her handmaidens following with choreographed steps. Another veil floated to the ground. The music swelled, her belly rolled.

He threw a glance to determine her position on the stage, and she responded to it greedily. Arms extended, she flew across the stage and fell to her knees next to him, leaned backwards, arched her hips, and simulated masturbation.

Matthew Pike dashed the sweat from his brow and returned to the musical score. It was a complicated piece.

Pike packed up the sheet music and slipped it between the sleeves of his leather case. From the wings he heard the sound of bright female laughter, Cockney voices. Someone tapped him on the shoulder. He spun on the piano stool and found Gabriel Klassen all but hidden behind an extravagant bouquet of red roses.

"Take these in to Margaretha, please, Captain." Klassen's guttural Dutch accent grated on Pike's nerves, set his teeth on edge, and took him back to places he wished he could forget.

"I am a piano player, not a delivery boy," Pike said, reaching for his cane and climbing to his feet. "You'll have to take them yourself—who are they from anyway?"

Klassen sighed and placed the flowers on the piano. "She will not be pleased. They are from the gentleman in the front row. He is becoming a pest to her, I think. Such a face. He looks like a corpse." The manager shuddered and Pike tried very hard not to sigh.

"I'll speak to him if you like. Is he waiting in the front entrance?"

"You would rather speak to him than Margaretha? It must be a coward who is more frightened of a woman than of a man." Klassen laughed nervously.

Klassen was more on the money than Pike would let on. He was a coward, with one woman certainly. His thoughts threatened to wander to Dody, as they had constantly during the last few weeks. He knew that the longer he put off contacting her, the less likely she was to forgive him. But something illogical seemed to have taken hold of him—the fear of fear itself perhaps—and seized him in a grip that would not let up. He glanced at the flowers on the piano. Perhaps he should send Dody a gift, something to articulate the words he was unable to say. But what? God, how useless he felt.

Klassen was looking expectantly at him. Pike flicked him a tight smile. "Tell me more about this man. I noticed he was here yesterday, too."

"He has been watching her since we arrived in London, sending her notes and flowers, giving me money to allow him to sit in on the rehearsals. He has already reserved a box for the first few nights of the performance."

"I wouldn't worry. I'm sure Margaretha can take care of herself."

Klassen gave a dismissive wave of his hand. "*Ach.* One lovesick admirer does not matter. It is not unusual; she attracts them wherever she goes. It's everything else that worries me. I told her we should never have changed the show, it's causing nothing but trouble."

"Our London fathers are still making a fuss over the Dance of the Seven Veils?"

"Indeed they are. Don't they realise how much we are compromising? This is nothing like the original; it's just a small portion of it. Nothing more risqué than any of the other acts she has danced countless times before on the London stage. But someone must have got to the musical director and frightened him off. He left me a note—his aunt is ill or some-such; he can no longer do the job—and the musicians are expected tomorrow." Klassen threw up his hands. "English-men and their scruples."

Pike headed for the stage steps, showing with his turned back that the manager's problems were of no concern of his. "Tomorrow you owe me a week's pay."

Klassen followed him. "Captain, wait and tell me this: what were you doing when I came across you in the tavern?"

Pike regarded him over his shoulder. "I was out of a job. I was about to ask the publican if he needed a piano player, but you got to me first."

"Yes, yes. And what will you do next week, when the orchestra starts, when we have no more need for an accom-panist for rehearsals? Will you start whoring yourself in the public houses again?"

"I take each day as it comes." Pike's footsteps rang on the steps at the edge of the stairs. He knew what Klassen was getting at—sensed what was coming next. He wondered how many of the hollow steps he would take before Klassen called him back: one . . . two . . . three . . .

"Wait there, Captain. I have something more to ask you." Klassen jumped like a dancer from the stage. "Margaretha and I, we both admire you greatly . . ." He licked dry lips.

"Yes?" Pike wondered when he had picked up the habit of making people so nervous. It was a handy skill for the inter-rogation room, but it seemed to happen these days whether it was his intention or not.

"We, that is, Margaretha and myself, were hoping you might take the musical director's place. You are obviously a talented musician. You are well acquainted with the score and we will pay handsomely."

Pike rubbed his chin and made a show of raising his eyes to the damp-stained ceiling. "How much?"

"Two pounds for the remaining rehearsals with full orchestra, then one pound per performance."

"Three pounds for the rehearsals," Pike countered, not wanting to appear too easy.

"Done." Klassen slapped Pike on the back. Pike's knee locked and he almost fell over. Damned knee. No longer just a reminder of the war, the pain would forever dog him as an opportunity not taken—in more ways than one. "Margaretha will be delighted."

"Shall I still have a word with the gentleman from the front row?" Pike asked.

"Please. But you must not put him off; he may have influential friends, and we need all the sponsors we can get."

"He obviously wants to impress Margaretha."

"As does Rear Admiral Millbank, a much more likely candidate, I think. If she pleases him, he will guarantee more bookings in the north of the country and, with luck, the Army and Navy Club, too."

"The admiral won't find fault with the performance, I'm sure."

"The contracts rest on more than the stage show. I need not tell you that." And then Klassen's eyes widened and he whispered, "Don't turn now, but the gentleman in question, the admiral, has just entered the hall."

"Is he carrying his briefcase?"

"Yes, Captain, cuffed to his wrist as usual. He must be a very important man."

Or a pompous fool, Pike thought, *one who endeavours to appear more important than he is.* Pike did not need to turn; he knew the rotund, snowy-haired Admiral Millbank well enough by sight. He doubted he would be recognised, but pulled his bowler over his brow just in case and feigned to notice something on one of the seats, a piece of litter perhaps, some distance from the admiral's rolling approach.

As Pike moved away, Klassen spoke through the side of his mouth. "Find out how useful that tall man might be. See what he has to offer us. I'll deal with the admiral."

Pike nodded, resigned. So now he was to be Margaretha's pimp. Well, he had done worse. He made his way down the side of the hall, his suit jacket slung over his shoulder, just as the admiral boomed out a dinner invitation to Klassen and the "dear lady."

Pushing sordid thoughts aside, Pike allowed himself the luxury of contemplating his new role in the exotic show. The greater part of the performance consisted of bits and pieces of music and dance that Margaretha had picked up during her travels in the East, but the climax was undoubtedly the Dance of the Seven Veils, borrowed from the Strauss opera. Any musician would leap at the chance to be musical director of this piece, even if it was only an excerpt. A part of him hoped he would find nothing incriminating against Margaretha and her troupe. If he did, the show was doomed to a limited season.

He passed through the hall's empty front entrance and found the man from the front row in the street, gazing longingly at a poster recently tacked to the exterior wall. The man stood fixed to the spot and stared as if mesmerised by Margaretha's image.

Pike cleared his throat to get the man's attention and

tipped the rim of his bowler. "Good afternoon, sir, I hope you enjoyed the rehearsal."

The man tore his gaze from the poster and stepped back. He was gallows tall and his face was flushed.

"Yes, I did, thank you," he stuttered, taking a handker-chief from his trouser pocket and mopping his brow with it. An ugly scar, like crumpled tissue paper, creased the side of his head and extended to the outer rim of his left ear. "You are the piano player?"

Pike put out his hand. "They call me the captain."

"That is all?"

"All that is necessary."

The man looked at Pike, one fraud regarding another. "Archibald Van Noort." The whites of his eyes, Pike noticed, were jaundiced yellow.

"You are Dutch, too?" Pike nodded to the poster.

"No, British with Dutch ancestry," he said, his eyes drawn once more to the poster of the near-naked woman. *He should enjoy it while he can,* Pike thought. It wouldn't be long before someone concerned about public decency ripped it down.

"Did she like the flowers?" Van Noort asked.

"Her manager was taking them to her as I was leaving."

"Just now I saw another man—a naval officer?—enter the theatre."

"Rear Admiral Millbank, one of the organisers from the Army and Navy Club. He's thinking of making a booking." Pike's reply was open, responsive. If he wanted to glean any-thing of interest from this man, he would have to give some-thing first.

Traffic rattled by, the jingle of harnesses, the sighs and gasps of motor vehicles. "Ah," was all the man said.

They stepped closer to the wall to allow a sandwich-board man to pass. The man wore the blue uniform of a Prussian soldier with a spiked helmet, his board advertising the latest invasion book. The country was obsessed with German spies, and not all of it was unwarranted, in Pike's opinion. There had been several sightings recently of mysterious airships floating over the east and south coasts near military installations, and several foreigners had been caught taking photographs at navy shipyards. There was even rumour that a heavily manned German vessel had been seen navigating the Humber, though it was long gone by the time the relevant authorities caught wind of it.

Pike looked to Van Noort for the faint flick of an eye, an increase in respiration—any kind of reaction at all—but saw nothing.

"I expect she'll send you a note," Pike said to fill the awkward silence.

The man's mouth twitched. "A note. Yes."

Pike snapped off his sleeve holders, shrugged into his worn suit jacket, and turned to leave. Getting to know this man and his motives was not going to be easy.

"Wait," Van Noort called as Pike began to make his way to the tram stop; miraculously these vehicles had not yet been affected by the strikes. "I have to ask you something." He looked directly at Pike. Away from Margaretha's image and no longer dazzled by it, he seemed quite lucid. "Forgive me for asking, but your knee is giving you trouble. I can tell by the way you walk, yet when you play the piano, it doesn't seem to worry you at all. I am a doctor, you see; I have an interest in such things. Are you aware that it is often possible to have those kinds of injuries repaired?"

Pike had not expected this. The man did not match his idea of a doctor at all. Then again, neither had Dody upon first meeting.

"No," he replied curtly. Assignment or not, he was sick of the attention his knee attracted.

"Shrapnel?"

Pike nodded. He was wondering if the doctor's disfiguring scar might also be a result of the war when a ragged boy of eleven or twelve appeared from the alley beside the theatre and tugged at the tall man's sleeve. "C'mon, Doc, it's time to go. 'Aven't you been 'angin' round 'ere long enough? We got work to do."

The boy passed between them. Pike felt the quick press of a hand against his jacket pocket.

"Just a minute, Jack; it's rude to interrupt," the doctor said.

The boy stepped away, put his hands on his hips, and began tapping his bare foot on the path. What was this all about? Pike wondered. The boy could not possibly be Van Noort's son. Did the doctor employ him to run errands—was he a courier of secrets?

Van Noort ignored the impudent child, saying to Pike, "I was in the army long enough, South Africa actually, to recognise a man of military bearing. It is not just your title that gives you away."

Strange that Pike was finding out more about this man now when he had ceased to try—or was it, perhaps, the other way around? "Van Noort," he pondered. "I thought your name was familiar."

"Yes, Dutch name, British Army, Boer War. You are bound to remember."

Pike paused for thought, wondering if perhaps they had even met. He felt a sudden burning sensation in his knee; saw the inside of a hospital tent pitched directly onto the veldt, the grass slick with gore. He closed his eyes briefly. If Van Noort had been a doctor in the war, this memory would be something they shared.

Van Noort frowned. "Captain, are you feeling all right?"

"Yes, fine, thank you." Pike maintained a grip by focusing on his next course of action. He hurriedly bade the pair good afternoon, returned to the cool entrance of the hall, and patted down his pockets. As he had suspected, his wallet was gone, stolen by the urchin. Luckily his warrant card wasn't in it. He noted the direction the oddly matched pair were going in the hall's front mirror and took off at a fast pace, leaving the building through its back entrance and rejoining the street some way ahead.

He waited in a doorway as they approached, then stepped out directly in front of them. His sudden appearance startled the man and terrified the boy, bleaching his face of all colour.

Pike said nothing but pressed down on the boy's shoulder with one hand, gesturing "give it over" with the other.

The boy swallowed and looked from Pike to Van Noort.

The doctor's face grew stern. Pike wondered if Jack was in for a clip behind the ear and prepared to intervene. But the doctor's lingering look of disappointment seemed to have more of an effect on the boy than any amount of cuffing. He turned down his mouth and dropped his head.

"Not again, Jack," Van Noort said with a sigh.

The boy sniffed, reached into the pocket of his oversized breeches, and handed Pike back his wallet, his gaze remaining fixed on a pile of cigarette butts near the gutter.

"What do you say to the gentleman, Jack?" Van Noort prompted.

"Sorry, sir. It won't 'appen again."

As the boy continued to study the dirty pavement, Pike and Van Noort exchanged barely perceptible smiles. Van Noort said, "The boy cannot help how he was brought up. We are trying to change all that, aren't we, Jack? The eighth commandment—remind me, please."

"Thou shalt not steal," Jack mumbled.

Pike wondered if he'd been set up; had the man, anxious to learn more about him, goaded the boy into stealing his wallet? Was the image of kindly guardian to troublesome waif an act? If it was, it was a very convincing one.

"Exactly, thou shall not steal," Van Noort said to the boy. "Run along now and I'll meet you at work. On your way call in at your mother's and tell her where you are going so she won't worry." Both men watched Jack disappear into the crowd. "Though I very much doubt she will," he added quietly.

A packed tram pulled up at the stop. "This is mine." Pike grasped the bar and swung aboard. "I'll see if I can arrange a meeting between you and Margaretha."

"I would be most grateful, sir." Van Noort paused. "Margaretha," he said as if savouring the texture of her name on his tongue. "So beautiful—why must she go by that ugly stage name?"

Pike looked down at the tall man with the yellowed eyes. The tram's bell rang. "Mata Hari?" Pike shrugged as the tram began to glide. "More exotic, I suppose."

Chapter Five

Dody left home earlier than usual and missed meeting up with Florence at the breakfast table. Although the sky hung pale and low and the temperatures remained sultry, she found that some of her languor had lifted. Tomorrow she was to present her research proposal to Spilsbury. It was not a genuine proposal per se; junior doctors such as herself and her colleague, Dr. Henry Everard, would never be given that kind of opportunity. But their mentor had thought it good practice for them to see what the groundwork of such work entailed; and if their proposals had merit, he'd said, he might hand them to a senior researcher for perusal.

Dody was cautiously optimistic that her paper would be well received. Spilsbury would not be as excited as she was—though with Spilsbury, one never quite knew—but she hoped it might raise her in his estimation and perhaps increase her responsibilities at the mortuary.

Even though the project would probably never happen, she could not help fantasising—seeing herself working in the famous laboratory at St. Mary's, its modern equipment at her disposal, surrounded by cages of valuable Wistar rats.

But for peace of mind, she needed a second opinion, which was why she had telephoned her old friend and chemistry tutor, Vladimir Borislav, to ask if he would mind checking some of her chemical formulas before she handed the paper in.

Despite the prestigious girls' boarding school Dody had attended, she had not been taught the required mathematics and science subjects for a medical degree, which meant extra swotting to pass her university entrance exams and some floundering during her first years of medicine. If not for Mr. Borislav's extra tuition, she might never have passed her pharmacology subjects.

Borislav's background as the son of Russian immigrants and her family's connections to Moscow had given them reason enough to continue a distant but amiable acquaintance—and since the Women's Clinic had opened down the road from his shop, she had been seeing more of the chemist recently than she had for several years.

Borislav must have heard the Benz idling in the street outside and opened the door of his ground-floor flat before she'd had the chance to raise the knocker.

He greeted her in European fashion with a kiss on each cheek.

"You're looking very well, cool and well. Yellow is certainly your colour," he said.

Dody wore a pale, buttery-hued cotton blouse with a stiff white collar. Her skirt was of a darker shade and a match for the ribbon she wore around her boater.

She smiled, thanked him for the compliment, turned back to the street, and waved at Fletcher to tell him she would not be long, then stepped through the door Borislav held open for her.

It had been a while since she had been inside her friend's flat, and she found the place lighter and airier than she remembered, the nicotine-coloured walls now adorned with floral wallpaper and tiles in the entrance hall instead of uneven floorboards. The austere ancestors who had lined the wall were no longer in view, their space taken up by landscapes of fragile watercolours painted by Borislav's late wife.

A multibranched electric chandelier of modern design added to the new-look hall. The ponderous morning meant it was left on, catching the bright hues of the leadlight front door and daubing the walls and floor with jewels of colour.

Borislav noticed her looking about and smiled. "The new electric system works wonders, yes?"

"It does indeed." *His chemist shop must at last be going well,* Dody thought, happy for him. She knew all about the years of struggle he had endured since the death of his wife, his neglect of the business, and its near collapse.

"Yes, it's taken a while, but I have at last lifted myself up by my bootstraps and given the shop and flat a revamp. You have not yet met my nephew, Joseph, have you? He is about your age and unmarried. I think you will like him." The chemist's eyes sparkled. Oh Lord, obviously it wasn't only her mother who thought she'd been too long on the shelf.

When Dody replied that no, she had not met his nephew, Borislav indicated his green velvet smoking jacket and the jaunty red fez with the gold tassel perched on his head. "As you can see, I am in no hurry for work. Joseph's a reliable lad with a bright head on his shoulders and the shop's in good hands. But enough chitchat. I believe you have something to show me? And I am also anxious for you to see my new parlour," he added with a chuckle.

Borislav's housekeeper, who must have been warned of Dody's arrival, appeared with a tea tray and led them to the parlour.

Dody gathered her notes together while Borislav poured the tea. After she had accepted a cup and declined the shortcake, she presented her paper to him.

He smiled, removed a pair of tortoiseshell spectacles from his top pocket, and began to flick through the pages.

"The pertinent part is towards the end, Mr. Borislav; I just need you to make sure I have the correct formulas."

He frowned, turned to the back page, and nodded. "Yes, yes, very good," he said, but with some reserve she noticed, puzzled.

Dody decided she wanted a biscuit after all. She glanced around the room while he read more of her paper, unable to keep her gaze on his deepening frown. She took in the ornate mantel clock, flanked on each side by Staffordshire figurines, the pile of pharmaceutical journals on an occasional table, and the upholstered chairs of red and white stripes. There was not much else to look at. Suddenly the small, newly decorated room felt stifling.

"So, Dorothy, you want to see if rats fed a certain diet will have a greater or lesser propensity to develop particular types of tumours?" he eventually asked.

"Indeed, but it is only the chemical formulas for the foodstuffs that I'd like you, please, to check. I did not expect you to have the time to read the whole thing." After another nibble of her biscuit, Dody felt compelled to fill the silence that followed. "I am inspired by the work of Johannes Fibiger and his hypothesis that certain tumours are caused by external influences."

Borislav said nothing for a moment. He handed Dody back her papers and removed his glasses. "A worthy cause, I'm sure."

Dody attempted to allay her anxieties with a nervous laugh. "That's all?"

"As you know, I am no research scientist, or even a doctor, just a humble chemist. I cannot give you any advice on the paper itself, only assure you that your chemical formulas are quite correct."

A "but" seemed to hang in the air between them. Borislav was holding something back; she was sure of it. The ring of the telephone put an end to further conversation.

When he returned from taking the call, he told her his special cold mixture was out of stock and that Joseph needed him to fetch some from the warehouse and bring it to the shop immediately. Borislav removed his fez and smoking jacket and replaced them with an outdoor coat and bowler from a hat stand in the hall.

"I'm so sorry, Dorothy, but I really must go," he said. "If there's anything more you wish to discuss, you know where to find me."

She barely had time to thank him as he hurried her to the door, pecked her on the cheek, and apologised again for his hasty departure.

Dody sank into the passenger seat of the Benz, her cautious optimism spoiled now by an undercurrent of unease. What was wrong with her paper? She and Borislav had known each other for ten years. He had never held back praise for her work—or criticism for that matter. She knew she could always count on him for an honest opinion. Why, then, was he holding back now?

She asked Fletcher to take her to the mortuary. Something told her this might not be such a good day after all.

Dody stood the required three feet away from the autopsy table next to her fellow assistant, Henry Everard. Like hounds on the leash, they strained for a word from the Great Man, either a request for assistance or an interesting note to take. Only when invited could they step over the white line that Dr. Bernard Spilsbury had personally painted on the green-tiled floor.

The assistants' struggle to view the proceedings was further hampered by the thick fug of smoke that almost engulfed their mentor. Dr. Everard's role was to ensure that Spilsbury was never without one of his strong-smelling Turkish cigarettes. Dody's part in the procedure was to act as secretary, translating Spilsbury's mutterings onto small index cards in terms that could be understood by the legal profession should the case go to court. Lacking in experience and formal forensic qualifications other than a diploma in general autopsy, Dody was rarely permitted to perform medico-legal autopsies in her own right and then only with written permission from Spilsbury. On rarer occasions still, and much to his chagrin, the less experienced Everard was required to assist her.

The angles of Spilsbury's face were classically handsome. Tall and slim, he was comparatively young for his senior position in the Home Office. His graceful movements over the bodies on the slab sometimes made Dody think of a conductor controlling a beautiful piece of music.

Spilsbury turned his head away from the body and allowed his cigarette end to fall to the floor. Everard crushed the butt into the tiles with the toe of his boot and fumbled in his pocket for a fresh one. Most women would say Everard was handsome, too, his dark good looks enhanced by a luxurious combination of trimmed side-whiskers and wavy, collar-length hair. Dody was not most women.

Everard inhaled. The cigarette paper crackled in the echoing stillness of the autopsy room. *Like resentment,* she thought.

He placed the cigarette between Spilsbury's lips.

"The background, if you please, Dr. McCleland," Spilsbury asked.

"This is Billy Kent, aged three, the third youngest of seven children belonging to Mr. and Mrs. Bert Kent of Whitechapel. Billy's death was regarded as suspicious by the family's panel doctor," Dody said. A panel doctor was one supplied by the newly introduced Health Insurance Scheme and who provided medical access to those who could not otherwise afford it. "The doctor called me in to examine the corpse at the family's tenement. He informed me that last year the couple lost another child to starvation and he was worried this death might be a case of insurance fraud."

Everard flicked a recalcitrant lock of hair from his forehead and turned his eyes to the mortuary room ceiling. "Why in God's name do these women continue to breed?"

Dody felt her spine stiffen. "The expense makes preventatives virtually unobtainable, Doctor. When you consider the appetites of their demanding husbands and that of a wife's obligation to obey, these women have little choice."

"Pregnancy is a natural state, Dr. McCleland," Spilsbury said, "one that should not be interfered with."

"But managed, surely, for the welfare of all."

The corner of Everard's mouth twitched. "You condone infanticide and abortion. Is that what you are saying, Doctor?"

Dody's teeth bit into the stem of her pipe; despite its empty bowl, it helped her to concentrate. Dr. Spilsbury saw the habit as unladylike and she was the only doctor not permitted to smoke in the autopsy room. "I do not mean that, Dr. Everard; you know that I do not," she said.

Everard's eyes widened momentarily. In anyone else the expression might have indicated jest, but she'd had enough disagreements with Everard to know full well when he was not joking.

If Spilsbury sensed the antagonism between his assistants, he never showed any sign of it. He shot them both a basilisk-type stare. "The autopsy room is not the venue for debate. Nor is this an acceptable topic of discussion between males and females."

How can conditions ever improve for the working classes without such discussion? Dody wondered, looking from one man to the other, barely managing to keep the thought to herself. They might be united in their goal to put a stop to criminal abortion and infanticide, but their reasons for it were quite different.

"Pass me the bucket, please, Everard." About to put out his hand, Spilsbury seemed to have second thoughts and shook off both his clumsy rubber gloves first. "Curse these wretched things, they mask all feeling," he muttered. Quick, ambidextrous fingers snipped loose the stomach and poured the contents into the bucket.

"This child looks like it was well on the way to starvation, too," Everard commented as he and Dody peered at the bucket's slime green contents.

"There's something in this." Dody pointed with the nib of her pen to smears of white amongst the green. "Shall I prepare a slide, Doctor?"

She took Spilsbury's grunt as a yes and moved to the instrument trolley for a spoon and a glass beaker.

"It's obvious what it is, isn't it?" Everard commented. "Flakes of lead paint—probably given to the child in some kind of drink—that's how it's usually done. And we've already ascertained that this corpse presents with all the signs of plumbism."

Indeed, the blue line across the top of the child's gums was identical to that of the girl Dody had recently seen in her clinic, Esther Craddock. "I don't think it is quite the usual method, Doctor," she said with the pleasure of proving him wrong. "The police found tablets in the parents' room, tablets which Mr. and Mrs. Kent claimed they had never seen before."

Spilsbury looked up. "Tablets? Where are they?"

"On the instrument trolley."

"Show me."

Dody took the box, tipped some of the tablets into her palm, and held them under the electric light for him to scrutinise. "They were found in a matchbox hidden under a pile of dirty clothes."

"Interesting," Spilsbury said. "They could indeed be lead.

Lead oxide. And the smooth surface, other than those two small dents"—he pointed out some tiny marks on the surface of one of the tablets—"indicate that they have been professionally manufactured using a pill press and not hand-rolled as per usual. Send them to the lab, Dr. McCleland, and make sure they do indeed match the contents of the child's stomach."

As she stared back down at the pills in her hand, a connection began to form somewhere at the edge of her consciousness. "These tablets are familiar . . ." She racked her brains and spoke her thoughts aloud. "A girl at the Clinic had some very similar. Esther . . ." She hesitated. Even amongst colleagues, doctors were bound to respect their patients' privacy. "A scullery maid, three months along. She had been taking lead for some time and wanted me to provide her with something more efficacious. I hope I have persuaded her away from that path." Dody paused. "And I'm sure I've come across something like them in the Book of Lists. Tablets taken by a woman who had also undergone physical abortion."

"Are you sure? This is not the norm. I've never known people like this using lead in tablet form." Everard joined the discussion under the light and severed the thread of her thought. "The poor are opportunists, using what they have at hand—paints, plaster, piping—whatever they think will do the job."

"Then someone is making the despicable task much easier for them, possibly instructing them with dosage, too. Inform the coroner, Dr. McCleland. Visit the family and see if you can find out where they got the lead tablets from."

"It might be worth asking the Whitechapel chemist, Mr. Borislav, if he knows the Kent family, or anything about the tablets' manufacture," Dody said.

"Yes, Vladimir. I've known him since university," Everard said.

"He tutored me at medical school," Dody said, her resentment of Everard's acquaintance with Borislav tempered by the knowledge that the chemist had little respect for her colleague.

"Women's medical school," Everard corrected her.

"He tutored students from many of the medical schools, Dr. Everard, sometimes even going to Edinburgh to lecture. He was not discriminatory."

"Well, jolly good for him."

Jets of smoke shot from Spilsbury's nostrils. "Go and see this Borislav chap then, Dr. McCleland," he said. "He's in the right locale and might have his ear to the ground. Since the tightening of the pharmaceutical laws, there has been a rise in street gangs selling all kinds of dangerous 'remedies.' Take one of the tablets and show it to him. Make a note to that effect and add this case to the Book of Lists. And see if tablets with these unusual indentations were indeed recorded there before our time."

Dr. Spilsbury was an enthusiastic compiler of lists; or rather he delegated the task to Dody. As well as lists of unscrupulous pharmaceutical suppliers, he'd recently had Dody working on lists of persons suspected of practising illegal abortions, infanticide, and baby-farming. The Book of Lists, started in a haphazard way by Spilsbury's predecessor, was growing more comprehensive weekly, and sometimes led to successful prosecutions.

Dody stifled a sigh. She admired the zeal Spilsbury put into the task of bringing such carrion to justice, and yet after years of university studies, numerous unpaid medical positions, and a diploma in autopsy surgery, she sometimes felt a coroner's clerk or agent of enquiry was more suitable for these duties than she. But she had worked hard to attain her position in the Home Office and was not about to complain and risk losing her one paying job, even if it was only part-time.

Spilsbury stepped aside from the table and ordered Everard to sew up the body, a procedure that could have been performed by any one of the lowly attendants. She smiled to herself when she caught Everard's low groan. Perhaps if Henry Everard had had to work as hard as she had to obtain his position, he, too, would have been more accepting of the minor tasks he was assigned.

Dody moved over to a wooden filing cabinet at the far end of the autopsy room and retrieved the heavy leather-bound Book of Lists. In it she recorded the details of Billy Kent's death and sketched a tablet with the unusual scorings. She was about to flick back the pages to see if similar tablets had been recorded before her time, when Everard let out a curse—"Hell's teeth!"—and held up his hand. Blood trickled from his finger and ran down his wrist, daubing the ashen corpse with drops of red.

Spilsbury cast his eyes aloft and indicated for Dody to take over.

She picked up the dropped needle and thread. "Disinfect that well, Dr. Everard," she said. "You know what damage a simple needle prick can do."

"I don't need you to point that out," he shot quietly. In a louder voice, he said. "Thank you, Dr. McCleland."

When she had finished with the corpse, she joined Spilsbury at the trough-like sink, where they washed their hands in silence with the leathery-smelling carbolic soap.

Conversation was not one of the pathologist's attributes. Recently, though, Dody had taken the opportunity to watch him testify in court and experienced once more the sensations that had sparked an earlier, short-lived, infatuation. At the mortuary he had less life about him than most of their patients, but in court, Dr. Bernard Spilsbury shone.

"You will visit Billy Kent's family this afternoon, Doctor?" he enquired.

"Yes, sir, and inform the coroner that he has a case."

"Good. If you find anything of further interest, I'll be in the lab at St. Mary's until about ten tonight. Tomorrow I leave for Edinburgh for two weeks. You will save all but the most routine cases for me."

"Will the trains be running, sir?" Everard called out.

Spilsbury turned to face him and dropped the towel he had been using on his hands. "Lord only knows. I'll go by automobile if I have to. Damned strikers—food left rotting on the docks, mobs in the street, starvation. Can't they see what they are doing to the country, to their own people?"

Dody remained silent. At first she had been in support of the strikers, who worked long hours often under intolerable conditions, until she'd begun dealing with the innocent victims—mainly the children, slowly dying of starvation. If the strikes went on for much longer, famine was predicted.

"They say the country's a whisker away from revolution, and a foreign war is the only way to fix the situation. God help us all," Spilsbury added.

Everard pulled the sheet over the body and joined them at the sink.

"Have you had the chance to peruse our papers yet, sir?" he asked.

"I have indeed. Very good, Everard."

Dody's heart skipped a beat. "Papers? I thought our papers weren't due until tomorrow."

"At the end of last week, actually," Everard said, flicking water from his fingers and reaching for a clean towel. "Because Dr. Spilsbury has been called away, he wanted them in sooner—did I not inform you of that, Dr. McCleland?"

"No, you did not," she said coldly.

Everard pressed a finger to his cheek. "Dear me, come to think of it, I didn't, did I? Frightfully sorry; sir, this is my fault."

Spilsbury nodded; evidently Everard's gallantry absolved him of all sin. Dody glared at Everard as they followed Spilsbury to his office, a large impersonal space off the autopsy room. Everard met her eye and shrugged.

Spilsbury lifted a sheaf of typed foolscap from his desk and handed it to Everard. "As it will be some time now before I can look at Dr. McCleland's paper, you may as well have yours back, Everard. Experiments showing that some foods are tumour-inducing in rats. Most interesting."

What? Dody all but gasped.

Everard must have noticed her look of shock. "Care for a look?" he asked with aggravating nonchalance.

She snatched the paper from his hand and leafed through it. Over the weeks he had openly quizzed her about her research paper. Once she had even caught him riffling through a draft copy she had left on a bench top, an act she'd put down at the time to harmless interest. She needed only a quick glance now to see that although the presentation was slightly different, much of the text was blatantly paraphrased from her own. More fool her for thinking her own profession above such deceit. No wonder Everard had orchestrated getting his paper to Spilsbury first.

Using all her powers of restraint, she managed to halt the accusation before it spilled from her lips. An altercation in front of their mentor would do more harm than good. Besides, it would be almost impossible to prove that she had come up with the idea first. She couldn't hand her proposal in now. What could she do?

Spilsbury said, "I can't guarantee that Dr. Eccles, our primary researcher in tumours, will be interested, but it is a feather in your cap, Everard, well done. As for your paper, Dr. McCleland, you may hand it in if you wish; otherwise, hang on to it until I come back."

"I might just as well keep it for a bit longer, sir," Dody said.

"Suit yourself."

Out of the corner of her eye she saw Everard smirk.

She whirled to face him. Now she understood Borislav's strange reaction to her paper; it was because Everard had shown him his first. That her old friend might have labelled her as the plagiarist was almost as upsetting as the crime itself.

"Yes, Dr. McCleland?" Everard challenged. When she failed to respond, he said, "Save us the suspense, then. Tell us something about your proposal."

She straightened and attempted to cover her inner fury with an outer aspect of cool dignity. She could not think clearly when she was angry and this answer required a quick, calm head.

After a brief pause, she said, "Mine also involves rats, only I am interested in seeing if the creatures can be trained to sniff out the tuberculosis bacilli."

Johannes Fibiger was also investigating the correlation between cancer and TB. The sniffing talents of rats had been but a passing thought of Dody's during the course of her reading and the idle observations of her new pets.

The question now was, could she really assemble the information and put the proposal together before Spilsbury's return? She had no choice. She had to.

Spilsbury shook his head in apparent wonder. "Marvellous, Dr. McCleland, marvellous. A cheap method of diagnosis that has the potential to reach masses."

Praise indeed! Dody could hardly believe her ears. For a fleeting moment she wondered if Spilsbury knew more about the conflict between his assistants than he revealed. *Playing us off against one another,* she supposed, *is one way of bringing out our best—or our worst.*

"Bravo," Everard said drily. "What interesting reading. I can hardly wait."

Chapter Six

The paper had taken several weeks to produce and now Dody had only two weeks to start and finish the new one. Despite the pressure, the more she thought about it, the more excited she became about her off-the-cuff proposal. The new challenge filled her with an electric charge she counted on to keep her going through the busy days ahead.

But there were still the day-to-day activities to contend with, and the first of her priorities was a visit to the Kent family. Accompanied by Florence, Dody descended the stone kitchen stairs to consult Cook.

Annie looked on in horror as, under Cook's supervision, Dody placed a large basket on the scrubbed kitchen table and packed it with a family-sized pork pie, ginger beer, a seed cake, four crisp apples, and a sweating chunk of cheddar.

"I thought we were having that pie for our lunch tomorrow, Mrs. C," Annie complained.

"By then it would 'ave walked out the larder by itself." Cook turned to Dody. "I'm 'aving a terrible time stopping things from going orf, miss. The milk on the doorstep was sour before I got the chance to bring it in this morning."

"Try not to worry too much about it, Mrs. Crabbe," Dody said, "and maybe order fewer perishables. None of us is hungry in this heat."

"I don't see why baby-killers should be treated so special," Annie huffed. She had been serving tea when Dody told Florence about the Kent case. No matter how often Dody chastised her, eavesdropping to Annie was as much a God-given right as her weekly half-day off. She wondered also how much the girl had taken in of her explanation to Florence of Everard's treachery—the whole lot probably. Perhaps it was time for another what-goes-on-in-the-house-stays-in-the-house lecture.

"We don't yet know the truth, Annie. A person is innocent until proven guilty." And besides, Dody thought, the food in the basket might help loosen hungry tongues. Not that she was particularly eager to see either of the wretched parents convicted of infanticide—if only the solution were that simple. What she really wanted was the unscrupulous supplier who had sold them the deadly lead medication and the know-how to use it.

"I don't think you should go there by yourself, Dody—let me come, too," Florence said.

Dody shook her head. "The place is a cesspool of germs. I wouldn't want you to get ill."

Florence grimaced. "No, you weren't at all well after the last visit."

"I was fortunate to get only a mild dose of English cholera.

I probably won't get ill a second time, but you would almost certainly be vulnerable. Don't worry, I can manage on my own."

Florence did not press the point, though she did grumble about being left alone with nothing to do for the remainder of the afternoon.

"Read your book, write to Mother and Poppa," Dody said.

Florence paused for thought. "I might see if Daphne's free to visit Lady Harriet Frobisher with me."

"The household struck with cholera? Don't have anything to eat or drink there, for goodness' sake. You'd be better off coming with me after all."

"I think they are just about over it now. Besides, it can't really be as dangerous as the place you're visiting."

Dody shrugged. "Perhaps not. Mrs. Crabbe, I need you to keep a variety of food scraps readily available at all times. Tell me in advance what you plan on leaving out for the pig man; I want first refusal on all kitchen waste—bread, cake, meat, fish, cheese, et cetera." She turned to Florence. "Before I start with the TB samples, I have to find out what food appeals to the rats the most, so I know how best to reward them for successful sniffing."

Florence, Cook, and Annie exchanged glances. "Dody," Florence said, holding up a finger. "We really don't want to see, hear, or smell anything more of your familiars, is that clear?"

The servants backed up their younger mistress with vigorous nods.

Dody sighed, outnumbered and suitably chastised. Back to the task in hand. She tested the weight of the basket: heavy.

She would have to ask Fletcher to drop her at the chemist, a quarter-mile or so from her destination. No good would come from the visit if the locals saw her being delivered by a private motorcar. Even motorised taxis were a rarity in that particular East End neighbourhood.

The High Street chemist was airless. Dody put down her basket with relief and pressed the bell on the counter next to a giant pestle and mortar.

Mr. Borislav emerged from the dispensing room and opened his palms in delight. "Two visits in one day: I am honoured. Are you still unwell? That pesky cholera has a tendency to come and go. Would you like some more Valentine's Meat Juice?"

"No, no, I am much better now, thank you."

"Your paper then—how was it received?"

"Actually, there are two things I need to talk to you about."

"And I have something for you, too."

"You do? Then please . . ."

"No, I insist, ladies first."

Dody drew a breath. "Mr. Borislav, I think you and I both know that you were shown two very similar papers."

"Ah." Borislav removed the spotted handkerchief that usually poked from his top pocket and dabbed at his damp forehead.

"How could you doubt me?" she asked with undisguised hurt.

"It was not you I doubted."

"Then why did you not warn me?"

"What good would warning you do? By the time I saw you, I knew Everard had already handed in his paper—what was done was done. Do you wish me to tell Spilsbury about it now?"

Dody frowned. "No, no, Spilsbury has no idea about the plagiarism. And I have been given an extension, which should just give me time to rewrite my paper. I'm only sorry that you were placed in such a difficult position."

"My heart dropped into my boots when I saw Henry Everard on my doorstep the other day, wanting me to check his proposal for him. He was at the same university and in the same year as my nephew, you know."

Dody waited with interest for him to elaborate.

Instead he said, "I think it is time you two met." He turned his head and called to Joseph in the dispensing room.

The younger man emerged, wiping his hands down his white coat. He was as tall as his uncle was short, his face as rugged as Borislav's was soft and round. But his smile was similar to his uncle's, and his identical spectacles caught the light in the same manner, adding a certain rakish charm.

"I have heard much about you, Mr. Champion," Dody said with a smile, liking him at once.

"Likewise, Dr. McCleland. My uncle speaks very highly of you. When I heard that your Clinic was opening down the road, I was hoping we would at last get to meet."

"I was telling Dr. McCleland how you knew Henry Everard at university," Borislav said.

Joseph paused as if to consider his words. "Indeed," and let the word hang. The lack of warmth, praise, any comment at all for that matter, told Dody more about his opinion of Everard than anything his uncle might have coaxed from him.

Borislav exaggerated a shrug. "How can I help that he was raised to be the gentleman?"

When their laughter had died, Joseph said, "It's been lovely to meet you, Dr. McCleland, but I must now tear myself away and return to work."

"Work of your own making, I would like to remind you," Borislav said. To Dody he added, "Joseph is working on a way of mass-producing poultices so we always have a ready stock. Frankly, I think it detracts from the sense of personal service our customers receive when they know the product has been made for them specifically."

"But far more efficient, Uncle. If you'd only allow me to employ an apprentice to help . . ."

"Be off with you!" Borislav said with an undercurrent of irritation in his voice that suggested his words were not entirely jest.

When the dispensary door had closed, Borislav said, "Change, change, change. I have to admit that Joseph has played his part in the shop's reversal of fortunes, but the customers can only take so much newness."

"You mean the proprietor can," Dody teased.

Borislav straightened his bow tie, then leaned across the counter towards Dody and returned to the earlier subject. "Everard was quite the wastrel, according to Joseph, and about the only thing Joseph did not miss from the university when he left it. It grieved me when I learned that you and Everard had been thrown together for work. Apparently he made no effort to hide what little respect he had for female doctors, even then."

Dody quirked her friend a smile. "I can cope with Henry Everard."

"Of course you can." He gave her hand a squeeze. "That's my girl. There was something else you wanted to ask me?"

Dody reached into her bag and put the matchbox of tablets on the counter. "These tablets were found at the premises of a suspicious death. We think they are lead."

Borislav picked out a tablet and examined it under a magnifying glass. The bright electric light shone down on his bowed head, his pink scalp shining through salt-and-pepper hair.

"Yes, they appear to be lead," he said. "How unusual—highly concentrated, I suspect. But I cannot tell for certain without tests."

"St. Mary's is conducting tests. I was just wondering if you had come across tablets with this type of unusual scoring before," Dody said.

"Not that I can remember, but I will check with Joseph. They were supplied in the matchbox?"

"Possibly; they were found in it. And the victim was from this area."

"Unfortunately there are many around here with the ability to manufacture tablets such as these. All it requires is some basic scientific knowledge, equipment, and a pill press such as you would find in all chemists, pharmacies, and apothecaries—sometimes doctors' surgeries. Even a doctor like yourself would be capable of manufacturing them . . ." Borislav broke off and rubbed his chin.

"What's on your mind, Borislav?"

"Oh, it is nothing, really. But—you are aware that lead is often used for criminal abortion?"

"Of course."

"Well, the lack of a specific container could indicate they

have been made without a licence by someone who did not wish to be traced. You can imagine how these tablets would appeal, especially if not diluted with superfluous ingredients. The higher potency means they have a better chance of working."

"More expensive?"

Borislav nodded. "I imagine so, but not too pricey or else the poorer classes would not be able to afford them. A rather strange fellow has been visiting me of late." Borislav paused and pushed his glasses up his nose. "Both Joseph and I have had occasion to serve him and we have both questioned his motives. He calls himself a doctor, though I have my doubts about that. He tends to buy supplies relevant to female needs, if you get my drift. I wonder if he might have something to do with these tablets?"

"The man practises obstetrics, you mean? Do you know his name?"

"Something foreign, I think." Borislav's Russian heritage made him no less suspicious of foreigners than most English. He shook his head. "I'm sorry, Dorothy, but that is all I remember. At times I have been driven to having words with him for pestering my female customers. I would go to the police if I had anything more conclusive."

"Will you let me know when he next visits—see if you can get his name for me and any other details? I might be able to find something about him in our Book of Lists."

"Ah yes, your record of suspicious persons."

"I've also seen tablets like this in the possession of a scullery maid I have been treating. I only had the chance for a quick glance, but they might have been scored this way. Perhaps she has had dealings with your foreign doctor? I will track the girl down and ask her some questions. I will not rest until I get to the bottom of this."

"Tread cautiously, Dorothy: asking the wrong kinds of questions in an area like this might not be such a wise move. It would be all too easy for you to kick over the wrong stone."

Dody heard the shuffle of feet, the clearing of a female throat. She stepped aside to let Borislav serve a customer, a plump woman of indeterminate age who ordered eight ounces of humbugs.

Borislav scooped out a clump of sticky sweets, weighed and bagged them, and exchanged friendly conversation with the woman about the close weather. Perhaps they would be blessed with a shower tonight. He finished up by trying to persuade her to part with tuppence for some soothing peppermint lozenges. She declined, her departure from the shop accompanied by the vigorous clanging of the spring bell on the door.

He turned back to Dody and shrugged. "Can't win 'em all."

She laughed.

"I am glad to see you cheered up. And now I have something that will really put a smile on your face."

He leaned across the counter and patted his top pocket mischievously. "Some weeks ago we had a conversation about the Ballets Russes . . ."

She stared at him for a moment, placed her hand on her chest to calm the sudden racing of her heart. "You didn't . . ."

"Indeed I did."

"Tickets to the ballet?"

"Due to cancellation; two tickets for tomorrow night, but only in the stalls, I'm afraid. Sorry about the short notice." Borislav smiled. "I take it you are still interested?"

"Oh yes, thank you. Of course I'm still interested!" Dody said, her thoughts hurrying over everything she had to get done. As for her paper, she could spend some time on it when she returned from the theatre. She must not let her concerns for that wretched assignment cast a shadow over the following evening: the Ballets Russes was the chance of a lifetime. "I'll pick you up at seven o'clock and we can have supper after the performance," Borislav said.

Chapter Seven

Her excitement over the ballet was soon forgotten when she entered the Kents' tenement building. So heavy was its press, Dody felt she could have pushed the stench away with her hands. It seeped through the tenement walls and floorboards like invisible fog, through window gaps and under doors. In the single-room dwelling belonging to the family, it gathered in greatest concentration in the vicinity of a dilapidated set of bureau drawers. Near these a red-faced Mrs. Kent dozed in a rocker, one breast drooping like an empty slipper from her open blouse.

Dody slammed the basket of food on the table. The woman gasped and opened her eyes.

"Blimey, Doctor, caught me napping." Mrs. Kent shoved her breast back into her blouse and struggled to her feet. Taking a rag from a bucket of water on the table, she wrung it out and dabbed at her face, her movements slow and delib-

ANTIDOTE TO MURDER 71

erate in the stultifying heat. Then she took a chipped cup and
dipped it into the same water, looking over the rim at Dody
with defiance as she gulped it down. Dody bit her tongue.
These people were sick of personal hygiene lectures given by
toffs who had no idea what life was like without indoor plumb-
ing, at the mercy of a single, erratic standpipe in the street.

The other occupant of the room, Mr. Kent, lay sprawled
half naked and snoring across the sagging iron bed. "Where
are the children?" Dody asked.

"John's at work and the others are playing in the street;
it's cooler there." Mrs. Kent plopped the cup back into the
water bucket and began to riffle through the basket's contents.

"John has a job?" That had to be something, Dody supposed.

"A good one—our John'll go far s'long as 'e watches that
lip of 'is."

"And the baby." Dody glanced around the room. "Where's
Molly?"

Mrs. Kent, busy lifting the pie from the basket, failed to
answer.

With a spasm of dread, Dody moved towards the bureau.
She didn't need the scenting talents of a bloodhound to recognise the smell of English cholera. "I told you to take her to
the London Hospital if she got any worse," she said, stooping
over the baby to feel her burning head.

"Bert an' me 'ave been sick an' all," Mrs. Kent said, spraying a mouthful of pie crumbs. "I mean look at 'im now"—she
nodded to the sprawled lump on the bed—"'e can barely move."

Dody's eyes rested on the empty bottle cradled in the
man's arms. Reading her expression, Mrs. Kent added, "For
the pain, love." She shot her husband a cautious glance, cut

a generous piece of pie, and put it back in Dody's basket. "Take that to my kids on yer way out, will you, miss? They won't get nuffink if it stays in 'ere."

Dody said she would and closed the basket's lid.

Sifting through a pile of dirty linen on the floor, she picked up the cleanest of the items, a hemless rag that might once have been a tea towel, and placed it over her shoulder to protect her fine cotton blouse. She lifted the listless baby from the drawer and settled herself on the only kitchen chair. "Has she been feeding?"

"Me milk's just about gorn, miss. I've been trying 'er with this." Mrs. Kent nodded towards a small milk jug sitting on the table next to the water bucket. "But she ain't interested."

Dody sniffed at the milk, amazed to find it still fresh. Taking a clean rag from the table, she twisted it into a wick and dipped it into the jug. With her little finger she prised open the baby's mouth and gently inserted the wick.

"Have you given her anything else?" Dody asked as she tickled the baby's throat, enticing her to swallow. "Anything from the chemist or apothecary?"

"We can't afford no fancy medicines," Mrs. Kent said, popping the cork from the ginger beer and taking a long swallow.

"I ask because lead was found in the stomach of your child Billy, probably from the tablets the police found here hidden in a matchbox."

Dody indicated an unopened blue envelope on the kitchen table. "I see you have received your summons—I'd open it soon if I were you; it will tell you where and when you need to appear in court. But listen carefully to me, Mrs. Kent. If you tell me now who gave or sold you the lead tablets, the enquiry will be a lot easier for you. Perhaps you purchased the tablets for yourself to prevent pregnancy and the child found and swallowed them. If that can be proved, Billy's death will be ruled as misadventure."

Mrs. Kent put the bottle down. "I don't know nuffink about lead pills," she mumbled, her eyes fixed on the baby.

"If you and your husband are found guilty of infanticide, you will go to prison. Or worse."

The rag-wick moved, the baby swallowed, and Dody felt her spirits rise. This child might at least have a chance at life. She handed the rag back to Mrs. Kent for a redipping. The woman's hands shook so she could barely get the wick into the milk. "Can't you tell me who gave you the tablets, Mrs. Kent?" Dody asked. "It really will be better for you."

"Who'll look after the little ones if we're both put away?" Mrs. Kent looked down at the baby, sucking now with more strength. A smile ghosted her reddened face. This was not the face of a bad woman, Dody realised, just an uneducated, deprived woman, one who might well have started life off in a bureau drawer herself.

"There's a bloke down the pub," Mrs. Kent began. "'E's a—" A hurled bottle cut the words from her mouth, crashing to the floor next to the table in an explosion of glass. Dody sprang to her feet and clutched the child tightly to her chest. The infant started up a feeble wail. "Mr. Kent, how dare you?" she cried, her heart galloping as she shielded the baby's head with her hand.

"And 'ow dare you come into my 'ouse and accuse me missus an' me of doin' our young'un in!"

"I saw the lead tablets in Billy's stomach myself," Dody said, willing the tremble from her voice.

"Well, we didn't put 'em there. The lad was always in the street, there's all types down there, anyone could've given 'im them as sweets."

"Then give the court the chance to prove it."

"Yeah, the court, maybe—but we don't need you messing about in our business, accusin' an' all. 'Er an' me didn't kill our kid and we don't 'ave the foggiest 'oo did. Now get out of 'ere while you still can. There's plenty other bottles under this bed, or do ya want the shit can?" He reached under the bed and slid out a brimming metal bucket. Dody backed towards the door, clutching the baby to her.

"I'm taking the baby to the London Hospital," she said to Mrs. Kent. "I'll give the staff there your details. Go and visit her tomorrow."

"Lady Harriet is not at home, Miss McCleland, Miss Hamilton, er, misses, ma'ams," the liveried footman said nervously.

Florence made a point of turning and looking into the street, where she counted one motorcar and two carriages, the chauffeur and coachmen of said vehicles lounging around under the shade of a horse-chestnut tree, smoking and talking as if they had been waiting awhile.

A door opened and closed somewhere within the red-bricked mansion and Lady Harriet appeared wearing rose pink. She glided up behind the footman. "Who is it, Frank?" she asked. The footman stepped aside. "Florence? Daphne? What a wonderful surprise! That will be all, thank you, Frank."

The women embraced. Not wishing to inhale any germs, Florence held her breath, letting it go only when she saw

Daphne breathing easily. Daphne was a nurse. She should know.

"Darlings, you must come in for tea. Miss Margaret Bentham is here, as are Lady Gloria Holt and Mrs. Chapman."

"Really? How marvellous. I haven't seen any of them for ages," Daphne said.

"We weren't expecting tea, Harriet. Please don't put yourself out. We just wanted to see how you and the household were—if you have all recovered," Florence said.

"Never felt better." Harriet's eyes shone. "Do come in, Flo, don't be such a spoilsport."

Never let it be said that Florence was a spoilsport. Surely the germs would have gone by now. She smiled. "Oh, very well then."

They followed Lady Harriet into her parlour to find their three friends seated around the tea table in a room of soft pastels and French-styled furniture. The scent of their mingled perfumes filled the air; shadows from the chestnut tree outside danced across the clean, bright walls. Frank was sent to fetch more cups despite Florence's continued refusal of tea. She was in a hurry to get going, to visit the apothecary who sold the Widow Welch's and give him a piece of her mind. If they stayed here much longer, she knew she would have trouble convincing Daphne, whose heart had not really been in the excursion anyway, to accompany her. Florence was not so foolish as to visit the East End on her own.

Florence continued to refuse the offer of sustenance. The others tucked in to cucumber sandwiches and light as light jam sponge with strawberries, and gossiped about a recent debutantes' ball. Did you see Mrs. Compton's gangly daughter stepping all over the toes of young Lord Such 'n' Such?

You'd think she'd never had a dancing lesson in her life, et cetera.

So trivial, Florence thought. They were all good eggs, but surely they could find something better to do with their time. What surprised her the most was how much Daphne seemed to be enjoying their company. Florence was even more surprised by what happened next.

Harriet left the tea table and turned the key in the lock of the door. "Wait, Harriet, we really need to get going," Florence said.

"Nonsense, Flo, the apothecary isn't going anywhere," Daphne answered. "We simply have to stay for this."

Harriet produced a dainty key from her pocket and unlocked the drawer of an elegant inlaid desk. From it she produced what looked to be an overly large silver cigarette box. Everyone, including Florence, leaned towards the table as Harriet sprung the lid to reveal a gold-plated syringe resting on a bed of silk alongside an ampoule of liquid and a rubber tourniquet.

One by one the ladies bared their arms and Harriet injected them with the substance from the ampoule. When she settled at Florence's side, Florence shook her head. The dreamy expressions of the women injected were discomforting, and she had no wish to join them. They were women without purpose, playing silly, childish games. Florence liked adventure, but this was beyond the pale. As for Daphne, she was a nurse and should know better. Dody was forever going on about how bad for one's health this kind of activity was. How could Daphne even think to do this?

Florence stood up. "I'd like to go now, Harriet. It's been

nice seeing you and I'm glad to find your household recovered from the cholera."

"Our tea parties are obviously not to Florence's taste," Mrs. Chapman said slowly, like a foreigner who had to think before pronouncing every word.

"Here," said Lady Gloria, reaching into her reticule, "maybe this is more Florence. Not everyone can tolerate the needle." At which she uncorked a small bottle marked ETHER and poured it over the bowl of strawberries in the centre of the table.

"I hear the strawberries are exceptionally good this year," Daphne giggled.

So even her friend was making fun of her. This would not do. Would not do at all. Florence unlocked the door herself. Turning she said, "I will see you, no doubt, at the next Blooms-bury meeting, Daphne."

Her flinty tone had the desired effect. Daphne, suitably shamed, looked down at her clasped hands. "Oh, yes. Of course you will, Florence."

Chapter Eight

Pike lived in a boardinghouse off Millbank Road, on a desolate, partially cleared patch of ground waiting for the completion of the new sewerage system and the extension of the Victoria Tower Gardens. Many of the area's slums had already been flattened and their occupants relocated to high towers of redbricked flats in nearby Westminster.

The local wharfs were dormant, too, but frequently, as Pike tossed and turned in his bed, he imagined them still operational. Sometimes he swore he could hear the creak of the winches, the thunk of crates, and the cursing of stevedores and lumpers, backs bent under heavy loads of timber and coal.

The area's state of limbo meant that his lodgings, destined for demolition, were cheap though surprisingly comfortable. The shabby exterior of peeling paint and warped boards was not reflected on the inside, which was clean and efficiently run.

The entry hall acted as an effective cordon sanitaire

against the dusty wasteland outside. The long oriental runner was of mulberry hues, the wallpaper dark green with lighter green stripes. Two chairs on either side of the marble hall table and the settee opposite were upholstered in creamy damask.

Pike found a letter from his teenaged daughter, Violet, waiting for him on the hall table and slipped it into his pocket. He would save it for later, when he was not in such a hurry, when he could give it the attention it deserved.

His private portion of the house consisted of a small sitting room and an even smaller bedroom, saved from the oppression of its dark varnished bed and wardrobe by pale textured wallpaper. Except for his clothes, a picture of Violet on the chest of drawers, and an old leather trunk, very little in the room belonged to him. The trunk held a few mementos of his military career: his Mauser automatic pistol—a German-made weapon he had taken from a dead Boer commando—captain's pips, uniforms, regimental photographs, and a few other things he should never have kept. The trunk's lock was getting rusty and the key would probably not turn now; he had not reopened it since locking it over ten years ago.

He put the letter from Violet on his bedside table and peeled off his dirty clothes. At his marble washstand he mixed up shaving cream in his mug and was about to lather over the thick stubble on his face when he stopped, brush poised. Perhaps he should leave the beard. The strange doctor had been at rehearsals again today. Occasionally the yellowed eyes in the front row had broken their hold on Margaretha and turned to focus on him. Pike had no idea what social circles the man mixed in or whom he might invite to accompany him to the rehearsals and performances. That he knew something of

Pike's war experiences was of no consequence, but it did matter that he was not identified as the serving police officer he was now.

If anyone were to enquire about the captain, they would have been told about the down-on-his-luck ex-military officer, a reserved gentleman who supplemented his pension by playing popular songs in the seedy pubs along the banks of the river. Clothes maketh the man and Pike knew this well. With only an outdated, shabby outfit and what he considered an ordinary face, he had blended effortlessly for years on the fringes of the dockside landscape, keeping an eye on the Yard's informants, sniffing out new leads on dead-end cases, and listening for talk of crimes yet to be committed.

He shaved his neck, making his beard appear more the result of careful management than of sloth, and after a quick wash, changed into a freshly pressed grey summer suit. As he straightened his silk cravat, he gazed in the mirror with satisfaction—piano tramp to city gent in less than fifteen minutes. Excellent.

His landlady, Mrs. Keating, had eventually grown tired of tackling him over his erratic sense of dress. It was not the only thing she had grown tired of.

He stood aside for her on the second-floor landing. She turned her head to the wall, the single feather in her dyed black hair quivering with indignation. "That's two nights in a row I've kept your supper warm for you, Mr. Pike. I won't do it again."

"I'm sorry, Mrs. Keating, I was unable to get word to you."

"Mr. Cross won't mind, I'm sure. He's always ready for a second helping," she said, a trail of eau de corsage lingering behind her on the stairs.

Poor sod, Pike thought to himself. Mrs. Keating's newest gentleman boarder had no idea what he was in for.

Pike caught a motorised omnibus to Horse Guards and called into the War Office, where he spent some time in the record archives before walking the rest of the way to Scotland Yard with an extra green-coloured file in his brief-case.

Humidity sucked the air from the atmosphere and left it with a heavy feeling of rain. In the gloomy hush, lethargic street vendors slung canvas sheets across stalls of flowers, fruit, and boxes of colourful sweets.

Pike was perspiring heavily by the time he reached his destination.

He entered the Special Branch offices through a side door of the Scotland Yard building and wended his way up the curling stairs and down claustrophobic passages to Superintendent Callan's office without, thankfully, bumping into anyone he knew.

Special Branch was considered an elite department, though Pike knew too well that his transfer to its suffragette arm was just a slap in the face, one step away from ignominious dismissal. It was like being asked to join the king's personal bodyguard and discovering your prime duty was to clean the royal boots. He had been told that his mild-mannered approach and nonthreatening appearance made him just the kind of officer the division needed to soothe those hysterical females.

Mild-mannered—was that what they really thought of him?

Until his daughter's involvement in the movement and his subsequent meeting with the McCleland sisters, he had viewed the suffragettes as little more than a trivial irritation. If they wanted the vote, hooliganism and vulgar heckling was not, in his opinion, the way to go about getting it. If their leaders were supposedly highly educated women, what should one expect of their more ignorant sisters? An extension of the vote to include all women would surely render the country more of a Bedlam than it was now.

But his attitude had softened somewhat on the broader issues of equal rights for men and women. Perhaps that had something to do with seeing the world his daughter would soon be entering through her eyes. Violet was a bright girl; he would like to see her doing something more valuable and fulfilling before marriage than attending mindless tea parties and debutante balls. Or perhaps it was observing the challenges that Dody McCleland had to overcome daily in order to practise the form of medicine she chose. Or perhaps he was just softening with age.

He reached Callan's door. Since the government interference into Pike's last murder investigation and his transfer from Scotland Yard, Callan had gone out of his way to restore their broken friendship. Sanctioning Pike's undercover operation during the lull in suffragette activity had helped, but it had not yet fully restored the sense of ease that Pike had once shared with his former friend.

"The beard doesn't suit, old man," Callan said, greeting Pike and pulling the visitor's chair out for him.

"An extra precaution," Pike said, smoothing his palm across the itching bristles. "I've met someone, an Englishman, whose behaviour is suspicious. I'm not sure of his connections.

He could even be in cahoots with the Dutch woman—he's certainly obsessed with her."

Callan's eyebrows rose. "What about Klassen?"

"Her manager? I've never met a less likely spy."

"Appearances are deceptive. You are the living proof." Callan smiled. Once Pike would have met the remark with a smile himself; now he betrayed no emotion at all. "As for that woman," Callan continued, running a finger along the inside of his collar, "she seems capable of anything. MO5 have asked us to keep an eye on her. Her postcards to Germany are regarded as highly suspicious. We have to humour MO5 and quash the rumours if nothing else—and she is Dutch, after all."

Pike agreed. Holland had close ties with Germany, and both countries had openly supported the Boers against the British in South Africa. "Even so, we need to follow this doctor up," Pike said. "He's not technically Dutch, but he does have the ancestry."

He removed the green War Office file from his briefcase and spread the contents on Callan's desk. "Dr. Archibald Van Noort," he read, running his finger across the lines of inky scrawl to pick out what he thought was relevant. "Born in Sussex in 1865, studied medicine at Oxford, and then a few years later set up rooms in Harley Street specialising in women's ailments. When war was declared in South Africa, he joined the Royal Army Medical Corps to broaden his medical experiences—seems his father-in-law, Major General Hawksworth, might have pulled some strings. Served with distinction in the RAMC, injured during the shelling of the Twenty-sixth Field Hospital at Dundee, and then returned to England to convalesce and resume his consultancy. That's it."

Callan tented his fingers. "Sketchy. What about the wife?"

"I'll talk to her when I find her."

"I can get my people to look further into the other records if it helps."

"Thank you. Rear Admiral Millbank seems to have taken a genuine shine to the dancer."

"Didn't think that would be too much of a stretch."

"He still knows nothing about me?"

Callan shook his head. "The less he knows, the less he can spill."

"Good, let's keep it that way."

"She's constantly pumping him for information, apparently—pressuring him to take her to the navy shipyards," Callan said. "He has been instructed on what he can and cannot say; mostly fantasy but the occasional smidgen of truth."

"When you see him next, ask him if he has seen her with Van Noort. The doctor might well be passing on the information she's gleaned from the admiral straight to Germany— wiring it in code or having it couriered, sent by diplomatic bag even. The last time I spoke to the doctor, he was in the company of a young ragamuffin. I saw no sign of the lad today. The boy might be his messenger," Pike said.

"It's possible, I suppose; try and find out. Meanwhile I'll get Customs to see if Van Noort has a passport. I'd like to know when he last left the country."

"Right," Pike said. "Your man's little talk with the musical director worked, by the way. He's disappeared and I'm to stay on for the performance proper at the Empire. Van Noort has booked a box for every night of the show, so I should have no trouble keeping an eye on him."

"Splendid. When does it start?"

"We have three days of rehearsing in the hall with full orchestra next week, and then the first performance is at the Empire on Thursday night, the beginning of a four-day booking. After that, they hope to get bookings for the Army and Navy Club through Millbank, provided there's not too much public outrage over the indecency, of course." Pike paused for thought. It had been his idea to plant the admiral, and so far the plan seemed to be working. But things were moving slowly . . . if he could only speed them up a little . . .

"What's on your mind, Pike?"

"That bloody briefcase the admiral insists on locking to his wrist."

"He's always done that; likes to feel important."

"Isn't he working on the fifteen-inch guns for the new Dreadnought? If the ship's blueprints were to fall into German hands . . ."

"Millbank isn't that stupid, nor is the Admiralty. I doubt they'd let him carry anything more important than his wife's shopping list."

"Well, we might know that, but Margaretha wouldn't and her contact wouldn't. Do you think the admiral is trustworthy?"

"I haven't had a problem with him so far. What are you suggesting, Pike?"

"With all due respect, sir, the admiral is a well-known braggart. He could be useful for more than just the planting of false information. We could use him to bait a trap for our spy."

"I'm listening."

"We could suggest that he be deliberately indiscreet, play up the importance of the papers in his briefcase."

"I think he probably does that anyway."

"Make him aware then that our spy—Van Noort, Margaretha, or whom-so-ever it may be—might make a move to try to steal the briefcase. Now," Pike thought aloud, "if there was just something we could do to that briefcase . . ."

Callan shook his head and smiled. "You and your love of intrigue and gadgetry. I have not forgotten it was your idea to catch Dr. Crippen by means of the wireless telegraph."

Pike smiled at last. His fascination with the rapidly developing techniques of criminal detection was what kept him in the force. His main problem was getting the old fogies holding the reins interested in them, too.

If only there was something he could place in the briefcase to make it easily tracked. He scratched his beard and ran through the possibilities in his mind: a wireless signal? No, too cumbersome. Something a dog could scent that the spy would not notice? Talk about the sublime to the ridiculous. And they could forget the time-bomb idea; couldn't risk the admiral being blown to smithereens . . .

Pike looked at Callan. "Back to basics, I think. A twenty-four-hour surveillance on that briefcase. Have you enough trained men?"

"I doubt it," Callan said without enthusiasm.

"Then borrow some from the Met—it's the only way, Tom. Someone is going to make a move on that briefcase, and we have to catch him or her red-handed."

"I'd hoped for something more imaginative from you."

Pike shrugged. What was Callan expecting, Sherlock Holmes?

Callan sighed. "I'll see if I can muster a team, but I can't promise miracles." He pushed back his chair and moved to a walnut drinks cabinet. Inside Pike saw neat ranks of bottles and sparkling crystal glasses, mirrored to appear like dozens. "A drink to success?"

Pike hesitated only a moment. Perhaps one day they would feel at ease with each other again. His career had suffered because of Callan, but he should be grateful to the man for giving him a break from those troublesome suffragettes.

"Brandy and soda, please." He should have taken advantage of the truce and called on the McClelands before he and Florence were at loggerheads again. A brave man would have found some way of explaining his abysmal behaviour at the hospital to Dody.

For a moment Pike lost himself in the memory of what might have been: soft brown eyes and the glossy pile of hair that tended to fall apart after a busy day. He found that her memory occupied his mind like a musical motif, anticipated with delight and mourned when gone. The bright intelligence of the woman, the bloody wilfulness, the stillness about her when she listened.

A sudden crack of thunder made Pike start, jolting him from his reverie and reminding him that he was not brave at all. "You all right, old man?" Callan asked as he handed Pike his brandy.

Pike took a gulp. "Fine. Thank you, sir. Damned weather. Hope it rains."

Chapter Nine

The Paddington Coroner's and Mortuary Complex was a modern structure boasting separate mortuary rooms for infectious and noninfectious cases and a well-lit postmortem room, separated from the civil side of the building by a viewing lobby. The self-contained building meant that the bodies no longer had to be carted between the different facilities as they had in the past—an inefficient process which rarely left them fresh for inspection.

Although, Dody reflected as she stepped into the yard, the odour about the place that day was quite reminiscent of the improvised mortuaries of the bad old days. The night's brief rainstorm had left nothing but steaming damp on the pavements and by afternoon the atmosphere was sultrier than it had been all week.

The heat and the strikes meant ice was in short supply. The drone of flies drew her gaze to the last of their precious store dripping from a pipe in the exterior wall, trickling into one of several drains embedded in the brick-paved yard. A bony dog sniffed at the overflowing dustbins stacked nearby, causing an unpleasant picture to form in her mind. She shook her head to dismiss it. Medical waste from these modern premises was supposed to be incinerated. In any case, Alfred, the senior attendant, fed the dog, so it wouldn't be that hungry—would it?

The yard was the only place Dody was permitted to smoke. She reached into her skirt pocket for her tobacco pouch and pipe and packed the tobacco into the bowl—not too tight—and took several relieving puffs. An afternoon in the office trying to sort through teetering piles of Spilsbury's neglected paperwork was more exhausting than a full day in the mortuary room. Smoke hung about her in the still air. From beyond the hearse entrance she heard someone hail a taxi, the clatter of a slowing engine, the slam of a motorcar's door.

Moments later a slight man wearing a greasy cloth cap entered the yard—surely this man had not arrived by taxi? Unaware of Dody's presence, he made as if to enter the premises through the back door.

Dody stepped from her place beneath the eaves. "Excuse me, sir. This entrance is for staff only; the public entrance is at the front of the building."

The man started, froze for a moment. He took off his cap and slowly turned. Dody found herself looking at a small man with a pushed-in face, the picture of misery itself.

"Sorry, missus," he said as if all the cares of the world rested on his shoulders. "But I've an appointment with someone in this place."

Poor soul must have come to collect personal effects or, worse, identify a dead relative, Dody thought. But while her heart reached out in sympathy for the man, they could not afford to have people off the street in this section of the coronial building. "That's quite all right," she said gently. "Just go to the entrance and state your business to the clerk at the front desk."

The man said he would, replaced his hat, and shuffled off, hobnailed footsteps ringing funereally across the paved yard.

A distant clock chimed four. Dody drew in a last breath of smoke and tapped out the remainder of the tobacco against the heel of her boot. It was time she left for home to prepare for the ballet. The ladies' cloakroom was at the civil end of the building, and she'd taken advantage of Spilsbury's absence by leaving her coat and bag in the more conveniently located doctors' common room. She would not have time to wash her hair when she got home before going out, but might still manage a bath if she was quick. It would be a good idea to ask one of the attendants to whistle her up a cab while she prepared to leave the building.

In the common room she dabbed scent behind her ears and straightened her tie and stiff collar in the mirror above the empty fireplace. The senior attendant, Alfred, shuffled in, clutching a bunch of fresh lavender. He stopped short when he saw Dody at the mirror, blushed, and took a step back.

"It's all right, Alfred, I've finished. Come in," Dody said.

"I don't like to disturb you, miss."

"I know I shouldn't be in here—you won't tell anyone, will you?"

Alfred gave her a crooked smile. "I'm beginning to lose count of all them secrets we share."

"Then just remember who got you this job," she teased. "Think how much better your chest is here than in that draughty old St. Thomas's Mortuary."

Alfred coughed, as if to remind her that he was not out of the woods yet.

Suddenly, they heard a commotion from the front of the building and raised male voices. Alfred and Dody rushed into the passage in time to see the small man she had directed earlier fleeing from the autopsy room through the door leading to the yard, clasping a heavy case to his chest.

"Stop him!" Everard yelled in pursuit. "He's stolen my bloody bag!"

Dody and Alfred rushed to follow Everard into the yard and from there to the street, where the man melted into a crowd of unemployed protesters. Everard's cries of "Stop thief!" were lost amongst the desperate chanting of the men. "Jobs for all!"

He returned to them beet-faced. "Damn and blast it. Didn't one of you see him enter the building, try to stop him?"

Dody did not answer him until they had returned to the comparative cool of the building. "I thought he was a grieving relative. I directed him to the front entrance," Dody said.

"How thoughtful of you. He still made it through to the back and right to my medical bag. It contained enough narcotic medicines to last my surgery for a week." Like Dody, Everard spent only part of his time at the mortuary. Unlike Dody's, though, his second role as a general practitioner also paid a substantial salary. "Alfred, call the police," he ordered.

"And then find me a taxi, please," Dody added.

Everard followed Dody back into the doctors' common room, where she collected her things. "You can't go yet. You have to stay and tell the police what you saw."

"If they need to talk to me, you can tell them where to find me. I have to get home. I have an important proposal to finish." A slight bend of the truth there; she did not want to be late for the ballet. She gave him a pointed look. "As if you didn't know."

Everard said nothing for a moment, but watched her gather her things. "In the doctors' common room again, Dr. McCleland?" he said finally.

Dody drew herself up to her full five-feet-four. "Quite obvious, I would have thought, Dr. Everard."

The skin of Everard's neck prickled red against the white of his winged collar. "Just as well the boss is away."

"I'm sure I can rely on you to inform him," she said. "Just as I should have expected you to plagiarise my paper."

Everard shrugged as if it were but a trivial matter.

"Are you not going to deny doing this despicable thing?" Deny her an argument even? Dody fumed, feeling the heat rise in her face. His arrogant stare, his erect posture suggested he thought he was merely exercising his rights. "If that is your right, what of my rights?" she added, not bothering to keep her voice level. Let anyone hear.

Everard waved his hand dismissively. "I don't think this will be of much concern when . . ." He hesitated, his face grave and nonmocking for a change. "Soon we will have far more worrying things on our minds than our papers and a stolen medical bag. The other day you mentioned seeing a young woman called Esther Craddock in your clinic—remember?"

Dody felt her breath stop. "I don't believe I told you her surname."

"No. Of course not. I made something of a deductive leap from the information you did impart. I was asking the clerk this morning about cases that might be linked to your lead tablets, and he mentioned this Craddock girl being found dead in her room on Friday night. The police are regarding her death as suspicious and there's to be a coronial enquiry."

"Here?"

"No, Bishopsgate—but if you saw her, you are likely to be summoned to attend the inquest. You'll get the details, I don't doubt, with the little blue envelope." He frowned. "Thought you might appreciate some prior warning."

Why the sudden consideration? Why the support of her interest in the lead tablets? Was Everard, in his own warped way, trying to make up for his previous actions against her? Dody swallowed her anger and directed her thoughts to poor Esther. She wasn't the first and she wouldn't be the last. "I have attended coronial enquiries before, Doctor," she said coolly.

"Maybe so, but not . . ."

"What?"

Everard pulled out his watch. "My goodness, is that the time? Surely the police should be here now. I must fly. Good luck!"

Dody watched his dark form retreat down the corridor. Good luck? Why on earth should she need good luck?

Dody had half expected Joseph to have taken his uncle's place for the ballet, and it was a relief to discover that Borislav had not taken his matchmaking to such lengths.

After the ballet, the two of them supped at a chophouse within easy walk of the theatre, dining on mutton chops, mashed potatoes, and parsnips. Dody was hungry; she had not eaten since luncheon and it was now past ten o'clock. She finished her meal, took a sip of wine, and glanced at the people around her. This was by no means an up-market establishment. She had not wished to be beholden to Mr. Borislav for an extravagant night out and had chosen the supper venue herself with every intention of paying her way. He would probably argue with her, most men did, and she would relinquish gracefully—it was all part of the game and at least he had let her pay him back for her ballet ticket.

The place was crowded with the noisy patrons of the theatre district. Dody surveyed the clientele. The rowdy beer-swilling group near the counter was made up of men wearing Sunday best suits and women with gaudy hats, doubtless from the music halls, their laughter every now and then punctuated by loud bursts of song. Men in evening dress and women in glistening gowns conducted earnest conversations with one another about the merits of the opera or the ballet. On other more shadowy tables, couples—the men often smart and young, the women painted and vulgar—caressed and whispered sweet nothings into one another's ears.

Borislav finished his meal and saw the direction of Dody's gaze. "They're probably from the latest show at the Alhambra, lively to say the least. I hate to think what this place will be like when the Mata Hari show opens—to be avoided at all costs I would think."

Dody smiled back at him. "I work in the East End, too, Mr. Borislav. I assure you I've seen it all."

"And now you have seen Nijinsky. That is something to tell your children."

"Children? I can't see myself married, let alone having children. But yes, seeing Nijinsky is something I will never forget. The music, the costumes were all superb. And poor Petrushka the puppet! Thank you so much for taking me."

"My pleasure," Borislav said.

"Did it remind you of home?"

"Not really, but I can forgive the lack of realism for its entertainment value. The colourful peasants were certainly nothing like those I remember from my childhood. When I look back, I see nothing but drab greys. Do you remember much about Moscow life?"

The McClelands had once been staunch members of the British community in Moscow. Her father, Nial McCleland, had made his decision to return permanently to his home country after the murder of his brother at Moscow University. That was the beginning of the end of the country, he'd said. Russia was going to the dogs.

"I remember bits and pieces," Dody said. "I was nine when I was sent away to school in England. My mother and her aunts always seemed to be involved in some way or another with helping the Moscow poor. I was too young to accompany them on their errands of mercy, but I do remember being told about my aunt visiting a peasant hut in winter that contained so little oxygen even a candle could not be kept alight. She thought the place deserted as a mausoleum until she found the occupants sewn into their clothes and hibernating on shelves above the woodstove."

"Ah, yes, the Moscow poor. Your family's charity. How

nice to be philanthropic, to wear peasant clothes and eat coarse black bread on a whim. Some of us had no choice, you know, Dody," he said gently.

Dody touched his hand. "I know how hard it was for you, but I assure you my family did, and still do, really care. My father is constantly writing letters, urging our country's intervention in Russian affairs before the situation blows out of control. He and my mother are genuinely sympathetic to the plight of the Russian repressed."

Borislav shot her a strained smile and gazed thoughtfully into his drink. "I remember desperately sitting on the hob as a small boy. I had no idea how it was that my breeches singed while the rest of me remained a block of ice." Borislav laughed, then shivered, despite the stuffiness of the room. He said no more. Whatever other memories had been stirred, he had no wish to share them with Dody.

Dody respected this need for privacy and did not probe. She knew enough of his background: the genteel poverty, the academic father banned from the university for holding radical views. She had given up inviting Borislav to meet her own family, with whom she felt he had much in common, reluctantly accepting his apologies and understanding his need for seclusion since the death of his wife. It was a privilege, she realised now, to be asked out by someone who shunned most social engagements.

"In fact, it was in Moscow that I determined to be a doctor," she said. "One of my aunts was an artist with an extensive knowledge of human anatomy. I remember watching her excise a tumour from a destitute man's face with nothing but a small penknife."

"And you decided that was the life for you?"

Dody laughed. "Well, yes, but it doesn't sound particularly romantic, does it?"

"I think you were always the realist, Dorothy. Otherwise how could you do what you do now?"

"I suppose so. And after the ballet's wonderful flight of fancy, it is back to reality for both of us tomorrow. I to a coronial enquiry—"

"And I to my shabby little shop," Borislav broke in.

Dody raised her hand in objection. "Don't belittle yourself, Mr. Borislav. You provide a valuable service to the people of the East End."

"As do you to your Coroner's Court."

"I feel I would be more use at the Clinic. I don't really see how I can help the court get anywhere closer to finding the person responsible for Esther Craddock's death."

Earlier she had confided to him her feelings of frustration and sadness at the circumstances of Esther's death, telling him how it made her even more determined to go ahead with her education classes at the Clinic.

"Were any clues found on the body?" he asked.

"I have no idea. The autopsy was performed by the police surgeon at Bishopsgate and I've not had access to the post-mortem report."

"They say that a criminal always leaves something of himself behind."

In response to Dody's look of surprise, he added, "I learned that from Joseph. He studied medicine for four years and was always attracted to the forensic side. Unfortunately my sister and her husband fell into financial hardship and he was forced to withdraw from university. At that time I was in no position to help him myself."

"But you have made it up to him now."

"I hope so. He seems to enjoy the job. It gives us both satisfaction."

"As does my job, despite the fact that the conditions are not always ideal."

"Surely you cannot complain about the excellent facilities at Paddington?" And then a look of understanding crossed his face. "Ah, I know what it is; in the company of friends you are permitted to say what you feel. It is not the magnificent modern facilities that you have a problem with, but those that reside within it—the living, I mean."

Dody laughed. "Yes, sometimes they make it hard for me. Dr. Spilsbury is a genius, they say the rising star of the forensics profession. He is quite eccentric and cool towards everyone and I don't think his treatment of me is because I am a woman. I'm sure he would never have employed me in the first place if he found that to be a problem."

"I wish there were more female doctors. The world would be a much better place if it were so." *What a nice thing to say,* Dody thought, raising her wine for a toast. "But on the whole," Borislav added, "I have lost faith in the medical profession—present company excepted, of course—and that is the reason I decided to give up tutoring medical students."

"And why this loss of faith?"

"The arrogance, I suppose, the kind of knowledge that makes men behave as if they are above God; men like Henry Everard, and with all due respect, my dear, the things I have also learned about Dr. Spilsbury. What a cold fish he seems." There was a slight bitterness in his tone and a clouding of his face that Dody thought might be due to the abrupt ending of his nephew's brief medical career.

He soon managed to rearrange his features into their usual amiability. "I might pop into Bishopsgate tomorrow if the shop is quiet and see how you are getting on at the enquiry," he said.

"If you see me nodding off," she said, "throw something at me."

Chapter Ten

The next morning Dody and Florence found themselves sitting on a hard bench in the improvised Bishopsgate courtroom—a school hall next door but one to the Bishopsgate Mortuary. It smelled of old flower water, dirty shoes, and mildew.

Florence put down her book and shifted on her seat. "I'm beginning to think this was a mistake," she whispered behind her hand. "I would be less bored at home and certainly in more pleasant surroundings. This place needs windows and fresh air. This bench is as hard as the ones at St. Andrew's in Moscow. Lord, remember those interminably long sermons?"

"Mother's reason for dragging us off to St. Andrew's was to keep in touch with the British community, which was a good idea in retrospect," Dody said. "Without their contacts, she and Poppa would have had a much harder time settling back into English life."

Florence huffed. "Well, I thought a Coroner's Court was supposed to be more interesting than a regular court. Nothing about this place has impressed me so far."

"Bishopsgate isn't as grand as Paddington, but you'll get an idea of how the system works—it can be quite exciting. Jurors are allowed to question witnesses and sometimes the spectators get rowdy, breaking into fights even. There's no accused, per se, but I guarantee it'll still be a lot more stimulating than the Magistrates' Court."

Florence exaggerated a shudder; she'd had plenty of experience with the magistrates.

On the bench opposite them a woman in a tattered bonnet wiped away tears with a greying handkerchief. An overweight lady in an elaborate hat flicked her way through a small diary, every now and then putting a pencil to her chin as if in deep thought. A gentleman, leaning over an opened newspaper, rustled and sighed and glanced at a gold watch dangling from a fine Albert chain. Dody recognised him as Dr. Burton, the police surgeon from the Whitechapel Division.

Dody pulled her gaze away from the other witnesses and gave her sister her full attention. "And if you think you are suffering now, Florence, spare a thought for the jury presently viewing the body." Florence peered about the entrance expectantly. "Not here, ninny, down the street in the mortuary."

"Why must they do that?"

"It's supposed to guide them in their quest to discover the cause of death. Frankly, I believe the tradition causes nothing but distress to the jurors as well as exposing them to harmful pathogens. I only hope the body is in a glass-topped coffin, and not merely resting on a slab. Dr. Spilsbury is actively lobbying against the unhygienic practice and does not approve of it at all."

"And therefore neither do you," Florence teased.

"I am not his sycophant," Dody said, thinking that once her sister might have been justified in calling her such, but not now. "Misreading, confusion, and inaccurate verdicts are inevitable when nonmedical people are forced to examine a corpse. It is common sense that the law must be changed."

"So he is human after all, is he, this Dr. Spilsbury of yours?"

Dody smiled. "He walks erect and makes full use of his opposable thumb. Indeed, I have seen him bend to tie a loose shoelace and swallow when he sips from a teacup."

A pale policeman swinging open the hall's double doors interrupted the sisters' conversation. Through the entrance stomped a dozen men of differing social classes, united by their unpleasant experience. Many held handkerchiefs to their noses, some still had their eyes half shut, and one portly gentleman clutched at his heart.

Dody rose to see if she could offer assistance, but was waved away by the constable. "He's all right, miss, quite well enough to perform his civic duty."

Dody exchanged glances with her sister and lowered herself back onto the seat. "Civic duty," she muttered. "Ridiculous."

The coroner, Mr. Carpenter, had a bulbous nose and a waxed moustache almost equal to the Kaiser's in curl, and he presided at the head of a long, baize-covered table, flanked on one side by the members of the jury. Dody sat in front of him on a bench reserved for witnesses, some of whom she recognised from the wait in the entrance.

Mr. Carpenter cleared his throat to indicate the start of

the procedure. His introductory address to the jury was curt. He named the deceased as nineteen-year-old scullery maid Esther Craddock, advising the jury that it was their duty to decide the cause of death: natural causes, suicide, accident, or murder; and if possible, the whys, whens, and hows. Then he called the first witness, Mrs. Godfrey Patel, the girl's former employer, to step up to the table they were using in lieu of a witness box. Mrs. Patel was the middle-aged woman Dody had seen in the waiting room. She wore a dress of flowing sweet pea hues which disguised her bulky figure in the same way the *papier poudre* on her skin disguised the lines of her face—without success.

Mrs. Patel told the jury that Miss Craddock had been in her employ at Bedford Square for approximately eighteen months until her dismissal a week earlier.

"And what was the reason for her dismissal, Mrs. Patel?" the coroner asked.

"My cook had been complaining about her slovenly work habits. I spoke with Esther myself, and when I asked if she was ill, she denied it. I guessed the cause of her slovenliness was pregnancy when, a few days later, she asked my permission to see a doctor even though she had said before that she was not ill. I questioned her again when she returned and received a mouthful of cheek for my concern. She gave me no choice but to dismiss her."

"Can you remember the date of her dismissal?"

Mrs. Patel took her time unfastening a small gold-mesh bag from around her wrist and consulting her miniature diary, holding it at arm's length from her eyes. "Yes, sir, August the ninth."

"And this was the same day that she went to the doctor?"

"It was."

"Do you know which doctor Miss Craddock visited?"

"I believe she went to a women's clinic, somewhere here in the East End. She never told me the doctor's name and there was no call for me to ask."

The coroner looked along the line of jurymen through his monocle. "Any questions for the witness, gentlemen?"

The portly juror, who seemed to have recovered from his earlier discomfort, raised his hand. He addressed the witness and identified himself as the jury foreman. "Madam, you have stated that Miss Craddock became slovenly whilst in your employ. Can you give us any other indication as to the young woman's character—say from the moment she took up position as scullery maid in your house?"

Mrs. Patel drew a breath, as if the heavy strings of beads draped across her large bosom were impeding her respiration. "Cheeky and wilful, sir."

At this there was a flurry of commotion from the witnesses bench. The thin woman in the tattered straw bonnet jumped to her feet and pointed her finger at Mrs. Patel. "Lying cow! My Esther weren't like that—" Before she could say more, a police constable was at her side, urging her to sit down.

Mr. Carpenter slammed his fist on the table. "Silence or face ejection from the court! You will have your say in due time, Mrs. Craddock." Mrs. Craddock folded her arms and sat back in her seat, legs extended, her loose-fitting bonnet teetering up and down like a seesaw. "It is important," the coroner continued, calm again, "that we explore the deceased's frame of mind before the unfortunate incident, and I'm afraid that not everyone"—he looked pointedly at Mrs. Craddock—"will like what they hear. It might be distressing, but I assure you, madam, this process is necessary to discover the truth." He turned to the foreman. "Any further questions for Mrs. Patel?"

"Yes, sir, as I was about to say," the juror again addressed the witness, "Mrs. Patel, was Miss Craddock's condition the reason for her dismissal?"

The witness raised her chin. "Indeed. No matter her nature, even if she had been a pleasant, hard worker, I would have dismissed her for this breach of trust."

Dody remembered a similar experience involving her mother. But while Mother had been disappointed with the behaviour of their Russian servant girl, she had still made certain financial provisions for her and her child. Louise was never one to follow society's norms.

One of the other jurors was clearly thinking the same thing and asked her about it. "Financial provisions?" Mrs. Patel looked at him, surprised. "I knew the girl had a mother to return to. I did not see her future outside my house as any responsibility of mine."

The jury seemed satisfied with this answer. The coroner glanced along the line of sombre men, and as no one offered any further questions, he dismissed the witness and called Esther's mother, Mrs. Martha Craddock, to the table.

Mrs. Craddock clumped towards the witness table in worn boots. Once she had given her name and been sworn in, she told the jury that she was a widow, a barmaid at the Crown and Anchor on Dorset Street and that she was provided with a small room in the attic of that establishment. On the night of August the ninth, she returned to her room after work and found her daughter, Esther, asleep in her bed. She woke her up, and when she discovered the reason for her dismissal from service, they exchanged angry words. When she asked her daughter who the father was, Esther had shrugged, indicating that she did not know. Nor did she seem to particularly care. She went on to tell her mother that everything was going to be all right because the doctor had promised to help her out. At this, Mrs. Craddock had slapped her.

"I shouldn't 'ave but I couldn't 'elp meself," Mrs. Craddock said. "That kind of 'elp is against the law, I told 'er, knowing what kind of 'elp she was on about. No doctor of good moral character would tell 'er that it wasn't."

"And you did everything in your power to dissuade her from returning to that doctor?" the coroner asked.

"I did, sir." Mrs. Craddock began to weep. "But I wish to God I'd never slapped 'er."

Dody stared at the pointed toe of her buttoned boot, only looking up when Mrs. Craddock gave the name of the doctor her daughter had visited: Dr. Dorothy McCleland of the High Street Women's Clinic, Whitechapel. Mrs. Craddock shot Dody a look of loathing as she spoke, and for the first time that morning, Dody felt a flutter of anxiety.

"What did the doctor do for your daughter during that first visit?" the coroner asked.

"She gave 'er medicine. Two lots she gave direct, the other she 'ad to get made up by the chemist. She was told to take the medicine and then come back in a few days."

Dody started in her chair. Two lots of medicine? That couldn't be correct. All she'd given the girl in the surgery was bromide.

Mr. Carpenter continued to question Mrs. Craddock. "Do you know when exactly?"

"No. I don't know when her second appointment was, but

she was much 'appier over the next couple of days, when she was waiting to see Dr. McCleland again.'"

"And then what?"

"On the Friday I came up to my room after work and . . ."

"Take your time."

"And I found her in my bed—a terrible mess—blood everywhere . . ." Mrs. Craddock put a hand over her eyes and began to weep. "I called the police. I could see she were beyond the 'elp of any doctor."

One of the jurymen trumpeted into his handkerchief and then asked, "Do you know the name of the medicine that the doctor gave your daughter?"

Mrs. Craddock shrugged. "Some were in a brown bottle, some were in a chemist's bottle, and the other were tied in cloth." She eyed the coroner. "The police took 'em all."

Surely, Dody thought, the police did not think she had prescribed the muslin-wrapped tablets?

"We will discuss this with the police surgeon tomorrow when he gives his testimony. Thank you, Mrs. Craddock, you may step down, but please remain at hand for the rest of the afternoon in case you need to be recalled."

As Mrs. Craddock retired, softly weeping, she was followed by looks of commiseration from several sympathetic jurymen. Dody turned to her sister. Florence met her eye with an air of unease that must have been a mirror image of her own.

"The court will now call Mr. Charles Robinson to the stand," the coroner announced.

Dody glanced up as a small wiry man passed her on his way to the witness table, disturbing the air with a draught of unwashed clothes and stale hops. At the witness table he gave his name and stated his occupation as hawker and newspaper vendor. Upon the coroner's questioning it was ascertained that Robinson had known the deceased since she was a child of about ten, though he had not seen her much over the last few years since she had entered service. His role in the hearing soon became clear.

"I was doing me job, selling the *Mail* down the High Street near the water pump as is my patch," Robinson began his version of events, "when I saw Essie—beg pardon, m'lord; Essie is what I always called her—passing by on the uvver side of the street. I gives her a whistle and a wave, but she 'ardly gives me a second look. Bent over double she was, an' looking miserable as sin. I crossed the road to say 'ello—it were the friendly thing to do, you see, yer honour—and she told me she was feeling right poorly. When I asked 'er what was wrong, she said she'd got some treatment at the Clinic and it weren't agreeing with her. She said she was 'eaded for the Crown and Anchor where 'er muvver worked and would probably be better after a lie down. I told meself I'd call in when I'd sold me pile and see if she was better, but I never got to do that seeing as a mate called me over to 'elp with a loose wheel—"

"What day was this that you saw the deceased?" one of the jurors interrupted.

"It were Friday August the eleventh, sir. I always know me dates, from the papers, see."

"What time?"

Robinson scratched his head, dropped his hand, and jigged from one foot to the other for a moment before answering. "About six o'clock or thereabouts, I fink."

"You say you saw her coming from the direction of the

pump, but you didn't actually see her coming from the Clinic, did you? You just told us what she told you—is that so?"

"Well, yes, no. I saw 'er, too, yes." Robinson swayed, became flustered, and tangled his words. Dody suspected he was drunk, drunk and unreliable—couldn't the jury hear what she was hearing?

"Coming out from the Women's Clinic she was, that old warehouse what was done up, near the fishmonger's," Robinson said.

Dody glanced along the line of sombre jurymen and felt a rush of nausea. She looked at Dr. Burton, sitting beside her. He pulled his eyes from hers and let out a breath. She turned quickly to her sister, desperate for the touch of a comforting hand, a whisper that everything was going to be all right.

But everything wasn't all right; she could see now exactly the course this inquest was taking. She fought the urge to call out to the court in her defence, knowing full well that a protest now would not help her cause. Besides, she had not been accused of anything yet. She would have to wait until she was called to the stand and meanwhile watch this bitter performance through to the very end. But at least she still had some time to prepare, to consult the Book of Lists and prove that someone was selling a unique form of abortifacient, and possibly performing physical abortions, too. A police constable approached Mr. Carpenter and handed him a note. The coroner sighed and looked at his fob, then back at the witness. "Thank you, Mr. Robinson, you may step down." He addressed the court. "The court will adjourn until three sharp."

Dody took hold of her sister's arm and steered her through the crowded hall entrance and into the street in search of a hansom or taxi.

"Please tell me we are going for tea. I'm parched," Florence said as they stood on the pavement not far from the hall, trying and failing several times to hail a cab.

"No, first we have to visit the mortuary and fetch the Book of Lists. There is something in it which will back up my theory about Esther's death."

"Then tea?"

"Then tea."

Florence told Dody to wait where she was while she reconnoitred the street at the back of the building in search of a taxi rank. The sound of a man clearing his throat startled Dody. She turned to find herself staring into the round face of Borislav. He lifted his hat. For once he was not smiling. "I heard it all from the back of the court. The girl Esther picked up your prescription for the lead antidote from me. I had not put two and two together until now. I'm not sure if it is of any relevance, but I will let the police know." Dody could not see what good that would do, but thanked him all the same. "I will also tell them about the foreign doctor. They may have a record of him if he has been seen in the brothels. If there is anything else I can do to help, Dorothy, you know where to find me. May I fetch you a cab, perhaps?"

"No, I'm quite all right, thank you; my sister is bringing one from the other street." Dody hoped she was correct. While she usually enjoyed Borislav's company, she could not bear the idea of polite conversation at this moment.

He touched the knot of his blue-and-white-spotted bow tie. "I have been keeping my eyes out for tablets similar to those that killed the boy, but to no avail, I'm afraid. Also, no more sign of the foreign doctor in my shop."

"It was worth a try. Thank you, Mr. Borislav." A motorised taxi pulled up at the kerb. Florence called from its dark interior for Dody to climb in.

"So that's your Mr. Borislav," Florence said as they merged into the traffic. "Can he do anything for you?"

Dody said nothing for a moment. Her head felt as if it were being squeezed in a vice. "Not now, please, Florence. I need some time with my thoughts. We will talk when we reach a teahouse."

Florence stayed in the cab while Dody hurried into the mortuary to collect the Book. In the autopsy room, she used more force than was needed to open the drawer in which the heavy tome was kept, wrenched it from its runners, and stared with surprise at the empty drawer in her hand. She slid it back in situ and opened the remaining drawers in the cabinet, finding an assortment of stationery items, but no book. The Book was her responsibility; she was the only member of staff who handled it regularly and she always put it back where it belonged. She hurried into Spilsbury's stark office and saw at a glance that it was not there.

She met Alfred on her way out. When she asked if he had seen the Book recently, he answered that he had not, but volunteered to ask Everard on her behalf. He returned saying that Everard had not seen it since Monday. Dody all but threw her hands in the air, barely suppressing the curses that wanted to escape from her lips.

"Could it have been stolen, do you think, Alfred, by that little man who took Everard's bag? The bag was taken from the autopsy room, after all."

"I suppose it could have, miss, and been placed in the bag. But what would anyone want with the Book of Lists?"

Indeed.

Everard entered the autopsy room. The only thing Dody did to acknowledge his presence was to straighten her posture. She would not grant him the satisfaction of seeing her in a panic.

"Never mind," she added to Alfred. "As to the Book's contents, I'm sure my memory serves me correctly."

As she exited the room, she heard Everard instruct Alfred to call the police and notify them about the stolen Book.

I t was some time before Dody and Florence found a respectable teahouse, an Aerated Bread Company shop in the courtyard at Fenchurch Street Station.

"Dody," Florence said as they settled at a table underneath the spread of an exotic palm. "Am I allowed to speak now?" She did not wait for an answer. "I don't like the way this inquest is going and I think I should call Mother and Poppa. If they are not told soon, they will read about it in the newspaper."

"No, Florence, they are run off their feet with their strike fund."

"I heard people in court saying the strike is about to end."

"There will still be hungry bellies to be filled for a while yet. I don't want our parents involved; they have enough on their minds."

"They always put family first; you know that."

True, Dody thought, *they never hesitate to act when Florence is in trouble.* Until now, though, Dody had never given them cause for concern. Typical that when she did it, she did it properly. This was no mere girlish scrape.

Florence reached for her hand. "Are you feeling all right? You look ghastly."

"I'm fine," Dody lied. It seemed she was not as immune to the English cholera as she had thought. Ever since her visit to the Kents', she had been feeling off colour and hoped this was not a precursor to another full-blown attack. Thank goodness she had dissuaded Florence from accompanying her to the tenement.

A waitress offered them menus. Emblazoned in red letters across the top of the card was an advertisement for Dr. Dauglish's healthy ABC bread, made with aerating carbon dioxide instead of yeast. Dody baulked at the thought—she had enough gas in her stomach already—and waved the menu away.

The tearoom clientele was predominantly female. The few gentleman customers sat with young ladies and were preoccupied holding dainty gloved hands and peering into fluttering eyes. The incongruity of the two gentlemen, one of them a uniformed policeman, striding purposefully around the table clusters to where the sisters sat, was noticed at once by even the most love-struck of patrons. All murmuring ceased; the only sounds were the rustling of gowns and the shift of chairs.

Dody recognised at once the bulky frame of Pike's former sergeant, Walter Fisher, a giant of a man in a badly cut suit. Fisher gave the sisters a small bow, attempted and failed to keep his voice low. "I'm glad I've found you, Dr. McCleland," he said, twisting his bowler in fighter's hands.

"You followed us?"

"Yes, Doctor. I tried to catch you outside court, but just missed you. I was sent to tell you that the inquest is to be delayed until tomorrow so certain items of, er, evidence can be processed."

The sisters spoke at once: "What evidence?"

"Oh, Sergeant Fisher, this is my sister, Miss Florence McCleland," Dody said.

"How do you do, miss?" Fisher paused to shake Florence's hand across the table. "It's Inspector Fisher now, Doctor," he said with an awkward smile.

"Of course, my mistake," Dody said icily. Pike had not told her in so many words, but she understood Fisher's promotion had something to do with his own move from Scotland Yard to Special Branch. "Congratulations, Inspector."

"I'm stationed in Whitechapel now, Doctor, and I am running the investigation into the death of Miss Craddock." He looked at Dody with an expression that was hard to place: part sympathy, part embarrassment, countered with more than a little officiousness.

"How unpleasant for you," she said.

"Yes, Doctor, it is—"

"And you found it necessary to break this news about the abeyance with a uniformed constable in tow?" Florence cut Fisher off, causing the young officer in question to lower his gaze to his shiny boots. "Drawing unnecessary attention to us in such a public place?"

"I'm sorry to cause embarrassment, Miss McCleland, but this procedure is necessary, I'm afraid, to inform Dr. McCleland that I will be searching her rooms at the Women's Clinic, and to invite her to accompany me."

The sisters exchanged glances. There was a moment of pin-dropping silence. A train rumbled from a nearby platform, accompanied by the sound of a cheering crowd celebrating the end of the strike. For many, their immediate troubles were over, but Dody knew hers were just beginning.

Chapter Eleven

Nurse Daphne Hamilton was sweeping the waiting-room floor when Dody, Florence, and the two policemen entered through the front door of the Clinic. Fisher asked Daphne for the patient register and spent some minutes examining it, the younger policeman reading the list of names over his shoulder.

Dody approached Daphne, laid her hand gently on her sleeve, and tried to smile, but her face felt like a wax mask. The waiting-room benches were askew, rubbish bins overflowed, and there was an odour of vomit in the air. "Lord, what a mess," Dody muttered.

The nurse blew hair from her face. "We've been run off our feet, Doctor, I'm so sorry. If you'd only left off visiting for half an hour, I would have had the place spick and span."

"No matter," Dody said, knowing that it did matter. She needed to prove to these policemen that she was not involved in some kind of shoddy, backstreet practice. "I want to show them my surgery. I'll have the keys, please."

Once the policemen had finished with the registry, she beckoned them to follow her. Leading them to one of several closed doors, she unlocked it, saying, "I share this room with two other doctors."

"Female doctors?" Fisher asked.

"Naturally," Dody replied tersely. "It's a women's clinic run by women. It is a place where female patients can come for free treatment and understanding."

Fisher cocked his head to one side.

"When I say understanding, I do not mean abortion, Inspector." There. She had spoken the unmentionable and felt surprisingly stronger for it. She gestured around the immaculate surgery. At least the staff had managed to get this room clean. "You'd better get on with it."

The sisters stood in the doorway while Fisher and his constable rummaged through the desk drawers and instrument cupboards.

"You need help," Florence whispered to her sister.

Dody stiffened. "I have done nothing wrong."

"We know that, but I know how the police work and I think they are out to frame you."

"You read too many detective books."

"Enough to know you need a lawyer."

"A lawyer is unusual for a coronial inquest. It would prove nothing at this stage but a guilty conscience."

"Pike, then."

"I don't know what he could do. If anyone, I need Dr. Spilsbury and he is away. I will fight this by myself."

Florence rolled her eyes.

Fisher straightened from his position at the instrument cupboard. "This cupboard does not seem to have much in it in the way of surgical instruments."

"We have our own instruments, Inspector. I bring mine from home when I work at the Clinic," Dody said.

"I would like to have a look at them then, if I may."

"And I would like to have a look at your warrant, please," Florence said.

"A search ordered by a Coroner's Court does not require a warrant, miss." Florence flexed her fingers, but thankfully remained calm. "Doctor," Fisher went on, "if you will be so kind as to open the medicine cabinet for me."

Dody moved to the corner cabinet and turned the key in the lock. Fisher reached for one of several brown bottles. "What's this?"

"What is written on the bottle: bromide."

The inspector unscrewed the lid, sniffed the bottle's contents, and passed it under the constable's nose. The young man nodded as if he recognised the odour.

"What is this bromide used for?" Fisher asked.

"It calms the nerves. It also provides relief for epilepsy."

"Miss Craddock was an epileptic?"

"No, in her case it was merely nerves," Dody said. "I also prescribed a chloroform mixture for the lead poisoning, which she picked up from the High Street chemist. Mr. Borislav remembers serving the girl: perhaps you should ask him about it."

Fisher said he would, replaced the bromide, and scanned the rest of the cupboard's contents. "We also found tablets in the girl's mother's room, which analysis showed to contain lead. I can't see a match for the tablets here."

"The girl was suffering from plumbism. I wrote that in her notes," Dody said.

"You don't dispense lead tablets?"

"Of course not—lead is a poison. Were these the tablets you found wrapped in cloth?"

"Yes, Doctor, I have them here." Fisher delved into his pocket and produced the muslin package, which he unwrapped, spilling half a dozen tablets into Dody's palm. At last she was able to get a good look at them. They were professionally made, compact and smooth but for two identical nicks on the surface of each one.

"Esther was carrying these tablets when she visited my surgery. She dropped them on the floor and I put them back in her pocket."

Fisher's eyes gleamed with interest. Lord, perhaps she should not have said that—should instead have distanced herself from the tablets altogether.

But it was too late now. "Tablets just like these were also found during a case of suspected infanticide," she said. "There's a criminal behind these tablets, Inspector, there has to be. I have seen reference to tablets like this in the mortuary records."

"That may be. But whoever gave her these was not necessarily involved in the surgical procedure that ended her life—which is what we are currently investigating," Fisher said.

"No, of course not; I am just urging you to see the bigger picture—that the person who supplied the tablets might also be the abortionist."

"Which, with all due respect, Doctor, is sheer speculation. That the tablets were not given to her by you *and* that you were in no way responsible for her death, is all I need to ascertain at this present point in time."

Dody felt the muscles tighten around her mouth, but tried to remain calm. This was as close to an accusation as anything she had heard so far. She had no memory of Fisher sounding so officious when he worked with Pike. His promotion had either gone to his head or he was mirroring his superiors' resistance to "newfangled" ideas about detection. Pike had always believed that a broader mind-set was required to sniff out hidden links. "I do not dispense tablets wrapped in muslin or in matchboxes, Inspector. Nor would any reputable doctor or chemist."

When they returned to their townhouse, a telegram was waiting for Dody on the hall table. She handed her gloves to Annie, tore the yellow envelope open, and read the message aloud to Florence.

> *HEARD ABOUT INQUEST STOP CEASE WORK FOR*
> *HOME OFFICE UNTIL MESS CLEARED UP STOP*
> *WILL RETURN TOMORROW TO SORT THINGS OUT*
> *STOP TAKE HEART STOP*
>
> *BS*

Despite what she had told Borislav after the ballet, she had not been sure how comfortable Spilsbury was with a female assistant, but this telegram vindicated her position. It proved that at least one man in the Home Office hierarchy considered her skills to be more relevant than her gender and that, above all, he believed in her. Dody felt weak with relief.

Florence put her arms around her shoulders. "There, there—you see? Everything's going to be all right now."

Dody tried to explain her feelings. "I think what has upset me more than anything is that they are trying to accuse me of something I would never contemplate unless to save the life of a mother. The oath I took compels me to preserve life at all cost."

"That's the difference between you and me, Dody; the things I'm accused of are usually true."

"I've been to enough inquests to sense where this is going. It seemed to be moving too quickly, the suspicion well and truly focused on me when I've not even given evidence. To call in that Robinson man as a witness was ludicrous. He was obviously drunk and didn't know what he was talking about."

Florence paused and placed her hand on her chin, her eyes sliding towards the telephone table. "Well, just in case Spilsbury cannot set things right immediately, perhaps . . ."

Dody guessed what her sister was contemplating. "No, Florence, no." Florence ignored Dody's raised hand, lifted the receiver, and asked the operator to be put through to the Special Branch section of Scotland Yard. Dody collapsed onto the hall chair, hands over her ears—although in reality she had every intention of listening to the exchange. Her sister asked someone if she could speak to Chief Inspector Pike, listened for a moment, said thank you, and then carefully put the telephone back onto its cradle.

"They say he's not available, won't tell me where he is. That's Special Branch for you—cloak-and-dagger nonsense."

"He was supposed to be taking leave after his knee operation to convalesce," Dody said. "I believe he was planning to help Violet prepare for the new school term." Dody lifted her chin, determined to remain calm and rational, although Florence's insistence on bringing Pike into this was making it increasingly hard to do. "I hope he is seeing more of Violet, for both of their sakes. She does not enjoy holidaying with her maternal grandparents."

"Brave of you to say that, darling," Florence said, "but you and I would still rather he were here, wouldn't we?"

The gentle tone had the opposite effect of what was intended on Dody. Pike's bolt from the hospital had more than adequately shown that he did not desire her help, and Dody had no intention of letting him think she needed his—Spilsbury's maybe, but not Pike's. Men did not have a monopoly on pride. She jumped from her seat and strode towards the morning room. "I don't need Pike."

The room was hung with thick green curtains drawn all week against the heat, and the fireplace was an empty black hole. Florence turned the electric switch and flooded the room with unforgiving light. Dody glimpsed her reflection in the mantel mirror, purple rings under her eyes, deep lines on either side of a pursed mouth. It was as if she had aged ten years. The fiasco with Pike, the day in court, and the subsequent confrontation with the police had taken their toll. The face in the mirror was that of a bitter, desperate woman.

And one she must take control of again.

"Sit down," Florence said. "I'll pour you a sherry and we'll try and make some sense of it all. No doubt Spilsbury will be able to extract you from this mess, but that shouldn't stop us from contemplating the fact that someone put Robinson up to that statement and that someone is trying to lay the blame for Esther's death on you."

"Not necessarily true. Robinson might genuinely have

been drunk and confused." Dody found herself playing devil's advocate. Objective impartiality was, after all, what she had been trained for.

"Then he should have been screened out as a witness," Florence said.

"Society has not yet come to terms with the notion of a female autopsy surgeon. I am a handy scapegoat—an easy way out of what might otherwise prove to be a time-consuming and costly case."

"I see. What they don't understand, they blame on the witch."

"Quite."

"Have you crossed paths with this coroner before?" Florence asked.

"No, but Mr. Carpenter would surely know of me. If I had only found that wretched book, I could at least plant the seeds in the jury's mind that there might be a correlation between the pills and the abortion deaths. Now they will just have to take my word for it."

They had not been talking long when Annie announced the arrival of the policemen.

"Not again," Florence said.

Dody sighed. "It was to be expected."

They led Fisher and his constable to Dody's third-floor rooms. The policemen weren't interested in the bureaus and wardrobe in the dressing and bedroom. Instead they made a beeline to her study. "I'd like to look at your instruments, please, Doctor," Fisher said.

Dody opened the glass doors of a display cabinet housing her surgical and specialist instruments in labelled leather

cases: OBSTETRICS, ORTHOPAEDICS, POSTMORTEM, OPHTHAL-
MOLOGY, and so on.

"Your women's, ah, tools, please, Doctor," he said.

She reached for her obstetric set and flipped the catch to
reveal varying sizes of specula and forceps, dilators and
curettes, resting in their individual niches on a velvet bed.
Fisher cast his eye across the row of gleaming nickel plate.
"Do you have any others?"

"My destructive instruments, yes." Dody reached for
another box and flipped the catch, pointing out the hook,
perforator, and transforator. Fisher seemed particularly interested in the hook, holding it up to the electric light and turning it through his blunt fingers.

"Looks like a crotchet hook," the younger policeman muttered, clearly horrified.

"What are these instruments used for, Doctor?" Fisher
asked.

There was no delicate answer to that question, nor any
that would lessen his suspicion of her. She braced herself.
"These instruments are used in the case of a severely
obstructed labour," she said. "The transforator crushes the
foetal skull and the hook is used to remove the foetus piece
by piece."

Florence gasped. Dody kept her eyes on Inspector Fisher,
hoping he now regretted his question.

Fisher tossed the hook back into its case with disgust. His
voice trembled slightly. "Could you perform an abortion
that way?"

"No, a dilation and curette would be performed on a
much less advanced foetus. The procedure I described is used

to save the mother's life in the case of obstruction. If an abortion was performed this way, the patient would most likely bleed to death."

"Which is what happened to Esther Craddock," Fisher reminded her.

"No one with any obstetric knowledge would make such a mistake. Miss Craddock was not in an advanced state of pregnancy. I expect she died from a perforated uterus."

"Do you have any more of these?" Fisher asked, pointing to the hook and transforator.

"No need," Dody said, looking at him levelly. "I hardly ever have to use them."

Chapter Twelve

Despite the suffocating humidity, Elizabeth Strickland shivered. She'd had to feign illness to get off work at the *Mail*'s typing pool and would have been almost home now if she'd caught her usual train. So far everything had gone to plan—Jimmy's plan, scribbled in haste on a piece of printing paper in an alley behind the newspaper building: omnibus times, routes, and street names. It was too risky for her to go to her local chemist, so he'd suggested this place, White-chapel, where his father had grown up. Whitechapel was miles from where she lived and, though geographically closer to work, felt another world away.

This chemist shop was even more lurid than the one they had at home in Lewisham. The window was filled with tall jars of all shapes and sizes holding coloured water of red, pink, emerald green, and blue. Gaudy as a gin palace, the shop was easily recognised by those who could not read. Elizabeth glanced down the street at the ragged children playing in piles of rotting rubbish. Groups of wan, grey people leaned in doorways; grimy lines of laundry stretched across the smaller streets and alleys. There would be no shortage of illiterates here.

She took a breath for courage and crossed the threshold, her arrival announced by a spring bell on the door. A long counter with a backdrop of well-stocked shelves stretched across the entire back wall. The shiny mahogany surface was jammed with commercial products, their garish signs advertising everything from custard powder, toiletries, and gripe-water to products guaranteed to "remove obstructions." A brass cash register, a set of scales, a large marble mortar and pestle, and a brass bell dominated the counter.

Elizabeth pressed the bell and the white-coated chemist appeared within seconds.

"Good afternoon, miss, what can I do for you?" He smiled pleasantly.

Elizabeth felt herself flush. Glancing around the shop to ensure there was no one else about, she whispered, "I need something for my courses. They seem to have stopped."

The chemist lost some of his friendly demeanour. "I'm sorry, but we don't sell that sort of thing here."

She hadn't travelled all this way to give up so quickly. Her words left her in a rush. "I've tried Widow Welch's—the whole packet—but they haven't worked." Jimmy had picked up the pills for her from the apothecary near the *Mail*'s office; they were the only things he could find purported to do the job.

"I see." The chemist looked her up and down. Perhaps now he could see how serious she was. His passive face revealed little, and she wondered what he was thinking.

Before leaving work, she'd changed into her second-best

dress: red and black with patterns of paisley swirls, so different to the drab grey she wore when working in the typing pool. The bright outfit was her attempt to make herself feel bright. So far the strategy had not worked. In her head she saw herself wearing it in a few months' time with her pregnant belly straining its seams. When her parents found out, they would throw her into the street, telling their friends at church that she'd died from the diphtheria that had taken her little brother.

Before she knew it, she found herself grabbing hold of the chemist's hand. "Please help me, sir," she cried.

He extracted himself and frowned for a moment, then glanced as if in great thought down the shop's aisle beyond the shelves and into the street. Elizabeth followed his gaze to a shadowy figure in a cloth cap peering in at the window display. Was the chemist's resolve faltering? Elizabeth's heart leaped with hope.

"I'm sorry, miss, there is nothing I can do for you."

And plummeted. Her nose fizzed, her face crumpled. She pulled the handkerchief from her sleeve and dabbed her eyes.

"Hush now; control yourself. Here comes a customer. Best make as if you are buying something."

Elizabeth was used to doing as she was told. Without thinking, she reached for a bottle of shampoo from a display near the counter. "And I'll have this, too, please, sir," she said, doing her best to keep the tremble from her voice.

As she fumbled in her purse for the money, she heard the heavy tread of a man approaching from behind. Had he been in the shop all along? Had he overheard the conversation? She panicked and dropped her purse. Coins clattered and rolled. Bobbing down to retrieve her money, she glimpsed smart, cuffed trousers atop a pair of shiny boots.

"No hurry," the chemist said as she scrambled for her coins. "Take your time and I'll serve this gentleman first. "Have you come to pick up your order, Doctor?" he asked the new arrival.

A doctor, oh no!

"Yes I have, but let's help this young lady first, shall we?" the doctor said, bending from a great height to help her retrieve her spilled coins. Elizabeth thanked him. He was tall and well dressed, but unfortunately featured with yellowed skin and eyes and an ugly scar on his temple. It took all her fortitude and good manners not to pull away. He dropped the last of the coins into her palm and she thanked him, insisting that he be served first. Elizabeth stepped back from the counter to rearrange her purse and gather together the money she owed for the shampoo.

The chemist ducked behind the counter and reappeared with a brown paper parcel.

Elizabeth watched the exchange. Impeded by shaking fingers, the doctor struggled with the knots. When he finally managed to unwrap the parcel, he took some time to inspect the contents, muttering like a wizard reciting a spell.

"Salves, salvarsan powder, cotton swabs, bottles of sterile saline, four brass syringes, and"—he counted out the remainder under his breath—"one dozen twenty-two-gauge needles. Where's the bromide?" he asked suddenly, his voice louder.

The chemist inspected the supplies strewn across the counter and wrinkled his forehead. "My mistake," he said, turning to the myriad bottles arranged on the shelves behind him. He selected a small brown one and placed it next to the doctor's pile of goods. "There you are. Someone needs calming, do they?" he asked.

"Sick people always need calming." The doctor turned to Elizabeth and smiled. She wanted to run away, but she had not yet paid for her shampoo and felt obliged to wait for him to finish his business.

"That'll be fifteen shillings and eight pence, please," the chemist said to the doctor.

Elizabeth could wait no longer. She extracted her money and clattered it on the counter, thanked the chemist, and hurried from the shop without waiting for her change. Outside she took some deep breaths. She must stop herself from crying—give the red a chance to leave her eyes before she got home. She dabbed her nose with her handkerchief and glanced at her reflection in the shop window. It would be no problem convincing Mother she'd been ill; the pale face and stooped shoulders said it all.

And then her attention was drawn from her own image to another on the rippling surface of one of the decorative jars. It was the reflection of the man she'd seen earlier, still loitering outside the shop. She turned and faced him.

The man gave her a little wave. He wore a dusty suit jacket with mismatched trousers. His cloth cap was pulled low over his face, but she glimpsed a pushed-in mouth and a flattened nose.

She nodded him a smile—because it was polite to do so, not because she felt like it—and prepared to cross the road.

"Oi, miss, wait."

She turned back to see the man holding up her handkerchief. He didn't hold the sodden fabric up by its corner as most would, but held it balled in his hand, as if he couldn't care less what it had been used for.

"What's wrong, love?" the man asked as he handed the hanky back.

"Thank you, sir, it's nothing. I'm all right."

The man had a weeping sore on the side of his face. "The chemist givin' you an 'ard time?"

"No, no, not really."

"Bloody toff, what would 'e know, eh?"

The shop bell rang; the doctor's form loomed in the doorway. The little man quickly stepped away from Elizabeth.

"Hey, you!" The doctor pointed his finger at the man and bellowed as if to a scavenging dog. "I know what you get up to, you and your gang. Leave the young lady alone. I'll be going to the authorities about you, mark my words."

"And expose yerself in the process? I don't fink so, Doc." The smaller man shrugged and turned to Elizabeth. "I've done nuffin, 'ave I, miss?"

"Preying on the weak and needy," the doctor harangued.

"You can talk an' all," the little man retorted.

Elizabeth looked desperately for a break in the traffic. She'd had enough of this place and needed to get away from these ghastly men.

As she was about to dash across the road, the doctor clutched at her arm. "What are you doing here? A nice girl like you shouldn't be in this area alone," he said.

She cricked her neck to look up at him. "Please let me go, sir, I have a train to catch." Before she could wriggle free, he pressed a business card into her hand. "If you find yourself in trouble, come to me."

"I'm no worse than you, mate," the smaller man bravely shouted from a distance. "Oh, yeah, I know all about you— least I ain't no *pre-vert*." He paused, as if searching his mind for an even worse insult. "Nor no Kaiser-Bill spy, never!"

Elizabeth didn't know what a pre-vert was, but she knew

what a spy was. The strange doctor certainly behaved in a suspicious manner. Could this be true? Was he really a spy?

"Everything's all right. Really," she said through the thumping of her heart. She shrugged from the doctor's grip and just missed being knocked down by a boy on a bicycle with a tray of fruit. Carts and delivery vans rattled by in a continuous stream, and crossing the road was now impossible. She joined in with a crowd of jostling people on the footpath, walking with them for some yards until she spied a gap in the traffic. Picking up her skirts, she slipped between a teetering furniture cart and a blistered old carriage and just missed having her shins rammed by a costermonger's cart. What a disaster this had been. She was no closer to solving her problem than she was at the start of her miserable journey.

The thunder of the traffic masked the small man's tread. She didn't notice him until he was almost on top of her, pulling her around by the shoulder and shoving his pug-like face into hers.

"Horse Feathers most nights till late. Ask for Dan."

Van Noort caught the omnibus from Whitechapel and disembarked at St. James. His own pounding footsteps echoed the beating of his heart and kept time to the desperate rhythm of his prayers: prayers for the unfortunate girl in the chemist; prayers for her exploiters; prayers for his wife—dear Matilda; and for Jack and his family and all those who suffered. The prayers went on through the list until he reached the Beast. What prayer for the Beast? There was one, he was sure, but he could not recall it. All he could do was hope that it would come.

With his destination in sight, his pace increased. He barely noticed his surroundings and cursed his feet for leading him on in such furious haste. He passed the venerable gentlemen's club, the hotel with the flags, dodged a pile of dog filth in the middle of the footpath, and strode by a building with window boxes of leggy geraniums, seeing them but not seeing them.

Instead he saw a line of verse unfurling in his mind and he clung to it like a falling man.

Now if I do that I would not, it is no more I that do it, but sin that dwelleth in me.

He slowed down slightly. Of course, his prayer: The Beast's prayer—that which absolves and justifies. He immediately felt the better for it. He mounted the steps of the Satin Palace with renewed vigour, his conscience clearer . . . at least for a while.

With its crystal chandelier winking through the glass above the door, this place could be mistaken for a respectable gentlemen's club itself. Van Noort nodded to the uniformed doorman, who unlocked the door for him. In less than an hour's time the door would be fixed open and the red lamp lit. Until then there was much work to be done.

Heading down the passage to the back of the building, he ran into Jack, barefooted as usual and wearing his trademark bargeman's cap. Jack dumped the heavy basket of linen he was carrying and greeted Van Noort with a cheeky smile. The brothel generated more washing than the laundress—an old whore who was no longer suitable for the shop floor—could cope with, and Jack worked in the laundry room as her assistant several evenings a week.

"Jack," Van Noort said as he reached into the store cupboard for his doctor's bag. The boy's smile faded when he heard the stern tone. "What are you still doing here?"

"A fella's gotta feed 'is family, Doc."

Van Noort opened his bag and began restocking the contents with supplies purchased from the chemist. "You are a child, Jack. This is no place for children. When we last talked, you promised you would find some other kind of employment."

"There's no jobs—what else can I do? Get a high hat and become a City tosser?"

Van Noort snapped his bag shut and endeavoured to keep a straight face. The boy had spunk, he had cheek—qualities that might just keep him alive. "You should be in school," he said.

"Then I would never've met you, would I, or been learned to read with one teacher all to meself. Some fings is just meant to be, Doc. Funny old world, ain't it?"

The brothel's proprietor, Harold Trevelly, came up from behind and put an arm around the boy's shoulder. The man dressed like a gentleman but spoke like a sewer rat.

"Are you lecturing my apprentice, Doctor?" he asked.

"Apprentice? What rot you talk, Trevelly. You're leading him on and you know it."

Jack broke in, "I don't care, really I don't, Doc. I like it 'ere and the ladies is real nice to me."

"Your soul, Jack, think what this place is doing to your soul."

"I 'ardly fink you're one qualified to preach salvation. Bloody lunatic," Trevelly added under his breath. To Jack he said: "And you watch yourself, son. Remember there's some what come 'ere 'oo give it both ways. We could even send you on to number forty-seven. A fresh-arsed young'un like you would go down there a treat."

Jack picked up the basket of dirty washing and hurried off down the passageway.

Van Noort stared down at Trevelly, a man so pitted by the pox his face looked like a gravel road. He represented everything Van Noort hated about himself; just another version of the Beast and one for whom there could surely be no redemption. There were times when he wanted to grab the man by his scrawny neck and wring the life out of him.

Trevelly mustered the women into a disorderly line in the passageway. From there they entered the large parlour with its leather armchairs, gilt mirrors, and elaborately carved mahogany bar. One by one they lay on the chaise for Van Noort to examine them. Fortunately none of them required time off, which meant Van Noort would be granted his satisfaction. Trevelly knew his doctor's weakness and exploited him as much as he did his whores.

When Van Noort had finished his work, he selected a small-breasted girl called Mee-Mee. The girl had glossy dark hair and an olive complexion and, when playing out his fantasy in one of the small back rooms, allowed him to call her Margaretha.

It was close to midnight when he eventually reached his own door. As his key turned in the lock, he offered the Lord a prayer of thanks. Once more his saintly wife, Matilda, had failed to bar his entry. There were times when he thought she understood him better than he did himself.

In the library he poured himself a brandy from the drinks tray and settled into his favourite wingback chair with the heavy family Bible resting on a table by his side. The ticking of the clock and the gentle crackle of his cigar were the only sounds in the large, comfortable room. Grey light from the street shone through a chink in the curtains and danced on him like a spotlight, isolating him, while all around the shadows crept.

As he sat he became aware of a euphoric sensation growing like a wave from his stomach and rolling upwards—the brandy and the relief provided by Trevelly's whore, he supposed. He did not fight the feeling but floated along with it. There was no foul-tasting cordite on the tongue and the sensations were pleasant for a change. They reminded him of how he felt before his first encounter with the Beast, when he was young and capable, in South Africa, where his skills were tested to the extreme. That piano player—not his patient, but he remembered him now—the young officer who had refused the amputation with his pistol cocked and pointing at the medical staff. They were all too tired to argue or call the MPs, and no one could blame him. Van Noort was busy with another patient—he would have liked to have seen the man's injuries for himself, but by the time he had finished, the orderlies had picked up the young officer and taken him to another tent to die.

The young man had defied them all by not dying. He had lived on to play the piano for Margaretha.

Just as, later, Van Noort had survived the explosion that shattered the field hospital and had lived on to conduct banal examinations of whores.

He glanced at the Bible by his side.

To every thing there is a season, and a time to every purpose under the heaven.

Funny old world.

Chapter Thirteen

Early the next morning another telegram arrived for Dody. Spilsbury had been unable to book a berth on the night train due to returning hordes of holidaymakers previously stranded by the strike. She calmly paid the telegraph boy, but when he had remounted his bicycle and headed back down the road, she screwed the paper tight in her fist, digging her nails painfully into her palms before throwing it into the garden. She would be facing the court alone. Until now, she had not realised how much she had been counting on Spilsbury's presence.

She forced herself to take some deep breaths and dashed the tears from her eyes with the back of her hand. It was imperative that she stop this, that she did not present to the court as a hysterical female. Even to her sister, she resolved, she must remain cool and levelheaded. Composed once more, she retrieved the paper ball from where it had landed on the box hedge and returned calmly into the house to break the news to Florence.

"Well, if Spilsbury can't be here," Florence said, "you must have some other support. Please let me see if I can trace Pike. If there is something sinister going on behind the scenes of this court, Pike is sure to find it."

"Pike's out of London, Florence. Besides, I have you for support and that's all I need."

Despite her brave words, Dody's anxiety deepened. She must have one last look for the Book at the mortuary.

For some inexplicable reason, Thursdays at the Paddington Mortuary were often quiet, and Dody seldom worked them. Even Everard was missing from the front desk, where he could usually be found at this time, gossiping with the clerks and going over the paperwork for the day's jobs.

In the autopsy room she found Alfred sharpening the blades of some rib-cutters. He stopped what he was doing when she entered and slid from the lab stool.

"It's all right, Alfred, don't let me interrupt you. I've just come for one last look for the Book."

"It's not 'ere, Doctor, and that's a fact. The police questioned all the staff and no one's seen it."

"Can it have been thrown away with the rubbish? Incinerated even?"

"No, miss. And the dog ain't et it neither."

Alfred was teasing her. He obviously had no idea how important that book was; that it might be the difference between her innocence and perceived guilt. She continued with her search, rechecking the places she had already looked in the hope that it had been returned, but to no avail. That ugly little man must have taken it; there was no other explanation.

Her continuing sighs of exasperation finally got through to Alfred.

"Well, there's something nice waiting for you at the front desk that'll cheer you up. Flowers and what looks like fancy marzipan fruits displayed in a box all pretty like. Your admirer ain't short of a bob, that's for sure. I don't know—why don't these young fellas just come out with it instead of spending all their money trying to impress?"

Now it was Dody's turn to blush. If this was Pike's apology, it was a bit late. "No admirer, Alfred. They are probably gifts from a patient—I'd say someone I have been treating at the Women's Clinic." Those patients, of course, could barely afford to feed themselves, let alone buy sweets and flowers.

"Then why didn't they 'ave 'em delivered to the Clinic?" Alfred muttered. He sat himself back down at the bench, picked up the chest cutters, and began to whistle a romantic music-hall tune:

The boy I love is up in the gallery
The boy I love is looking now at me . . .

Dody needed no more of this irritation. She left the autopsy room and stalked to the front desk to collect the bouquet of roses and the box of sweets. The note was printed in ink and minimalist—typical Pike. Why could he not express his feelings?

I'm sorry.

He might well be sorry, but that wasn't going to help her now, was it?

*   *   *

Later that morning, Dody entered the hall where the inquest was being held. Unlike the previous day, there were now a number of expectant reporters seated behind the row of witnesses. This was no longer a simple, routine enquiry; something of public interest was anticipated, and the gentlemen of the press had caught the whiff of scandal.

Henry Everard settled on the bench next to her. She could only guess why he was here today—he had come to witness her fall from grace. A cramp gripped her stomach. She suddenly felt sick.

"I'm sorry, Dr. McCleland," Everard said when he read the expression on her face. "Like you, I am obliged to obey a coronial summons."

Dody met his eye. "Dr. Spilsbury will not be impressed at this public show of antagonism between his staff."

"Look, we must put your accusation of me behind us."

"My accusation? Your plagiarism."

"Is not the issue here. I have been called as a character witness and I plan on doing my best for you."

Dody stared at him, open-mouthed.

"It's what's called making amends," he added.

An eternity seemed to pass. "Thank you," she said at last, the words almost sticking in her throat. She sat stiffly on the witness bench, puzzling about his real motives, and waited for the proceedings to commence.

First, Inspector Walter Fisher was asked to explain what he saw in the room above the Crown and Anchor public house. He described a scene of bloodstained sheets and hysteria.

Then the police surgeon, Dr. Anthony Burton, took to the witness table. The police had called him to examine the body where it had been found in the attic room, and he had later performed the autopsy at the Bishopsgate Mortuary.

"To anticipate a little," said the coroner, "did you arrive at an immediate opinion as to the cause of death?"

"Yes. From the postmortem examination and the analysis taken at the time the body was found, I came to the conclusion that the deceased died from the effects of a mismanaged criminal abortion."

"Have you any doubt that criminal abortion was really the cause of the deceased's death?"

"No doubt whatsoever."

"Please explain your findings, sir."

"There was a considerable amount of blood on the sheets and soaked into the mattress, enough to conclude at the scene that death was due to exsanguination. Upon further examination at the mortuary, I discovered the blood loss to have been caused by several tears in the deceased's uterus—commonly called the womb—wall and a pierced uterine artery."

"Could these injuries have been caused by anything other than an abortion?"

"Unlikely. To add more weight to my findings, I discovered remnants of foetal tissue still adhering to the uterine wall."

"How do you think the injuries were inflicted?"

"Because the neck of the uterus is clamped tight during pregnancy, a long thin instrument would have been inserted to dilate it. The instrument would also have been used to scrape the lining of the uterus. It was during this procedure that the womb was perforated."

"Knitting needles," said a juror who had not spoken before. "I hear they use knitting needles."

The coroner looked to Dr. Burton.

"Indeed, knitting needles are often used in the case of an illegal procedure, but not in this instance, I feel."

The juror, more excited now, called out again, "Then what, sir, what was used?"

"The nature of the tears to the uterus indicate the use of a surgical hook."

A hook? Dody thought. No wonder the policemen had been so fixated on hers.

"There are also other marks on the uterus that suggest other medical instruments were used," the surgeon continued. "I conclude that someone with access to medical instruments and some knowledge of surgical procedure performed this disastrous operation."

Mr. Carpenter allowed several long seconds for the medical officer's conclusion to register with the jury before saying, "And how long would such a procedure take?"

"Anything from twenty minutes to one hour."

"And would the deceased have been capable of walking home after this?"

"A short distance, yes, but with extreme discomfort."

"She would have been bleeding?"

"The uterine artery was damaged but not severed. She bled out slowly."

Dody could contain herself no longer and jumped to her feet. "Sir," she addressed the police surgeon. "Do you not agree that a hook is an inappropriate instrument for a pregnancy of this duration?"

"It did cross my mind, yes. A case of overkill, certainly."

Some of the jurors snickered. The surgeon covered his mouth as if he might snatch back the unintentional pun.

"So, possibly performed by an amateur," Dody said, as if to herself, hoping to get the same thought ticking in the brains of the jury. "Did you find the deceased to be in good health otherwise?" she asked, louder again.

Dr. Burton looked to Mr. Carpenter, who indicated that he could answer the question.

"No, Dr. McCleland, I did not think further examination was relevant."

"Lead poisoning," Dody said through pursed lips, thinking that Dr. Burton's autopsy could not possibly have been conducted to Dr. Spilsbury's standards. "She was suffering from lead poisoning. She had already attempted abortion by ingesting lead and was showing all the symptoms. Professionally manufactured lead tablets were also found in her possession—not supplied by me, I might add." She turned to Inspector Fisher. "Tell them please, Inspector, tell the court about the lead."

Fisher nodded his head. "Yes, sir, Mr. Carpenter. Professionally made tablets were found, and we have no evidence that Dr. McCleland supplied them, despite Mrs. Craddock's supposition."

"The abortionist might have supplied the lead first," a juror called out.

"Yes." Dody seized on the juror's words. "That is what I suspect."

"To suspect is not good enough for my court, Doctor," the coroner said, directing his monocle at Dody. "You may speak further on the subject when it is your turn to testify. Thank you, Dr. Burton, you may step down, but please remain on the premises. The court will adjourn for fifteen minutes."

During the short break, Dody discovered that her parents had arrived, having caught the train from Tunbridge Wells. Dody barely had time to glare at her sister for summoning them before a crowd of reporters converged upon the small family group as they stood grasping one another's hands outside the school hall. For a moment Dody was relieved that the reporters' attention was on her father. Until she saw the direction their questions were heading.

"Is it true that your group encouraged the unions to take strike action?" a reporter in a crumpled linen jacket asked.

"Are you also encouraging revolution amongst the working classes?" asked another wearing a brown homburg.

"Fabians believe in reform, not revolution," Nial McCleland replied calmly.

"You are socialists?"

"In a manner of speaking—we believe in equality and justice for all, independent of class."

"All, meaning female suffrage also?"

"Of course."

"Your younger daughter is a champion of this cause, I believe."

"I am very proud of Florence and her activities, yes."

"And it seems your elder daughter, Dorothy, is taking the cause one step further, providing women with the means of shirking their God-given responsibilities by disposing of their babies for them," Homburg Hat said.

Dody clenched her fists. Both sides of the suffrage movement twisted their arguments, but this was surely the most obscene of all.

"That is preposterous! How dare you?" she shot at him.

"Equality for all, I say," the crumpled reporter sneered.

Her father looked aghast. He put out his hand and pulled Dody close. "This is not the Criminal Court yet, my dear. Your family's reputation can have no bearing on the outcome." An usher appeared outside the hall and jangled a small hand bell. "Come." Nial McCleland drew himself up and addressed his party. "The proceedings are about to recommence."

As she turned to enter the building, the crumpled reporter hurried over to her and leaned forwards so only she could hear what he had to say: "*A whistling woman, a crowing hen, are no use to God or men,*" he chanted. "Much like a female autopsy surgeon, eh, Dr. McCleland?"

For the first time in her life Dody learned what it really meant to hate another human being. Fortunately she was not holding a pistol. If she had been, she might not have been responsible for her actions. She turned her back on him and hurried to the ladies' cloakroom just before her bowels turned to water.

Dody moved over to the witness table for the swearing in. As she gave her name, she glanced at the sea of faces before her. Florence sat a few rows from the front, between Mother and Poppa. Poppa as usual wore his Russian peasant garb: a coarse wool shirt, embroidered jerkin, and baggy trousers tucked into knee-high felt boots—just this once she wished he would dress like other Englishmen. Thank God Mother wore clothes more appropriate to her class: a high-collared lace blouse and a pale pink trumpet skirt. Her lace-adorned hat, Dody took pleasure in seeing, was wide enough to block the view of the obnoxious reporters who had insulted her.

Dody explained her medical qualifications to the court— her initial degree at the London Royal Free Hospital School of Medicine for Women, her postgraduate experience at the New Hospital for Women, and then the graduate diploma she had completed the previous year in Edinburgh.

"In what discipline, Doctor?" the coroner asked.

"Autopsy surgery, sir. I now work for the Home Office as assistant to Dr. Spilsbury."

A ripple ran through the court.

"I've never heard of a female autopsy surgeon before. It is a part-time occupation, I believe," the coroner said.

"Yes, sir, I divide my time between the Home Office and the Whitechapel Women's Clinic. It was there that I last saw the deceased."

"Explain the visit, please, Doctor."

"I had never seen the young lady before. She came to the clinic in an agitated state. I noticed she was showing signs of lead poisoning. I questioned her about this, asking if she had taken the lead to promote miscarriage. She denied this, denied she was pregnant even, but upon further examination I confirmed my suspicions, establishing that she was towards the end of her first trimester. Upon hearing the news, she became violent and demanded that I do something about it. I told her that while I could not—*would* not—abort the baby, there were other things I could do to help, and after hearing this, she settled down."

"And what is it you did to *help*?" The coroner glanced at the jury and theatrically raised his eyebrow.

"I counselled her on the available support services—organisations that would help her during her lying-in, for example—and then gave her a bottle of bromide and instructed her in the dosage. Then I asked her to come and see me again this week so I could give her more counselling once she'd accepted her condition."

"And what is bromide used for?"

"It calms the nerves."

"Did you give her anything else?"

"I wrote her up a prescription to ease the symptoms of her lead poisoning—chloroform half an ounce and glycerine two ounces. She still denied taking lead to cause miscarriage, but I could tell by her symptoms that she had. I told her she would need to visit a chemist to have the mixture made up."

"And neither of these medicines is used to induce miscarriage?"

"Absolutely not."

The coroner glanced at Dr. Burton on the witness bench. Burton nodded his head.

"And you did not see Miss Craddock subsequently?" the coroner enquired again of Dody.

"I did not. Mr. Robinson was mistaken to think he saw Miss Craddock leaving the Women's Clinic on August the eleventh. All our patients are recorded in a register and her name is not on it. The register was examined yesterday by the police and they can vouch for my words."

"At what time does the Clinic close?" the jury foreman asked.

"Five o'clock, sir."

"The deceased was seen at six o'clock. Could she not have attended the Clinic after hours with her name therefore not recorded in the registry?"

"She was not attended by me, I assure you."

"Can you account for your movements at this time?"

"I was at home studying."

"Did anyone see you when you arrived home?" Mr. Carpenter asked.

"I let myself in. It was my maid's afternoon off. I did not see anyone until after seven when my sister returned home."

The coroner sighed and opened a folded piece of paper from the table in front of him. Dody found herself holding her breath. Someone must have tipped Mr. Carpenter off. How else could the proceedings have transpired with such precision, such speed?

And then the coroner confirmed her suspicions. "I have received several letters since the death of Esther Craddock, all anonymous, unfortunately. I think you will see when you read them, why this line of enquiry was necessary. The letters are all along these lines: *Sir, For the interest of morality and female safety you must investigate the practices of Dr. Dorothy McCleland.*" He paused as if he had some difficulty reading the note. "*Not only does she conduct classes amongst working-class girls in the area of pregnancy prevention, but she has also been performing criminal abortions in the Whitechapel Women's Clinic. For the sake of the morality of our working classes, I urge you to act upon this information.*"

When he had finished reading the letter, he gathered together a bundle of similar papers and instructed the usher to hand them to the jurymen to read. From the spectator's section of the hall, Florence cried out in protest. "Lies, those letters are lies! My sister would never do that!"

Dody felt the hall spin. Through a veil of mist she saw the figure of her sister being led away from the court by a policeman. Her mother sat in stunned silence with her hand over her mouth, her husband gripping her arm.

Once the contents of the notes had been digested, the coroner addressed the jury:

"As you can see, gentlemen, the nature of these letters

gave me no choice but to open this coronial enquiry. With a focus on the activities of Dr. McCleland." He removed his monocle, briefly recapitulated the evidence, and then requested the jury to consider their verdict.

Everard climbed to his feet. "I was summoned to this hearing, sir, but I have not yet been given a chance to speak."

The coroner looked surprised and shuffled through his notes in a slight state of confusion. "And you are?"

"Dr. Henry Everard. I work at the Paddington Mortuary with Dr. Dorothy McCleland."

Mr. Carpenter pulled a sheet of paper from his pile. "Ah yes, so you do. What do you have to say? Be quick about it, sir."

"That I was asked by the Coroner's Office to provide a character reference should any suspicion fall on Dr. McCleland, which does now appear to be the case."

"Feel free to do so, then."

Everard cleared his throat and addressed the jury. "I find it hard to believe the contents of those letters. The Dr. McCleland I have worked with for the past three months took the same Hippocratic Oath as all physicians. I feel absolutely confident in my assertion that, despite her feminist leanings, Dr. McCleland would refuse to perform an abortion under any circumstance other than to save the life of the mother—"

"She believes in contraception, don't she?" a man's voice called from the public benches. Someone whose wife she had counselled at the Clinic, perhaps?

"Contraception is not the same thing as abortion—" Everard started, before being shouted down.

"Against the laws of nature!"

Other men jeered their agreement; some even shouted, "Same difference!"

"If she weren't doing a man's job, she wouldn't 'ave got 'erself into this mess!"

Everard's done nothing to help my cause, Dody thought with increasing panic. Had he known it would be received this way?

A shout from the back: "Baby killer!"

"Silence!" Mr. Carpenter slammed the gavel down. "Please sit, Dr. Everard. You have said enough."

Dody dropped her head into her hands.

Everard touched her on the elbow. "I'm sorry, I tried," he whispered.

"The jury will now consider their verdict," Mr. Carpenter proclaimed after he had settled the crowd with threats of ejection.

A solemn hush fell upon the court, broken only by the whispers of the jurymen as they consulted and, Dody was certain, by the agitated beating of her own heart. The spectators gazed in awed expectancy from Dody to the jury, who took but a short time to reach their conclusion. At the end of five minutes the foreman announced that they were agreed. In answer to the coroner's formal enquiry, the foreman stood up and said, "We find that the deceased met her death by mismanaged criminal abortion, in all probability caused by the actions of Dr. Dorothy McCleland."

"Thank you, gentlemen," the coroner replied. "The case will now be referred to the Central Criminal Court at the Old Bailey."

Chapter Fourteen

Dody was charged before a justice of the peace and her case sped through the Magistrates' Court the next day, leaving her legal advisors with plenty of time to prepare her defence for trial the following month. If she had been of a lower social class, she might have had to spend time in prison during this period, but bail was granted for thirty pounds and paid by her father. It wasn't often the McCleland family were grateful for their country's social inequalities.

The following week, towards the end of a long day, she sat in the morning room with her mother and sister, Annie bustling around, gathering up dirty teacups and uneaten Dundee cake. The curtains were drawn and the room was in semidarkness. An oil lamp flickered from the writing desk. Flames from a pair of silver candelabra on the card table made the long shadows sway.

In deference to the Fabian motto, "A simple way of life,"

the sisters were obliged to regress to a lifestyle without electricity or modern conveniences when their father was in town. The Benz was kept out of sight in the mews, and Fletcher was forced to exchange his chauffeur's uniform for his old coachman's livery.

Nial McCleland insisted on using a tin bath in front of his bedroom fireplace despite the modern bathroom on the second-floor landing and on more than one occasion had chastised Annie for using the portable dedusting pump instead of a feather duster. His opinions were progressive on so many topics, but he was adamant in his contention that on the domestic front the old ways were always the best ways.

Louise McCleland was not as hardy as her husband. When she had dealings with the authors and artists of the Bloomsbury set—Nial had no time for them despite the fact that some of them were also Fabians—she visited her daughters without him. On these occasions she took every advantage of the modern facilities, thought the townhouse a tremendous treat, and was rarely seen without a smile on her face. Not so today, however.

Louise picked up the dog-eared newspaper from the settee next to her and handed it to Annie to dispose of. HOME OFFICE DOCTOR TO STAND TRIAL FOR CRIMINAL ABORTION, the headline on page three proclaimed.

"I don't know what you two are still looking so gloomy about," Florence said to her mother and sister when Annie had left the room with the laden tray and the newspaper tucked under her arm. "Dr. Spilsbury has returned to London to bat on Dody's side and we all know he barely ever loses a case."

True, Dody thought. Upon his return to London, Spilsbury had been granted permission to perform another autopsy on

Esther's body and to review Dr. Burton's findings. While he had agreed with the police surgeon that a person with basic medical knowledge had performed the procedure, he declared the accusation against Dody preposterous and circumstantial. He confirmed Dody's diagnosis of Esther's lead poisoning and guaranteed her his support, promising that he would stand by her as a character witness in the trial should the need arise. Without Spilsbury's declaration of faith, Dody knew she might never have made it through the nightmare of the last few days.

"What of Henry Everard?" Florence asked. "Will he also come forward in your defence again?"

"I sincerely hope not," Dody said. "He hardly helped me during the inquest, did he? I think Dr. Spilsbury must have forced him to testify." She turned to Louise. "Everard resents me, Mother. He has no time for female doctors, let alone autopsy surgeons, and sees me as a threat."

And her heated debates with him about pregnancy prevention had done nothing but damage her cause. If only she'd kept her opinions to herself. On second thought, she doubted it would have made much difference. There was nothing she could do to change her gender and that was surely his biggest problem.

"Dr. Everard stole Dody's idea for a research paper, Mother," Florence said.

Louise looked with surprise from one to the other of her daughters.

"Could he have done it, Dody—written the letters, I mean?" Florence added.

"And risked his career? I don't think so," Dody said.

"But perhaps some enquiries could be made anyway,

dear?" Louise suggested. "I seem to remember one of you telling me about a policeman acquaintance who you thought a slight cut above the rest."

Florence broke in before Dody could reply. "Chief Inspector Pike is away on leave. When he read about Dody's case in the newspaper, he phoned immediately, even offered to return to London to help, but Dody refused to talk with him." At this she shot Dody a sharp look.

He had also sent those flowers and sweets—sweets so disgusting she had taken one bite and dumped them in one of the mortuary dustbins. These had been followed a few days later by a detailed apology, though she had not confided this to Florence. He'd said he understood if she wished to put an end to their friendship, but would she at least consider admitting him to the house so they could discuss her case? He had signed his note "With affection," and for the briefest of moments her heart had stopped.

But still she had not replied.

"Police involvement is for my legal advisors to organise, if they think it necessary," she told her mother and sister. "Besides, Pike is the wrong kind of policeman; he does not deal in matters such as this."

Louise looked to Florence with a raised eyebrow, as if to ask her younger daughter if there was something else she should know about this man. Florence, to her credit, did not elaborate.

Dody would not be drawn into any more discussion about Pike. Her mother would be horrified if she knew Dody had ever thought of him as much more than an acquaintance. Louise would probably have been less distressed to discover that Dody had been consorting with a Tory politician.

"It must be a relief to Mrs. Craddock that her daughter's body has at last been released for burial," Louise McCleland said, thankfully leaving talk of Pike behind. Florence followed her mother's lead in trying to buoy Dody's spirits with positive news.

"And Daphne told me that the Kent baby has been discharged from hospital, fully recovered. If not for you, she would have died. You see, Dody, the news is not all doom and gloom."

Dody left her chair and began to pace. "I know what you are both attempting, Florence, Mother, and I appreciate your trying to cheer me up. But I am a realist, and I know the Kent baby's troubles are by no means over. What has she been discharged to? What are her chances of survival in a family of such poverty, with parents who have probably already yielded twice to the temptation of infanticide?" Dody stopped pacing and faced them. "If I do go to trial, I will at least be able to draw public attention to the appalling conditions of the working classes, largely brought about by their inability to control their pregnancies."

"Lord, Dody," Florence said, "if you spout off like that, they really will think you are an abortionist."

"I am not alone in my opinion; there are many who feel the same. Only last month I met a woman called Marie Stopes at the Natural History Museum. She is a professor of palaeobotany at the University of Manchester and is all for birth control—she sees it as a form of women's rights. I am aware that this is a divisive issue amongst the suffragettes, but Florence, you are an educated woman. You of all people should be able to understand the differences; birth control is not abortion."

Florence folded her arms. "Dody, I've told you this a hundred times. Birth control makes a mockery of marriage, makes it no more than legal prostitution, giving men even more reason to exploit their wives, put pleasure before responsibility—"

"For someone who openly declares she will never marry, you suddenly seem to have a high opinion of the institution," Dody said sharply.

"Yes, there are those for whom I consider marriage to be perfectly acceptable; it is just not for me, that's all. For me it would be a distraction from the Cause. Marriage is not something that should be taken lightly, and contraception only adds to its risk, making people care too much about lust and none of its consequences."

Dody clenched her fists; quite aside from the problems of the poor, how could Florence talk like this when only a few years earlier she had herself been involved in an affair with a married man? True, she had not known the man was married at the time and had fallen for his romantic looks, his poetry, and his lies. But imagine if she had become pregnant. She must have been very lucky, or practising some form of contraception. Now, as a result, she was off men entirely. With her own experience scrubbed from her mind, she seemed unable to understand how hard it was for others to fight the attraction of love. Even Dody, with her limited physical experience, could empathise; she yearned even for something that, at the age of thirty, had probably passed her by.

The last line of Pike's note slipped into her mind unbidden.

She set her jaw. "There's none more zealous than the newly converted."

"Dody, Florence." Their mother held up a finger. "Enough

of that. We all know how divisive this debate is. Personal attacks and splitting hairs will do nothing but harm. At least until the end of the trial, concentrate on what you do agree on and that is Dody's innocence. This debate about contraception and marriage is getting us nowhere. Please, girls, kiss and make up."

Dody and Florence fell silent. Their mother was right, of course; she usually was. Florence sat with her head bowed and her hands twisted. Dody looked over to her sister. She could never cease to love and admire Florence, even though there were times when she felt like shaking her until the blinkers fell from her eyes. She must cease discussion of contraception, at least until the trial began. And then? Well, if she had to go down, she would not go down silently—she might as well be sent to prison for something she really was guilty of.

Dody met her sister's eyes. Florence offered a cautious smile and they opened their arms to one another.

"That's better, girls," Louise said.

They finished their embrace and settled back into their chairs. A short while later Nial McCleland strode into the room looking as if he had just come from the field—hair awry, spikes of untrimmed beard poking in all directions—oblivious to the uncomfortable silence he was breaking.

"I've spoken to Sebastian Carmichael, my lawyer, you know, and he's going to join us for dinner to discuss strategy." He moved towards the drinks trolley and offered them all a sherry. Dody shook her head. Her stomach still felt fragile from her latest bout with the cholera. She'd sent to the chemist for more Valentine's, and settled for a dose from a sherry glass.

"I thought you were dining with the Thompsons tonight?" Florence asked her parents.

Louise and Nial exchanged glances. "No dear, that engagement has been cancelled," Louise said quietly.

"Some problems at their country house, I believe. Had to leave the city in a hurry." Their father's tone was loud and stilted. He had never been a good liar. The "scandalous behaviour" of the McCleland girl was the reason the dinner party had been cancelled, Dody was sure of it. She wondered how many more of her parents' friends would ostracise them.

"Don't worry, my dears," Louise said to her daughters as she took a glass of sherry. "I have the utmost faith in Sebastian. He's certainly got your father out of one or two scrapes in his time."

But did Dody really want a radical lawyer on her side, one who had defended anarchists and revolutionaries, suffragettes, unsuccessful suicides, and homosexuals? Oh, Lord. Her innocence seemed inconsequential with a man like that fighting her case. Her career was ruined regardless of whether she won or lost.

"Bother," Florence said as she looked to the mantel clock. "I shall miss him. The truce is over and we're having a protest in Leicester Square tonight. I've helped organise it, so I have to be there." Florence moved over to where Dody sat on the chaise. "I'm sorry I won't be able to hear what Sebastian has to say, but I will be here with you in spirit."

"I'm almost tempted to go with you," Dody said with a weak smile, even though she suspected she would not be well received by the righteous members of the Bloomsbury suffragettes. Since the coronial verdict, the hate letters had poured in from every social and political spectrum, including suffragettes, suffragists—those who supported female suffrage through peaceful, constitutional means—and of course, the antisuffragettes. Earlier that day, a small crowd had gathered for some hours outside her house, only giving up when the "baby killer" failed to appear. Dody was a prisoner in her own home.

"Nonsense, Dody," her father said. "We McClelands never run away from a fight."

Dody had no intention of running away, and she would tell her legal advisors that. But she wondered if her father knew the exact nature of the fight in which she was embroiled. It went much deeper than the black-and-white conflicts between Capital and Labour he was so often asked to mediate. There was more than money and conditions at stake here.

Criminal abortion not only took the life of a developing child and threatened the life of the mother, but affected the very souls of all those involved. That Dody should be accused of something so abhorrent made her feel physically sick.

Chapter Fifteen

Outside the theatre, visibility was grainy. The streetlamps would make little difference until the descent of night proper. It was not yet time for the music halls to spill their audiences into the street, and the still air carried the raucous applause and even the words of the songs to Florence and her group waiting outside the Empire Theatre.

I'm not too young, I'm not too old
Not too timid, not too bold
Just the kind you'd like to hold
Just the kind for sport I'm told
Ta-ra-ra Boom-de-aye!

"Disgusting," Florence's colleague, Miss Jane Lithgow, said.

"Not nearly as disgusting as what's going on here," Florence replied, nodding to the poster of the partially clad Mata Hari tacked to the wall beside the Empire's front entrance.

"I agree. That woman is a traitor to our sex. She has no right bringing her foreign pollution to our shores." Jane handed Florence her basket of eggs, reached for the top of the poster, cried out, "Votes for women, chastity for men!" and rent the thing down the middle.

"Bravo!" cheered Florence and her companions.

Their opposition, a group of painted women standing on the other side of the promenade, shouted obscenities and called them "prying prudes." The women were waiting to offer themselves to those of the theatre's male patrons who had been enjoying Mata Hari's performance unescorted. If what Florence had heard about the show was true, the men would be well and truly primed.

The small group of suffragettes attempted to drive the street women from the promenade, prodding them with their wooden signs, trying to send them on their way with gifts of money or suggestions regarding how they might reform their ways. The women wouldn't budge, not when many of them had hungry children to feed or pimps to beat them for failure.

Florence and Daphne stepped away to distance themselves from some of their more vocal companions. "How many times," Florence said to Daphne, "have I tried to point out to the others that it's not the prostitutes we should be targeting, but the men who are using them?"

"Cast aside your shackles and join the fight for female suffrage—" Jane cried.

"Back to your ol' man, prying prude!"

"Don't ya please 'im, love?"

"Want some lessons?" another coarse woman called out, waggling her tongue obscenely at Jane.

"If the men weren't so driven by lust, there would be no demand," Daphne said.

Indeed, Florence thought. The prostitutes needed saving and their customers reforming, which was why women needed to be granted equal voting rights. A female vote, women members of parliament even, was their only hope to temper the rash, immoral, and corrupt behaviour of men.

Daphne dug Florence in the ribs. "I say, Flo, I have a splendid idea. Why don't we sneak around to the back of the theatre to surprise the performers as they leave? Mata Hari will know better than to exit from the front. I mean, it's not as if she hasn't been mobbed before."

That's more like it, Florence thought. The street women might be victims of the system, but Mata Hari certainly wasn't.

Florence glanced over at Jane Lithgow, the Bloomsbury Division's second-in-command since the events of the previous year had all but shattered their group. Jane had given up on her heckling and was sorting through her basket, holding eggs up to the light to identify the most rotten. Florence had never liked Jane, but circumstances had forced them to form a shaky alliance. The woman was a prying prude to the extreme, and Florence could not discount the possibility that she might have been behind some of the hate letters Dody had received. Florence needed no excuse to distance herself. "What a splendid idea! I'll get us some eggs."

"No need, Flo," Daphne said, holding up a string bag of tomatoes. "I got these from Cook just before I left home."

They whispered their intentions to some of the others and

then scurried down the alley separating the theatre from the building next door. The further they travelled, the darker and more dingier their surroundings became. The smell of effluent from leaky drains almost made Florence gag. Her eyes strained, scanning the cobbles for dustbins, piles of manure, and the legs of a drunk protruding from a doorway.

The theatre backed onto a small cobbled yard, just large enough to take a lorry or cart. A ramp paved the way to a huge delivery entrance door. Rusted iron steps parallel to this led to the smaller backstage door set in a wall of soot-blackened bricks veined with twisting metal pipes. This yard was a reflection of the theatre's black heart, Florence decided. The rest of it, the lavish front lounge, entrance, and promenade, made the place nothing but a whited sepulchre.

"How is Dr. McCleland?" Daphne asked as they waited there in the gloom.

"She has an experienced lawyer behind her. Poppa thinks the charges will be dropped before she gets to court. But she is understandably upset and quite ill from the worry of it."

"I can only imagine how she feels. I helped her once with an abortion—the mother was haemorrhaging, would never have survived carrying the baby to term. It was dreadful, and Dr. McCleland was no less affected by it than I was. I know she would never be involved in anything like this, and I hope I get the chance to testify." Daphne paused. "Flo? You haven't told Dr. McCleland about the, er, tea party, have you? I had only tried it once before, you know, and I don't intend doing it again. Only, if your sister was to hear about it, I'd probably be in huge trouble and—"

Florence turned to her friend, whose round face glowed like the moon through the descending darkness. "Of course not, silly goose. But *please* don't do it again. Where did Harriet get the stuff from anyway, do you know?"

"I think the first batch was left over from her husband's cholera treatment. As for the second, I have no idea."

"Well, let's not worry about that for now: first things first. Daphne, I've been thinking," she said and then paused, trying to adopt a tone that would not make her sound like a child about to devise a mischievous prank.

"Yes?"

"If I could find the true abortionist, I'd be able to save Dody's reputation and bring this whole affair to an end—even sooner than her lawyer, I suspect—as well as ridding the streets of one more ruthless killer of women and children."

"But how would we do that?"

Florence liked the sound of "we"—it was what she had been fishing for. Besides, Daphne owed her a favour now. "Well, we know that he or she operates in the Whitechapel area, don't we?"

"Yes, but that's about all. There must be dozens of abortionists in the area: old ladies with knitting needles, amateur doctors, and disreputable midwives. Criminal abortion is a lucrative business, Flo, and we only find out about it when something goes wrong—"

Daphne's words were swallowed by the sound of thunderous applause. The theatre shook to its foundations, and the yard was flooded with yellow light.

Chapter Sixteen

The crowd hooted and roared. They were not cheering for him, of course, and Pike did not care. He was not a natural showman and disliked the attention. His mother, a talented pianist herself, had attempted to school him for a career she could never have as a woman, and the pressure to perform had driven him from home. He had joined the army to avoid the audition she had organised for the Royal Academy and to spare her the disappointment of his almost certain rejection. He took his final bow on the stage and murmured a prayer of thanks to God for allowing him to follow his instincts.

He had enjoyed the rehearsals, but judging by this opening night, the performances were bound to be anything but satisfying. Perhaps he was too much the perfectionist. The oboe was breathless and out of sync with his colleagues, the lead violin scratchy and off-key. And the drummer, Ahmed—or whatever it was the little Cockney called himself—had not once looked up for his prompt, resulting in a pounding rhythm more akin to African tribal than the exotic mysticism of a sultan's dancing harem. Lucky for him the crowd couldn't have cared less; it wasn't the music they had come for, after all.

Pike exited stage left, away from the heat of the lights and into the cooler, darker embrace of the wings. He was in a hurry to leave. Dody had refused to answer his telephone calls or his note, and the only course of action left was to call in person. If she barred his admittance—as she might—he would do whatever it took to muscle in on the investigation. Inspector Fisher owed him that much at least.

He paused for a moment to look back upon the stage. Face flushed with triumph, Margaretha tipped her head back and extended her arms to the rose petals and calling cards raining down from the dress circle. Her handmaidens had already helped her replace most of her costume, but her enticing shape was still visible through the thin folds of veils.

A brazen youth mounted the stage, presented her with flowers, and greedily eyed her breasts. *Not again,* Pike muttered as he strode back under the lights, reaching the youth the moment before he lunged. The audience booed and hissed as if he were the villain of a children's pantomime. To their disgust, he put the young man in a headlock, dragged him to the edge of the stage, and shoved him from the top of the steps into the arms of his jeering mates.

He needed to get Margaretha safely ensconced with the admiral before he could go about his other business, and this wasn't helping her speedy departure. Taking her by the hand, he marched her from the stage and into the wings. "That's enough," he said. "Any more of that and we'll have a riot on our hands."

"Oh, Captain, you are such a killjoy."

"Someone's got to look after you." Pike glanced around backstage where stagehands were hauling in backdrops of pyramids and painted elephants. "I don't know where Klassen's got to."

"Flirting with one of the ushers, probably. But darling, I didn't know you cared."

"Where will I be if you are lynched?"

Margaretha pouted and ran her hand up the firm buttons of his waistcoat. "*Godverdomme*, Captain. Have you got ice in your veins? Am I just a meal ticket to you—meat and potatoes?"

"No." He removed her hand and patted it. "Lobster and champagne—which is what you will miss out on if you keep the admiral waiting."

"Bah, the old man is such a bore. Ships, ships, and more ships; that is all he ever talks about."

"I thought you wanted him to take you to Portsmouth."

"Well, yes, of course. Anything for an outing, a chance to get out of this miserable, stinking city."

And the chance to look over the latest Dreadnought being built at His Majesty's Shipyard, no doubt, Pike thought. "And don't forget Klassen wants you to sweet-talk him into sponsoring the Army and Navy Club tour." Margaretha pulled a face and snatched her hand from his. "Please get yourself dressed," he said. "I'd like to get home and go to sleep as soon as possible."

Margaretha swore again in Dutch and stalked in a thundercloud of veils down the passage towards her dressing room. Pike pushed his way through a floating crowd of half-dressed chorus girls and looked over the various gentlemen visitors who had bribed Klassen for backstage visits.

He spied Van Noort standing a head taller than most, bat-

tling his way through the throng towards Margaretha's dressing room. Their eyes connected. Van Noort raised his hand.

They met outside the door marked with a painted star.
The tall man gripped Pike's arm. "Well, did you ask her? Did
you ask?"

While Margaretha was still high on his list of suspects, it
confounded Pike to think that this pathetic Van Noort creature could also be a threat to national security.

"I'm sorry, sir. Mata Hari is unable to meet you," he said.
"She's very grateful for the flowers, but says she can't take
your money." Pike extracted the envelope of money the man
had attempted to press upon Margaretha after the final
rehearsal from his trouser pocket. "She asked me to return it."

Van Noort reached to take it, but his shaking fingers failed
to close and the envelope fell to the floor, spilling its contents.
"Can you taste them?" he murmured, leaning into the passage wall in a faint.

Pike retrieved the scattered notes and straightened. "Taste
what?" He looked at Van Noort. The man's face was masklike,
his eyes glazed. A twitch began at the corner of his mouth and
crept its way up both cheeks. And then his lips began to smack
and his eyes to blink as if he was having some kind of a fit.

"The guns, the guns—" he cried, massaging the scar on
his temple. Sweat streamed down his face, and he launched
into a monologue of gibberish.

Alarmed, Pike took Van Noort by the arm and guided
him to a wooden chair set against the wall. He looked about
him. The backstage throng were paying them no attention;
they had other things on their minds. After loosening the
man's collar, Pike grabbed a passing stagehand by the arm
and asked him to fetch a glass of water. Gradually Pike sensed

that whatever had gripped the doctor was loosening. Van Noort straightened, took a sip of water, and then mopped his brow with a handkerchief.

"I'm sorry for the disturbance. It's something I cannot seem to help," he said quite lucidly.

Pike handed him the envelope of money. "You've plenty there for a taxi. Better get home and have some rest."

"Yes, yes, of course, thank you." Van Noort climbed to his feet and took a few wobbling steps. Pike beckoned to the hovering stagehand and told him to escort the gentleman from the premises and help him find a cab. As Van Noort turned to leave, Pike said, "The guns. What did you mean by the guns?"

Van Noort stared at Pike. He finally said, "You should know, you were there—weren't you?"

The ragged boy Pike had seen with Van Noort at the tram stop suddenly appeared at their side. Pike searched his mind for the boy's name. "Jack, how did you get in?" he asked.

"It's all right, the manager has given him permission to enter. He knows Jack is with me," Van Noort said. "Find me a cab, will you, lad?"

"Sure thing, Doc. Off ya go, mate," Jack told the stagehand. "I'll 'andle this." He pulled Van Noort's long arm over his own shoulder.

The child's done this before, Pike thought as he watched man and boy disappear into the crowded passageway. He shook his head, puzzled for a moment, and then turned his mind to more important things: Margaretha.

He tapped on her dressing room door and entered at her command. The floor was strewn with petticoats, underclothes, and feather boas. She sat at her dressing table in a silken robe of oriental design. The lightbulbs around the mirror shone down upon a cornucopia of makeup pots, crystal bottles of scent, tubs of powder, and wilted flowers. On a small table next to this sat her elaborately carved water pipe, similar to the ones Pike had seen in the Sudan. Mata Hari revered the object not only for its decorative appearance; its soporific fumes had almost overcome Pike on more than one occasion.

She removed her jewelled headdress, looked at Pike through narrow eyes, and took aim. With a sweep of her hand, she sent the headdress flying through the air straight at him. He dodged and it smashed to the ground. Shattered faux rubies dotted the dressing room floor like drops of blood.

"Shall I call your maid?" he asked with deliberate calm.

"I heard you outside with him, that slobbering oaf! I don't want anything to do with him. Tell Gabriel to cancel the remainder of his tickets."

"Can't be done. He's paid in advance. Shouldn't Betty be here now, helping you to dress?"

"I sacked her. She was stealing from me. Gabriel will find me another maid." She ripped the pins from her hair, tossed them onto the dressing table, and seized her hairbrush. "Sometimes I feel I am nothing but a whore, a prisoner of you men, with Gabriel and you as my pimps."

The hairbrush caught in a clump of hair at the back of her head. She yanked it, crying out with pain and frustration as the brush became even more tangled.

"Careful, you'll hurt yourself." Pike moved in on her from behind and relieved her of the brush's handle. With as gentle a touch as possible, he attempted to extract the brush from the tangled nest of hair. "You shouldn't have sacked your maid," he said. "She should be doing this."

Her shoulders curled as his fingers brushed against the

skin of her neck. She lifted her hand to his, but he avoided her touch by moving to another knot. "You tease me," she said.

To prove that this was not the case, he ripped the brush out of her hair with a yank that made her gasp.

Glancing in the mirror, he saw there were tears streaming down her cheeks. Pike closed his eyes briefly; the torture of women was not to his taste. Did she really want him this badly? Pike doubted it; to his mind he was nothing but ordinary—poor, ordinary, and half crippled. This woman could have almost any man she wanted. She got through more lovers than most women got through silk stockings, confound it. She only wanted him because she could not have him, because, unlike most men, he refused to succumb to her allure. Was this the personality trait that drove her to espionage, he wondered—the love of a challenge, the glory of success, the adoration of men?

He tossed the brush back onto the table. Trying to understand her would not get his job done. "Hurry up," he said, "the admiral will be waiting."

"Pimp!" The brush thumped against the door as he closed it behind him.

It didn't take long for the others to follow Florence and Daphne's lead. Soon there were almost as many of them waiting outside the back of the theatre as there had been at the front; protesting suffragettes, young men lusting for Mata Hari, and a starstruck group from a nearby restaurant who had heard the commotion and wanted to join in the fun.

Mata Hari's appearance at the top of the back steps caught Florence by surprise. She was expecting the woman to appear as in her poster, wearing more jewels than clothing, but the spotlight on the back door illuminated a tall, lithe woman, fully dressed—although the silken blouse visible through her open summer coat was cut a little lower than respectable. Her figure-hugging skirt appeared so tight at the ankles that it made her take Geisha-like steps, and she descended the iron stairs leaning heavily into the arm of the gentleman in white tie and tails escorting her.

"That's the conductor," Florence heard one young man say to his companion.

"What I wouldn't give to be in his shoes tonight," the friend replied.

As they reached the bottom of the steps, Mata Hari pulled a feather from her hat and began to tickle the conductor's cheek in a manner most provocative.

Florence dug her elbow into Daphne's side. "Give me some ammunition." She reached into Daphne's bag and selected the softest tomato she could find. More suffragettes followed Florence's lead, screaming out their protests. Reinforcements, led by Jane Lithgow and her rotten-egg brigade, joined them from the front of the theatre.

A group of ushers came running down the steps and linked protective arms around the pair. The conductor took the dancer's hand and shouted something above the din, then indicated the taxi ranks in the neighbouring street with his cane.

Florence took aim with her tomato and, with a strength gained from years of playing Fabian hockey, struck the silk hat from his head. The man touched his bare head with surprise and glared angrily into the crowd, seeking the direction from which the missile had been thrown.

Florence drew her breath with a gasp, blinked, and looked again. Mentally, she shaved off the beard.

Pike.

Of all the duplicitous men she had known, she would not have expected this from him.

In that instant Pike recognised her, too. He put his fingers to his lips and tried to hush her.

Florence was damned if she would be hushed. "Pike!" she screamed with righteous indignation, her blazing anger lifting her voice above the din. "You traitor, you cad, you . . . you . . . crippled weed!"

Pike whispered something to Mata Hari, placed her into the care of one of the ushers, and pushed his way through the crowd to Florence's side. Before she knew it, he had tipped her back in his arms and forced his lips to hers, pressing her screams of protest into silence. When they broke for air, he rubbed his cheek against hers. "I told her you were a friend of mine," he said, sotto voce. "Florence, listen, please, don't call me Pike. This is not what it seems."

Florence's head was still reeling from the unexpected kiss; it was a long time since she had been kissed like that. And by Pike, of all people—the very cheek of it! She drew back and walloped him hard across the face. Pike flinched, grabbed hold of her hand, and glowered down at her. He was not a tall man but in this instant he appeared to Florence like a giant. In the tension of the moment she was vaguely aware of Daphne Hamilton creeping up behind him, hefting her VOTES FOR WOMEN sign above his head. "Meet me in one hour at the Queen's Hotel, in the Oyster Room, and I'll explain—"

His words were cut short by a sharp crack and the sound of splintering wood.

*   *   *

The classic white front of the Queen's Hotel stood out from the dark leviathan shapes of the buildings around it. Pike hesitated on the bottom step. Florence deserved to know what was going on, and in any case, there was nothing to lose now—he was certain the covert operation was ruined. His explanation to Margaretha in the hansom on their way to the Ritz had been weak, and in the flickering light of the cab's lamp he'd read the suspicion in her eyes. She was sure to tell Gabriel Klassen about the scene outside the theatre, and her accomplice, too, if she had one. Perhaps that was not a bad thing; it might spur them to act. The admiral had been well briefed; he might be a buffoon, but he was still a patriot and more than happy with using his briefcase as bait, provided talk of his escapades did not reach his wife.

As Pike stood on the steps, he felt a great, cleansing wave of relief wash over him. He was free now to help Dody in any way he could if she would let him. He need not creep to her house under cover of darkness, worried someone might recognise the quiet police officer as Mata Hari's conductor; he could visit her tomorrow, in respectable daylight.

Of course, there was still one other hurdle to overcome, and that was to convince Florence of his integrity. Despite their differences, the sisters were close. If he could win over Florence, he might have a chance at winning Dody over, too.

He mounted the steps with a new resolve, handed the doorman a penny, and entered the hotel's plush interior. The Oyster Room stayed open late and was popular with theatregoers, offering light oyster suppers, clam chowder, and assorted specialities from the grill. The interior was dimly lit and smoky, and it took a moment for his eyes to adjust. He saw her, finally, at the far end of the room, wearing a dress of mauve brocade. She was sitting alone at a table next to a window facing the busy, flickering square. He handed the maître d' his stained hat and made his way over to her past a table of boisterous young Guards officers. Florence refused to acknowledge his presence. Even when the maître d' pulled out a chair for him, she would not turn her head from the view.

Pike cleared his throat. "May I order you something? I can recommend the oysters."

"I'm not hungry."

Pike beckoned to a waiter. "Two glasses of Krug, please, and a dozen oysters natural."

"I told you I wasn't hungry," Florence said.

"I am."

Pike did not have to wait long. The plate was soon in front of him. Florence looked from the oysters to him. "Rather expensive, I would imagine, for a policeman's purse."

"As you've probably gathered, I've been employed elsewhere recently."

"Selling yourself, you mean?" she responded coolly. The oysters seemed to wriggle about on their beds of ice.

"I assure you, it's nothing like that."

"Then you'd better explain."

Pike leaned across the table. "Firstly, I need to know how your sister is."

"Good of you to ask."

"Florence, please. I know about the inquest and have been worried sick."

"You don't seem unwell. If anything, I would say you are quite in the pink."

Pike put his hand to the back of his head and probed the lump, testing her mood with a slight smile. "Actually, I've got a thumping headache."

"Good, you deserve it." She failed to smile back. "I don't like the beard; it makes you look sinister. I think it illustrates your true nature. You probably never had any intention of helping my sister—how could you, when you've been so busy consorting with harlots?"

"Florence, I've been on special assignment, undercover, and that's all I can tell you. You can believe it or not, the choice is yours." He pushed his chair from the table to leave. His head hurt, he was tired, and he had lost his appetite. He did not have the time for this. Besides, if he had to explain his behaviour to anyone, he would rather it was to Dody.

The beaded trim of Florence's dress danced in the lights of the candelabra and reflected in her eyes. "Spies?" she enquired in a stage whisper that had Pike looking around the restaurant in a panic. "If you don't want the whole restaurant to hear me, you'd better sit back down, hadn't you?"

Pike reluctantly sat. The waiter poured the champagne, and Pike took several swallows before the fizz settled.

Florence said, "I have read all about the German threat and I am full bottle on it." Pike could almost see the thoughts chasing one another through her brain. "I take it you mean German spies? They say there are thousands of them in the country at any given time, disguised as butchers and bakers and businessmen even."

"Yes, I've read that in the shilling shockers, too."

"Must you be so obtuse? You know very well that what I am saying is not some kind of fiction."

It was at times like this that the age difference between

Dody and her sister became glaringly obvious. This was a game to Florence, much like the protests and stone-throwing she got up to with the suffragettes. Had she no idea of the real danger the German threat posed? "No, not fiction. German spies on our soil could indeed be the precursor of an invasion. The Kaiser's jealousy of Britain is getting out of control—he's building up his armaments, setting his neighbours' teeth on edge, and demanding Germany's 'place in the sun,'" he said, endeavouring to get the seriousness of the situation across.

She clasped her hands and peered earnestly into his eyes. "It's Mata Hari, isn't it? She is Dutch and surely has German sympathies. It is no surprise to me that she's one of them. They say she is dangerous, wanton, and promiscuous—she certainly seems to fit the bill . . ."

Alarmed at her enthusiasm, Pike furtively looked around the room and raised his hands for her to stop. "Slow down and please keep quiet. I can neither confirm nor deny what you've said. And don't tell anyone about this conversation or your suspicions, despite the fact that the operation is almost certainly at an end now."

Florence looked contrite. Her eyes dropped to the rising bubbles in her champagne glass. "Because of me? I am sorry, Pike."

"Don't be. Part of me is relieved."

"You will visit Dody tomorrow morning and explain?"

"I'll explain what I can. Yes."

"And tell her why you reneged on your knee operation? I'm afraid she's taken it very personally."

Pike had no answer to that. He might be able to explain his extracurricular activities to Dody, but to explain the other issue was a matter easier said than done.

Chapter Seventeen

He lay on a stretcher in the operating tent after a three-day journey across the veldt in an oxcart. The hospital tent he was carried into was so small they could barely fit the operating table between its two poles. His tongue stuck to the roof of his mouth; his body cried out for water. He stared longingly at the row of pannikins on the dressings stand, tried to reach out for one, and found he could barely lift his hand. Flies pattered across his face, and he did not have the strength to bat them away.

An orderly leaned over him, peeled the stinking dressing from his right knee, and called the doctor over.

"That left leg will have to come off," the doctor said.

No, not the left, the right leg, Pike tried to say, but the words would not leave his mouth.

"There's no anaesthetic," the orderly said.

"Cowards don't deserve anaesthetics."

The remains of his ragged trousers were cut from his left leg. Above him the surgeon hefted a great axe. Then he realised this wasn't the surgeon he'd seen earlier. This one had the face of Dody McCleland. She leaned over and kissed him long and deep, one moment looking like her sister, the next looking like herself. "It has to be done, Pike," she said, resuming her position with the axe.

"No, no!" Pike cried mutely. He wriggled and strained and, just as the orderly moved to hold him down, fell with a crash from the operating table.

He awoke on the floor of his bedroom in a tangle of sweat-soaked sheets. "Just a dream, just a dream," he murmured to himself. It hadn't been like that at all. But despite his reassurances, the dream had opened a curtain in his mind on events he had no desire to remember.

First there was the fighting that transformed the dusty veldt into a butcher's shop, painting it red with the spilled blood of both sides. White stars of shrapnel smoke dotted the landscape; big guns boomed. Shredded eucalyptus leaves released their medicinal odour while imbecilic British commanders sent hundreds to their deaths. It was in one such skirmish where the British troops had been led into an ambush—boxed in on each side of a high ravine—that Pike had been hit. His batman had led his horse from the lines and taken him to a field dressing station. Indian stretcher-bearers had next loaded him onto a bullock cart and transported him to the field hospital. His companion in the cart was a sergeant with similar injuries to his. The stench from their legs grew with each hour they spent on the rutted dirt track. By the time they reached their destination, Pike could not say which of them reeked the most.

They were both feverish and in a dreadful state when they arrived at the village of tents that served as the field hospital. The sergeant was examined by the doctor, who, after waving the flies away, declared that he had no time for intricate surgery—the leg would have to come off.

Pike saw it all from where he lay on the stretcher waiting his turn.

He saw orderlies hold the sergeant down. He saw the young doctor under the watch of an older man—Van Noort—reach for his surgical saw and press it against the sergeant's bone. The sergeant screamed; the doctor said, "God damn it—the bloody thing won't cut!"

For a moment the young doctor had looked around the tent in a state of panic. Then his eyes fell on a big ripsaw which the women had been using to make splints. After washing the saw in a bucket of water, he cut through the bone as if it were butter. Fortunately by then the sergeant had lost consciousness.

The older doctor clapped the younger one on the back. "Well done, George. I'll leave the other to you then," he said and he exited through the tent flaps.

"Next!" the younger doctor ordered as the sergeant was carried away. It was then that Pike had drawn his pistol.

The medical staff had more than enough casualties to attend to and no time to argue with a belligerent lieutenant, even if he was the holder of the DCM, and took him to another tent to die.

But he hadn't died. Having found him unfit for frontline duty, the military promoted him and sent him to help supervise the running of the internment camp at Bloemfontein, where Boer women and children were imprisoned to prevent them from providing succour and supplies to the guerrilla forces. It was then that his nightmares had really started: the waking nightmare of starving children, overcrowding, and pestilence and disease that left people dying like rats. The British authorities could barely see to the needs of their own forces, let alone those of enemy civilians.

Pike's protests over conditions in the camp fell on deaf ears, and little fuss was made over his resignation. A crippled officer wasn't good for the reputation of the regiment anyway, despite his chest full of medals. Joining the police had seemed a natural progression from the military. *Strange,* he thought, *after last year, I am now not only an embarrassment to the army, but to the police force, too.*

He shook his head and hefted himself from the floor. He needed a bath, but the sounds of running water and singing from the bathroom at the end of the landing put paid to that notion. Moving over to the marble washstand, he poured cold water into the bowl from the jug, stripped off his nightshirt, and sluiced himself down. He inspected his face in the shaving mirror. Florence had said the beard made him look sinister. Dody would probably think the same, and he couldn't afford that. After trimming his beard with scissors, he mixed up the shaving soap and applied a thick lather to his face, stropped his razor, and carefully removed the offending growth.

He dressed, adjusted his cravat in the wardrobe mirror, and slung his jacket over his shoulder. As he made his way downstairs, the savoury aroma of kedgeree grew stronger. In the dining room he piled up his plate, took a seat at the large polished table, and was about to take his first mouthful when he felt a tap on his shoulder.

"There's a telephone call for you, Mr. Pike." Mrs. Keating looked annoyed. She hated the newly installed telephone with a passion—how it always rang at mealtimes and the space its closet took up in her fine front hall.

Pike excused himself from the other lodgers and retired to the telephone. "Pike," said the crackling voice on the other end of the line. "It's Callan. We have an emergency. Get to the Ritz immediately. The operation's off."

Chapter Eighteen

Dody had slept badly. Her digestive condition continued to flare, necessitating several trips to the WC, and she'd been up since dawn with the first gatherings of the mob in the street outside her house.

It was mortifying that her parents had had to see this. They had departed early to attend to some urgent farm business, leaving for the station by the back door.

As they kissed her good-bye, they had promised to return as soon as possible to support her for the trial.

Dody tried to distract herself from the mob's chanting by working on her paper, but found it impossible to concentrate. The paper was probably a complete waste of time now. She had been barred from the mortuary until the end of the trial and had no idea when she'd get the chance to hand it in—if at all. If convicted, she would surely never work as a doctor again.

Sensing the scrutiny of a pair of beady pink eyes, she looked

up to see a whiskered nose twitching at her through the bars
of a cage. Edward Rat had been confined to sturdier lodgings
since he had been identified as the ringleader of the last escape.
Now he resided on her desk, and his increased contact with
her meant he was tamer than ever. Dody imagined herself in
his place, looking out from the wrong side of the bars.

*To sit in solemn silence in a dull, dark dock, in a pestilential prison
with a life-long lock . . .*

A tremble surfaced from somewhere deep within her
body. She shuddered and opened the cage door. Edward Rat
would be allowed a short exploration of her desk.

Exercise period in C block.

She returned to the journal she was scanning for articles
on TB research but instead came across a paper on surgical
knee repair. Here at last was something that held her attention.
It was impossible not to think of Pike as she studied the article
with her head propped on her hand. The writer recommended
a vertical incision to open the knee joint and then provided a
step-by-step guide for the removal of shrapnel. This technique,
Dody realised as she looked at the date of the paper, had been
documented before the development of Röntgen's X-ray
machine. With the help of the X-ray, which Pike had already
had, the operation would be even more straightforward.

Engrossed at last in her reading, she barely heard the
quick, energetic footsteps on the landing and a knock on her
study door. Not that Florence ever waited for permission to
enter.

Dody hastily put the rat back in his cage and slipped it
out of sight under her desk. "Good afternoon, Florence." She
never understood those who chose to miss the best part of the
day by sleeping through it.

Florence must have detected the starchiness in Dody's tone and said defensively, "I deserved a lie-in. I had a very late, but very successful night." She dabbed the back of her hand on her forehead, careful not to disturb the meticulous pompadour that took Annie half an hour to arrange each morning. "Goodness, but it's stuffy in here," she added, apparently not noticing the ratty odour about the room. "Another overcast day, with not enough blue for a sailor's suit—we might as well be living in equatorial Africa."

"Since when have you been to equatorial Africa?"

"I've read enough about it in the *National Geographic* magazine to know that I never want to go there." Florence moved to open the sash window. "Let us pray it rains again soon."

"Don't open it—I can't bear the chanting."

Florence peered down into the street at the crowd. "I know what you mean: loathsome reporters."

"No, I don't think they're reporters. They look too rough. Paid troublemakers, I think."

"Put up to it by reporters, then—do I look all right, by the way?" Florence turned from the window and twirled.

This morning she wore a striped batiste dress in blue and white, to which she would add a hat and matching parasol when she went out. Florence and her group of suffragettes always made a special effort with their dress to belie the dowdy spinster stereotype the antisuffragettes had concocted.

"Enchanting as always," Dody said.

"Thank you." Florence looked out of the window again to the jostling, pushing group of hooligans below. "I hope Pike has the common sense to use the mews entrance."

Even the mob seemed to fall silent.

"Pike? Florence, what are you talking about?"

Florence flopped onto the Queen Anne chair opposite her sister. "I met him last night outside the theatre. You are never going to believe this, but he was conducting the orchestra for that dreadful Mata Hari creature, the woman we were protesting against. I barely recognised him."

All Dody could do was cover her mouth with her hand and stare.

"At first I was furious, especially when he kissed me—"

"He what?"

"Don't worry; it was just a pretend kiss. He explained it all to me later, in the Oyster Room. He's coming to see you"—she glanced at her wristwatch—"any time now, to tell you everything he's been up to. It's all very hush-hush. He also wants to help you."

Dody turned from her sister and faced the wall. The only thing that seemed to have registered with her was that Pike had kissed Florence. He was supposed to be helping his daughter Violet prepare for the start of the school term, filling tuck boxes and buying uniforms. Instead he was consorting with dubious women and kissing her sister. Did she really know this man? How could she when he appeared to lead such a secret life? And he expected her to accept his offer of help—who did he think he was?

"Did he seem well?" she could not help enquiring.

"He has grown an ugly beard, and it doesn't suit him. It makes him appear villainous."

"I mean his health, Florence."

"Oh, that, well, yes. His limp is as bad as ever. He was a fool not to have the operation, and I imagine he regrets it now.

There is also some grey at his temples—whether or not it was there before, I don't know. You would probably be a better judge of that than me."

"I don't need Pike's help. I'm going to help myself," Dody said. "Last night the lawyer said the best way of having my case dismissed before trial was to find out who really did perform the abortion that killed Esther Craddock."

"Yes, that is just what we, that is, Daphne and I, were saying."

"Poppa's lawyer wants to hire an agent of enquiry."

Florence looked taken aback. "One of those sleazy fellows? I would have thought an officer of Special Branch would be more appropriate, and a lot more discreet."

"Well, it looks like I have no choice: your Special Branch officer is not here, is he?" Dody heard the crack in her voice and hated herself for it. "What time did he say he'd be coming?"

"He said midmorning. Perhaps he was put off by the mob?"

"Or perhaps he never intended coming in the first place." She put her hand out to her sister. "I really appreciate everything you've done, Florence—your support and your attempt to bring Pike in to help—but do you know, I really don't think there is anyone, Pike, lawyers, police, or agents of enquiry, who can help me any better than I can help myself."

"But how? What do you intend to do?"

"Before her abortion, Esther Craddock had been poisoning herself with professionally made lead tablets. When the tablets failed to work, it stands to reason that she went back to the supplier for something stronger. In all likelihood, the supplier was the one who referred her to the abortionist, or—"

"The supplier might be the abortionist as well. Yes, it makes sense, though that Fisher didn't seem to think it worth following up," Florence finished.

"It's a long shot, but at the moment it's all I have." Dody left her chair, picked up her shopping basket, and moved to the door. "Supplier, abortionist, whoever it is, they are obviously worried enough about me to try and have me sent to prison, get me out of the way. I'm sure they stole the Book of Lists, too. Perhaps I have been asking the right questions after all."

"Where are you going?"

"I'm going to see someone who might be able to give me some more information about the tablets."

"But what if Pike comes while you're out?"

"I can't wait in all day for something that may never happen."

Florence rose to follow. "Then we'd better leave via the mews, and wear veils over our hats—the sun is hot enough to warrant them—so we are not recognised."

"We?"

"Yes, Dody. I'm coming, too."

Chapter Nineteen

Pike's dread increased with each step along the plush carpet to the hotel room door. He repeated a phrase in his head—*I told them to warn him, I told them to warn him*—a feeble attempt to ease his overwhelming sense of responsibility. The admiral was an eager participant in the plan, he told himself. Not only had he grasped at the chance to serve his country, but he'd been more than willing to satisfy his baser instincts as well. He had been on high alert and had been warned of the danger. What, then, had gone wrong?

A uniformed constable stood guard outside a corner suite at the end of the corridor, where a small man in a brown suit paced to and fro. The small man looked up at the sound of Pike's tread and hurried to meet him.

"And you are?" Pike asked coldly. The man pulled out his warrant card and handed it to Pike. "Detective Constable Appleby." Pike slowly mouthed every syllable. He'd been briefed by Callan earlier on who the man was, what he had and had not done.

Pike looked closely at Appleby and noticed a purpling bruise around his swollen left eye. The detective delved into his waist-coat pocket and removed a gold sovereign. "Here, sir, take this. I was going to give it to the widows' and orphans' fund."

"As you still will," Pike said without taking the money. "Tell me what happened."

"I exchanged places with Detective Constable Simpson out-side the dining room when the admiral and the lady were about halfway through their meal. I sat in the hotel lobby so I could follow them upstairs when they'd finished. I caught the lift imme-diately after the one they were on, and as I stepped out on their floor, the admiral accosted me. Quite aggressive and drunk."

"He assaulted you?"

"Yes, well, but I'd rather not make anything of it."

I bet you won't, Pike thought.

"He didn't mince his words, told me to take the money and get lost, go down to the bar, anything but hang around the corridor—said he could handle matters himself."

Stupid old fool, Pike thought to himself. What did the admi-ral think he could do alone? "Had you or Simpson seen any-thing that aroused your suspicion?"

"No, sir."

"And your instructions?"

"To sit in the dark in the adjoining room with the door ajar to keep an eye on the admiral's room and to watch if anyone else was to enter it."

"And the admiral objected to that?"

Appleby shrugged, brushed a pale thread from his jacket sleeve. "Must have."

Pike stared pointedly at the man for a moment. "What are you not telling me, Appleby? What did you do to upset the admiral?"

Appleby paled. "Just a small misunderstanding, sir."

"I'm sure." Pike pushed past the detective and flicked his warrant card to the constable guarding the door. A pungent smell assaulted him as he entered the room. The admiral lay naked on the giant bed, body arched, the back of his head jammed between the mattress and the bed head, his blackened face contorted into an agonised grimace.

Trying to avoid the hideous eyes, Pike leaned over the body and examined the handcuffs fixing the dead man's hands to the head of the bed. They were police issue, similar to those usually attached to the admiral's briefcase.

Pike straightened and glanced around the opulent white, gold, and scarlet room. There were two others present apart from himself, an elderly sergeant and a police photographer. A constable sat with Margaretha in the adjacent room, where Detective Appleby was supposed to have been stationed for the night. As a courtesy, the hotel had provided the room for continuing use of the police. Pike had already spoken to the twittering hotel manager and suggested it was in the Ritz's best interest to cooperate.

"The admiral usually kept his briefcase cuffed to his wrist; I can't see it anywhere," Pike said to the sergeant as he pushed through the dead man's clothes with the toe of his boot. "Have you made a thorough search?"

"Ah, yes, sir. Left the briefcase under the bed where I found it. I didn't want to touch it; know what you Special Branch chaps are like."

Pike ignored the sergeant's attempt at a jocular tone and

dropped to his knees. Bone ground on bone. He suppressed a grunt of pain, slid out the case, and placed it on the bed.

He inspected the latch. Damaged, prised open by a small knife by the looks of it. With a handkerchief wrapped around his hand to prevent contamination by his own prints, Pike opened the lid and gazed at the case's contents: a copy of yesterday's *Times* and a fountain pen, but none of the planted documents. He picked up the pen and immediately felt the black ink seeping through his handkerchief. There was an ink stain on the newspaper where the pen had rested. The gathering of fingerprints would now be even more arduous than usual.

"Damn it," Pike cursed. He threw the pen back into the case and made his way to the bedroom sink.

"What was supposed to be in the briefcase, sir?" the sergeant asked.

Pike did not reply, but scrubbed at his hands under the running water until the black trickle turned to grey. The sergeant should have known better than to question a Special Branch officer. Fortunately the genuine blueprints of the Dreadnought's new fifteen-inch guns were residing safely in the Admiralty strongroom. The stolen papers were fakes, but the fewer who knew that the better. The prospect of the Germans wasting time and resources on plans that were at least four years out of date had given the British military authorities much satisfaction.

"Who raised the alarm?" Pike asked as he dried his hands on a fluffy white towel hanging next to the sink.

"The woman in his bed"—the sergeant coughed—"discovered the admiral like this when she woke up early this morning. She ran screaming into the corridor and told the maid, who contacted the hotel manager. He located your man, who had fallen asleep in the lobby and who in turn called Special Branch." He paused. "And here you are, sir."

"Yes. Here I am."

How could Margaretha not notice someone dying in such a violent manner beside her in the bed? Although, Pike conceded, having witnessed Margaretha's condition after a hashish binge, perhaps it was possible she slept through the admiral's death throes.

"Did she say whether, when she ran out into the corridor, the door was locked or unlocked?" Pike asked.

"I'm afraid I didn't ask her that, sir."

Pike tried to hide his frustration, stepped from the room, and examined the brass plate under the door lock. Several thin lines scored the polished sheen of the plate. He licked his finger and rubbed at one, causing it to fade. Brass fittings were polished every day in this kind of hotel; these scratches were new.

Returning to the sergeant, he said, "I think the lock was picked." He pointed to a heavy key on the bedside table. "That's the door key, still where it was placed after one of them locked up last night."

He scanned the room again. Women's clothes spilled from a gilt chair next to a table where Margaretha's water pipe stood. The smell of stale smoke in the room suggested it had been used within the last few hours. Dirty blobs of water surrounded the pipe and two empty champagne glasses rested next to it. An empty bottle of French champagne lay under the table.

"See if you can lift some fingerprints from the champagne bottle, briefcase, and table—and try not to touch them yourself," Pike said to the sergeant.

The sergeant sighed. He was old-school and had not taken to the new innovations in crime detection that always so intrigued Pike. But, Pike thought soberly, he'd not been able to think up any bright ideas this time. *Please God*, he prayed, *help me find justice for the admiral and make up for his death, even if I can't make up for the blood of Bloemfontein on my hands.*

He stepped aside for the police photographer to set up his tripod, and soon the chemical smell of flash powder had replaced the sweet pungency of hashish and the bleachy odour of lust. When the photographer had finished, Pike brushed away the residual flash-smoke from the air and pulled the sheet over the body. The arrival of the police surgeon was imminent, but the dead man deserved some dignity in the interim.

He lifted the admiral's braided jacket from the floor and went through his pockets, finding a cigarette case, a hand-kerchief, some loose change, and a small key.

The key fitted the lock of the handcuffs, which he unlocked. The admiral's arms flopped to the bed, and Pike tucked them under the sheet.

On the bedside table next to the key there stood a small, unlabelled jar. He unscrewed the lid, sniffed the contents, tipped some of the brown tablets into his palm, and showed them to the sergeant. "Any idea what these are?"

"No, sir, but the surgeon is on his way. He'll know them."

Pike slipped two of the tablets into his pocket. "I might be able to get them identified sooner." He still planned on visiting Dody once he'd finished here and would ask her then—if she was talking to him, of course.

He found nothing of interest amongst the female articles of clothing: a blue satin blouse, a tight hobble skirt, and various items of risqué underwear, which he had seen more often than not strewn across Margaretha's dressing room floor.

* * *

When she saw who he was, Margaretha went for him like a wildcat, tearing at his cheek with her sharp talons and ripping red furrows through his skin before the constable could wrestle her to the bed.

"Shall I cuff her, sir?" the young man asked.

Pike nodded and dabbed at his bleeding cheek with his handkerchief, bright red blood joining inky black stains. "Then leave us, please."

The constable closed the door. Pike sat on the end of the bed and regarded Margaretha in silence. Her right arm hung from the cuff attached to the head of the bed. The lacy neck of her silken negligee had been stretched during the scuffle, leaving one small but perfect breast exposed.

"Cover yourself up," he said.

She lunged as far as the cuff would let her and spat at him. Her aim fell short and the blob landed on the eiderdown. "You do it," she said, hatred gleaming in her coal dark eyes. "You've always wanted to touch me; now's your chance."

The contrived smile made his skin crawl. "These kinds of games might have worked with the admiral, but they don't work with me," he said.

Pike moved to the window and pulled back the net curtain, rubbing a hand across the back of his neck in an attempt to ease the tension. Below stretched the wooded meadows of Green Park, through which women under lacy parasols strolled arm in arm with men in boaters and striped blazers: a world far removed from the one he was in now. Opening the sash window, he inhaled the tickling scent of mown grass and felt himself begin to calm.

"Tell me what happened," he said without turning from the view.

"Laat me met rust!" Leave me be! Pike had learned enough Afrikaans in South Africa to understand this much Dutch.

She reverted back to English. "Then I shall tell you right now, Mr. Piano-Playing Policeman, that I did not kill him."

"Let me decide that. What happened after I dropped you off at the hotel?"

"We dined late in the restaurant here—a magnificent meal prepared by M. Escoffier himself."

"And how was the admiral's mood?"

"Very jolly, especially when I tantalised him to his peak under the table."

Pike ignored that. "Could he have eaten anything that made him ill?"

"We had the same meal. As you can see, I am perfectly well."

"And then what?"

"We went up to our room."

"I believe the admiral had a confrontation with a man in the corridor."

Margaretha rolled her eyes. "The admiral said he was spying on us." Her features lightened. "Ah, one of yours, of course. I should have guessed that filthy little man was one of yours."

"The admiral knew about him. Amongst other things, the man was supposed to be your protection." At her mocking laugh he said, "Please explain."

"We had just begun to enjoy ourselves in our room—"

"With champagne and hashish."

"No, the hashish came later—when we heard a strange

noise from the walls between the rooms. The admiral found your little friend here, in this room"—Margaretha pointed to a painting on the wall depicting a reclining Venus—"at a peep hole, watching us."

Pike moved to the adjoining wall and pushed the picture aside. Sure enough, a neatly bored hole through the wall zeroed in on the big bed next door. Bloody Appleby was in for it now. He couldn't blame the admiral for sending the scoundrel on his way with a shiner; he would have done the same himself. And the bribe? Nonsense, the money was probably from Appleby's own pocket. He'd see to it that Appleby lost more than his sovereign.

"And then?"

"The admiral was feeling inhibited, so I persuaded him to have some puffs of my pipe. It had the desired effect—we made love over and over again until we fell asleep. The rest you know, I think."

Hearing the catch in her voice, he allowed himself to turn from the wall. Thankfully she had covered herself up and was busy patting at her tears with the bed sheet, finally behaving as a woman ought after suffering such trauma.

"Did you or the admiral lock the bedroom door?" he asked, adjusting his tone to remove some of its earlier sting.

Margaretha shrugged. "Who knows?"

"Did you see anyone else who looked suspicious, other than the policeman?"

Again she shrugged, "When you are in love, you only have eyes for your sweetheart. Then again, you probably know nothing of love, do you? Or is it men like Gabriel Klassen who are more to your taste?"

Love? Is that what she called her liaisons with the admiral? He rubbed his hand across his brow. This task would be easier if she had been nothing but a stranger to him.

The sergeant put his head around the door. "The police surgeon has examined the body, sir, and reckons the pills are strychnine. Says he thinks the admiral died from strychnine poisoning."

"Thank you." Pike returned to the woman. "You heard what he said?"

Her sudden pallor said she had. She tugged against the handcuff. "You think I poisoned him?"

"Yes, I do, unless you convince me otherwise. I think you distracted the admiral and then poisoned him to allow your accomplice to steal the contents of his briefcase. Perhaps you didn't mean to poison him, perhaps you didn't know quite how lethal the strychnine was—"

"He took the tablets himself!" she screamed, tugging at her chain like a wild beast. "After smoking the pipe!"

"Why would someone deliberately poison himself with strychnine? It's a ghastly way to die, agonising."

"*Ach*, I don't know, I don't know."

Pike paused and regarded her coolly. "You can't be very impressed with your accomplice, leaving you to take the blame for all this."

"What are you talking about? I have no accomplice." Her eyes welled with tears and her face took on such an overwhelming look of misery that his softer side almost believed her.

But she was a performer, he reminded himself. "I'll give you some time to think this over," he said. "Take her to the cells at the Yard," he said to the sergeant.

Chapter Twenty

The sisters removed their veils as soon as they were clear of the mob of agitators and walked through the faded grandeur of Bloomsbury to Museum Station where they caught the underground train to Aldgate. As far as Dody knew, Florence had not visited the East End since her terrifying pursuit by a deranged killer the previous year. They linked arms, Florence thrusting her rolled parasol before them like a lance, and stuck to the longer, safer route towards the High Street, avoiding the gloomy maze of winding streets to the left and right, though they might have got them to their destination quicker.

Two hundred years earlier, Huguenot refugees had established the area as a centre for silk manufacturing, but during the previous century the domestic industry had suffered such decline that it was now almost nonexistent. The fine terraced houses and mansions belonging to the master weavers had deteriorated into smoky slums and penny lodging houses, and the precinct was now a rookery of crime and depravity.

They passed the dripping water pump at the junction of Fenchurch and Leadenhall Streets, where people queued with buckets. Approaching the High Street, they glimpsed the tall white steeple of Christ Church rising above the slums of Commercial Road—the detached finger of God, heedless to what went on below. The parks were closed at night and sleeping in the streets was illegal, so the homeless had no choice but to walk all night and sleep in the parks by day. In her mind's eye Dody saw the street women, many of whom she treated at the Clinic, dozing beneath yew trees or stretched out upon the benches of "Itchy Park," their children swarming around or playing knucklebones with grave pebbles.

Florence relaxed her grip on her parasol when they approached the comparative safety of the High Street. A street stall outside Borislav's shop attracted her attention, and she began rummaging through piles of secondhand clothing.

"We're organising a fancy dress ball to raise funds for the movement; I might find something suitable in here," she said.

Dody was relieved at Florence's distraction, though the sallow-faced vendor didn't seem too impressed at having her stock of practical clothing labelled "fancy dress." Reluctant to let her sister know just how unwell she was feeling, Dody wanted time alone in the chemist's. The meat juice didn't seem to be working and she needed something stronger.

To her surprise, she discovered the CLOSED sign hanging on the shop's front door. She cupped her eyes to the glass. Looking beyond the garish bottles of coloured water, she caught some movement and recognised Borislav's nephew, Joseph, sweeping the shop floor.

Dody banged on the window and waved to get his attention. Joseph propped up his broom and opened the door a cautious crack. When he saw who it was, he flung it wide and ushered her in. Something crunched beneath her feet. She looked down to see the floor awash with sticky substances, scattered powders, and broken glass.

"My goodness, what's happened here?" she asked. "It looks as though an elephant's been let loose in the place."

Joseph scowled, and slammed the head of the broom onto the ground. "We were robbed, that's what. After taking what they wanted from the back room, they decided to leave a calling card." He pointed to the debris then started pushing it towards another pile already waiting at the wall for disposal. "Could be worse, I suppose. At least the old man wasn't hurt too badly."

"Mr. Borislav?" Dody had assumed the break-in had been at night when the shop was unattended. She looked towards the counter with concern.

"He's all right, Dr. McCleland; he's in the back room making an inventory of what was stolen."

She found Borislav sitting on a high stool at his workbench, adding the final touch to a list of supplies. An angry bruise was evident on the chemist's forehead as soon as he looked up.

She rushed to his side. "That looks nasty; let me put something on it."

Borislav gave a dismissive wave. "Don't fuss, Dorothy. Joseph has done enough of that for both of you."

"What happened?"

"Nothing that has not happened before, only this is the first time I've caught them at it. It's the drugs, you see; they always want the drugs. A couple of roughs came into my shop this morning just before I opened up, when the streets were still quiet. They forced me into the dispensing room, where I gave them what they wanted. Regardless, they still left me with a bump on the head and a smashed-up shop."

"You called the police?"

"Yes, and they asked me to write a list of what was taken."

Dody glanced over his shoulder at the list: morphine and raw opiates, strychnine, arsenic, medicinal brandy, as well as various ingredients and suspension agents used in the manufacture of tablets. She waited for more commentary from Borislav, but none came. Whoever stole these drugs must know what to do with them. Many of the items were raw and useless on their own without some kind of mixing or manufacture.

She considered this for a moment. "Could these have been used for the manufacture of lead tablets?"

"I don't even stock lead," he said impatiently, pointing to his list. "As you see, lead is not on my list."

"But some of the ingredients, such as the suspensions, could be used in the tablets' manufacture."

Borislav sighed and said wearily, "No mention was made of lead by the police or by me, Dorothy."

Dody realised what he was thinking, that she was attempting to use his misfortune to somehow reverse her own. In his opinion, the two events were barely related. Or were they? Perhaps, but this was not the time for an interrogation.

With no further probing from Dody, he said, "I got a good look at the men, though, and gave the police their description. One was short and swarthy, the other tall with a long unkempt beard. They warned me not to go to the police."

Dody smiled. "Which only strengthened your resolve." This was so like Borislav. "Please, let me look at your injury."

"If you insist." He huffed, but closed his eyes and allowed Dody to tip back his head. In the middle of the discoloured lump she spied a small streak of grazed skin.

"What did they use?"

"A wooden spar of some kind."

"You were lucky." Her gaze automatically dropped to his forearms. "Any defensive injuries? Please, roll up your sleeves."

"My arms are fine. It happened so quickly," Borislav said. "One held my arms behind my back as the other struck, giving me no time to ward off the blow at all."

"Thank heavens they only struck you once."

The chemist nodded and rubbed a hand across his tired face. "But look, Dorothy, I have a lot to do here, and I'm sure you did not pop in to hear my troubles or pass the time of day. Do you require something for the Clinic?"

"No, I will pay for this myself. Are you able to mix me up a powder of citrate of potash and bicarbonate of soda? I'm happy to do it myself if you tell me where you keep the ingredients."

"Someone has a stomach complaint?"

"Yes." Dody did not wish to elaborate.

"Leave it to me." He stood, reeling slightly. Hearing voices from the shop floor, he glanced in the mirror angled towards the front door. "It seems that Joseph is being distracted by yet another young lady," he said with some irritation.

"That will be Florence, my sister. Why don't you come out and meet her?"

He touched his head. "No, if you don't mind, I'm not

feeling particularly sociable today. Pop back in half an hour and collect your medicine, eh?"

The sisters recommenced their journey down the High Street. When they came to the fishmonger's, they held hands and counted like schoolgirls—"One . . . two . . . three!"—and dashed through a swarm of flies hovering around the gutbuckets waiting for collection by the cats'-meat man.

There were few motor vehicles puttering about the East End. They crossed the side street, dodging horse-drawn vehicles and handcarts and entered the Clinic from the High Street side, pushing their way through a queue of destitute women. A visit to the doctor was an unaffordable luxury for the unemployed, and Dody felt a surge of pride that she and a handful of female doctors had at least made medical care possible for some.

The sisters blocked their ears to the profanity-laced protests at their queue jumping and arrived at the tall admissions desk.

Daphne Hamilton looked with surprise at the two well-dressed women below her.

"I'd like you to put this up on the notice board, please, Daphne, but make sure you also inform potential attendees verbally." Dody handed the nurse a notice she had drawn up during the sleepless hours of the early morning, informing the patients at the Clinic that she would be available for Friday evening consultations as usual. Also, that Tuesday evening lectures on health and hygiene were pending.

Florence raised an eyebrow to Daphne. When she received nothing but a shrug in return, she folded her arms as if to say she expected this kind of plan from her sister, but surely not her friend as well. Dody felt tempted to leave her there while she attended to the rest of the day's business, but she was not that cruel. She knew too well her sister's squeamishness to a profession that dealt with squalor, poverty, and hideous disease.

They bade Daphne good day and continued their journey to the Kents' decrepit tenement.

Dody recognised one of the Kents' elder children, John, a boy of about twelve with a pale, feral face, wearing a bargeman's cap. She'd first met him when she had been called to the tenement to view the body of his brother, Billy. The boy lolled idly against a wall watching some smaller girls playing with a skipping rope and chanting a rhyme:

Jack the Ripper's dead
And lying in his bed
He cut his throat with Sunlight Soap
Jack the Ripper's dead.

"Good afternoon, John, how's the family?" Dody asked.

The boy neither changed position nor doffed his cap. "You're the doc 'oo was called when Billy died, ain't ya?"

"I am: Dr. McCleland. I believe your baby sister has been discharged from hospital," she said.

The boy grunted.

"Did you hear what he said, Dody?" Florence asked loudly, one hand cupping her ear. "Because I did not."

John thrust a grubby hand towards Dody. "Why should I talk to 'er? Me dad might swing 'cos of 'er."

"Suspected infanticide," Dody murmured to Florence,

deducing from John's response that the case had been heard and the findings doubtless unfavourable for the family. "Are either of your parents home, John?"

"Dad's taken off. Ma's upstairs, but yer won't get nuffink outta her."

Upstairs they found Mrs. Kent slumped over the kitchen table next to an empty gin bottle. A child of about two, obviously soiled, sat on the floor gorging itself from a jar of jellied eels. Florence put her hand to her mouth, unable to hide her horror.

Dody touched her sister on the arm and whispered, "Do you feel sick?" Florence stoically shook her head. "Good girl." Dody swallowed down a rush of nausea herself. "I'd like to have a look at Molly, Mrs. Kent."

"'Elp yerself." The woman nodded towards the bureau.

Dody found the baby sleeping soundly in the open bottom drawer. Her temperature was normal and she appeared clean and well fed.

Dody pointed to the gin bottle. Mrs. Kent could not meet her eye, but she did attempt to pull her frazzled greying hair into some kind of order.

"John got paid yesterday, love," she said by way of explanation. She picked the toddler off the floor, laid her on the bed, and began to clean her up with a wet rag from a bucket. The child whined and squawked, desperate to return to her eels.

"Have you still money left to buy milk for the baby?" Dody asked her.

"John takes care o' that."

"And your husband?" Dody asked, raising her voice against the crescendo of wails. "Where is he?"

"Done a bunk straight after the inquest, before the rozz-ers could get 'im—doubt as we'll see 'im again. Tosser."

No wonder John looked so miserable. He was probably now the family's sole wage earner.

"God in heaven." Florence, until now unexposed to the machinations of poverty Dody had come to know so well, sank pale and speechless onto the edge of the bed, as far from the odiferous toddler as possible. Her summer dress of blue and white looked as clean and fresh against the filthy mattress as a water lily on a stagnant pond.

"I have to find out where your husband got the tablets that killed your child Billy," Dody said. "You have nothing to lose now that Mr. Kent has vanished. He might never reappear to face the charges."

Mrs. Kent licked her dry, cracked lips and looked Dody up and down.

Dody asked, "You want me to pay you for the informa-tion?"

The woman nodded, lowered the child gently to the floor, and handed her back the jar of eels. Silence at last.

Dody delved into her purse. All she had left was a gold sovereign and the sixpence they needed for the train home.

Mrs. Kent snatched the sovereign from her hand and bit it with her teeth. "'E got the pills from a bloke in a pub."

Dody's heart sped. "That's what you said before. I gath-ered then that you wanted to tell me more."

"What I said, a bloke in a pub."

"Did this man have a name?"

"'Ow should I know?"

"What did he look like?"

"An ugly bugger, according to Bert, but I never seen 'im."

"Which pub?"

"One hereabouts, I 'spect; Bert wouldna gone far."

"But *which* pub?"

"Gawd knows."

Dody caught Florence's eye. This was a useless exercise. "Time to go," she mouthed.

"Don't spend that sovereign all at once," Florence said to Mrs. Kent as they headed for the door. "Save it for winter to buy boots for your children."

"Wouldn't fink of nuffink else, love," Mrs. Kent said with a gap-toothed smile.

The sisters left the tenement and returned to the street. The girls were still playing with their skipping rope and chanting their morbid rhyme. John, though, was no longer leaning against the wall half asleep, but talking with a small man, thin as a rail and wearing a greasy cloth cap.

"Ask 'er yerself," John said to the man, nodding to Dody.

The man turned and doffed his cap. "Good afternoon, Dr. McCleland. Miss."

"You wanted to see me?" Dody asked. The man looked familiar, but she could not place him.

Restless eyes jigged above a flattened visage, bony fingers worried at the worn cloth of his shirtsleeve. He dropped his gaze. "No, sorry, ma'am, I must 'ave been mistaken." At that, he turned tail and scampered away down the street.

Florence whispered, "Most suspicious; a spy, do you think?" Dody pretended not to hear her.

"What on earth did he want, John?" she asked as her gaze followed the man's retreating form.

John shrugged. "Dunno. 'E 'appened by just as you went upstairs. Said 'e needed to know what you wanted with Ma."

"And what did you say?"

"That you was checkin' up on Molly."

Puzzled, Dody nodded good day to John and took her sister's hand. And then she remembered where she'd seen the man before. He was the man who had stolen Everard's bag, and possibly the Book of Lists, too. It was the caved-in brow and the flattened nose that jogged her memory, despite his manner being so different. The movements of the man she had seen outside the mortuary yard were slow and languid, weighed down by unspeakable sadness, or so she had assumed. That he had something to do with her case was undoubtable; that he might have been following them, disconcerting to say the least.

"Let's go home, Florence," Dody said. "And on the way I'll pick my medicine up from the chemist."

The mob was still congregated outside the front railings of their house, so the sisters entered from the mews. Annie met them at the scullery door in quite a fluster. Cook had made scones for tea and had been taking it out on the maid for not informing her when her mistresses would be home.

"No one likes cold or reheated scones no matter how hungry they are," Annie said.

They handed Annie their bags and the parasol with their apologies and then proceeded to the morning room, where a sumptuous afternoon tea was laid out for them.

Florence played mother and poured the tea but refused the scone offered by Dody.

"I'm not very hungry, thank you, Dody," she said. "But don't let me stop you."

Dody's appetite had finally returned—they'd done a lot of walking. She took a scone and told Florence about having seen the man they'd encountered outside the tenement before. Like her, Florence had not been aware of him following them. But they both agreed that with the East End as crowded as it was, he would have been very hard to detect.

Dody's brooding was interrupted by Annie's announcement that Chief Inspector Pike was in the kitchen, having also entered through the mews. "Shall I show him into the morning room, Miss Dody?" Annie asked.

A door closed on Dody's thoughts and sent her mind blank.

Chapter Twenty-One

They spent some time on small talk, with Florence doing most of it. Dody tried to keep her eyes off Pike's raw, scratched cheek. She wondered what had happened; the striped wounds looked to have been inflicted by a woman's fingernails. And then she decided that she did not want to know.

When Florence was called away to take a telephone call, they sat for an interminable time in awkward silence, looking at each other as if across an abyss. They broke the silence at the same time:

"How are you, Pike?"

"Are you well, Dody?"

And smiled awkwardly.

"You're looking pale," Pike said.

"I don't feel pale."

"Apparently Violet, too, has been under the weather,"

Pike said in an unconvincing attempt at a conversational tone. "In her last letter she mentioned that her grandmother is giving her marrow bone jelly to strengthen her blood— perhaps you should try it?" When Dody failed to reply, Pike said, "I'm sorry. I suppose I shouldn't be giving a medical doctor dietary advice."

Dody could not help smiling. She knew Pike's daughter well enough to guess that she would not be eating her grand-mother's disgusting concoction. She was probably throwing the marrow out of the window or burying it in an indoor pot plant.

Florence breezed back into the room. "What's this about Violet?"

"Pike says she's pale," Dody said.

"I hope it's not because she's become a vegetarian."

Pike looked from one sister to the other, mystified.

"She told us so in a letter," Florence explained.

"She never mentioned it to me," Pike said.

"There are lots of things that fourteen-year-old girls don't tell their fathers," Florence said knowingly. It did not seem that long ago to Dody that her sister was one herself and leading their parents a merry dance.

"Violet will be the first to tell you that she is now fifteen," he replied with a slight smile.

"Is she enjoying the holidays with her grandparents?" Florence asked.

"They lead a quiet, country life. I think Violet prefers the city."

"Then you must invite her down to London for the week-end. She can stay with us, can't she, Dody?" Florence sug-gested.

Dody nodded, doubting Pike would take up the invitation. While he was fond of Florence, he was not fond of her radical ideas, and Violet's involvement with the suffragettes had already exposed her to danger once. Dody didn't doubt that right at this moment Pike was blaming Florence for his daughter's vegetarianism. Strange, how well she had learned to read him.

And if he thought she was looking pale, he should look in the mirror. The skin on his face was taut with worry, the creases under his deep blue eyes deeper than she remembered. Something was bothering him, but she was not conceited enough to believe it might be renewed contact with herself. A case, she decided, it must be a case.

"Surely you can spare one weekend for her now that your top secret operation is at an end," Florence went on.

Dody noticed the pulse beating at Pike's temple and knew Florence was on dangerous ground.

"Thank you for your invitation," Pike said. "But when she visits the city, we usually stay in a small hotel near Hyde Park. It's very comfortable and only a short walk to the bandstand, which she very much enjoys—she is passionate for Gilbert and Sullivan."

"We're not that far from the park," Florence persisted. "Only an omnibus ride away."

"Mm." Pike flicked them a smile, put his cup down, and rose from his chair, moving towards the large bay window that looked into the street. For a moment he stood there, silent. Unlike some men, Dody reflected, Pike's presence didn't fill a room; it became a part of it.

He twitched the curtains and peered at the chanting mob. "How long have they been doing this?" he asked.

"On and off since the coronial verdict," Dody said, perched on the edge of her chair.

The conversation about Violet had been a distraction, but now that they were back to the reality of her situation, she felt the spring coiling inside her once more. The roaring mob did not help matters; their numbers had grown since earlier that morning.

"I attempted to question some of them at your back door," Pike said.

"They are keeping vigil at the mews now?" Dody asked, aghast.

"I'm afraid so. I showed them my warrant card and they took off. But they'll return to the back entrance, I'm sure, now they know where it is."

"They're definitely not reporters?" Florence asked.

Pike shook his head. "Paid troublemakers." He withdrew from the window and sat in the winged chair opposite Dody. Florence was right—there was a sprinkling of grey in his dark hair now.

"I only know what I've read about your case in the newspaper reports," he said. "It surprises me that the court chose to focus such heavy suspicion on you when the evidence is clearly so circumstantial. Then again, it was Mr. Carpenter presiding, wasn't it? The man does have a reputation for idleness. He probably wanted to pass the case on as quickly as possible." He reached into his coat pocket for a notebook and pen. "I'd like to help you, Dody, if I can and if you will permit it."

Tired though he seemed, the antique blue of his eyes was as intense as ever, and the obvious sincerity of his words caused a warmth to open up inside her. She swallowed and nodded her head. Of course she would permit it.

"Are you happy with how the police are handling the case so far?" he asked.

"I'm not sure yet, Pike. They have gathered evidence—"

"If that's what you call a few bottles of medicine," Florence interjected. "And try as they did, they couldn't link the crime to any of Dody's own surgical instruments."

"But I think the coronial decision rested largely on the word of the witnesses," Dody said.

"And the letters," Florence added.

"Hardly a tight case. No surprises there—Fisher is new to the job, inexperienced . . ." Pike looked as if he was about to say more, but stopped himself. "Please, tell me about the trial," he said.

As soon as he put himself in policeman mode, he seemed to lose his awkwardness. He questioned Dody about the details of the inquest and the names of the witnesses, writing her answers in his notebook, now perched on his knee.

"Did Esther give you the name of the child's father?" he asked.

"I don't think she knew."

"She was a dollymop?" Pike cleared his throat as if he had made a faux pas. "I'm sorry, Dody, I mean was she a part-time prostitute?"

The slang term did not shock Dody, and it amused her to think that Pike thought it would. "It would not have surprised me—not with the wages she was paid," she said.

When Dody explained the nature of the letters that had sealed her fate, he ceased writing and snapped his notebook shut.

"That's it then," he said with some satisfaction. "You are being framed."

"That's what my lawyer seems to think. He says if we can prove it, my case may never go to court."

"He's right. Have you any idea who might have sent those letters?" Pike asked.

Dody hesitated. She had asked herself this question over and over again during the sleepless nights following the hearing. "Dr. Spilsbury has in the past received death threats," she said. "An expert witness whose evidence frequently sends men and women to the gallows is bound to have enemies. But I am no more than his assistant; I sometimes support him in court, but in the main I deal with the paperwork and assist when required with the autopsies, and that's about it. Up until now I have never been aware of any animosity personally directed at me."

"But you had been asking questions about the lead tablets?"

"A few enquiries, that is all. I was going to speak to Esther again, but she died before I got the chance to see her."

There was a long pause while Pike considered this. Dody met her sister's eye and Florence spoke for both of them. "You don't think Esther Craddock was deliberately murdered, do you, Pike?" she asked.

Pike shrugged. "Well, Dody's the autopsy surgeon. Can it be proved that the girl's injuries were deliberately inflicted?"

"That had not crossed my mind," Dody said. "In a case like this it would be impossible to tell the difference between accidental or deliberate damage."

"Well, let's put that possibility aside for the time being," Pike said. "Can it be something to do with your stance on contraception? The newspapers made quite a thing of it."

Dody appreciated the forthright way Pike had asked the

question. She had been wondering how she was going to bring up the topic without embarrassment, and now realised she need not have worried.

"I have been somewhat vocal on that matter, I suppose. I can see that someone with a savage sense of irony might enjoy seeing me convicted as a so-called abortionist," she said.

"There's a doctor who works at the mortuary with Dody called Henry Everard. He's made life quite difficult at times, hasn't he?"

"Yes, Florence, he has," Dody said quietly, her mind back in the school hall and his useless defence of her.

"He plagiarised her paper," Florence told Pike, "and almost caused a riot in court."

"Did he now?" Pike paused. "I take it the letters were delivered to the coroner by hand?"

"I believe so," Dody said.

"Handwritten?"

"Typed."

"Ah, now that holds some promise. Where are the letters now?"

"With my lawyer."

"Can you get hold of them and give them to me? I'll return them to your lawyer directly. You see, it's often possible to trace the source of typewritten documents to the machine they originated from—not many people would know that."

"How clever," Florence said.

"I think I can get hold of them." Dody glanced at the curtained window. "If they let me leave the house."

"We'll come with you, won't we, Pike?" Florence offered.

Dody looked at her fob. "It's too late now, the office will be closed."

"Then let's have a drink to celebrate our reunion. It's been too long, hasn't it, Pike?" Florence glided over to the drinks trolley and poured them each a sherry.

Pike produced a silver cigarette case from his suit pocket, flicked the catch, and offered it first to Dody, who took one, and then to Florence, who declined. Curiosity got the better of Dody. When he bent to light her cigarette, she asked, "What happened to your cheek?"

"I was attacked by a murder suspect," he said.

"Oh, do tell," Florence said with relish.

"Her lover was poisoned with strychnine, but she swears the man took the pills himself. Absurd."

"Bizarre," said Florence.

"Quite."

"Took them himself?" Dody queried. "It is possible, you know, Pike."

He drew deeply on his cigarette. "Why would anyone want to do that? It is a terrible way to die. I'm sure the victim wasn't suicidal, and even if he was, there must be many less painful alternatives."

"In small doses, strychnine is not a poison," Dody told him. "In fact, it is considered by some to have curative qualities as well as being a powerful aphrodisiac when mixed with zinc phosphate and gold chloride. In that form it goes under the name *nux vomica*."

It was rare for Pike to become flustered. Dody enjoyed watching him struggle with his thoughts—the creasing of the brows, the rubbing of the forehead, the stubbing over again of his cigarette butt in the ashtray. "An aphrodisiac, you say?" he said at last. "I suppose that is possible. He was an elderly gentleman; his passions probably exceeded his capacity."

Pike's gaze moved from Dody and settled somewhere midway across the room. "So she might have been telling the truth after all," he said as if to himself.

"You look relieved," Dody said, glad, too, that she had discovered the cause of his anxiety.

"I am, in a way. I still have more details of the case to sort out, but your information has been a great help. Thank you." He turned and stared deeply into her eyes.

Dody felt the heat rise in her face. "My pleasure."

Florence sprang to her feet. "You will stay for dinner, won't you, Pike?" Pike opened his mouth as if to protest, but Florence cut him off.

"I'll just pop downstairs and tell Cook." This was an unnecessary move, the call bell was hanging right by her side, but Dody appreciated the opportunity for some time alone with Pike. Their silly pride had led to more than two wasted months and there were many questions she needed to ask. She hoped he could be persuaded to stay.

"Meanwhile, if I may, I'll put some antiseptic cream on your scratches." She rose to fetch her Gladstone bag from the hall before he could object.

"Here, please move to the light," she said when she returned, directing him to a chair next to the standard lamp. From her bag she removed antiseptic lotion and gauze swabs.

"This nux vomica—it can be purchased legally through a chemist or pharmacy?" Pike asked.

"Yes, but it is only legal in small quantities, and the strychnine side of it is recorded in the poisons registry."

"So, to substantiate my suspicions, I would need to find the dead man's name in the supplier's book?"

"Technically, yes, but legally he could not have been sold

a lethal dose. Indeed the tablets are usually sold individually. He may have obtained them from an underhand operator." Dody's thoughts tripped over each other. "In what kind of container were the tablets found and was it labelled?" she asked, smearing a gauze swab with antiseptic lotion.

"Labelled? No. I found them in what looked to be a cosmetics jar."

"How many?"

"Over twenty."

"Definitely illegal then. This will sting a little," she said, dabbing at Pike's cheek. "Illegal supplies are dispensed in any containers that come to hand: matchboxes, food packets. Esther Craddock's were wrapped in muslin," she said.

"I have a sample of the tablets in my pocket. Would you mind having a look?"

"Certainly, but let me finish here first." She put her hand on the side of his head and tilted his cheek to the light to ensure she had not missed any of the scratches.

He covered her hand with his. "It's all right now, don't fuss." He took a breath. "I've missed you, you know, Dody."

She turned her hand in his and squeezed back. "And I you. I'm sorry I didn't reply to your calls. Stubborn pride. Stupid of me."

"It is I who was stupid." He rose from his seat and gently wrapped his arms around her.

During the nightmare of the last week, she had refused to admit her need for him, even to herself. Now she wondered how she could have been so stubborn, so certain she was right.

"Are we friends again?" he asked as he pressed his cheek against hers.

They had never been in one another's arms quite like this

before. She breathed in his clean, comforting scent. He felt so right; he smelled so right. Lord, the feelings he stirred when he was close to her—if this was how it felt to be supported and cherished, she did not want to let him go.

"We could be more than friends—if you wish it, that is."

The words slipped from her mouth without thought. Good God, what must he think of such forwardness? Even her free-thinking mother would not have condoned such a brazen invitation. She was wondering how she might take the words back, when he tightened his embrace and murmured into her ear, "Of course I wish it."

He was moving his lips towards hers when a scream reached them from the street. Pike knocked her to the ground and threw himself on top of her just as the front window shattered, spraying their backs with shards of glass. "Stay down," he said, covering her head. Dody smelled petroleum fumes, heard the crackling of fire, felt the press of Pike's body on hers.

There was a sudden *whoosh* and he jumped to his feet.

The door flew open and Florence rushed into the room, crying, "The curtains are on fire!" Pike pushed her to the floor next to Dody, ripped off his frock coat, and started beating the flames with it. "Stay down, both of you!"

Neither sister obeyed. Florence tore flowers from a crystal vase and successfully doused one of the curtains. "I'll run downstairs and get more water," she said as she rushed off.

"There's someone hurt in the street. I'm going to help," Dody called as she picked up her bag and ran from the room.

"No, Dody, no!" Pike cried.

"The fire's under control; there's no need to stop me."

Pike threw his hands into the air. "But the mob isn't—stay here!"

Dody dashed into the hall and flung open the leadlight door. She flew down the steps, across the short path, through the gate, and into the street.

A straggle of troublemakers took off at her approach, bolting across the road and disappearing into the cool shadows of Cartwright Gardens. She found the man alone, huddled in the foetal position on the footpath outside the front of her house. Several vehicles pulled over to the side of the road to observe the goings-on. Passengers and drivers gawped from motorcars and carriages.

The man on the ground moaned, "I'm burnin' up, I'm burnin' up."

"It's all right. I can help you. I'm a doctor."

"It hurts, miss—"

"That's the risk you take when you throw firebombs through windows."

Dody looked up from her crouched position to see Pike looming above her, blocking the murky sky with his back.

"Likely he dripped fuel onto himself when he was making the bomb, and when he lit the petroleum-soaked rag, he flared up, too."

Pike's theory seemed to explain the man's injuries, the charred shirtfront, the weeping flesh that oozed beneath one of his ragged sleeves.

"Help me bring him inside," Dody said.

Pike remained where he was. "He could have killed you."

Dody repeated her command and rolled the man onto his back. She drew a sharp breath as she stared down at the familiar, concave face. "I've seen this man before," she said, "once hanging around the mortuary and again today in the East End. I need to talk to him."

Pike bent to examine his face. The man clamped his eyes shut. "I've seen him before, too, during my Scotland Yard days. In fact, we're well acquainted, aren't we, Mr. Dunn? Dr. McCleland, meet Daniel Dunn, known troublemaker and thief."

"Whoever he is, he needs medical attention," Dody said.

Dunn's eyes popped open.

"Wait just a minute, Dody," Pike said, his gaze not wavering from the man. "Why were you here causing a disturbance and firebombing Dr. McCleland's house? Who put you up to it?"

Dunn screamed and tossed his head from side to side. "I dunno, I dunno!"

He brought his uninjured hand to his chest. Bony fingers twitched at the fabric of his shirt. And then, before they knew it, he'd jumped to his feet, a steel blade flashing in his hand.

Pike pressed Dody to take a step back. "Don't be a fool. Drop it," he said, his eyes fixed on the trembling knife.

"Your burns need seeing to, Mr. Dunn. You need to be taken to the hospital," Dody said. It was worth a try, despite her feelings that the man's strange, electric charge seemed to have eclipsed all sense of reason. "Left untreated, you might die."

She tried to take a step towards him. Pike gripped her arm and held her back.

"I'll die if I do and I'll die if I don't—what difference does it make?" Dunn shrieked.

Pike called to one of the gawping motorists, "Fetch the police," and took a step closer to the injured man. The motorist, Dody noticed, made no attempt to move. This was probably more entertaining than anything on offer at the Variety.

"Pike, be careful," Dody cried.

And then a zippy little black Crossley pulled up, honking its horn. The driver, wearing cap, goggles, and scarf, flung the front passenger door open and yelled, "Get in!" to Dunn.

Dunn took advantage of Pike's distraction and let loose a kick to his bad knee. Pike hit the footpath with a curse. Dunn threw himself into the black motorcar, which then chugged at speed towards the main thoroughfare, Euston Road.

Pike was on his feet in no time, commandeering one of the other idling vehicles, a baker's van, and its driver. Before Dody knew it, she was left alone on the footpath, her eyes straining as she followed the van disappearing into the bustle of the street.

Chapter Twenty-Two

Pike focused on the car they were chasing until his eyes hurt. The road was jammed with almost identical black motorcars, hansoms, and taxis, and they lost sight of the Crossley on several occasions.

"Oi, Chief Inspector, looks like he's heading east to Pentonville Road. Should 'ave known him for an East-Ender, sewer rats, the lot of 'em," the driver, Cuthbert, said.

But just as they passed the twin arches of Kings Cross Station, Dunn's car took a sharp right, changing south down Grays Inn Road, parallel to where the chase had originated. And then they turned right into Guildford Street. Pike understood the Crossley driver's intentions as soon as he turned left at the Foundling Hospital. Here the road was much narrower with smaller streets wavering from it like wispy roots. The baker's van would have difficulty getting through if they became any smaller.

They came upon a delivery cart piled with empty barrels at a standstill halfway through the brewery gates. The cart was overloaded, too high to pass under the hanging sign, and several barrels had crashed to the road and split. Even if the road were wider, Pike thought with exasperation, they would never have got past this crowd. Workmen yelled as passersby stopped to scoop up the frothing liquid, carrying it away in shoes, hats, and anything else that came to hand.

Pike ignored the throbbing of his knee and jumped from the van, cursing as he landed in a river of beer. He handed the driver sixpence, telling Cuthbert there would be more where that came from if he would wait.

Then, on the other side of the cart, Pike saw something that made him smile. Luck at last! Under his gaze and as if to his will, the Crossley backfired, began to slow, and then puttered to a halt at the top of the cobbled lane, its engine flooded with beer, Pike supposed. He silently cheered. Give him a bicycle or a horse over a motorcar any day.

The driver leaped from his stricken vehicle and, with the tails of his white coat flapping, attempted to crank-start the car. Dunn remained in the vehicle until he saw Pike hurrying towards him. He shouted a warning to the driver then lurched from the passenger door. The driver turned quickly. He was of about average height, Pike noted, with no distinguishing features visible on account of the motoring outfit.

The flying crank missed Pike's head by a whisker. He changed direction, deciding to aim for the target of least resistance. Daniel Dunn stumbled towards an alley. Pike closed the distance in no time and tackled him to the ground.

Dunn did not require much restraining; a hand on his collar was the only force required to navigate him to the van.

Pike shoved him in next to Cuthbert and then hopped onto the running board, using the higher vantage point to scan his surroundings. He saw no sign of the goggled motorist with the flapping white cotton coat.

Pike dismissed Cuthbert outside Dody's house with another sixpence and his heartfelt thanks. With Dunn's good arm draped around his shoulder, Pike commenced to haul him up the steps.

"I want the doctor to have a look at you here before the police take you to hospital," Pike said in a low, steady voice. The sooner they could get some information from him, the better.

"I don't wanna go to no hospital," the man whined.

"You might die if you don't." Pike paused for a breath; this was hard work. "Then again, you might also die if you fail to answer my questions."

Pike abhorred the bullyboy policemen he came across so often, and rarely put the boot in himself, but there were occasions when even he believed the end justified the means. This man could have killed Dody and there was still someone out there who might yet succeed. He needed a name.

"What questions?" Dunn asked.

"Who paid you to firebomb the doctor's house?"

"Dunno."

"Was it the same man who picked you up here in the motorcar?"

Dunn paused. "Maybe."

Pike gripped the man's burned arm until he screamed. "I dunno, I dunno!"

Pike hissed him silent as the front door opened and Dody appeared on the porch. "Of course you know—you might be an idiot, but you have to know something about the man who employed you." Again Pike moved his hand. The man released a bloodcurdling scream before he had even touched it.

"No, Pike!" Dody said with a raised hand and a fierce look. "I know we need answers, but that's not the way—let's get him into the house first."

Pike turned his eyes skywards. He'd lost his chance now, damn it.

Between the two of them they lifted Dunn up the front steps into the house and lowered him onto the chaise in the morning room. The room smelled of burned fabric. The parquetry floor was puddled with water and the oriental rug was sodden underfoot. Annie was attempting to mop up and grumbling to everyone who got in her way. She gave the man on the chaise a sharp look and wrung the mop in the bucket as if she wished it were his neck.

Pike felt the same way.

Florence looked first at Dunn and then at Pike. "Well done, Pike," she said, then turned her attention to Fletcher, who was busy hammering boards across the jagged window-pane. "And after you've done that, Fletcher, you can fetch the glaziers."

"Everyone, please clear the room. I need space," Dody ordered. "Annie, the floor can wait. Get me a large bowl of water, bicarbonate of soda, and some soft, clean rags; Florence, telephone for the police." *She would have made an excellent army officer,* Pike decided.

Soon, Dody and Pike were alone in the room with Daniel

Dunn. Dody gave him some laudanum from a sherry glass and waited for the drug to take effect.

Pike took out his handkerchief and wiped his face clean of sweat and soot, flicking the tablets from the admiral's murder scene to the floor. Dody picked them up and examined them.

"Those are the tablets I was telling you about, identified on the spot by the police surgeon as strychnine," Pike said.

"He managed to do that very quickly, I must say. I would have ordered a laboratory test."

"The police surgeon is old-school, like so many of my colleagues. He tasted them."

"How dangerous." She turned the tablets over. "Ah. I should be surprised, but somehow I am not." She pointed out some strange indentations on the tablets' surface. "I've seen these markings on tablets before—lead tablets distributed from pubs in the East End for abortion and infanticide. These marks are also identical to those on the lead tablets that Esther Craddock was taking."

"They are from the same supplier?" Pike asked.

"I think so; at least they were produced by the same press."

Pike smiled. "Now that is the kind of proof I'm looking for—for both of our cases. But I suppose it now means we will have to inspect the presses of every dispensing chemist in the area."

"It's not that simple. Some doctors still make their own tablets and apothecaries do, too." A moan from her patient caught her attention. "But let's forget about that for a moment. The laudanum should have taken effect by now and it's time I got to work."

Pike shook his head at her ability to block out her own problems to tend to the needs of another.

She cut the sleeves from Dunn's arms and exposed patches of angry, weeping flesh. "My house is cleaner than a hospital. Tended here first, we will reduce the chance of infection," she said as she worked.

The man responsible for employing Dunn must have something to do with Dody's accusation, Pike thought as he watched her deft fingers, *might even be the abortionist himself.* Getting the truth from the injured man would be a much simpler solution than testing every pill press in the East End. And yet there was something niggling his mind, gnawing away at it— something that he had not yet had the chance to discuss with Dody.

Somehow, everything seemed too simple. Why should someone go to all this trouble to frame Dody, kill her even, to stop her from getting to the source of some illegally produced lead tablets? There was no doubt about it, abortion and abortifacients were handy earners—he'd dealt with enough cases during his time at the Yard to learn that—but compared to other moneymaking rackets, the proceeds of such sales would surely be small fry.

His instincts told him they were up against something more powerful and more fearsome than Dody had imagined. Pills like those found in the admiral's possession showed that the supplier covered a broad spectrum of problems and that he did not limit himself to the needs of the working classes. It was imperative to get some answers from Dunn.

Florence and Annie returned to the room with the items Dody had requested. Dody dismissed them both, telling Pike when they'd left that neither girl had the stomach for medical emergencies.

Pike watched, awed by her professional calm and wincing

as, with steady hands, she used forceps to pull threads of burned fabric from the oozing wounds. She added several teaspoons of the bicarbonate to the water, swirled it around, and soaked as many rags as would fit in the bowl before applying them to the burned areas of Dunn's arms and chest. Chalky water dripped all over the chaise.

"Annie will be furious; she is constantly cleaning this chaise." Her lips rose into a delightful smile. Despite his frustration, Pike could not help responding with a smile of his own. Before he had got to know them, he remembered what a colleague had said about the McCleland sisters, how he considered the younger to be the more attractive of the two. That was true to a degree; Florence was stunning and turned heads wherever she went, her allure only increased by her obvious lack of interest in men. But Dody was different again; hers was a quiet, thoughtful beauty, a natural beauty, and her indifference to it made it all the more radiant.

He tore his eyes away from Dody's face. Dunn seemed calmer now, more relaxed.

"Feeling better?" Dody asked.

Dunn nodded. "A bit. But I'll 'ave more of that stuff now, if you please, Doc."

Dody hesitated, then glanced at Pike. He got the message and drew back. He'd failed to get the truth from Dunn his way—perhaps a softer method of interrogation was called for.

"Mr. Dunn," Dody said, "I'll give you some more laudanum if you tell me who paid you to bomb my house."

"Gimme the stuff first."

"After you've told us who you are working for."

Dunn clamped his jaw and shook his head.

"Things will be a lot easier for you if you cooperate," Pike said.

Dody picked up the laudanum bottle and poured a measure into the sherry glass. "Tell us first," she said, holding the glass just out of Dunn's reach. Caught by the light, the liquid in the glass released an inviting, reddish-brown glow.

"I can't, 'e'll kill me!" With a cry of desperation, Dunn lunged for the glass and would have fallen from the chaise if Pike had not caught him.

Dody slowly poured the powerful painkiller back into the bottle and pressed down the cork.

The injured man closed his eyes and began to moan.

Florence put her head around the door. The police were waiting to see them in the hall.

A sense of duty forced Pike to decline the invitation to dine with the McCleland sisters. His day was not over yet, and his conscience would not allow him to enjoy the evening with the death of the admiral weighing on his mind, not to mention the possibly wrongful incarceration of Margaretha. After Dody's revelations about the strychnine tablets, he was beginning to believe the dancer might have been telling him the truth. Had the admiral's death been caused by misadventure, and not murder at all? There was a certain cold comfort to that notion, even though it did not solve the mystery of the missing papers. There was still a spy in the midst of Margaretha's dancing troop; of that he had no doubt.

He yawned. It had been a long day. Had the admiral only died that morning? It seemed like a lifetime ago.

The hansom swayed. Pike put his work-related problems aside and relived the memory of that brief moment alone with Dody before the explosion. She had told him she would like to be more than friends. Or had she? The bomb came so soon after she had uttered the words that he might have misheard or even imagined them.

The cool of the cells and the sight of a miserable Margaretha through the door's grille drove thoughts of romance from his mind. She was still half-dressed as he had left her that morning and huddled beneath a ratty blanket on the plank bed. Dried tears had carved runnels through her face paint, and the skin beneath her eyes was stained as black as a panda bear's. The sight triggered an idea; it was a wild one, but worth a try.

He wrote down Gabriel Klassen's name and the address of his hotel for the constable. "Get someone to contact this man and tell him to bring her in some clothes." The constable said he would and ushered Pike into the cell.

Margaretha sat bolt upright on the bed.

"Leave the door unlocked and send some coffee in, too, please, Constable," Pike said.

"Are you sure, sir? She's a wild one."

"I think she might want to listen to what I have to say." He spoke to the constable, but looked at Margaretha. "She might be out of here by morning if she cooperates."

Margaretha pushed a clump of hair from her face and regarded him suspiciously.

He pulled a chair out from the rough table and invited her to sit. She held the blanket tight around her chest. She had a look about her that Pike had seen more often than he cared to remember: the look of a woman who had been abused, intimidated, and exploited by men for most of her life.

"We need to talk more about those tablets the admiral took," he said.

"I know nothing about those bloody tablets. I told you that."

"I have to find out where the admiral got them from."

"*Achnier.* How am I supposed to know?"

"Do you realise just how close to a prison sentence you are? Tell me, Margaretha, tell me, please—where did he get those tablets from?"

Her arms flailed. Desperately she looked around the cell as if the answers could be found inscribed on its dank grey walls. "He mentioned something about the East End. He said you could find anything in the East End if you were prepared to pay for it. I know he used to visit the area sometimes—he brought the smell back with him on his clothes."

Pike waited patiently for more, but nothing came.

The fact that she did not attempt to pull names from a hat made Pike inclined to believe her. "Different tablets but with the same markings have been distributed around the East End and used to murder children," he said.

If he'd hoped the fact might stir some emotion in her, some empathy for someone other than herself, he was out of luck. She took the cigarette he offered her, leaned back in her chair again, and blew a smoke ring.

"I can tell you nothing more," she said, turning her head away from him.

"But you are sure the admiral took them himself?"

"How many times do I have to tell you—yes, yes, yes!"

A constable appeared with a tin coffeepot and two mugs. For a moment Pike wondered if he could trust her not to throw the scalding coffee in his face. To his relief she circled cold hands around the mug and hunched into her blanket. He gave her a few moments to savour the drink before reaching into his pocket and putting one of the strychnine tablets on the table.

"Had the admiral taken these kinds of tablets before?" he asked.

"Yes, he usually takes one when he is with me."

"Only ever one?"

"Until last night, yes."

"What made last night different?"

"The hashish maybe; the distraction of that odious little man perhaps. He had never tried my pipe before. I think it made him reckless, adventurous. The handcuffs . . ." Surely that was not the stain of a blush Pike saw creeping up Margaretha's neck? "He had never required that sort of entertainment before either. And he kept gobbling down the pills—to savour the enjoyment, so he told me."

"You took them to be aphrodisiacs?"

"If that is the English word for them, then yes."

It came to Pike then that if she had mentioned the word *aphrodisiac* initially, he might have been more inclined to believe her. He looked her in the eye and nodded and she relaxed into her chair.

"I can still press the point that you were a willing participant in the theft of the briefcase's contents. You could easily have opened the door to an accomplice," he said, blowing a smoke ring himself. Manipulating the suspect's mood was all a part of the interrogator's technique. Give her hope for release and then take that hope back again. "I suppose you might eventually get used to this kind of place."

"Bastard!" she spat.

Pike continued to question Margaretha for the best part of half an hour and a second pot of coffee, getting no further with the business of the stolen papers, until finally a constable put his head around the cell door. "Mr. Klassen is here, sir, come to deliver the lady some clothes. He'd like to see her, with your permission."

Pike climbed stiffly to his feet. He nodded as Margaretha's manager entered the cell.

Klassen gasped when he saw who was before him, almost dropping the bundle of clothes he was carrying. "Captain. What are you doing here?" The manager looked dishevelled, as if he'd dressed hastily in clothes left piled on the floor.

"Detective Chief Inspector Pike to you, sir," the constable said.

Pike was too tired to offer Klassen any kind of explanation. "Margaretha can tell you all about it when you take her back to her hotel," he said.

"You are letting me go?" Margaretha asked.

He nodded. "For the moment, and on the condition that you report back to me here at the Yard, at noon. See that she does, please. Klassen, I'm releasing her into your custody. A good sleep in a soft bed might be just the thing to jog her memory."

Klassen continued to look bewildered. "Margaretha, what have you done?"

"I have done nothing, you stupid man!"

Pike rubbed his eyes; he could not take much more of this. Klassen muttered some apologies and offered Pike his hand.

Pike had already registered the incongruity of gloves on such a stuffy night and now he noticed a small spatter of black on Klassen's shirt cuff. Perhaps his idea had not been so wild after all.

Pike clamped hold of the man's arm and ripped off the glove. The skin of Klassen's hand was stained the same faded grey as his own, a souvenir from the leaking pen in the brief-case.

It looked as if he had found his spy.

There were no crowds tonight and the hansom dropped Van Noort directly outside the theatre doors. That alone made him uneasy. He told the driver to wait while he read the sign on the door:

DUE TO UNFORESEEN CIRCUMSTANCES, THE MANAGEMENT REGRETS TO ANNOUNCE THE CLOSURE OF MATA HARI AND THE DANCE OF THE SEVEN VEILS.

His head buzzed. He hammered on the barred doors. A foul wave of sensation rolled up from his stomach and smeared his tongue. Exploding shells and the screams of ripped men shattered his skull. He leaned against the theatre wall and dropped his head. Not again.

Finally the fit passed. Bitter disappointment took its place.

He felt a hand on his shoulder. "You all right, guv? Can I take you someplace else?" the cabby asked.

Van Noort removed his top hat and wiped the back of his hand across his forehead. "Er . . . yes. The Satin Palace, St.

James, please." He took a step and would have fallen had the cabbie not caught him. "I'm afraid I will need some help."

The cabby took him by the arm, gave him a boost up the cab's step, and closed the knee-door.

Jack was acting as the Satin Palace's doorman. Trevelly had acquired for him a ridiculously large braided green coat and a top hat that would have dropped over his face if not held up by the handles of his ears.

The boy opened the doors with a flourish. "Welcome to the Satin Palace—oh, it's you. 'Ello, Doc. I don't fink we need you tonight, sir."

Van Noort did not have the energy to give lectures. "Is Mee-Mee free?"

"I believe she is, sir. Would you care to partake in a drink and some merriment in the lounge first?"

"For God's sake, Jack, it's me you're talking to."

The boy shrugged. The big coat failed to move.

Van Noort grasped the boy by the chin and tilted his face towards the light.

"Have you been crying, son? Trevelly beaten you again?" He reached out his hand with the intention of gently probing the boy's bruised cheekbone. Jack pulled back. "Better pay the cabby, sir."

Van Noort gave the kindly cab driver a generous tip then followed Jack up the marble steps and into the Palace. He must think of a way to get the child away from this evil place.

But he had needs to satisfy, and the sin that beset him always came first.

Chapter Twenty-Three

There was no sign of the mob the next day and Pike's contemplative silence only seemed to intensify the eerie quiet of the morning room. He sat opposite Dody in the winged chair, his bad leg propped on a footstool, a cup of coffee growing cold on the table at his side. She moved over to where he sat, crouched, and took his hand.

"You do not look to me like a man who has just captured a German spy. This is a win for you, surely, Matthew."

Pike squeezed her hand. "If only it were that simple. The case has left an unpleasant taste in my mouth. Is . . . Margaretha . . . guilty, innocent, or merely a victim herself? Klassen maintains he worked alone; he said Margaretha never told him anything overt. He told us he subtly questioned the admiral himself and then transcribed what he gleaned in invisible ink onto musical scores, which he posted to Germany. The false papers from the briefcase were found in his room—

he admitted breaking into the room when the couple were asleep. He was planning on condensing the papers and sending them to Germany the same way as before."

"And you find it hard to believe that Margaretha was not involved in any of this?"

Pike pushed his hand through his hair; he seemed so tired, so defeated. Then again, staying up all night to interrogate Margaretha's manager couldn't have helped.

"I don't know what to believe," he said. "With Klassen maintaining her innocence, we don't have enough evidence to hold her. He is not so very different from other men after all, it seems. She still managed to cast a spell over him."

"Perhaps you will have to accept that her innocence—or guilt—is something you might never prove."

"She will be deported, never allowed to return to this country again."

"I'm sure Florence will be happy to hear that."

Pike smiled tiredly. Dody walked over to the newly repaired window, through which heat from the street seeped. Charred curtain fabric crumbled beneath her fingers and an acrid smell filled her nostrils.

"And there's still that." Pike pointed to the window. "Do you realise how close you were to being killed?"

"We were all in danger, Matthew."

"But it was you they were after. You are no longer just being framed. They want you out of the way permanently."

"I am aware of that." Though Dody had not thought about her situation in quite such blunt terms. His words gave her a sudden chill.

"Your parents are staying in Sussex?" Pike asked.

Dody had telephoned them to say there was no need to

hurry back to the city. She had told them with an exaggerated optimism that the police were close to finding the man who had written the letters, and once they had discovered his identity and obvious calumny, charges against her would be dropped. She had not mentioned the attack or the damage to the house.

But she could still see where Pike's question was going. "If you expect me to go running off to the country and to the protection of my parents, you don't know me as well as you think."

Pike climbed painfully to his feet and limped to her side by the window. He touched her shoulder lightly, briefly. "Did I say that? Would I dare to say that?"

"Not if you know what's good for you."

"I rest my case."

She looked into his troubled blue eyes. "What else is worrying you?"

"I've had some enquiries made and discovered the approximate value of lead tablets sold on the street. They amount to little more than three shillings a dozen—slightly dearer than rubber preventatives."

Dody thought back to Esther Craddock's horror at the price of French letters. "Expensive for a working-class girl," she said.

"Still, comparatively cheap, and not lucrative enough to kill for, surely. I need to speak to Inspector Fisher about this. I fear we might be up against something bigger than we thought, perhaps an organised gang with a speciality for things medically related."

"My friend Mr. Borislav, the Whitechapel chemist, has been robbed several times this year."

"Which supports my suspicions. Tell me, Dody, any-thing. Anything you might be privy to that might give the gang reason enough to first frame you and then attempt to kill you."

"As far as I'm concerned, the death of Billy Kent and the lead tablets are the only noteworthy case I have been involved in recently."

"Yesterday you mentioned someone at the mortuary called Everard."

As distasteful as it was, even she could no longer keep ignoring the obvious. "Yes," she said. "I suppose his plagia-rism has shown that he is quite capable of theft and trickery—but it does not necessarily connect him to this gang you're talking about. His bag of drugs was stolen recently . . . Oh, surely he would not stoop so low?"

Pike said nothing, but his eyes searched her face. He retrieved his briefcase from where it rested on the chaise. "True, all I have is supposition," he said. "But I have to tell you now that we have had some definite luck with the typed accusations." He handed her a bundle of papers. "Here we have the originals—the lawyer's office was closed, but Fisher contacted him at home and persuaded him to open up and hand the letters over." He reached into his case and produced a single sheet of paper which he handed to her. "And this is a sample document from the Paddington Mortuary." He handed her another paper. "The autopsy report for the Kent child—I noticed the similarities immediately. All the docu-ments show malformed lowercase *g*'s. The top halves of the uppercase *S*'s are also noticeably thicker. The typewriting machine has left its fingerprints. These documents were all produced from the same machine."

Dody's stomach contracted painfully. The room was sti-flingly hot. "Go on."

"It's a handy point of reference," he said, taking the doc-uments back from Dody and returning them to his briefcase. "But I have to play this carefully. I can't trample too much in Fisher's jurisdiction. I'm hoping my history with him might count for something. I will suggest he interviews the mortuary staff as soon as possible. You said earlier that you had seen Dunn there—that he was seen fleeing with stolen property, in fact. I will make sure that Fisher is supplied with his picture to show around."

"The staff?" Dody queried, horrified. "What will Dr. Spilsbury say? He will be furious to have them in any way involved in my case. I have always tried to keep a low profile. I have to if my professional life is to continue. This will destroy everything—I can't allow—"

Firm hands gripped her shoulders. "Dody, take a breath, please. Plainclothes officers will question the staff discreetly with as little disruption to the mortuary routine as possible. Through no fault of your own, you are already in the spotlight. The damage has been done and you have to face the fact that your enemy might be someone who works in the mortuary. You don't want this trial of yours to go ahead, do you?"

She shook her head and realised then how silly, how hys-terical she must have sounded. She put it down to the linger-ing effects of her illness and sat to collect herself for a moment. From the hall she heard the whirr of the grandfather clock as it prepared to strike the hour.

When she spoke again, her voice, she was pleased to note, sounded quiet and even. "Of course not, Matthew. Do what you have to do."

"I contacted the local police to retrieve the broken-down motorcar, but by the time they arrived to collect it, it was gone—spirited away. Does your colleague Everard own a motorcar? Could he have been the driver I was pursuing?"

Dody thought carefully. No matter how much she wished to believe Everard was not behind this, she had to remain objective. "I have heard him discussing motorcars with Dr. Spilsbury. He is interested in them, but I have no idea if he owns one or not. I can't imagine it, though. They are fearfully expensive, and Everard's salary is not much more than mine." *Despite the fact he is my junior,* she thought wryly. "Though, of course, he does work as a private practitioner also."

"I will have enquiries made. This is all a good start and will give me more leverage when I question Daniel Dunn. I'll throw Everard's name at him and see how he reacts."

Dody rose from her chair. "You are going to see him now at St. Thomas's? I will fetch my hat."

Pike took hold of her arm. "Dody, I said I have to question him. You might not like my methods."

"As long as you don't use torture, I don't really care."

Pike relaxed. "All right then."

They took some time finding Daniel Dunn's ward, and when they did, the place was a scurry of activity, clanging bedpans, and rattling trolleys. Dody finally managed to grab the attention of a flustered-looking nurse to ask her what was going on.

"We've had a sudden death, ma'am. I'm sorry I can't help you now," she said, about to rush off until Dody took hold of her arm.

"I am a doctor; please tell me the patient's name," she said.

The nurse hesitated—she might never have dealt with a female doctor before.

"And I am a police officer." Pike flashed his warrant card.

The nurse paled. This was an announcement she understood. "We had two that passed in the night, sir."

"This last one, then, the one you are in a fluster about," Pike said.

"Um, Mr. Daniel Dunn, sir."

Dody suppressed a gasp.

"Where is he now?" Pike asked sharply.

The startled nurse nodded to a screened-off bed about halfway down the ward.

Dody and Pike hurried over. "Hello in there," Dody called.

"You can't come in here, ma'am," a woman's voice called from behind the screens.

Dody pushed the screen aside and found a middle-aged nurse putting the final touches to the laying-out of the body of Daniel Dunn. She glimpsed the flesh, caught a brief flash of cherry red skin, before the nurse covered the head with a sheet.

"I am a Home Office doctor and this is Detective Chief Inspector Pike. We need to examine the body." Dody attempted to push past the nurse, but the woman remained planted to the ground like an immovable oak.

Pike said, "Please step aside and give the doctor access. While she examines Mr. Dunn, you can tell me what happened."

His tone had the desired effect. The nurse dropped the limp hand she had been washing and tucked it under the sheet.

She moved to Pike's side, straightened her veil, and smoothed down her apron. Dody barely had room to move. She did not wish to examine the body while the nurse was present—who knew what hysterical rumours she might spread—and remained where she was, listening to the exchange.

"The note in the night nurse's report indicated that he seemed well enough," the nurse told Pike. "And his burns didn't seem to be bothering him too much. She last checked him at about two this morning and found him to be sleeping soundly. Then when she went to take him his morning cup of tea at about seven, she found him dead in his bed. That is all I can tell you, sir."

"No one heard him cry out, saw any suspicious persons near his bed?"

"Apparently it was pandemonium here last night. Several of the patients were taken ill, so their doctors needed to be fetched."

"Who was Dunn's doctor?" Pike asked.

"Dr. White, but he was not one of those summoned. As far as I know, no one attended Mr. Dunn last night."

A tremolo of a voice called out from the other side of the screen. "'E yelled, sir, I 'eard 'im meself." Dody and Pike stepped out and found themselves being addressed by a prickly faced old man propped up in the neighbouring bed.

"Please tell us what you heard and saw"—Pike glanced at the name on the bed—"Mr. Bingham."

"The nurse 'ere wasn't wrong when she said it was pandemonium—for a while anyway—more like Charing Cross Station if you ask me, doctors and nurses flying about everywhere."

"About what time was all this?" Dody asked.

"Between about three and four or thereabouts, miss."

Well after the nurse last checked on Dunn, she thought.

"What was Mr. Dunn doing while all this was going on?" Pike asked.

"Trying to sleep through the racket, I s'pose, like I was. And then one of the doctors came over and said something to 'im. 'E spoke as if he knew 'im and give 'im something 'e said would 'elp 'im sleep. I called out, 'I'll 'ave what 'e's 'avin',' but 'e paid me no mind."

Which was just as well. Dody had only needed a brief glimpse of the body to decide almost certainly that Mr. Dunn had been poisoned.

"It can't have been Dr. White you spoke to, Mr. Bingham." The nurse turned to Pike. "I assure you, sir, Mr. Dunn's doctor was not called into the ward last night."

Pike flicked the nurse a tight smile. "Thank you for your help; we'll call you if we need you."

"And please tell Sister that this man's body must be sent to the Paddington Coroner's and Mortuary Complex without delay," Dody added.

The nurse's hand went to her throat. "You suspect foul play, Doctor?"

Dody said nothing, but glanced at Mr. Bingham and then back to the nurse—not in front of the patient. "Oh, yes of course, Doctor," the nurse said as she scurried off.

"Did you see what this doctor looked like?" Pike asked the old man.

"Nah, didn't really try. 'E was carrying a lamp and I shut me eyes against the light. Just caught a flash of white coat, that's all."

"And then what?"

"Not long after that, Mr. Dunn cried out. I 'eard the squeaking of the bedsprings as if 'e were thrashing around, and then 'e fell silent. I thought 'e must've 'ad a bad dream or somefink. Didn't think much more about it till morning when I found out 'e'd clapped 'is clogs."

"Thank you for your help, Mr. Bingham," Pike said. He and Dody returned to the body and drew the screens around themselves.

Each raised an eyebrow, releasing a simultaneous breath.

Before she examined the corpse, Dody paused for a moment as she always did. She had not cared for Dunn in life, but in death he took a different aspect. It was the same with every corpse she examined, as if the very emptiness of the vessel somehow proved the existence of something beyond it. It was a privilege to sense this—so many of her colleagues viewed a corpse as just one more slab of meat—and all she had left of a Christian upbringing. She prayed scientific rationalism would erode no further the remnants of her once solid belief.

She took her light reflector from her bag and slipped it over her head, drew back the sheet, and opened the dead man's mouth with a wooden spatula to expose a jagged row of tobacco-stained teeth. She inhaled. Somewhere, mingled in with the other foul odours of the dead man's mouth, she caught the whiff of almonds. And then something lodged in one of the man's back molars caught her eye.

"Pass me my forceps, please, Pike."

Pike rummaged about in her bag for a moment, then handed her the instruments. It took some jiggling to dislodge the gelatinous object, which she held up between the teeth of the forceps for Pike to see.

"What's that?" he asked.

"It looks like the remains of a gelatine capsule," she said as she dropped it in a specimen jar from her bag. "It needs to be tested, but—"

"You have an idea what it might have contained," Pike finished for her.

"Yes. Cyanide," she all but whispered.

"What makes you think cyanide?" Pike asked. She heard his footsteps, felt his presence directly behind her.

"The colour of his skin, the rapid nature of his death, the slight odour of almonds about his mouth."

"He said he would be dead whether he received treatment or not. He knew he was in danger, that someone would stop him from talking," Pike said. "That someone must have had quite a hold on him. You sensed that yesterday, didn't you? That's why you tried to entice him to tell the truth with the laudanum."

Dody nodded. "There was something about his twitchiness, the sores on his skin."

Pike said no more; he had no need to. He took hold of Dunn's unburned arm and turned it over. The red discolouration of the skin did little to hide the puncture marks.

"A morphinomaniac," Dody confirmed. "So corrupted he would have been easy to control and manipulate. This adds credibility to your theory that some kind of organised gang might be behind all this."

"Yes. The abortions, the abortifacients—I fear they were just the sideline of a much bigger business, one whose foot soldiers are controlled by powerful nostrums."

"Everard surely has nothing to do with this." A doctor, so far from the profession's true path?

Sensing her despondency, Pike placed his hands on her shoulders.

"We don't yet know whether Everard is involved or not. But I assure you, we will soon find out."

"Thank you, Matthew." The warmth of Pike's hands and his reassuring words brought comfort, though they could not remain in such proximity. What if an observer noticed the position of their feet beneath the screens? Under different circumstances, this might have been amusing. But now it was time to be businesslike again.

Reluctantly she stepped away from Pike, folded down the sheet, and exposed the top half of Dunn's body. "As you can see, the cherry red colour has spread to the whole body. The cyanide shuts down the ability of the red blood cells to carry oxygen and they rise to the surface. He must have been given a large dose for it to have taken effect so quickly."

"Would Everard have access to the drug and be capable of using it?"

"Undoubtedly."

"'When a doctor goes wrong, he is the first of criminals,'" Pike murmured. Much as she did not wish to hear them, Conan Doyle's words did hold more than a modicum of truth.

"And you're sure it's cyanide?" he asked.

"Almost. Not everyone can smell the marzipan odour of cyanide. I am one of the lucky ones who can. Dr. Spilsbury can't and usually summons me when he suspects it. "

Pike clenched his jaw at the mention of Spilsbury's name. There was no love lost between the policeman and the pathologist. The two men had been thrown together during the Dr. Crippen investigation the previous year and the resultant hanging of the doctor for the murder of his wife. Pike had always been suspicious of the forensic evidence that had led to Crippen's conviction, believing Crippen to be innocent of the crime. Dody and Pike had had numerous arguments on the matter with Dody refusing to entertain the idea that her mentor might have been mistaken.

She had always thought Pike's animosity was more than just professional rivalry, that he suspected some kind of romantic involvement between herself and the eminent pathologist. Perhaps it was time to put that assumption to rest, to show Pike that he was in the wrong.

And as for her former conviction that there was not enough room in her life for a career and romance, well, perhaps this time it was she who had been in the wrong.

Chapter Twenty-Four

That evening Pike accepted Dody's invitation to dinner. For a change Dody made a special effort with her dress, picking out a gown of emerald green silk with a daring low bodice softened by a fine net underblouse ending at her elbows.

Annie was at last permitted to do Dody's hair and spoon her into a corset. The stays manipulated her top half into the fashionable S-bend that forced its devotees to adopt a forwards gait when walking, which was the reason Dody tended to avoid it whenever possible. Admiring herself in her dressing room mirror, she dashed away concerns about how bad it was for her spine. Just for once she wanted to surprise Pike and remind him that a woman did not have to sacrifice her femininity to do a man's job.

She sat at her dressing table and dabbed scent on her wrists and behind her ears. She was attempting to screw in place some glittering Fabergé earrings when Florence entered the bedroom with barely a knock, her burgundy gown whispering around her ankles, her dark hair piled high and decorated with tiny ribbons.

"You look exquisite," Dody said, glancing in the mirror at her sister before returning to do battle with her earrings. Her hands shook; fixing them was proving an impossible task.

"As do you. Pike will not recognise you. And he is here, by the way, waiting in the drawing room."

Dody felt a shiver of excitement. "Already?"

"He must be keen."

Dody caught Florence's smile in the mirror and dropped her earring on the glass-topped dressing table. "Oh, bother, I can't do this."

Florence retrieved the earring. "Here, let me," she offered, and attended to both ears in a matter of seconds.

"Thank you. I'm afraid the last week has left me in a state," Dody said, holding out her shaking fingers for her sister to see before pulling on her gloves.

"Well, it's almost over now. Pike told me he will be visiting the mortuary personally on Monday to see how the interviews are going—he'll sort everything out, I'm sure. Now, turn to the light," Florence ordered. "I need to apply just a tinge of powder under your eyes to hide the dark circles." Dody reluctantly obeyed. She did not wear powder often, but in this instance she could see that needs must.

Florence pinched her cheeks. "That's better; you're not so pale now. Tomorrow is another day. Let us not spoil the evening with talk of trials and hideous death. Let us talk of good things, such as how glad I am that you and Pike have made up."

Dody smiled. "I'm glad, too."

"So, you do have feelings for him?" The daring question gave them both pause.

"Whatever feelings I have, I have never felt like this before. Certainly not for Rupert."

Rupert had been paying court to Dody the previous year. Flattered at first, she had accepted his attention and chaste kisses, but he had certainly not stirred her as Pike did. Until meeting Pike, she was not even aware that she'd had passion to stir. Was she falling in love with him? Perhaps she was. The very thought suffused her body with a warm glow.

"Thank goodness. Rupert was only interested in using Mother's influence to better his career," Florence said.

"And his plays were quite awful."

When their laughter had died, Dody began, "Florence . . ." and then stopped. There were things she wanted to ask her more experienced younger sister, but had no idea how to go about it. Love was one of the few topics that Florence knew more about than she did.

"Yes?"

"What does it feel like to . . . I mean, what do I do about these feelings I have for Pike?"

"My advice is to have nothing to do with men at all. They are only trouble and grief." The twinkle in Florence's eye belied her serious tone.

"You can't generalise like that. You can't compare Bobby Stratford to Pike, surely." Stratford was the married man who had nearly ruined Florence when she was just seventeen years old. "They are poles apart, barely of the same species."

"I agree. Pike is very straightlaced."

"And Bobby had no laces at all!"

"He was a poet, an artist—people like him must not be confined by society's ridiculous restrictions."

The defensive tone surprised Dody. She thought Florence had recovered from her attachment to that wretch. "Indeed," she countered, "his sort turn promiscuity into an art form."

"But it still stands to reason that Bobby behaved like he did. It was just unfortunate for me that I did not understand it at the time."

"You were lied to. And you were seventeen. I am thirty. I have made no such mistakes to learn from."

Florence put her hand out to Dody. "I understand your curiosity, and I am hardly in a position to judge. It must be hard for you with most of the men you have ever touched lying before you cold on the slab. Follow your instincts. I think you can trust Pike. In fact, I am sure you can."

Dody was overly aware of the rustle of her dress, the beating of her heart, and the pinch of her shoes and corset—she had felt less self-conscious at her university admissions interview. When Pike rose from his chair, she found herself dropping her eyes like a nervous debutante.

"You both look delightful," he said, kissing first Florence's hand, then lingering a second longer over Dody's. She made every effort to banish her childish insecurities. This would not do. Dr. Dody McCleland, Britain's first female autopsy surgeon, was not going to allow herself to turn to jelly over one man's appreciative gaze. She forced herself to meet his eyes. How dashing he looked in his cream brocade waistcoat, matching bow tie, and black tailcoat.

He poured them a sherry.

"So, Pike, *distasteful* as it obviously was to you," Florence said teasingly, "your infiltration into Mata Hari's troupe was worth it. Your success is being bandied all over the evening newspapers."

"On the contrary, Florence, not distasteful at all."

Florence's eyes flashed. "Typical. Men!"

"Quite. In my case, conducting a full orchestra was a new experience and most educational."

Florence took breath as if for a stinging retort, noticed Dody's smile, and relaxed into easy laughter. "I suppose I deserved that," she said.

They toasted Pike's success. Dody was glad to see he had managed to put the morning's disquiet behind him.

"Klassen is fortunate we're not at war with Germany," Pike said. "If we were, he would have been taken to the Tower and shot. As it is, he faces a lengthy prison sentence."

"And Mata Hari?" Florence asked.

"She will be deported back to Holland," he said. "Though I expect she will be brought back to testify further down the track."

Annie called them in to the dining room. Over dinner Dody joined in with Florence's accounts of what it had been like to grow up in a family of Fabians. They told Pike of the artists and literary guests who frequented their parents' homes and the high regard the artistic community had for their literary critic mother. They also told him of their father's insistence that every guest participate in a Fabian hockey match before enjoying the family's hospitality—an endurance test of sorts—to see if they were worthy company.

"Somehow I don't think I would make the grade," Pike said with a fleeting smile.

"Nonsense, Pike," Florence said. "If you think your knee will prevent you from playing, all you have to do is stand in the paddock as an obstacle. Poppa's rules are very flexible."

Dody doubted that was what Pike had meant. As Florence continued to explain the conventions of Fabian hockey to Pike, it struck Dody that her parents, who accepted most people with open arms, might possibly not allow Pike through their front gate, let alone into their house. His distant gaze while Florence talked on indicated to Dody that he was probably aware of the situation, too.

It wasn't his class that would be the problem—her parents were constantly battling the absurd British class system—it was his status as a policeman that would cause them the greatest unease, a problem increased tenfold now that Pike was with Special Branch. Special Branch officers had spied on her family when they had first settled back into England from Moscow, certain they were out to spread subversion and revolution. Dowdy little men had stared at them through binoculars for hours from the shrubbery, stolen their letters, and pumped their servants for information. The experience had left the McClelands with a bitter taste for the English police.

But perhaps she was jumping ahead of herself on this issue. There was still a lot more territory to explore before taking Pike home to meet her parents.

They dined on soup, saddle of lamb, and trifle. Fletcher wore his chauffeur's uniform while he helped Annie wait at table. They had no need for a butler or a footman in their small, unconventional household.

Pike entertained them with stories of the regimental reviews he'd had the dubious honour of accompanying with piano at various postings in India, the Sudan, and South Africa.

She would have liked to hear about his war experiences, how he had injured his knee, but dared not ask. She suspected that that part of his life was closed to her and anyone else who had not been there.

"Buttercup had only been on stage for about five minutes," Pike went on, "when he shifted his position and ended up falling through the rotting timbers of the bolted trapdoor. The crowd loved it, of course."

"I imagine they did," Dody said, laughing.

Soon after dessert, Florence surprised them both by jumping to her feet. "It's been a delightful evening, but I'm afraid I have to go out now."

Pike stood.

"Where on earth are you going at this hour?" Dody asked.

Florence glanced at Pike then back to Dody. "Oh, you know . . ."

"Not more plotting, surely?" Dody asked.

Pike put his hands over his ears. "I hear nothing."

"I'm just visiting Daphne; we have a few things to sort out," Florence said. "It's all right, Pike; we are not planning anything illegal. But I will be home late and will use my key to get in. Dody, tell the servants not to wait up."

And with a slide of burgundy silk, she was gone.

Pike sat down again. Dody found herself staring at him through the candlelight. The more she got to know Pike, she realised, the more attractive he became.

"Well?" he asked softly.

"Well?" Dody repeated. "Shall we take our coffee in the morning room?"

The servants had been sent to bed. Dody and Pike stood in the morning room by the light of the standard lamp. Side by side, arms brushing, they examined with feigned interest the photograph of an elderly relative on the mantelpiece.

Pike took the photograph from Dody's hand and put it back on the mantel. He put his arms around her and drew her close. She did not resist.

He kissed her gently at first and she did not hesitate to return the kiss, pressing her body against his in a response that felt like hunger. He pulled her down onto the chaise and she felt the beat of his heart—a *beating* heart—through the silk of her dress and the stiff barrier of his shirt.

She longed to feel the smooth warmth of his skin, imagined herself undoing his tie, the studs of his shirt, and waistcoat buttons—so many buttons—and slipping her palm into the gap.

She could not go to her grave untouched by a man. She wanted, she needed, to give herself to Pike. Below his starched bib she found a button. She hooked her finger beneath it and felt a small patch of skin.

He covered her hand with his and gently held it back from further exploration. With a groan, he buried his face in her neck. "We can't go any further with this, not here, not now," he murmured.

What did he mean?

"Because of our work? We could be discreet. No one need know," she said as she rubbed her hand against the taut muscles of his neck, spreading her fingers into the soft damp of his hair.

He took a deep breath and straightened beside her on the chaise, winged collar askew, pulse beating wildly at the base of his throat. "No, not that."

What then? She lowered her head. With a burning feeling of shame, she busied herself with adjusting the crooked bodice of her dress. What had happened? What had gone wrong? What kind of fool had she made of herself?

"I understand," she whispered. "I have gone too far and you no longer desire me."

"Good God, woman, of course I desire you," he all but choked. He leaned towards her and cupped her face in his hands. "I love and desire you more than any woman in the world. But I also respect you and I will not take advantage of you. You are a rebel, yes, but not in matters like this. If we were to do as we want now, you might hate me for it later and I could not stand that. There will be plenty of time to fulfil our desires, if"—he hesitated, as if unsure whether to go on—"if we are married."

Her own heart seemed to stop beating. "Married?" she whispered. This was a proposal? Marriage to Pike was something that had not crossed her mind. Lovers, yes, she had fantasised that. But marriage?

She got up from the chaise, moved to the newly repaired window, pulled back the curtain, and strained to see past the shadows of Cartwright Gardens.

He approached her from behind and encircled her with his arms. She watched his reflection in the window through eyes blurry with tears.

"I don't know, Matthew," she said truthfully.

"We wouldn't want a stiff Victorian marriage. Ours would be a union of equals—I love and respect you too much for it to be anything else. You could continue your work at the Clinic if you wished. I would never stand in your way."

"And the Home Office?"

He paused. His silence told her this was another story. She wondered if he had given any thought at all to having a wife who, for the better part of the week, reeked of death.

"I do not have much to offer you, and we could not live as you are accustomed on a policeman's wage. But you would never be short of love. Please tell me that you love me and that what I desire is what you desire, too."

She turned in his arms to face him. "I don't know what to say."

He brushed his finger across her lips. "Just tell me that you love me."

"I do love you, Matthew," she said with all her heart, gazing into his face with one hand on his chest. "But this marriage proposal is unexpected. Please give me time to think."

His hold loosened. "You didn't seem to have any hesitation in considering me as a lover." His words were spoken levelly, but the look on his face made her think of a calm lake ruffled by a cool breeze.

"That is not quite the same as marriage." She moved over to the electric switch and flooded the room with unforgiving light.

Pike left the window and slumped onto the chaise. "Are you really prepared to swap roles completely with men? Advocate that women behave as they do—take lovers instead of husbands? Is marriage to me such a degrading thing?"

"No, no, I did not mean it to sound like that." She rushed to sit at his side and took his hand. "I just need more time—surely you can understand? I am still establishing my career as one of a small handful of female specialists. Marriage now will put an end to that, to my independence. I would always wonder what might have been . . ."

Pike swallowed. "So your answer is no?"

"Please, Matthew," she said desperately, "can we not just forget marriage and live for the here and now?"

He squeezed her hand back, his body sagging. "Of course I understand. But as for the here and now, that is not how I live, Dody—can you understand that?" He ran his hand over his mouth as if wanting to take his words back. "I have made a fool of myself. Forgive me."

"No, no, you are never a fool, Matthew; it is me. You surprised me and I've been clumsy and hurtful. I beg you to forgive me."

Even through her pain, Dody knew she must be grateful to Pike. In the heat of the moment, it would have been too easy to continue what they were doing without a thought for contraception, to become a doctor who did not practise what she preached.

He kissed her hand. "There is nothing to forgive. Why don't we just blame Florence for leaving us unchaperoned and then forget this ever happened?"

She smiled through her tears. "Yes, let's do that."

But how could they?

Chapter Twenty-Five

MONDAY 28 AUGUST

For two nights Dody had grappled with various scenarios, none of them comforting. Marrying Pike to the displeasure of her parents and the end of her career. Or the alternative: rising to the top of her profession, making a difference, proving that a woman was as capable as a man.

Being lonely, missing Pike.

Of course, he might come to share or at least accept her terms, but then, if he did, how could they function professionally together?

Perhaps she would find someone who, unlike Pike, had nothing to do with her work and would be happy to love her without the restrictions marriage would automatically impose. Modern, unmarried women of her age and class did take lovers. Her parents—often operating just barely on the fringes of polite society themselves—would not be concerned for long, provided she remained discreet. But that scenario required that she could bear the thought of giving herself to any man other than Pike. That she could even dally with the thought of being with another man shamed and repulsed her.

What kind of a world do I live in? she'd thought as she'd buried her face in her pillow, finally allowing the bitter tears to flow. Why couldn't she have the man she loved and continue with her career? What price must one pay for love?

Monday morning she did her best to put Saturday's disastrous night behind her. She had told Pike that she would meet him in the mortuary yard and she intended on being punctual.

Pike seemed surprised to see her. He shook her hand with a formal greeting and a stiff bow. "Dr. McCleland."

Dody hated hearing him address her so formally. The touch of his hand brought with it sudden, unbidden sensations.

"Fisher and his men are interviewing the staff now," he said, "and I do not wish to interfere with his procedure—this is his case after all. He has orders to report to me here when he's finished."

She now wished she had not been so punctual. She had no desire to show her face while the interviews were being conducted, and the mortuary premises were still out of bounds to her. Waiting there with Pike was more painful than she could have imagined. They stood in uncomfortable silence, listening to the sound of the Benz fading down the street.

It was another close morning, and the rising heat had

done nothing to dissipate the sulphurous fog that wound its way around the yard. As they waited for Fisher, Dody kept her eyes on what was going on outside the mortuary gates; at that moment men in rubber boots were hosing away the horse manure from the road.

She glanced at Pike, noting the dark circles under his eyes and the way he leaned heavily on his cane. He looked as tired as she felt and there was a vague odour of whisky about him. Had he barely slept for the last two nights also?

Under different circumstances she would have been proud to show Pike around her place of work. It was a relief to find the yard much tidier than when she had last stood under the eaves, smoking her pipe. The strikes were mostly over, there were no overflowing dustbins, and the stench was easier on the nose. The stray dog seemed to have vanished. Perhaps Alfred's wife had finally allowed him to take the pathetic creature home.

To break the silence, she told him about the dog. Pike nodded. He didn't seem able to bring himself to say anything, and she gave up trying for conversation.

Finally, Inspector Fisher and another plainclothes detective slammed through the back door and clumped across the paving to meet them. Dody looked from Fisher to Pike as they coolly shook hands. There was some kind of unpleasant history between the men, she knew that much, and it dated back to their time together at the Yard. Well, she would probably never know what now. There was a lot about Pike that she would never know now, and he about her. Her hopes of sharing their past and present, their dreams and aspirations, had been stronger even than her desire for physical intimacy with him. Now it seemed as if they might not even remain friends.

Oh, God, what had she done?

"Any results, Fisher?" Pike asked.

"Yes, sir. We talked to most of the staff. The head clerk told me Everard borrowed the typewriting machine on several occasions before the inquest. Dr. Everard was also seen by one of the staff in a local public house giving Daniel Dunn an envelope. The staff member recognised Dunn as the man who had earlier stolen Everard's medical bag and had assumed Everard was paying to get it back. I checked with the Bishopsgate coroner, sir, and on that same day Dunn handed a similar-looking envelope to the clerk there. Everard might well have written the letters, sir. It is common knowledge in this place that he bears Dr. McCleland some resentment."

"He has admitted to writing the letters?" Pike asked.

"Not as yet, sir, but his association with Dunn casts doubt upon his character. In fact, I feel that perhaps the two of them were in collusion over the stolen medical bag."

"Does this mean the charges against me will be dropped?" Dody asked, her spirits finally beginning to buoy.

Fisher glanced at Pike and then smiled at her hesitantly. "I will speak to the magistrate myself and file a motion to dismiss."

Was Fisher trying to make things up to her or was he settling some kind of debt with Pike? Whatever his motives, she was grateful.

Pike's eyes shone. He lifted his hand to hers—how she longed for his touch—and then let it fall. "Congratulations," he said.

Her heart felt squeezed; one side pressed with sweet relief; the other with loneliness and regret. "Thank you, Inspector," she said to Fisher.

"Good job." Pike patted the inspector on the arm. "Though it seems to me you still don't have enough to charge Everard with."

"No sir, but enough to justify bringing him in for some lively questioning. "

"Where is he now?" Pike asked.

"With a constable in the police van."

"Go with him to the station and wait for me there. I'll inform Spilsbury about this personally."

"May I talk to Dr. Spilsbury first?" Dody asked. "I would like to tell him my good news."

Spilsbury was in his office. Dody knocked and entered. The pathologist stood up quickly from his desk. "Dr. McCleland," he said, blinking. "What are you doing here? These premises are out of bounds to you. If you wanted to discuss your case, you should have written or telephoned."

"I wanted to tell you personally, Doctor." She smiled. "There will be no trial—the charges against me are to be dropped." It took a moment for her words to register. Spilsbury did not smile back, but she could tell by his loosening posture that he was relieved. "The coronial suspicion of me rested largely on the typed letters of accusation, and it has come to light that someone in this mortuary wrote the letters accusing me of conducting criminal abortions, and that someone here has criminal connections."

"Not Everard, surely? I was told that they've taken him

away—can you believe it? Have you any idea why? Surely he has nothing to do with any of this?"

"I expect Chief Inspector Pike will tell you what's going on. In the meantime, sir," she added quickly, "may I return to work?"

"Yes, yes, of course. The charges against you were preposterous, appalling. And now Everard? Is there no end to the shame? It's almost as if someone has a vendetta against this place. Forensic pathology is coming ahead in leaps and bounds; we have too many places and not enough men to fill them. Everard has a wonderful career ahead of him." Spilsbury rubbed his chin and spoke as if to himself. "I can only hope he has not thrown it away over petty jealousies."

Dody did not hide her surprise. "You were aware of Everard's feelings towards me?"

"Of course. I had to pull him into line on occasion. In fact, I had him in this office not long ago and told him to pull his socks up. Told him to pay more attention to his learning and stop trying to constantly get the better of you."

"Thank you, sir, I appreciate that. I never knew—" Dody might well have not spoken.

"I mean it is obvious that one day he will be promoted above you. He is a man, with a wife and family to support. That is the way of the world. I told him you would probably leave to marry sooner or later, and if not, the pressure of the work would finally get to you—understandably, of course. Ours is not a job for the fainthearted."

Dody could take no more of this; the emotions she'd spent days trying to control at last burst their banks. She filled her lungs with air, hardly recognising the shrieking voice that followed as her own. "And what of my career—my career was almost ruined! Have I not proved to you that I am more than adequate at doing my job?" Damn the consequences, she should have yelled like this months ago.

"Of course you have proved it, I have no complaints other than—"

"Other than what, sir?" she snapped.

"That you can be too emotional. Which you are proving at this very moment." He bent his head and shuffled some papers. "We have a case that might interest you," he said, handing her some notes as if the last minute had not happened. "Read the preliminaries. A body was sent to us from St. Thomas's yesterday afternoon with suspected cyanide poisoning. You may assist me with it if you wish. Meet me in the autopsy room in about ten minutes."

Of course she wanted to assist him. The body was undoubtedly Daniel Dunn's and she was desperate to have her cause of death confirmed.

"Yes, Dr. Spilsbury." What else could she say?

She excused herself and hurried from the office then went and stood in the middle of the autopsy room. It was hard to believe that she had shouted at her mentor. She wasn't sure if she should be feeling relieved to have got away with it, or angrier still at her obvious impotence. For the amount of good it had done, she might just as well have stood there like a frightened little mouse and said nothing at all.

Dody shook her head and looked around at the neatly parked trolleys, the instrument cabinets, the sink, the marble slab, and the shelves of specimen jars and microscopes. This place, once a second home to her, now felt like an alien and hostile world. Florence had always said one had to suffer to be a true feminist and she was right. But how much easier it would be to be more like Florence—vent her frustrations by hurling bricks through windows, vandalising golf courses, and throwing eggs at politicians. Unlike her sister, though, she had never believed that violence was the path to female empowerment—nor yelling, as she had just proved. There had to be a more effective way.

She thought back to the exultation she'd felt when Spilsbury had first offered her the job as his assistant. She was sure she had been chosen on merit, but it was obvious now that that had not been the case. Spilsbury had employed her because he had an urgent need for an assistant and no men were available at the time. Autopsy surgery was not a popular medical speciality.

Now it was clear that the recruitment of Everard a few months after hers had sealed her fate—she was destined to remain little more than a secretary for the remainder of her career.

How could she have been so naive? Of course a male employee would be given preferential treatment over a female. Of course Everard would have been promoted above her as soon as he had obtained the necessary experience.

But if her fate was sealed, and Everard already knew it, why had he written the letters? There was no further gain for him, only risk of discovery. Could he hate her so much? Why? It made no sense.

Start again. Why would he accuse her of being the abortionist? Because he was the abortionist himself? Surely not, but it was the most obvious answer. Pray God the police could sort this sorry mess out.

She dashed away a tear. She must continue as if the conversation with Spilsbury had never happened. Charges against her were about to be dropped, and that surely was cause enough for celebration. She had spent the last two nights shedding tears for Pike, but she would not shed them for her job. She would make these premises familiar again and find a way to demonstrate her worth. If Everard was sent to prison, Spilsbury would have no choice but to rely on her skills until the next man applied for the job, and she would face that prospect when it came.

The swinging door batted open and Alfred rushed in. "Oh, miss, it is good to see you again—but I can't talk now, I have to see Dr. Spilsbury. There's a great commotion at the front of the building. Dr. Everard is being taken away in a police van."

"It's all right, Alfred. Dr. Spilsbury knows about it."

"But what's 'e done?"

"I expect he is just helping the police with their enquiries." She forced a jubilant smile. "And in the meantime, Alfred, the charges against me are to be dropped and I am back at work." Alfred grabbed her hand in both of his and pumped enthusiastically, his eyes shining.

"How have you been since my absence? Has the place been running smoothly?" she asked.

"Oh, yes, indeed, Doctor. I managed to acquire more ice, and our other supplies are plentiful again now the strikes are over."

"I'm glad to hear it. And the yard is certainly looking cleaner. That dog you were so fond of, did your wife agree at last to let you take it home?"

"Oh no, miss, that was very sad. I found the dog dead in the rubbish pile, all filthy and twisted."

Dody frowned. "I'm sorry to hear that. When was this?"

"The day after you left, miss. I think he must have eaten something bad."

Dody said nothing, but patted the old man's arm. It was puzzling, though. Whatever the animal had eaten, presumably from the rubbish pile, must have been highly potent to affect the iron constitution of a stray dog.

The clatter of a rolling trolley and the whoosh of the swinging door put an end to further contemplation of the subject.

"Good morning, Doctor," a young porter said as he wheeled a covered body alongside the slab. "One-two-three-up," he chanted as he and Alfred transferred the body from the gurney to the slab. The two men speculated as to why Everard had been taken away by the police and Dody tried to pay them no heed as she peeled back the sheet to reveal the cherry red countenance of Daniel Dunn.

"Please tell Dr. Spilsbury that we are ready to commence," she said to Alfred. At that moment, another figure entered the autopsy room. It was Pike come to talk to Spilsbury.

Pike met Dody's eye and nodded. She acknowledged his presence with the hint of a smile. Conscious of his lingering gaze, she unhooked an apron from a peg and picked up her notebook and pen.

"Time to get back to work," she said to Alfred in a voice that was loud and clear.

Chapter Twenty-Six

Pike would never have proposed marriage to Dody had he still been obliged to spy on her sister. But after his somewhat accidental capture of the German spy and the subsequent praise from his superiors, suggestions were made that he might like to return to his former position at Scotland Yard. He had accepted the offer gladly, and it was this that had spurred him to ask Dody to be his wife.

In the light of her reaction, though, the arrest of Gabriel Klassen looked but a hollow victory. On his way home from Dody's, he had called at a public house and attempted unsuccessfully to wash away his sorrows, wondering how fate could deal so much with one hand and then take it all back with the other. Come Monday his head still throbbed and he longed for the day to end, but first he had to get through the interview with Dr. Everard.

He finished reading Dody's note written on mortuary stationery, which she had handed to him when he had vacated Spilsbury's office. The note was solely about the case, and her signature came with no endearments. He closed his eyes for a moment and rubbed the paper's texture with his hands, as if it might bring some part of her to him, and then reluctantly slid it across the table for Fisher to read.

Esther Craddock's death and the murder of little Billy Kent were loosely linked to the admiral's murder through illegally manufactured tablets—he knew that much. While not strictly Special Branch concerns, Callan had given Pike permission—another reward for his success—to take over from Fisher and lead the investigations. Fisher did not appear to resent the fact and nor should he, Pike thought with some bitterness. If it weren't for him, the inspector would not be carrying the rank that he did.

Pike had transferred directly from the army to the police, where he had assumed immediate officer status and the resentment of the men. Fisher had once been his most trusted assistant and his only ally in Scotland Yard. For the sake of monetary gain and promotion, he had betrayed Pike to his superiors for attempting to keep Violet's name out of a murder investigation, and that was what had led to Pike's exile to the Suffragette Division.

Fisher read Dody's note and passed it back to Pike. Pike stared at Everard for a moment, deliberately trying to disconcert him. He folded the note carefully into a tiny square and returned it to his pocket. This latest information from the mortuary was more grist for the mill and he wanted Everard to know it.

The doctor mopped his brow with his handkerchief despite the cold atmosphere in the cell. "I want my lawyer," he said.

"You are not under arrest, sir," Fisher said. "A lawyer is an unnecessary expense at this stage."

"Just questions and then I can go?" Everard looked hopefully from one man to the other. "Ask away then."

Fisher removed the pencil from behind his ear and licked its tip. "Did you give false information in the form of anonymous letters to the coroner implicating Dr. McCleland in the death of Miss Esther Craddock?" he asked.

"Certainly not."

"These letters." Pike took the bundle of letters from his pocket and spread them on the desk. "Look at them carefully, please, sir. Do you recognise them?"

Everard ran his tongue around his lower lip and glanced down at the documents before him. He leafed his way through all four and snorted. "You really think I would write something with such appalling grammar and spelling? *Doktor Doroty Maclleland is responsible . . .*" He tapped a line of type. "Surely, Chief Inspector, you can credit me with a little more pride of presentation than that."

From the moment he had laid eyes on Everard, witnessed the flick of his long fringe, Pike had labelled him a pompous ass; and now he was proving it. "It is not the spelling or the syntax I am interested in, but the content. How do you feel about Dr. McCleland's presence in the mortuary?" he asked.

"I am not happy about it. I believe that a woman's place is in the home—do you not agree, Chief Inspector?"

"My opinion is not relevant."

"I feel like most men, I think."

"You resent her?"

"I simply do not believe that a woman should be doing a man's job."

"She threatens your future?"

"Not at all; Dr. Spilsbury has assured me my position is quite secure."

This tallied with Dody's note and failed to throw Pike. All along he'd felt there was more to Everard's motivation than thwarted ambition. "You borrowed the chief clerk's typewriting machine on several occasions leading up to the Craddock inquest," Pike said.

"The clerk is a muddle-headed old fool," Everard said. "Yes, I did borrow the machine a few weeks ago when I was attempting to type up a paper—I can show it to you if you wish. It's about tumours in rats. I made such a hash of the thing that from then on I resolved to employ someone to do my typewriting for me—there are certain firms that hire out women especially for the purpose."

"So, women do have their uses?" Pike could not resist the jibe.

"Of course they do, but just not in the medical world—other than as nurses, of course."

"I still believe you wrote the letters, Dr. Everard," Pike said. "I put it to you that you not only wrote them, but you also paid Daniel Dunn to deliver them to the coroner at Bishopsgate and you might also have paid Dunn to steal your briefcase. I'm absolutely certain that you paid Dunn to cause several disturbances outside Dr. McCleland's house and incited him to throw a bomb through her window."

Everard reddened. "I did nothing of the kind. I don't even know any Daniel Dunn, nor was I even aware that he was the man who stole my bag." He jumped to his feet. "I've had enough of this. I need to go home." He glanced over to the locked cell door. The police officers remained seated, and he had no choice but to drop back into his chair. "I thought I wasn't under arrest," he muttered.

"You own a Crossley motorcar," Fisher said.

Everard frowned. "Yes, yes I do. But what has that got to do with anything?"

"You picked up Daniel Dunn in your motorcar after he was injured during the firebombing. Later, as I followed you in the baker's van, you threw a crank at me," Pike said.

"Oh, God." Everard put his head in his hands and ran his fingers through his hair. "This is a nightmare."

"What is that supposed to mean? Is that a yes, or a no?" Pike asked.

"No, I did not do any of that. A Crossley is not an uncommon motorcar. There are plenty around the London streets."

"It is a relatively uncommon vehicle, sir," Fisher said, his interjection coming as some relief to Pike, who knew little about motorcars. He had not even thought to record the vehicle's number during the pursuit; a mistake he would not make again.

"Where were you between five and seven p.m. on Friday, August the twenty-fifth?" Pike asked.

"I was at home. My wife and servants can vouch for me."

"You weren't loitering near Cartright Gardens in your motorcar, hoping to get a glimpse of Dunn's handiwork with the firebomb?"

"I told you I was at home."

"Did you lend your motorcar to anyone?"

Everard opened his mouth to speak and then closed it again. "No."

Pike narrowed his eyes at the doctor, who seemed to have so much to hide. "What have we got so far, Fisher?" he asked, keeping his gaze fixed on their suspect.

"Suspicion of perverting the course of justice through criminal libel, suspicion of inciting a disturbance, criminal damage endangering life, and violent avoidance of arrest, sir."

"Should we add murder to the charges, too, Dr. Everard?" Pike asked.

Everard paled, and jumped again to his feet. "I don't know what you mean. I have murdered no one. This is plain bloody nonsense and you can't prove any of it!"

"Sit down, please. Mr. Dunn was found poisoned in his bed on Saturday morning at St. Thomas's Hospital. I have just received a note from the mortuary confirming that the poison ingested was cyanide. A man was seen visiting him just before he died and that man matched your description." Not true, but worth a shot. "For the last time," Pike said, "sit down please, Doctor."

Everard dropped back into his seat. Under the table, his foot began an agitated tap. "I haven't visited St. Thomas's for months."

"You deny the murder charge?" Pike asked.

"Of course I bloody well do." Everard folded his arms and turned away, muttering, "This is absurd."

"Did someone coerce you into helping him? Did you perform the illegal abortion on Esther Craddock, too?" By rapidly switching the subject matter, Pike hoped to forestall a formulated response.

"I did not."

It was time for some fearmongering. Pike turned to Fisher. "How vehemently he denies the charges that could have him dancing at the end of the hangman's rope."

"He's guilty, sir."

"Of course he's guilty," Pike snapped and turned back to Everard. "I can see why you might have begrudged a female doctor lording it over you at the mortuary, even been prepared to set her up for something she did not do. But I don't understand why you would go so far as to murder for the same reason—surely the risk to you is too great? And you do have something to do with all this; of that I have no doubt. Do you have an accomplice, or is it you who is the accomplice, Dr. Everard? Who, if not you, was driving your motorcar on the evening of Friday the twenty-fifth of August? What kind of hold does this man have over you that you would be prepared to swing for him?"

"No hold, no man, no comment."

Pike sighed, gathered up the letters, and put them back in his pocket. He wasn't going to break this man today; Everard's barriers were too rigidly fortified.

"I need to send word to my wife, Pike. When can that be arranged?" Everard asked.

Pike glanced at Fisher and back to Everard. "No comment."

As the cell's door banged behind them, Pike said to Fisher, "Charge him over the letters, give him some time to stew, and then grant him police bail—nothing too hefty, mind, I don't think he can afford much—and then let him go. Have him watched around the clock. I want to know what he does and who he sees."

"Yes, sir."

Pike began to make his way down the passageway until the sound of Fisher clearing his throat made him stop and turn.

"One more thing, sir," Fisher called out.

"Yes, what is it?"

"I just wanted to say that it is a privilege to be working with you again, sir." When Pike made no reply, the big man shifted his weight from one foot to the other. "And I feel you deserve some kind of explanation for my recent behaviour."

"I'm listening."

"Remember my wife, Mary, sir? You kindly sent a hamper when you learned of her sickness."

"I remember. Consumption, wasn't it?"

"Yes. She passed away a few months back."

Pike felt the hard set of his shoulders slacken. "I'm sorry, Fisher." He remembered them as a devoted couple.

"I should never have done what I did, sir. But I thought there was hope for Mary, you see. There was an apothecary who supplied her with medicine, said it would cure her. It was very expensive—the stuff had gold in it—and it seemed to be working. But there was no way I could continue to afford it on a sergeant's wage. Superintendent Shepherd always had it in for you, didn't he? He promised me a hefty bonus and promotion if I could find anything against you—"

"And you did."

"If you want to report me, that is your right."

"There is nothing to report you for."

"I also stole money that was meant for an informer."

"I didn't hear you say that, Inspector."

They stood for a moment in awkward silence. Fisher had

broken the law for the woman he loved. Pike had always prided himself in being an honourable man. Arrogantly, perhaps, he had always thought himself above temptation. But he had proved more than capable of bending the rules to keep his daughter out of a police investigation. What else would he do for love? Would he do what Fisher had done to save someone he loved, Dody say, from unnecessary suffering? Of course he would.

"I'm glad I was able to have the charges against Dr. McCleland dropped," Fisher said, interrupting the train of Pike's thoughts. "I also regret my part in what must have been a very upsetting experience for her. I will do my best to find the abortionist and get to the root of what is going on here."

"I'm pleased to hear that, Inspector. As will I."

There was nothing else Pike could think to say. The events of the last forty-eight hours had left him feeling as if he'd been wrung through a mangle, the words squeezed out of him.

He put his hand out to the inspector.

Florence leaned against the shop wall next to Daphne to catch her breath. Her feet were killing her. Crowds of people filled the footpath on their way to an open-air market down the street. A cabby pulled up a few yards away and hooked a nosebag around his horse's ears. Florence took a deep breath, exhaled, and listened for a moment to the rhythmic grind of teeth on oats.

"How many have we visited now?" she finally asked.

Daphne pulled a list from her shopping basket. "This will be number five out of a possible six chemists, apothecaries, and pharmacies in the Whitechapel area."

"With no luck in purchasing any ready-made lead tablets and enough Widow Welch's to open a sweet shop."

Daphne examined Florence, reached for her face, and tucked a loose tendril of hair under her hat. "You're beginning to look quite weak and pathetic, Flo. Are you sure you want to keep doing this?"

"The more weak and pathetic I look, the less I have to act."

"That's the ticket." Daphne smiled encouragingly.

Both women wore simple dresses borrowed from their maids and small, unadorned hats. It felt strange to be going out with none of the usual regalia—cartwheel-sized chapeaux, parasols, and long gloves—and Florence felt naked and defenceless. Then again, that, too, helped her with what she saw as her very convincing performance as an unmarried woman desperate to rid herself of her unborn child.

Daphne played her part as supportive friend extremely well, too—not having to act much at all.

Even though the charges against Dody had been dropped, Florence knew the experience had left her sister wracked with anguish. Maybe this was also behind the illness that had been plaguing her. Despite the wonderful evening she purported to have had with Pike, she'd appeared haggard and tearstained at breakfast for the last two mornings.

Florence hated doing nothing and felt she had to help in some way. What a boost it would be to Dody if they identified the manufacturer of the lead tablets. Dody had said the tablets were more than likely distributed in the local public houses. But it was still worth investigating the drug dispensaries as well, and this was surely the most effective way. Florence looked at the apothecary's across the road, Zimmerman's—the man she had wanted to investigate days earlier when Daphne had been waylaid by Lady Harriet Frobisher's tea party. She indicated to Daphne that they should enter.

The apothecary was like none of the other shops they had visited thus far in their quest. The electric lights rigged up behind the coloured bottles in Zimmerman's shop window made the place as alluring as a sweet shop. A curling bell above the door tinkled as they entered. They skirted baskets of berries and sacks of dried goods with their strange, foreign smells. Florence felt like Dr. Livingstone hacking his way through the jungle as she pushed her way through medical hardware hanging in clumps from the ceiling, enamel bedpans and rubber hoses, and bunches of aromatic herbs.

The lighting over the counter was dimmer, as if to deliberately obscure the more nefarious contents of the bottles and jars on the shelves above. Several unborn hedgehogs shared a jar of preserving fluid; their neighbour, a curled grass snake, stared out through opaque eyes. Next to these, a stuffed stoat, teeth bared as if ready to pounce, guarded other jars containing less identifiable lumps of sloughing tissue and rubberised bone. Surely, she thought, there could be no better indication that this was the place.

Florence presumed it was Zimmerman himself leaning on the counter. The man adjusted his skullcap and smiled. "What can I do you for, miss?"

"I need something to help me. I am with child." Florence rubbed her padded stomach and gave Zimmerman what she hoped was a knowing look.

"Vitamins, minerals; or is it iron you need to strengthen your blood?"

"No, nothing like that," Florence whispered, more urgently now. "I mean I need something reliable to get rid of the baby. Surely you have something besides Widow Welch's?"

Zimmerman frowned. "You won't find anything stronger than that in my shop, young lady."

"Not even lead tablets?"

"I would not risk my licence. Get out of here before I call the police."

The man lifted his hand as if to strike. Florence cowered and reached for Daphne's arm. The trouble she would face from Dody if the police became involved was not worth imagining. They scampered from the shop like a pair of frightened dormice.

"There is one last shop, Flo," Daphne said as they continued down the street, "just a bit further down, not far from the Clinic. Let's make that lucky last and then call it a day."

"Mr. Borislav's shop?"

"Yes, that's it. I'll have to wait outside, though. I sometimes get supplies for the Clinic from him and he might recognise me. Do you dare?"

"Well . . ." Florence hesitated. "I did call in the other day with Dody. He is a friend of hers and I really can't believe that he would be a supplier of abortifacients, I—"

"Oh, that's a shame. I feel very sorry for him, about the tragic death of his wife, I mean, and I'm sure he is a very nice man, but we shouldn't let our personal bias get in the way of our professional investigation." Daphne and Florence shared the same enthusiasm for detective literature.

Florence brightened. "But Mr. Borislav didn't see me—we weren't even introduced. I spoke to his nephew." Florence paused. "If Joseph is serving at the counter, though, I'd better not risk it. But if it's Borislav at the counter"—she gave a dismissive wave of her hand—"he won't have a clue who I am."

"That's settled then." Daphne nudged her with her elbow. "Go on." Florence took a deep breath and crossed the shop's threshold.

The chemist was empty, but the sound of angry male voices reached Florence from somewhere behind the counter. As she edged closer, she noticed the door leading to the dispensing room was ajar. The voices became clearer, a young man, Joseph, and an older one—Mr. Borislav, she guessed—and they were arguing.

"I've had just about enough of your moneymaking schemes," Borislav said.

"If it were not for my innovations, we'd be on the street. As for that doctor from the mortuary who's always hanging around—why put up with him when you have me to help? Can't you give me just a little bit of credit for the shop's renewed good fortune?"

"You have proven good at the book work, I'll grant you that."

"I have to protect my investment somehow. Can't you see, Uncle, the only way we can prosper is to diversify."

"Like Boots, you mean, turn ourselves into a lending library? For goodness' sake, Joseph, it'll be tinned salmon next, then tin-openers and!"

"In order to survive, we have to damn well offer our customers that something extra that the competition does not provide. You're blind, old man, totally blind to what's going on under your very nose. Aunt Gertrude's been gone for six years, it's time to—"

The voice stopped, as if the men were suddenly aware of another's presence.

Borislav burst through the door from the back room, saw Florence, and tried to compose himself. He looked at her over his tortoiseshell-rimmed spectacles and moulded his mouth into a smile. "Good afternoon, miss, what can I do for you?"

When Florence explained her predicament, his pink complexion deepened. "I think it would be more appropriate for you to consult your sister on this matter, Miss McCleland," he said. "I am afraid I'm unable to help you."

Bloody hell.

Chapter Twenty-Seven

TUESDAY 29 AUGUST

At the sound of her mother's brisk footsteps on the stairs, Elizabeth Strickland drew her knees to her chest and buried her head beneath the bedclothes. The mattress sagged as her mother sat down. Elizabeth smelled the starch from her fresh cotton blouse. No fancy perfumes for Mrs. Arthur Strickland and certainly no makeup. Heaven forbid she was mistaken for a trollop.

"Elizabeth, dear, isn't it time you got ready for work?"

"I'm not feeling very well, Mama. I think I have a touch of the cholera."

"Oh, my poor lamb. In that case I will pop down to the surgery and see if Dr. James is free. You can't afford to be missing much more work. They'll be sacking you soon, mark my words." Elizabeth sat bolt upright in bed, pulling the sheet to her chin lest her mother notice the swollen breasts pushing against her flower-sprigged nightdress.

"No, Mama, please. Let us wait and see how I am tomorrow before summoning Dr. James; just give me one more day at home to rest. Besides, today is sewing circle and I know how little time you have to finish the church kneelers."

Elizabeth read the conflict on her mother's face: whether to be a good mother or a dutiful parishioner. The parishioner won.

"Well, if you're sure."

"Go, Mama." Elizabeth looked to the clock on the wall. "Your friends will be waiting."

It was a warm day, but it had rained quite heavily in the night. Mud, churned up by rumbling carts, splattered many of the shopfronts. A boy tossed a bucket of water against the fishmonger's window, lashing it like sea spray. *The fish must feel at home*, Elizabeth thought. Not that she cared. Elizabeth hated everything about fish: their smell, their gaping mouths, their jellied eyes, and the prick of their scales. Not to mention the shiny film of blood that coated their gills.

She pushed open the door. It was hotter in the shop than it had been in the street. Shards of ice covering the fish were shrinking before her eyes. Come afternoon, the stock would be as warm as the customers.

A heavy woman with a grey bun and a bloodstained apron stood behind a sloping slab of fish. "What can I do for you, love? Want some fish?"

Elizabeth shook her head, lost for words.

The woman looked her up and down. "'Im upstairs, then?"

"Yes, please, ma'am. My name is Elizabeth Strickland

and I was told to meet the doctor here." The woman smiled, showing a row of blackened teeth. "Call me Mother, if you like." She rubbed the side of her nose with a scaly finger. "Told no one else about this, I 'ope."

"Not a soul."

The woman guffawed, grabbed a big flat fish by the tail, and pointed to the orange spots on its back. "Sole," she said.

Elizabeth tried to smile and failed.

"Mother" flicked the sign to CLOSED and beckoned Elizabeth to follow her up several narrow flights of stairs until they came to a small landing. The woman tapped on a door to the right of the stairwell, opened it, and pushed Elizabeth in. "This 'ere's Elizabeth Strickland, Doctor," she said to a man sitting behind a large desk.

"Thank you, Mother, you may go now," the man said.

Mother closed the door behind her, clumping footsteps fading down the stairs. Alone in the room with the man, Elizabeth started to shake.

"You have the money?" the man asked without lifting his head from the open book in front of him.

She nodded, unable to get her words out, her throat constricted from all the days of crying.

"Put it on the desk then," he said. "There's a good girl." Elizabeth reached into her pocket for the money and clunked it down. The coins were hot from her hand and it felt as if she were parting with a piece of her own body. The tears began to well again.

The man went for the money, sliding it across the leathered top of his desk and into his palm. "No more crying; this will soon be over. Climb onto the bed and let me examine you." When he finally met her eyes with his, she noticed how dead they were—as dead as the fish for sale downstairs. She felt a spasm of fear. Was she really doing the right thing? What choice did she have, though?

The doctor took her by the hand, holding it high as if she were a posh lady about to mount a carriage, and led her to a high bed. Leather straps were attached to poles at each corner of the mattress and Elizabeth wondered what they were for.

"Just relax down onto the pillow now," he said as he helped her up.

With a flick of a switch, the stained white ceiling disappeared, replaced by a blinding electric light that swallowed the shadows of the dingy room. She could no longer see his face, but felt his fingers fumbling with the buttons of her dress. As instructed, she'd not worn a corset. His fingers were cool against her burning flesh. He palpated her breasts and worked his way like a spider to her stomach.

"You took the pills?" he asked.

"Yes, sir."

"No symptoms at all?"

"Um?"

"Did they make you cramp or bleed?" he asked impatiently.

"Cramp. But only a bit."

"You are still with child. Do you remember what we discussed?"

Elizabeth nodded. The man pushed the light away. "I'll put you to sleep, and when you wake up, it will all be over. You'll stay here for a few hours before going home, just to make sure there are no, er, complications."

Something cool and rubbery was placed over her nose

and mouth, some kind of mask. Out of the corner of her eye she saw him reach for a bottle and slowly drip the contents over the mask. "Breathe deeply and tell me about yourself. What do you like doing best in the whole world?"

Other than being with Jimmy? Well. "I like family sing-songs, sir."

Her voice sounded funny through the mask, like she was speaking from the depth of a cave.

"Sing me one of your favourite songs."

Elizabeth liked the romantic songs best but she worried that the man would laugh at her. It was romance, after all, that got her into this mess in the first place.

"Go on," he urged.

"All right then." She began to sing in a high, quavering voice:

Let me call you "Sweetheart," I'm in love with you.
Let me hear you whisper that you love me, too.

The darkness began to crowd in on her. "Doctor," she said, "will it hurt?" She felt muddled and light-headed. She wasn't sure if she was thinking, saying, or singing, if he was a doctor, Jimmy, or the devil himself.

Chapter Twenty-Eight

Dody held the dripping red paisley dress over the mortuary sink to examine it. The dress was labelled SEL-FRIDGES; the material, while not overly expensive, was too fine for your typical East-Ender. A faded brown stain spread from the middle of the back and travelled to the hem. The garment had not been in the Thames long enough to disguise the stain's true nature—blood.

Dr. Spilsbury stooped over the girl's body. He had been silent for some time now. The only sound in the echoing room was from his autopsy instruments: the brisk scraping of the bone saw, the snip of the rib-cutters, and the drip of watery blood into the drain beneath the slab.

"Where was the body found, Inspector?" Dody addressed Fisher, who stood near the swinging mortuary door as far away from the slab as possible.

The body was reasonably fresh and virtually odour-free

save for the fetid smell of the river. Nevertheless, Fisher still answered through a handkerchief over his nose and mouth. "She was pulled out of the river last night by a lighterman near Temple Pier," he said. Temple Pier, as the crow flies, was only about a mile away from the Clinic, Dody realised.

"Why wasn't the body taken to the Bishopsgate Mortuary?" she asked.

"I sensed it would be of interest to you here, Doctor, and arranged for it to be delivered to Paddington."

"Thank you, that was very considerate." *He is still trying to make things up to me,* she thought, touched.

Spilsbury looked up from the body. "Had the corpse been weighted down or tied, Inspector?"

"A rope, sir, attached to her ankle. You'll find it in the sack of clothes that came with her."

Dody removed a coarse rope from the hessian bag and held it up.

"The body was attached by that rope to a heavy metal wheel found resting on a sand bar," Fisher went on. "Whoever put it there either did not know about the sand bar or misjudged how close to the surface it appears at low tide. The lighterman saw her hair just below the water and thought at first it was seaweed."

Our man's making silly mistakes, Dody thought. Interesting. Back to the dress. Dody felt something at the bottom of one of the deep pockets, put in her hand, and removed a printed calling card. Dropping the dress back into the sink, she hurried over to Inspector Fisher with it.

"Look, Inspector, a name."

Fisher held the soggy card at arm's length. The name was easy to read; the card had not been in the river long enough to suffer much damage. "*Dr. Archibald Van Noort. Number seventy-seven Harley Street.*"

"She probably intended on seeing this Harley Street specialist to correct damage done," Spilsbury said, throwing his heavy gloves to the floor with a splat.

Dody sensed the owner of this dress was not the type to visit a Harley Street specialist, but kept the thought to herself. That a Harley Street man might be responsible for the damage done was a notion Spilsbury would find hard to entertain. *Not too different,* she thought, *from my own earlier difficulty in believing that Everard would stoop as low as he has.*

"Sew her up, Alfred," Spilsbury said as he moved to join Dody and Fisher at the door.

"What have you discovered, sir?" Fisher enquired.

"She was dead before she was tossed into the river," Spilsbury said. "The lack of water in her lungs tells me that she did not drown; this was no suicide. The cause of death was exsanguination. She bled out from a pierced uterine artery as a direct result of criminal abortion." He turned to Dody. "This case bears striking similarities to the Esther Craddock case. There are still remnants of placental tissue adherent to the uterus wall, and the girl also shows signs of plumbism."

Dody's heart leaped. "Then it might be the same person who operated on Esther."

"It might be."

"When did she die, Doctor?" Fisher asked.

"Anytime between yesterday afternoon and late last night," Spilsbury said.

Fisher had told her earlier that Henry Everard had only just been released from jail that morning. He could not have done this. Dody felt light-headed with relief.

"May I examine the body please, Doctor?" she asked.

"If you wish, but I think you will find that I have not missed anything."

Heaven forbid. "I'm sure you haven't, sir, but I would like to see it for my own experience." Dody moved over to the body. Alfred abandoned his suturing and stepped aside to make way for her.

She pulled back the girl's lip and saw the telltale blue line on the gums. Then she cast her eyes along the pale, marbled corpse. This was not the body of a street woman or a servant: the hands were unblemished, the body well nourished.

"Do we know her identity?" Spilsbury asked the inspector.

"Her description matches that of a Miss Elizabeth Strickland from Lewisham, sir. Her parents reported her missing to their local police station at about six o'clock last night."

"How old was Miss Strickland?"

"Seventeen."

"You'd better see if the parents can identify the corpse. This may well be her."

"I'll get on to it right away, sir. Good morning, Dr. McCleland." Fisher put his shoulder to the swinging door.

"Inspector, wait. There is more we need to discuss. We have ascertained that the girl was suffering from plumbism before her abortion, yes?" Dody queried.

He turned and nodded.

"The supplying of the lead then was the first action against the pregnancy. The remnants of lead in her stomach were too dense to suggest it had been ingested in anything but tablet form—a form that we have already ascertained is relatively unusual. When this did not rid her of her child, can we speculate that she opted for the same extreme measures as did Esther Craddock?"

"I suppose so, but with all due respect, Doctor, *speculation* is the right word for it. We do not have the evidence to prove it."

"Absence of evidence isn't evidence of its absence," Spilsbury said. "Dr. McCleland is saying that the two may be linked. Surely, as you have nothing else to go on, this connection is worth pursuing?" Dody could have hugged him. "Find the manufacturer of the tablets, Inspector, and you might find the abortionist."

"Which is what I decided to do when I was under investigation," Dody said quickly. "I started making enquiries and discovered the tablets were being distributed in the public houses in or around Whitechapel. Someone must have purchased the tablets for this young lady." She pointed to the body on the slab. "I can't imagine her loitering about in a public house on her own. She probably asked her young man to get them for her. If you can find out the name of the father of her child, we might get some answers."

Fisher gave a resigned sigh. "I'll put some men onto it right away, Doctor."

"Will you also be visiting the man whose name is on the calling card?" Spilsbury asked.

"My orders are to report to Chief Inspector Pike, sir."

"This Van Noort is a Harley Street specialist," Spilsbury said. "I think it prudent that a doctor accompanies the police during the interview, to translate medical terms if necessary. You can do the honours, Dr. McCleland. Contact Chief Inspector Pike and arrange it with him. Give Dr. McCleland the card, Fisher. A gentleman from Harley Street is, of course, above suspicion, but he might still be able to shed light on the matter. I want this murdering abortionist stopped."

"Yes, sir." Dody took the card from Fisher and put it in her apron pocket. The thought of being thrown back into Pike's company after Monday's uncomfortable meeting was mortifying, but she was going to have to bear it. Her feelings for Pike were not the issue here. Her purpose was to find the man responsible for the death of this poor girl and the murder of her unborn child, and to stop him from killing again.

She said good-bye to Inspector Fisher, told Alfred he could continue with his suturing of the body, and returned to the clothes in the sink. She gleaned nothing of interest from the lace chemise other than the garment's reasonable quality, which suggested Elizabeth Strickland was a member of the respectable lower middle class. Criminal abortion pervaded all classes, as should sensible birth control practices. Anyone could make a mistake, no matter what her level of income or education—as Dody had come perilously close to proving herself.

Picking up the bloodstained drawers, she felt along the drawstring. Something at the eyelet jabbed into the skin of her thumb. A dot of blood appeared on her thumb and a small opaque protrusion—a sliver of glass perhaps. The last thing she needed was an infection. Taking a magnifying glass and some fine forceps from the shelf above, she extracted the object and examined it.

It wasn't glass.

"Dr. Spilsbury, would you mind having a look at this, please?" Spilsbury joined her at the sink. "I have just pulled it from my thumb and I think it's a fish scale. It was in the eyelet of her drawers."

"How odd," he said, holding out a specimen jar for her. She tapped the scale on the lip of the jar to dislodge it from the forceps.

"The girl's dress would have billowed in the water and a fish could have brushed against her and lost a scale. Or maybe someone was cleaning fish nearby," Dody said.

"Send the scale to the lab for confirmation. They might be able to identify the fish." He gave her one of his rare, chilly smiles. "Every little detail is worth noting. Good work, Dr. McCleland."

Dody hurried home to bathe and change her clothes. She was in the hall, about to go upstairs, when the sounds of voices in the morning room caught her attention. She opened the door to find Florence engrossed in conversation with Daphne. They immediately stopped their chatter. Daphne climbed to her feet and smoothed her dress.

"You can relax, Daphne," Dody said with a smile. "You are not at work now."

Daphne sank back into the winged chair but continued to look ill at ease.

"What are you doing home at this time of the day?" Florence asked.

"Just home to bathe and change before going out again."

"Have you heard . . ." Florence hesitated. "Have you progressed any further with the case? Found the source of the lead tablets?"

"Spoken to Mr. Borislav?" Daphne blurted out.

"No, why should I?" Dody asked, perplexed. "A while ago I asked him about the tablets, but we have not spoken on the matter since."

Both women looked relieved. Dody did not have time to stop and talk, but made a mental note to ask Florence about it later. She pulled the bell and asked Annie to prepare a bath for her with plenty of lemon juice to help neutralise the odour of the mortuary.

After her bath, she changed into her pale yellow outfit. Now that she was clean and fresh, she decided not to battle with the sweaty public transport system. She asked Fletcher to take her to the Medical Licensing Board so she could examine Archibald Van Noort's credentials, and then on to Scotland Yard.

She had not visited Pike since his move to the Special Branch section of the castle-like New Scotland Yard building. His office was small and poky, not much bigger than a water closet, with barely enough room for the boneshaker bicycle balanced across two filing cabinets. No matter how determined he was, without the operation she could no more see him riding that thing again than she could see herself behind the steering wheel (or was it a rudder?) of a flying machine.

He stood when a constable showed her in, one hand on his desk for support. She suspected he was still feeling the effect of Dunn's kick and hoped his knee had not suffered further damage. A few days earlier she would have offered to examine it for him, but sensed that any kind of advice from her now would be unwelcome.

"Inspector Fisher told me you were handling the case," Dody said, trying for a nonchalant tone. "With your Mata

Hari assignment over, I thought you might be taking some leave."

"Yes, I should have. But this case is close to my heart." The intensity of his gaze made her own heart lurch. "I have been given permission to pursue leads in the deaths of Craddock, Dunn, and now Elizabeth Strickland, with Fisher as my assistant."

"Just like old times." She shot him a tentative smile.

"Forgive me. I seem to have forgotten my manners. Please sit down." He pulled out the visitor's chair for her. Not wishing to waste time with idle talk, she waited for him to settle back behind his desk and then got straight to the point, producing Van Noort's card from her reticule.

Pike gave a pronounced start when he read the name aloud. "I know this man."

"You do? From where?"

"He was obsessed with Mata Hari, always hanging about the stage door. He told me once that he was a doctor in the South African war. There was a time when I thought he might have been my spy."

"I've just come from the Medical Licensing Board. Van Noort was struck off the list over five years ago."

"But he has continued to practise?"

"The card found in the girl's pocket suggests it. A Whitechapel chemist recently complained to me about a doctor with a foreign name harassing his female customers." Dody shrugged. "I can't help but note that Whitechapel is where it all started."

"Van Noort introduced himself to me as a doctor," Pike said.

Dody paused. "You came to know him quite well?"

"Well enough to know he is an odd fish—I saw him once having some kind of a fit."

"Can you describe the fit?"

Pike opened his palms. "A dazed look, gnashing teeth, facial contortions, nonsensical mutterings—"

"Did he fall to the ground?"

"No, but the fit appeared to weaken him. He was forced to lean against a wall and took some time to recover from it."

"Did he remain continent?"

"I believe so."

Dody thought she knew the type of fit Pike was describing, but would not jump to conclusions without a physical examination of the man. "I am anxious to meet him."

"As am I to renew our acquaintance," Pike said, leaving his desk to assist Dody with her chair.

"You think he might be our abortionist—even have something to do with the drug gang?" she asked.

"I can't say just yet." The walls were close; they brushed against one another at the door. Pike's face creased into a smile. "But let's see what we can find out." How she would grieve if she never saw that smile again.

Chapter Twenty-Nine

Dody was glad to see how focused Pike was on the job in hand. He was being professional, though something in his manner still held remnants of Monday's hurtful aloofness in the mortuary yard. Then she had yearned to hold him in her arms and share with him the joy of her exoneration. Now she wanted to take him in her arms and drive his pain away—their pain.

Well, she would never know unless she tried. Instant rejection would surely hurt less than this lingering, painful distance. She slipped her hand through the crook of his arm as they walked towards the underground station, well prepared for him to cast it off. Instead he reached over with his other hand and gently squeezed her fingers. She felt the warmth of his touch through her glove. When he turned his head and met her eye, she wondered if he knew the smallest part of what she felt for him.

They settled into their carriage and she looked around her. With a motorcar at her disposal, she had little call to use the underground.

"How filthy and noisy it all is," she said to Pike. "I hate to think what it was like when steam trains dominated." As it was, the rumble of the electrical system, supposedly cleaner and quieter, still hampered conversation. She and Pike said little, but sat close. As she gazed about her, she marvelled at the diversity of the train's occupants: from barrow boys to well-dressed women on shopping expeditions. Everyone paid the same fare and could sit where they wished. This was London's first experiment with classless travel, and it seemed to have caught on.

They came out at Oxford Circus, crossed Cavendish Square to the clatter of rising pigeons, and strolled in silence, arm in arm down Harley Street. The long, straight road was lined with Georgian buildings. Dutch elms stood outside each house, giving the street an air of cool and shady tranquillity. Brass specialists' plates winked in the dappled sunlight.

They climbed the steps of number seventy-seven. Screw holes visible below the number on the door showed where a brass plate had once been fixed. Pike paused halfway, closed his eyes, and drew a sudden breath.

"Your knee is paining you?" Dody asked before she could stop herself.

Pike flicked her a smile. He leaned on the railing and pointed with his cane to the plaque. "What would the plate have said?"

"Probably his name and initials indicating that he was a member of the Royal College of Obstetricians and Gynaecologists."

"So he could be a skilled abortionist."

"He could do the job, yes, without a doubt—and that puzzles me. Even if he were the criminal abortionist, why would a man so eminently qualified make the kinds of mistakes he seems to have made? Esther and Elizabeth were butchered; there was no skill . . ." She thought for a moment. "Unless of course he suffered a seizure while working."

Pike nodded and tapped the knocker onto the glossy black door. A maid appeared, glanced at them, and said, "I'm sorry, sir, ma'am, but Dr. Van Noort's clinic is no longer operating."

The maid must have assumed they were a childless couple seeking treatment—what other explanation for a man accompanying his wife to the obstetrician? Dody felt herself colour and stared down at her walking shoes.

Fortunately Pike seemed to have no idea of how things might look to the maid. He lifted his hat. "This is a personal matter. I am an old friend of the doctor's here to pay a social call." Pike patted his pockets. "I'm afraid I have forgotten my calling cards, but tell him the Captain and Dr. Dorothy McCleland wish to see him."

"Very good, sir. Please come in."

They followed the maid into a wide high-ceilinged hallway from which a walnut-banistered stairway curled towards a spacious landing with a row of dark wooden doors. The maid led them into a tastefully furnished parlour that might once have been used as a waiting room. Dody could imagine chairs along the wall now occupied by a chintz settee. A world away from the waiting room at the Women's Clinic, she mused. One consultation fee here would probably have equated to about a month's rent on the Clinic's premises.

No fire burned in the duck's-nest grate, but the room had

a welcoming feel, enhanced by the greeting of the pleasant-faced woman who joined them. The faded blond hair and the fine lines around her eyes put her somewhere in her late forties. She introduced herself, and her bright smile lifted years from her face. Dody warmed to her immediately.

"I believe you are an old friend of my husband's. Are you from his army days, Captain?" Mrs. Van Noort enquired.

"Our acquaintance is more recent than that, ma'am."

"Well, I'm afraid he is not at home. I'm sure he will be disappointed to have missed you."

"Really? Your maid seemed to think he was here."

"Sally was mistaken. My husband comes and goes often these days. It is hard to keep track of him."

The smallest delay in Pike's response betrayed his suspicion. "Can you tell me when you expect him back?" he asked.

"Why don't you both sit down?" Mrs. Van Noort suggested. "Sally will fetch us some tea. Sally?"

"Yes, ma'am," the maid replied, leaving the room. Oddly enough, Mrs. Van Noort did not seem anxious to get rid of them.

Dody and Pike sat alongside each other on the chintz settee. Dody felt uncomfortable with the deception and spent some time adjusting her skirt. It was a relief when Pike said, "Ma'am, my name is Chief Inspector Pike and I am with Special Branch. Your husband knew me as the captain." Pike pulled his warrant card from his inside jacket pocket and showed it to her.

Mrs. Van Noort frowned at it for a moment, and then turned her gaze to Dody.

"And I am a doctor with the Home Office."

"We are investigating a series of incidents," Pike said,

"and were hoping your husband might be able to help shed some light on them for us."

Mrs. Van Noort lowered her eyes to fingers that twisted on her lap. "I do not know where my husband is or when he will be back. As I said before, he comes and goes at whim."

After a moment's thought, she rose from her chair. Moving to the mantel, she picked up a photograph of an officer dressed in the uniform of the Royal Army Medical Corps. She passed it to Dody. A fair young man with an angular face stared back at her from a silver frame.

"That was my husband before he left for the war in South Africa. He was not the same man when he returned." She paused, as if to say something more, then stopped herself.

Dody handed the photograph to Pike, who indicated with a tip of his head that this was the Van Noort he had met.

"In what way was he changed, Mrs. Van Noort?" Dody asked.

The woman glanced at Pike and back to Dody with the tiniest shake of her head. The maid returned with the tea tray and placed it on an inlaid card table near her mistress.

Pike rose from his chair. "May I impose on your maid to show me around the house?"

Mrs. Van Noort touched her throat. "But your tea?"

"Not for the moment, thank you."

"Why do you wish to search my house, Chief Inspector?"

"Solely for the purpose of eliminating your husband from my investigation."

Pike's vague answer would not have satisfied Dody, but strangely, it seemed to offer Mrs. Van Noort some form of relief. "As you wish. Sally, show the chief inspector anything he wants. Start in the basement and work your way up."

"Yes, ma'am." The maid closed the door behind them, and Mrs. Van Noort poured the tea in silence.

"Was there something you wished to tell me about your husband in private?" Dody asked, blessing Pike's insight.

Mrs. Van Noort turned her head away and took a sip of tea. "This is hard for me. I have been expecting a visit from the police for some time now—my husband follows his heart, Doctor, and is therefore not as careful of regulations or reputation as one might wish. Nevertheless, it is still a shock. When rehearsing this scene in my mind, I had always resolved to tell all. I had no idea how hard it would be when the time came—to speak to a man about it, especially."

Dody gave an encouraging smile. "We are alone now. Let us take advantage of that."

"Of course. But first of all, Doctor, can you tell me what you think my husband is involved in?"

"We think he might be able to provide us with information. His card was found in the pocket of a dead girl who died from injuries sustained during a criminal abortion."

Mrs. Van Noort covered her mouth. It took a moment for Dody to realise that rather than attempting to hide an exclamation of horror, the woman was in fact covering a sigh of relief.

"And you think my husband was somehow involved? Of all the crimes he could have committed, I assure you illegal abortion is the most preposterous. We were unable to have children; we see children as a precious blessing denied to us. My husband is also a deeply religious man and a dedicated doctor. He could no more take a life than you could." Mrs. Van Noort paused and looked closely at Dody. "But of course I realise who you are now. I thought your name sounded familiar. You are the doctor at the centre of the inquest into the death of that scullery maid. The charges against you have been dropped, I believe." She put down her cup, moved over to Dody, and took her hand. "You poor girl, how awful it must have been."

Dody squeezed the hand that held her own. "Thank you," she whispered, unable to trust her voice. After the events of the last few weeks, it took no more than a sympathetic tone to leave her on the verge of tears.

"I can see why you would want to find the true criminal, but I assure you that it is not my husband," Mrs. Van Noort said, returning to her chair.

"I'm afraid I was unable to find his name listed with the Medical Licensing Board," Dody said, pausing to allow the words to register. "Has your husband been practising without a licence? Is that why you have been expecting a visit from the police?"

"Your tea must be cold, let me refresh it." Mrs. Van Noort made as if to move.

Dody held up a palm to stop her. "Mrs. Van Noort, the police will eventually discover whatever it is your husband has been up to. I'm afraid they can be quite relentless in their pursuit." She took a stab in the dark. "Did his deregistration have anything to do with his epileptic seizures?" Mrs. Van Noort looked to the ceiling as if to prevent tears. Dody continued gently. "I know that nothing they could say or do to me was going to stop me practising my profession. Had my career been totally ruined, I still would have found somewhere to practise—behind prison bars if necessary."

"Once a doctor always a doctor, I suppose. Archie can't seem to help himself."

Dody waited patiently for Mrs. Van Noort to continue.

"His physician said his problems were due to an injury sustained during the war."

"Where exactly was this injury?"

Mrs. Van Noort indicated an area on the side of her head, the temporal area. Dody had not come across such a case since medical school, but as Mrs. Van Noort talked, the signs and symptoms of temporal lobe epilepsy came back to her in almost textbook form.

"He is selective with his work, of course, performs no dangerous or complex medical procedures, and he knows what to look out for these days," Mrs. Van Noort said. "His body gives him a warning—an odd feeling, a strange taste in his mouth—that a fit will soon be upon him. The seizures became so frequent he was forced to close down the practice. He had a turn in front of a patient. The lady was not injured, but she made a complaint, and the Board decided his illness compromised patient safety and struck him from the list. Funnily enough, we still have people making enquiries of the clinic. It was closed years ago, but my husband's good reputation lingers on."

The poor woman had to have something to cling to, Dody supposed. "But he continues to practise?"

Mrs. Van Noort shifted her gaze from Dody's. "Yes."

"Where?"

"Does it matter?"

"I'm afraid so."

Mrs. Van Noort looked pained, as if what she was about to say required great effort. "He treats harlots, Doctor. Women whom few doctors want to touch. He examines them for signs of . . . disease . . . and administers simple treatments.

Drug therapies, mostly, I have taken care to discover. As I say, he came back from the war a damaged man . . ."

Her last sentence was left to hang in the air, as if Dody was expected to fill in the gaps herself. She was no mind-reader, but her knowledge of temporal lobe epilepsy was beginning to give her an idea as to what the woman was alluding to. No wonder she had not wanted Pike to hear any of this. His questions would have undoubtedly been too painful and embarrassing to answer.

"Pregnancy is an occupational hazard with the women your husband attends. How can you be so sure that he does not perform abortions on them, too?" Dody asked.

"In the course of your medical experience, Doctor, I am sure you have noticed that even the most unbalanced have certain parameters they will not cross—they will not step on the cracks in the footpath, they will not eat anything that is green—things that might not make sense to us, which do to them. My husband is not completely unbalanced. I know he would rather take his own life than that of another. The saddest thing about it is that he is sane enough to hate himself for the other . . . things . . . his condition compels him to do. He is a tormented man, Dr. McCleland."

"I think I understand," Dody said. But while understanding, she did not see how this torment made him any less capable of performing an abortion than any other doctor who had gone wrong. The woman's love for her husband might well have blinded her to the truth. "But it is still important that we find him."

"I'm afraid I have no idea where he is, my dear—in some house of ill repute as likely as not."

"I appreciate your candour, Mrs. Van Noort."

"I want you to help him."

"I hope that we can."

Pike returned to the room with a pill press tucked under his arm.

"I found this in your husband's study, Mrs. Van Noort," he said. "May I borrow it for a while? I'll return it undamaged as soon as I have run some tests."

The woman looked to Dody, who encouraged her cooperation with a nod.

"Very well, Chief Inspector; if you think it will clear my husband's name."

Pike bowed. "Thank you. We will do our best. In the meantime, when your husband returns, please urge him to come and see me." He handed her his card.

"We need to find somewhere to talk, Matthew," Dody said as they headed away from number seventy-seven Harley Street.

"We do indeed," said Pike.

Archibald Van Noort paced the length of his parlour. "They suspect me of what, Matilda?" he asked again in disbelief.

"Criminal abortion, Archie; please tell me it isn't true."

"Surely you don't think—"

"I don't know what to think anymore. But I would never have let the policeman search the house if I had known you were home."

"Sally saw me. I came in just before our visitors arrived. I was tired and went straight to bed in my dressing room.

When I heard the voices on the stairs, I hid behind the curtains. But criminal abortion—that is preposterous!"

"They know you are practising without a licence. Your card was found in the pocket of a dead girl."

"What girl?"

"I don't know—they didn't tell me her name. Can you remember handing anyone your card recently?"

Van Noort shook his head. "I see so many unfortunate girls."

"Prostitutes," Matilda clarified.

Van Noort pressed the heels of his hands into his eyes. Matilda knew everything, understood more than he deserved, and yet he could still not meet her eye for the shame of it. "No, no, prostitutes are not the only ones who get themselves into trouble—though they are, of course, the hardest to help. The most I can do for them is to warn them to keep away from backstreet operators—there's a gang of ruffians out there who deliberately lure the girls into undertaking dangerous treatments. And, of course, I encourage them to change their ways. It's not as useless as it sounds. I have had some successes."

"But why give these girls your cards? You are no longer a registered doctor. It was only a matter of time before the police came calling."

"My dear, I don't need you to point that out. But my card gives me more credibility. When the women and girls see *Doctor* before and the initials after my name, they trust me."

"Well, I wish you had never done it. The police are sure to come back."

There was a sudden banging at the door. "Back upstairs," she whispered urgently.

He was halfway up the stairs when she called out in relief, "It's all right, it's only Jack."

Only Jack, thank God. Not the police, or worse, those men from that filthy street gang. Only Jack.

"What are you doing here?" he asked gruffly. "Is something wrong?"

It took a lot more than a rough tone to hurt Jack's feelings. "'Ello, Mrs. V, Doc," the boy said in his usual cocky manner.

"Take your cap off inside, Jack," Matilda said. He did as he was told and she hugged him. "Are you here to stay this time?"

"I want to, Mrs. V, you know I do, but it's 'ard, see, wiv Dad now gone."

Van Noort had not told Matilda where he had met Jack. She might not be so keen to have him in the house if she knew where he spent so much of his time.

"I understand." Matilda bravely hid her disappointment. "Would you like some biscuits and lemonade?" she offered kindly.

"'S'aw right, Mrs. V, can't stop now." Jack turned to Van Noort. "Somefink terrible's 'appening above the fish shop—'ere, read this." The boy handed Van Noort a grubby piece of paper.

"What's this? Did that rascal Dunn give it to you?" Was this a trap?

"Nah, word on the street's Dunn's gone to meet 'is maker. Though I reckon 'is maker will probably soon be frowing 'im back to where 'e come from."

"Don't make light of it, Jack. Judgement will eventually befall us all," Van Noort said as he digested the note's contents. "So, who did give you this?"

"Just some ol' biddy from the fish shop. Said she thought there was somefink bad going on upstairs and knows you take an interest in this kinda fing."

"You've read this?"

"Course." Mee-Mee the whore had been teaching Jack his letters, and he was proving to be a quicker learner than any of them had expected.

"Should I call the police?" Matilda asked.

"No, but I will if I catch the blaggard at it."

"At what?" She looked from one to the other, confused.

Jack twitched at Van Noort's sleeve. "We gotta go now, Doc, before it's too late."

"I'll explain later, my dear," Van Noort said.

He retrieved his hat and jacket while Matilda headed for the kitchen, returning with a handful of biscuits. "Put these in your pocket, Jack, and be careful."

Chapter Thirty

The sun blazed down on them as they walked, and Pike had no breath for talking. Sweat streamed down his face, and Dody had to slow her pace for him to keep up, his cane *tap-tapping* on the footpath. Feeling the heat herself, she suggested they stop at Debenham and Freebody off Cavendish Square, which like many of the larger draperies, had a luncheon room especially for ladies on serious shopping expeditions.

Pike excused himself to make a telephone call while Dody freshened up in the cloakroom. They met again at the restaurant's entrance, and the waiter found them a table.

Dody was relieved to find the atmosphere between the two of them had returned to much as it had been before their disastrous evening together.

He placed the order: a dandelion and burdock drink for Dody, ale for himself, and a plate of sandwiches to share.

He took several swallows of ale and immediately looked the stronger for it, listening intently as she recounted her conversation with Mrs. Van Noort.

"Poor woman," he said, drawing his brow. "But you think she was still keeping things from you?"

"She left so many gaps, which only my knowledge of her husband's particular form of brain damage can begin to fill."

"And that is?"

"I think he suffers from temporal lobe epilepsy due to damage to that part of the brain. Sufferers' symptoms vary. Some exhibit sudden outbursts of unexpected aggression, agitation, and grand mal fits. But from what I gather of his wife's descriptions and yours, Van Noort seems to experience aura-like phenomena accompanied by incomplete though violent seizures."

Dody thought back to Spilsbury's comments that certain topics should never be discussed openly between the sexes. Would Pike feel the same? Now was as good a time as any to find out.

"Patients with temporal lobe damage are often left with heightened libido and religious mania, the combination of which must result in terrifying internal battles."

Pike made no reaction. The notion of "proper" conversation between males and females did not seem to enter his thinking. Their minds seemed to meet on so many levels, she hoped that somehow they would find a way to cast aside the barriers that separated them.

"He did strike me as a religious type, and his lust for Mata Hari seemed incongruous, to say the least," Pike said.

"The man is also suffering from some kind of hysteria as a result of his war trauma." Dody looked at Pike. The more she reflected on his behaviour at the hospital, the more she thought he might be suffering from a similar affliction.

He refused to meet her eye and helped himself to an egg and cress sandwich from the platter. "The head injury and peculiar behaviour I can believe. The hysteria, as I understand, is due to a lack of moral fibre."

A common idea amongst men of Pike's cloth, Dody mused, and a terrible misconception. It confounded her to think that he might see this in himself. She did not think she had met a more courageous or principled man. Unfortunately this was not the time or the place to take the matter further.

"As for his drastic change in sexual behaviour," she continued, "he would hate himself for being unable to control his urges."

"He is a rapist also?"

"No, I don't think he is. It is a certain type of woman who would trigger his lust and the type of woman he seems to favour would be more than willing. As long as he could pay, there would be no need for force."

"I've seen him on at least two occasions in the company of a young lad. You don't think . . ."

Dody saved Pike the discomfort of continuing. "No, I don't think so. He and his wife were devastated when they discovered they could not have children. He is possibly just exercising his paternal instincts."

Pike shuddered. "I hope you're right. Though it is possible his wife knows him less well than she thinks."

"Yes, that is possible." Dody took a sip of her cool drink. "And what of you—other than the pill press, did you discover anything else in the house?"

"As a matter of fact, I did." Pike paused. His eyes shone; he was pleased with himself.

"Will I have to use torture to extract the information?"

"I will tell you gladly. You are proving most helpful—I am glad Spilsbury forced you to come along." He smiled.

"Hardly forced, but go on."

"He was in the bedroom, hiding. I sensed he was there and then I noticed the toes of his boots behind the curtains. He has a"—Pike waved a hand through the air as if trying to catch a word—"a peculiar presence about him. I acted as if I had not seen him, but telephoned the Yard as soon as we arrived here. I've asked Fisher to assign some men to follow him and I can only hope he doesn't vanish before they get into position."

"But what good will following him do?"

"If he is innocent, it will be for his own protection. If he is guilty, we might catch him in the act. Meanwhile, I'll have the pill press tested and see if it produces the same kind of indentations as found on the illegal tablets."

"Much as it pains me to say it, I don't believe he is innocent."

"The man is of unsound mind—any lawyer worth his salt will be able to prove that. If he is guilty, he will be prevented from committing such crimes again and he will be helped. I guarantee he will not hang."

Pike insisted Dody take the last sandwich from the plate. She was not hungry and still suffering from intermittent bouts of cholera, but she forced it down with the remainder of her drink. Dispiritedly she said, "And there's still Borislav's account of a doctor with a foreign name in his shop."

Pike sighed. "Vague conjecture which we must not allow to blinker our investigation." It was strange that they both wished Van Noort to be innocent. Perhaps, in different ways, they both had sometimes walked in his shoes.

They needed a change of topic; the case was making them melancholy. And there was still the other matter weighing on Dody's mind. She might as well broach the subject; she had nothing more to lose now.

"At about the time of the inquest, I received flowers and a box of marzipans with a brief, unsigned note of apology."

His eyebrows rose. "You have a secret admirer?"

"Is that such a surprise?" she asked with some pique.

"No, no, forgive me. I didn't mean it to sound like that."

"I have no idea who the gifts were from. I thought"—she paused for a breath of courage—"at the time the gifts must have been from you, but now I'm not so sure."

"I assure you, Dody," Pike said, covering her hand with his. "I have never kept my admiration of you secret."

Chapter Thirty-One

The young lady from the river has been officially identified by her father as Elizabeth Strickland," Fisher said to Pike as they bounced along in the dispatch van to Everard's house. "I sent men to interview her work colleagues and it did not take long to find her young man. I interviewed him this morning, and he was distraught and quite cooperative after I told him he would not be charged with procuring abortifacients if he provided us with information."

"Good. And?"

"He bought the tablets at the Crown and Anchor on Dorset Street. Naturally he was not given the seller's name, but he described him as having an ugly mug—as if he'd been kicked by a horse, he said. I made further enquiries and believe the name of the man to be—"

"Daniel Dunn?"

"The same, sir. I had Dunn's premises searched but found no tablets nor tablet-making equipment."

"And the pill press I took from Van Noort's study is perfectly smooth; it did not produce tablets with the pitted surfaces. So, who the devil was Dunn working for, Fisher?"

"I don't know, sir, although I am following the idea that he was involved in some kind of a gang, with possibly Van Noort and Everard at the top of it."

Again Pike wondered what the connection might be between the two doctors. What kind of a hold, if any, did the older man have over the younger?

"Have you heard from the men watching Van Noort?" he asked, aware of how stretched the surveillance team was, with but one pair of men assigned to each suspect. He could only hope they were more reliable than the men who had been assigned to the late admiral.

Fisher grimaced. "I'm afraid he'd already left the house by the time they got into position. A streetsweeper saw him leaving earlier in the company of a young lad."

"Damn—but someone is still watching his house?"

"Yes, sir."

That was better than nothing. Considering the time it took to organise such matters, it came as no surprise that they had lost him. If Pike's knee had not been playing up so much, he would have hung around and followed the man himself. But, he reminded himself, that would have meant leaving Dody to make her own way home and he was glad he had been able to escort her. Towards the end of their lunch she had looked quite unwell. When they reached her door, she had promised him she would rest, and he hoped she had kept her word.

"What about Everard? Any movement there?"

"No, sir. He has not been seen since after he was released from the cells and returned home to his wife. Their house has no telephone for us to listen in to, and as far as my men can tell, no notes have been sent out or delivered."

Pike said nothing. Could it be that there was no connection at all between the two? It was possible Van Noort had performed the disastrous operation on Esther Craddock independently and Everard merely used the death to stir up trouble for Dody.

But who had employed and later murdered Dunn? No one at the hospital had been able to give them a description of the poisoner. He seemed to have blended in with the other doctors visiting the ward on that chaotic night. Everard might have got away with this, but surely not Van Noort with his long gangly legs, sallow skin, and peculiar mannerisms. Van Noort was one of the most unusual-looking men Pike had ever met, and even an overworked nurse would surely have noticed him.

Fisher had a few more solid facts for him. "The Everards live in a semidetached residence within walking distance of the Paddington Mortuary," he said as they chugged past the modern coronial complex. "They have two children, a boy of four years and a girl of two. They employ a maid, a cook, and a nanny." Outside the van window, neat semidetached homes with well-kept front gardens passed by. "We're almost there, sir."

"How can he afford three staff on his wage?" Pike mused.

"Like Dr. McCleland, Everard's work at the mortuary is part-time. He has rooms close by from which he works as a general practitioner."

"But he must be stretched."

"I wouldn't know about that, sir. But he could not have killed Dunn. I sent some men to his rooms to make some enquiries. On the morning that Dunn was murdered, Everard was delivering a baby. He had been up all night with the mother—it was a difficult birth."

"If his wife and servants verify that he was home on the afternoon of the firebombing, that leaves us with nothing but the letters he still denies sending."

"Are we barking up the wrong tree then, sir?"

"Everard's guilty of something, Fisher. Of that I am sure."

The police van dropped them outside a red door in the middle of a neat row of Queen Anne–style semidetached homes. Harley Street this was not, but the area had a pleasant, middle-class feel that Pike found appealing. An image of Dody came unbidden: opening the door to him, pulling him into the cool of the small hall, and covering him with kisses, children's toys scattered on the stairs behind her. He sighed. Perhaps he was seeking the unobtainable; perhaps he was more like Margaretha than he cared to think. He feared that Dody could no more fit into his world than he could into hers. He shook the thought away as the red door opened for them.

The maid showed them into a cramped parlour and introduced Mrs. Henry Everard. Beside him, Fisher drew breath. Pike hoped he managed to hide his surprise more effectively as Mrs. Everard held out her hand from the confines of a wheeled invalid's chair. No wonder the Everards needed all the domestic help they could get.

Henry Everard entered the room collarless and in his shirtsleeves, stopped abruptly in the doorway, and bristled. "What the hell are you doing here?"

"Henry, please," his wife said.

Everard pushed past the police officers and took his wife's hand. "I'm sorry, my dear," he said, "but I think they have come to bully information out of you." He shot an accusing look at Pike.

"If you mean by enquiring of your wife your whereabouts on the afternoon of the twenty-fifth, you are correct, sir."

"My husband was with me, Chief Inspector."

No surprises there, Pike thought, Everard had probably briefed her already. The servants might tell a different story, though. Paltry wages would surely be a measure of their loyalty when confronted with the weight of the law. "Have a word with the servants, please, Inspector," Pike said.

Fisher gave a start, drawing his mind back from other things. The woman maintained her composure, but must have noticed his eyes scanning her wheelchair. "In case you are wondering, Inspector, I was semiparalysed in a carriage accident about eighteen months ago."

Fisher stuttered some apologies and left the room. Pike admired Mrs. Everard's frankness, as well as the open shine of her green eyes. She was an attractive woman despite being crippled. Her brown hair was unfashionably short—practical and easy to cope with, he supposed. But his sympathy for her did not extend to her husband, who had succeeded in making Dody's life a misery over the last few weeks. He would not allow these kinds of emotions to temper his questioning or distract him from his purpose.

"If your husband was with you on the afternoon of the twenty-fifth, can you tell me who might have borrowed his motorcar?" he asked.

Pike watched the couple carefully; they made no eye contact or gave any other noticeable signals. "I have no idea,"

Mrs. Everard answered. "The motorcar is rarely used; it was a gift to Henry from my father. We find it unreliable and expensive to run—Henry barely knows how to drive it, isn't that right, dear?" Everard dropped his head. "He just likes to polish it."

"I did not lend it to anyone," Everard muttered like a sulky child.

"I would like to look at it then," Pike said.

"Very well." Everard heaved a sigh. "Follow me."

They met up with Fisher in the hall. According to him, the servants had confirmed what their mistress had said, that Everard had been at home on the afternoon of the fire-bombing.

They followed the doctor through the garden to a converted stable backing onto a lane at the rear of the property. As Pike trod the path bordered by urns of vibrant blooms and reclining marble cherubs, he wondered if he might be able to strike some kind of bargain. Everard was hiding something—that much was obvious—but if Mrs. Everard could persuade her husband to tell them all he knew, such as who it was driving his motorcar, his sentence might be reduced.

At the stable Everard drew the heavy bolts and pushed aside the creaking door, revealing a vacant space bordered by a wheelbarrow, a stack of dirty terra-cotta pots, and a pile of empty hessian sacks.

"As you can see," Everard said, poker-faced, "the horse has bolted."

Fisher reddened and took a step towards Everard. "Why didn't you tell us that in the first place? What the hell's happened to the bloody thing?"

Pike straightened from his examination of an oily patch on the ground. "A motorcar was kept here until recently."

"Indeed one was—until it was stolen," Everard said. Fisher flexed his fingers. "As my wife said, it was a gift from her father, one of his last gifts before he died. She was sentimentally attached to the vehicle. I did not want her distressed by its theft and chose to keep the matter from her. I trust you will do the same." He shrugged as if the matter were out of his hands.

Fisher had had enough. He grabbed the man by the front of his waistcoat. "You could have said this earlier when you were first questioned and saved us a good deal of time. You're making this up as you go along, covering for someone else, damn it."

"Let go of him, Fisher," Pike said, understanding fully how his colleague felt.

Fisher released his grip, and Everard made a show of dusting himself down. Pike said, "You are not taking this seriously enough, Dr. Everard." He nodded towards the house. "It seems to me that you have a lot to lose here."

When they returned to Mrs. Everard in the parlour, Pike asked, "Is your wife aware that you might be charged with murder—at the very least, as an accessory? For her sake, you must tell me what I need to know. Tell me about the man you are in league with. Frankly, I do not believe you are responsible for Dunn's murder and the deaths of the two young women, but I think you know who is." He glanced from husband to wife. "And I think that is the same man you lent your motorcar to."

Mrs. Everard held out her hand to her husband. "Henry,

please, whatever you have done, I forgive you for it—just tell the police what you know."

Her cooperation with the police despite her obvious love for her husband reminded Pike of Mrs. Van Noort; he marvelled at how two obviously flawed men could have such intelligent, loyal wives. Perhaps a female influence on parliament would not be such a bad thing after all.

"All right," Everard said through clenched teeth, "I wrote the bloody letters, but that is all I did." Mrs. Everard gasped and brought up a hand to cover her mouth. Her husband would not or could not bring himself to look at her. "Are you satisfied now, Chief Inspector?"

"On whose instructions?" Pike asked.

"My own—and you know why. I resent the woman."

"I think you were told to write the letters by the man who borrowed your car."

Everard turned his back on them.

"Tell us who borrowed your car," Fisher said.

"I've got nothing to tell you," Everard said with a heave of his shoulders.

Pike removed Van Noort's water-stained card from his jacket pocket and tapped Everard on the back with it, obliging him to turn. "Do you know this man?"

The doctor took the card and looked at it, then handed it back, his countenance unchanged. "No. Never heard of him."

"But there is someone whom you are in league with—you admit to that?" Fisher barked.

"I admit to absolutely nothing except the letters."

"Cooperate with us now and you might be able to avoid a lengthy prison sentence," Pike said.

Everard folded his arms and said nothing.

Mrs. Everard dropped her head into her hands and began to weep.

"Look, the poor woman's too upset for us to continue," Pike said under his breath to Fisher. "Let's leave them alone and maybe she'll talk him out of this stubborn mind-set." Louder, he said, "Mrs. Everard, if you or your husband have anything else to divulge, please contact me." He handed her his card. To Everard he said, "A bailiff from the courts will be visiting you shortly to notify you of your appearance before the magistrate to face charges of libel and perverting the course of justice. I suspect a murder charge might also be pending. Good day to you both; we will see ourselves out."

On the front porch Fisher said to Pike, "Well, that was most unpleasant."

"Unpleasant indeed, but worth it; he admitted to the letters."

"But why did he write them?" Fisher asked.

"Because someone pressured him into it, someone who might be using Mrs. Everard's unfortunate situation to his advantage." There were no boundaries to what a man would do for the woman he loved—Fisher would know that.

"Is it worth keeping the men in position?" Fisher nodded to a man up the street, propped against a lamppost with an open newspaper.

"Absolutely. They must follow him when he leaves the house."

"Do you expect him to leave, sir?"

"I have no doubt about it. He is facing the prospect of prison and he will need to make provisions for his wife. His silence must be worth something to someone."

* * *

A short nap had left Dody feeling refreshed and her stomach a little more settled, too. These continuing bouts of English cholera were debilitating, and puzzling—she should surely be immune to it by now. Some dry toast might help. She washed her face in her bathroom and redid her hair. She was losing weight, she noticed, as she tightened her belt another notch. Taking the new bottle of effervescent powder Borislav had made up for her from the medicine cupboard, she added three teaspoons to a glass of water and drank it down. It was a triple dose, but today she needed something stronger than the meat juice she had been relying on to keep herself going.

Annie met her on the stairs. "Chief Inspector Pike is in the morning room, Miss Dody. Are you up to receiving visitors?"

"Yes, thank you, Annie, I'm feeling much better. Please bring us some tea."

In the morning room, Pike rose from his chair. He put his hand out to take hers and held on to it. "You still don't look well. You need to see a doctor."

"I *am* a doctor," Dody scoffed with good humour.

"And I am a policeman. Look at the mischief my daughter got up to last year under my very nose."

"All right, I see your point. Our professions sometimes blind us to things that others can easily see. There's another doctor at the Clinic, Nancy Wainright. I will see her tomorrow—does that satisfy you?"

"Yes," Pike said, unable to keep from touching her arm. "I would hate for you to get worse. I don't think I could bear it."

"I won't get worse, but thank you, Matthew, I know you care and I am glad of it."

He smiled faintly then dropped her hand when Annie entered with the tea tray.

Over tea, Pike told Dody how Henry Everard had admitted writing the letters, and about his dire domestic circumstances.

"No wonder he was so driven," Dody remarked. "His poor wife. I had no idea. I put so much of my energy into disliking him, I didn't give much thought to his personal circumstances. I should have known better."

"You are an astonishing woman, Dody," Pike said, shaking his head. "In your situation I would find it hard to be so understanding."

"It is over, that is enough. And I would prefer to think that no man is entirely bad—or entirely good."

"But it is as if the devil has him round the throat," Pike continued, "and he won't say a word to make things easier for himself. If I'm not careful, he's likely to throw in the towel and confess to everything whether it be true or not."

Annie entered the room once more, this time with a note on a silver salver, which she presented to Pike.

"I told my staff they could find me here—though why they did not telephone, I don't know. I gave them your number." Pike paused to read the note. "Good God," he said, jumping to his feet. "Annie, who delivered this?"

"A messenger boy on a bicycle, sir."

"Is he still there?"

"Long gone, I 'spect."

"Go into the street and get me a cab immediately."

"No, Annie, tell Fletcher to bring the car around," Dody said, anxious at the alarm on Pike's face.

"Fletcher's out, miss; taken Miss Florence shopping," Annie said.

Pike handed Dody the note and rushed from the room. Dody followed him into the street. He turned as if to tell her to stay, then stopped himself with an exasperated sigh, knowing full well that he could not say or do anything that would stop her. While they waited, Dody read the note. If they wanted to catch their abortionist, the anonymous correspondent wrote, they would find him operating at this very moment in rooms above the fishmonger's in Whitechapel Road. They must hurry before it was too late.

"Fishmonger's," Dody said aloud as they hurried to the main road, where the chances of flagging down a cab would be greater. "I found a fish scale in Elizabeth Strickland's clothing. We thought it must have come from a fish in the river."

"The river is too filthy for fish. I don't know when one was last caught in the Temple Quay stretch of the Thames," Pike said.

Dody pressed her palm to her forehead, "Of course, how stupid I—" Her stomach contracted painfully and she gasped, doubling over.

Pike took her arm. "Dody, what is it? Are you all right?"

She straightened herself and smiled to put his mind at rest. "I am quite all right. I'm just annoyed with myself."

He looked at her doubtfully, but said only, "Even if you had known that, I doubt it would have led us to this particular fishmonger's."

Fortunately a motor taxi was the first vehicle to stop. Pike flashed his warrant card at the driver and told him to make haste.

"How long does such a procedure take?" Pike asked as they settled onto the vehicle's dimpled backseat. Dody linked her arm through his and held on to him tightly. Her stomach was feeling most peculiar and the movement of the taxi threatened to unsettle it further. "Twenty minutes to an hour, depending on how developed the foetus is. God, I hope we're not too late."

"But he does not deliberately kill them, does he, Dody?"

"He would not be much of an abortionist if he did. I'm presuming Esther's and Elizabeth's deaths were accidental—but who can tell?"

"Then I'm staking my hopes that she is alive and that he is still on the premises, cleaning up."

Fifteen minutes later they were hurtling past the blur of colours in the front window of Mr. Borislav's chemist shop and lurching to a halt outside the fishmonger's. The shop door was locked and hung with a CLOSED sign, and the marble slab in the front window was bare of fish.

"This shouldn't be closed now," Dody said, cupping her eyes against the glare and peering into the darkened interior. "Or is it because a procedure is being performed?" She caught a flicker of movement behind her and turned to see a figure scampering towards the back of the shop. "John Kent, is that you?" she called.

Pike looked perplexed. Dody did not have time to explain how she knew the boy.

John whirled around. "'E's been too long up there, too long!" he shrieked, a red spot emblazoned on each pale cheek. "I gotta get in."

"What's going on here, Jack?" Pike asked.

"The doc went upstairs to 'elp, wouldn't let me come. But 'e's been too long and somefing bad's 'appened—I know it."

"Get in the taxi and wait for us there," Pike ordered.

"But I got to 'elp!"

The boy was almost hysterical. Pike gave him a sharp slap to the face and told the taxi driver to hold him. Within seconds John was gripped by a pair of thickset arms and shoved onto the backseat of the cab. "Lock him in if you have to," Pike said, "and wait here."

Dody followed him to the back of the building, where the stink of rotting fish met them at the open back door.

Chapter Thirty-Two

Pike flung open a dented wooden door on the third floor of the upstairs landing. "Good God!" he exclaimed, feeling the colour drain from his face.

Van Noort looked up from a welter of gore. Blood seeped into the mattress, the source a pale female figure, partly clothed, stretched out and still across the bed.

"She was like this when I got here, I swear it; I was trying to revive her, trying to stem the bleeding," Van Noort stuttered. "She had a faint pulse when I arrived, but now . . ." Van Noort stopped when he realised who he was talking to. "Captain? What are you doing here? I don't understand."

"Police. Move away from that bed."

Dody kneeled down beside the filthy bed and felt for the girl's pulse then pushed aside the girl's clothing to examine the body.

"The girl might be all right," she said. "The uterus has been packed, much of the blood flow is stemmed," she said.

"Archibald Van Noort," Pike said, "I am arresting you for suspected criminal abortion."

Van Noort's voice rose. "Jack brought me a note—that I would find an injured girl here, and if I moved quickly enough, I could save her life." Van Noort gulped a breath.

Dody rearranged the girl's clothing to cover her body. "We need an ambulance. Now."

Pike caught the tremor in her voice. About to dash down the stairs to have the taxi driver fetch an ambulance, he turned to see Dody sway and turn the colour of the girl on the bed.

"Dody!" Pike caught her just before she collapsed to the ground.

"Sorry, Matthew," she said weakly. "Can't get up. My stomach—"

Pike was no newcomer to the paralysing grip of fear, but nothing in his experience had prepared him for this. The sight of Dody collapsed upon the floor, retching, her hands and clothing bloodied by her examination of the girl, was more than he could bear. What was wrong with her? Surely she had seen worse than this in the autopsy room?

Van Noort's eyes vacillated from the stairs to Dody, from possible freedom to probable imprisonment.

"Damn it, man," Pike cried. "Prove to me that you did not hurt that woman on the bed—stay here and help me with this one!" It was a calculated risk, but he was almost sure that Van Noort was not responsible for this abortion. The notes they had both received, the timing—someone wanted him blamed for the girl's condition.

Dody was lying on her side with her knees drawn up to her abdomen, the remnants of her afternoon tea in a pool by her head.

Van Noort hesitated for only a moment. "First we have to move her away from this mess."

Between them they dragged Dody to a cleaner patch of floor. Van Noort took a pillow from the bed and placed it gently under her head. He urged her to straighten her legs and asked her what she had eaten.

"The dog," she muttered, "the dog . . ."

"What is she talking about?" Van Noort asked while he gently palpated Dody's abdomen. "Surely she has not been eating dog?"

Pike tossed his bowler onto the floor and clawed his fingers through his hair. Then he remembered. "She mentioned a dead dog at the mortuary." Why hadn't he paid more attention? How was that tied in with this?

"We have to work out what she has eaten." Van Noort examined Dody's lower eyelids and peered into her mouth. "The mucosa has no colour at all. That makes me think she has been poisoned."

"Then we must get her to a hospital," Pike said.

"There may not be time. I want to make her expel as much poison as I can before any more is absorbed into her system." Van Noort turned Dody's head to the side and rammed his finger down her throat.

Pike closed his eyes but could not block out the sound of Dody's agonised retching. Then it was over and Van Noort was gently wiping her face with a handkerchief. Dody was trying to talk. Pike dropped to his knees by her side and bent his ear to her lips.

"The marzipans sent to me at the mortuary." She struggled. "Must have been poisoned. The dog ate them from the rubbish. Died."

Pike stroked Dody's clammy forehead. God, he had not seen a woman this ill since Bloemfontein. He closed his eyes against the memory and fought the panic as it rose in his throat.

"Did you eat any of the sweets?" Van Noort asked her.

"Just one. Threw the rest away."

"But you were ill?"

Dody groaned.

"I suspect she has been taking the poison in other forms, too," Van Noort said. "This is an acute attack. Take heart, Captain. In some ways acute is easier to treat than chronic."

"I took some medicine before we left home . . . an extra dose . . . felt so dreadful . . ." Her voice faded to a whisper. Pike could barely hear her. She doubled up again and cried out in pain.

"It's all right, my love, I am here." Pike stroked the hair from her face. "Please tell me it is not strychnine—dear God, tell me that it is not," he demanded of Van Noort in a harsh whisper.

"She'd be dead by now if it were strychnine. Strychnine is too obvious; that would be the choice of a desperate man. Arsenic poisoning is more subtle and easily mistaken for common infections of the gastrointestinal tract."

In his head Pike told God he would do anything, anything in his power, to save this woman. What a priggish fool he had been not to take her love when it was offered. "Tell me what to do," he said.

"If it is arsenic, there is an antidote. Pull yourself together, man—there is hope." He reached into the pocket of his frock coat then wrote something down on a piece of notepaper he found there. The hand that held the note began to shake.

"Watch . . . watch out for the chemist . . ." Van Noort broke off and his eyes glazed.

Good God, Pike thought, *he can't be having a fit now.* He grabbed the doctor by the shoulders and gave him a hard shake. "The chemist, what about the chemist?"

Van Noort passed a hand across his brow and became lucid again. "The chemist will know what all this means. Make sure the quantities are exactly as written—too much is as bad as too little. Now hurry, we have no time to spare. I'll see if I can get her to expel more of the poison."

"How can I trust you not to take off?"

Van Noort shrugged. "You can't. Go."

Pike had no choice. His crippled knee was forgotten; he could not remember when he had last run with such speed. He was at the pharmacy in moments, slamming his fist upon the counter bell.

The white-coated chemist appeared from the back room. "All right, all right, I'm coming, where's the fire?"

"Police." Pike's breath left him in rasping gasps. "Urgent. I need you to make this up now." He slid Van Noort's note across the counter.

"Arsenic antidote, eh? What symptoms is she showing?" the chemist asked, noticeably paler than he had been.

Pike grabbed at his hair, tried to clear his muddled thoughts. "Um, stomach pain, vomiting . . ." Then his mind fired to life. He had not mentioned the sex of the victim—how did this man know it was a she? He said no more and forced his head to clear itself of panic. What had Van Noort been trying to tell him about the chemist?

Pike followed the chemist into the dispensing room, on his guard now. "Show me the ingredients before you mix them up," he said.

The man waved him away, flustered. He took hold of a ceramic jug and poured the contents into a bottle. "Water," he said.

"I can see that. Get on with it."

The chemist collected an armful of bottles but, shaky with haste, dropped several of them as he lowered them to the counter. With cold realisation, Pike knew why.

He grabbed the chemist by the lapels. "God help me, it's you!"

The man's arm shot up with the bottle he was holding and Pike felt a shattering blow to the back of his head; he dropped to the floor amidst a spray of glass. Then he heard a grunt of pain, not his own, and felt a sudden, suffocating weight as the breath was knocked out of him. It took a moment for Pike to realise his assailant had been undone. He edged himself out from beneath the chemist's body, spat blood, and squinted up at his rescuer.

Jack stared down at Pike, grinning from ear to ear. "Doc said you might need an 'and," he said, and dropped a pestle the size of a police truncheon to the floor. He helped Pike to his feet. Together they ripped the braces from the chemist's trousers and trussed him like a sheep, and then began a desperate search amongst the debris for Van Noort's list.

It was not to be found. Pike desperately tried to remember the listed ingredients. "Magnesium, ferrous . . . ferrous what?" He threw up his arms. "For God's sake, help me, Jack."

"This it?" Jack pointed to one of the bottles the chemist had previously set out on the bench.

"Good lad. We'll take them all for good measure. The doctor will have to concoct the antidote for himself." As Jack placed the bottles in a metal pail he found under the sink, Pike inspected the label of the bottle the chemist had hit him with. The glue on its back was still attached to shards of broken glass, but the label was legible. He searched the shelves and found another bottle of magnesia. Then he picked up the jug of water.

The chemist began to moan—he was waking up.

Pike thrust the jug to Jack for him to carry. At the dispensary door they almost collided with another man in a white coat.

"Help me, Joseph!" the chemist called out from his position on the floor. "We are being robbed!"

Pike lowered the pail of bottles and braced himself for a fight. He need not have worried.

"In here, Inspector," the younger white-coated man called dispiritedly over his shoulder.

Fisher entered the dispensary with two constables, one of them gripping Henry Everard by his jacket collar. Pike had never been so glad to see his inspector.

"Mr. Vladimir Borislav is our man, Chief Inspector." Fisher paused, looking around him at the damage. "But I see you have met."

"What brought you here?" Pike asked.

"Mr. Everard here led us to him," Fisher said proudly. "Turns out he's been blackmailing Mr. Borislav all along. This time he was intending to threaten Mr. Borislav with exposure unless he agreed to support Mrs. Everard financially while he was in prison. We were closing in when we met up with Mr. Champion outside the shop."

Champion addressed his uncle. "I did not want to believe what they said. The abortions, the drugs—what would Aunt Gertrude think?"

Borislav turned quite puce and struggled against his bonds. "She'd be alive now if it wasn't for a butchering doctor. And how many even poorer women are abandoned by this so-called *profession*? We were happy—we had everything." Tears streamed down his face. "When the baby . . . the doctor . . . Incompetent, bloody drunk . . . couldn't even *get here on time*." He put his head up; pride and fear were at war in his eyes. "I may have made mistakes, but I was at least trying to make these women's lives easier." His tears redoubled. "I did not want them to die. That man"—he pointed waveringly at Everard—"knew *everything*. He calls himself a doctor, he's too high and mighty to help women in trouble, but he blackmailed—"

Before Borislav could say more, Everard broke free of the constable, rushed over, and gave him a hefty kick. The constable pulled Everard away.

"You told those women you could help them and they died," Joseph moaned.

"My success rate speaks for itself," the winded Borislav gasped. "I provided a service those women needed."

Pike could not afford to stop and hear what more there was to be said. He wanted answers, but they would have to wait. He moved over to Champion and showed him the pail of bottles. "Are these the correct ingredients for an arsenic antidote?"

Champion examined each bottle and took out two he said were unnecessary. "Magnesia, liquor ferri-persulphatus, and water—correct now."

Borislav groaned. "Dorothy was not supposed to . . .

Please, Joseph, give them a sedative for her, too. She should sleep while the antidote does its work."

Pike felt something warm running down his cheeks. He swiped it off with his hand and realised it was blood—cuts from the broken glass.

"Are you all right, sir?"

"I'm fine," he said to Fisher, "but Dr. McCleland is not. Send one of your men for a van and stand guard over these two. Jack, follow me to the fishmonger's."

Cool fingers on her neck brought Dody back to her senses. "Matthew?"

"He's on his way, Dr. McCleland," Van Noort said, "with the arsenic antidote."

"And the girl on the bed?" she asked.

"Her pulse is getting stronger by the minute."

Dody shivered violently. The disfigured face above her began to swim. Another spasm gripped her stomach. She cried out. If this was death, pray God for its sweet release.

Van Noort stroked her head. "Hush now. Listen. Help is at hand and I must leave you now. Good-bye and good luck, my dear." Van Noort moved towards the window.

Thumping feet; Pike's voice. "Stay where you are, for God's sake, Van Noort." In her weakened state on the floor, Dody could not see what was happening. She sensed a desperate urgency in Pike's voice, but was beyond caring. "Jack, stay with him," Pike instructed. "Sit on him if you have to."

Pike's hand gripped hers and pressed it to his trembling lips. "It's all right, Dody, the good doctor is going nowhere."

She heard the murmur of Pike's voice as he spoke with

Van Noort, the clunking of glass, and the pouring of liquid, and then her head and shoulders were cradled in Pike's arms. "Drink this, my love, and try to keep it down," Pike said.

The antidote tasted foul and she struggled to suppress her gag reflex.

"I've put the sedative in the mixture. She should sleep through the worst of it," Van Noort said.

Pike gently lowered her head to the floor. The sounds in the room were distant, as if she were listening through water. The original taxi had long gone. John/Jack was sent to fetch another while Van Noort and Pike talked in subdued voices. They spoke of war, of constant fear, of revulsion for their own kind. The choke in their voices broke through the roar of the sea in her head.

And then there was a shout from Pike, and the shatter of breaking glass followed by a long and terrible silence.

Chapter Thirty-Three

Pike's eyes had always mesmerised Dody; now it was his lips she could not tear her gaze from. Not too thin and not too fat, well-defined, beautiful, kissable lips. His face began to waver. She lost focus and forced herself back with a jolt. "What was that about the fishmonger's woman?"

Pike leaned across the bed and gently kissed her. "Too much talking—you can hardly keep your eyes open. Sleep now."

"No, Matthew, please don't go yet." She seized his hand as he made to move. "I need to know everything. Don't try to spare me. Anyway, I remember now. You said the woman at the fishmonger's knew Borislav was doing abortions in her upstairs room, but was paid to turn a blind eye, or so she told you, but you suspect she was more involved. She's in custody now and you hope to prove her active involvement. You see, I was listening. But I need to know more. I need to understand how Everard fitted into things."

Pike smiled. "Very well, if you're sure you're all right."

"Go on."

"When Everard was in his fourth year at university, he was keeping company with a chorus girl. He got the girl pregnant and performed a successful abortion on her, which he boasted about to his friend Joseph Champion."

"And Champion in turn told Borislav?"

"Indeed. Family circumstances meant that Champion was forced to withdraw from university and go to work with his uncle, Borislav. Borislav's business was in bad shape, his wife had just died—were you aware of the details?"

Dody shook her head. "He never spoke about it."

"She was some years younger than he was and pregnant with their first child. There were complications during the birth and the doctor arrived late, obviously intoxicated. Mistakes were made; the woman and child were lost. Borislav's resentment of the medical profession increased; more so when his nephew was forced to withdraw from university. He gave up teaching medical students and decided to provide what he saw as vital services the medical profession wouldn't touch. He began by supplying illegal drugs—opiates and poisons. He also tried to convince his East End customers to use contraception, and when that didn't work, he graduated eventually to criminal abortions."

"Which is where Everard came in?"

Pike nodded. "Borislav asked, hypothetically, how such surgery might be performed. Everard had already made contact with him regarding the drug business, finding out all about it from one of his private practice patients, a society matron who asked him for morphine. She had been a Borislav customer, but he had cut her off for nonpayment. The society matron led Everard to Dunn, whom she had met through Borislav, and Everard jumped at the opportunity to be a part of this undoubtedly prosperous venture."

Dody shook her head in dismay. A doctor and a respected chemist, manipulating vulnerable people for profit. She could hardly credit it. "So they were in business *together*? Borislav had so little respect for Everard."

"It's pretty clear the good doctor left Borislav little choice but to cut him in—Everard could easily have turned the whole network over to the police. Borislav decided to pay him off and hoped he'd be satisfied with that. But Everard was not satisfied; he wanted more. When Esther's body was discovered, he realised Borislav was behind it and used her death to simultaneously endanger you and blackmail Borislav. Borislav, to his credit, did try to get you out of the firing line and turn suspicion on Van Noort, though he was also happy to make you very ill rather than risk your continued investigations into the dented pills."

"I thought my symptoms were the return of the cholera."

"As he hoped you would. He kept your symptoms just uncomfortable enough to impede your work—the marzipans, the meat juice. He did not imagine you would drink so much more of the effervescent mixture than prescribed."

Other than Poppa and now Pike, Borislav was one of the few men Dody had felt totally at ease with; he was her friend, or so she had thought. An educated woman like herself should have seen through him, seen the greed and anger beneath. Strange; throughout history, it seemed, women *and* men had been blinded by their own needs and duped by the opposite sex. No amount of equality could rectify that.

She bit her lip. Pike squeezed her hand as if he knew what she was thinking, as if to show that she could trust him.

Dody fought back tears. "Go on," she urged him. "Borislav ran a gang? We were right about that?"

"We were. He ran a network of roughs, many of them morphinomaniacs, like Dunn, who, as well as the cheaper remedies favoured in Whitechapel, sold stolen drugs to a wealthy clientele in the West End. Nothing like a syringe of morphine to liven up a ladies' tea party. Borislav and Everard staged the robbery at his own pharmacy to justify the missing drugs to Joseph."

That explained the lack of defensive injuries on Borislav's arms, Dody thought. She said, "I suppose the tighter pharmacy laws are better than the old days, when people got opiates as easily as ale. Now at least they have to get them through prescriptions. Though it has, it seems, created an underground market. Something new for criminals to do! Is that why Everard's bag was stolen?"

"That was largely a clever ruse to hide the true intention of the visit, which was to steal the Book of Lists. It's vanished by the way; probably at the bottom of the Thames by now. And Borislav did have a suspicious mark against his name, from a couple of years ago. Everard had seen it and organised the theft before you got the chance to look. Dunn was something of a double agent; he worked for Borislav—and was terrified of him—but he had been recruited by Everard as a source of information initially and then later to help bring you down. An addict belongs to anyone who'll provide him with a dose."

"Has Borislav said any more?"

"Not much more than what he told me originally in the back room of the chemist shop. He's hardly said a word—though he seems genuinely remorseful on your account. Most of what I learned is from Everard and the thugs he was able to name."

"Borislav didn't . . ." Dody almost choked on the words. "He didn't deliberately kill Esther to stop me talking to her again, did he?" When Pike failed to answer, she forced some strength into her voice. "Answer me, Matthew; I'm not a child."

Pike got up from the bed and began to pace the small room.

"Please tell me," she urged. "I asked you not to spare me."

Pike sat back down and said gently, "We can only speculate that Esther's death was deliberate. There was no reason for him to murder Elizabeth Strickland, however, and her death most probably was accidental. He knew we were getting close and I suppose he lost his nerve."

"Can you prove that Borislav murdered Dunn?"

"It's common knowledge amongst his gang that Dunn was murdered to stop him talking. Borislav's lost control now and his thugs are willing to speak against him. He will hang on their testimony alone, I'm sure of it."

Dody suppressed a shiver. "But Everard murdered no one."

"He tried, may I point out, to murder you. Had you been convicted—and he genuinely thought you might be—you might have hanged. He still faces a prison sentence, but it will, I'm sad to say, be considerably reduced in the light of his cooperation. He will probably also gain the court's favour by claiming he picked Dunn up in his car to save him from Borislav's clutches—when, in fact, he was using Dunn to get to both you *and* Borislav." Pike shrugged.

"His poor wife . . . is there anything you can do for her?"

Pike sighed. "Dody, I am police, not Salvation Army. She has supportive relatives. They will see to it that she does not starve."

There was something else she needed to ask, but her eyelids were getting heavy and she was having trouble holding on to the threads of her thoughts. If she rested her eyes for just a minute, perhaps she could gather the tangles up again. "Van Noort . . ." she began.

"Hush now," Pike said and placed his finger across her lips. "Sleep."

And for once she obeyed his wishes without further question.

She was sleeping peacefully when Pike kissed her forehead, murmuring that he would soon return. Footsteps in the corridor caused him to straighten and retreat into the shadows of the room. A couple of late middle age, whom he recognised from photographs in the townhouse as Dody's parents, hurried over to the bed with Florence in tow. They were too distracted to notice Pike inching towards the door; he had no wish to eavesdrop on an intimate family gathering.

Mr. McCleland went straight to Dody's side.

"Hush, don't wake her, Nial," his wife admonished.

"She's so pale," he said as he bent over his daughter, his face almost hidden behind his shaggy beard.

"Don't worry, Poppa," Florence whispered. "The doctors are expecting a full recovery. She should be home within a few days." And then she spied Pike. "Ah, Pike, stay where you are. I'd like you to meet our parents."

"Not here, dear, we might wake Dody. Let's step outside

for a moment," Louise McCleland whispered. Her hair was grey under her wide-brimmed hat, and she met Pike's gaze with eyes the same violet hue as her younger daughter's. But her mannerisms were all Dody, from the tilt of her mouth to her sensible, calming countenance.

They all stepped into the corridor, where Florence introduced them. "If not for Chief Inspector Pike, Dody might not be alive now," Florence said.

Pike took Florence's lead. He kept his manner stiff and formal. "I am more inclined, miss, to give the credit to the late Dr. Van Noort," he said.

"The poor fellow who jumped to his death?" Mr. McCleland enquired.

Pike closed his eyes briefly. "The same, sir," he said.

"He was of unsound mind, Poppa," Florence said.

"But that does not make it any easier or right, does it, Chief Inspector?" Mrs. McCleland responded.

"No, indeed, ma'am, it does not. I was hoping he could have been helped. His only crime, after all, was practising medicine without a licence."

"Such a shame. Thank you, Chief Inspector, for all you have done." Mrs. McCleland put her hand out to him.

"Indeed. Please don't feel you have to stay, we don't wish to hold you up," her husband added. There was no hostility in his voice, but it was obvious that Mr. McCleland was keen to have his family to himself, and Pike could not blame him for that.

He bowed and bade them good day.

He was about to step out into the street when he heard hasty footsteps from behind. "Pike, wait," Florence said, reaching for his arm. "I've said nothing to Mother and Poppa, but I can hardly bear the thought that so much of this is my fault."

Pike had never seen Florence look quite so miserable. He took her by the arm and guided her to a wooden bench against the wall near the admissions counter.

"It's my fault," she said again, twisting her gloves in her hands. "It was my stupid idea to try and discover who had manufactured the tablets, and it was my actions that alerted Mr. Borislav and spurred him into laying the trap. I thought he would not know who I was."

"Don't blame yourself, Florence," Pike said. "Many things have happened to get us to this point and yours was just a small part of it." He could only hope that she had learned from her mistakes and would not take police matters into her own hands again.

"And Dr. Van Noort—I feel responsible for his death, too," she said.

Pike rubbed his hand over his eyes and down his face. His skin still stung from the myriad tiny glass cuts. "The man had attempted suicide before," he said tiredly. "If not now, he would have succeeded further down the track."

Pike found himself unable to control the sudden shudder that wracked his body.

"Pike, are you all right?"

"I almost talked him out of it, you know. He was on the ledge about to jump when I returned to the room with Jack. I persuaded him to climb down. We gave Dody the antidote and I sent Jack to find a taxi. During that time we spoke about the war; I think it helped him to talk. And then suddenly, there he was, rushing for the window again before I could stop him. I only hope Dody was unaware of it. She'd drunk as much of the antidote as she could take and was, I think, unconscious by that time."

Florence squeezed his arm. "You are a good friend, Pike, not only to poor Dr. Van Noort and to Dody, but to me, too."

Tuesday 5 September

It was a still, overcast day and fitting for a funeral. Dody, who had only been out of hospital for a day, held on to Florence's arm and looked across the grave to Mrs. Van Noort. The widow exhibited a combination of grief and relief, as a person helplessly watching a loved one slowly dying of an incurable disease might at the close. Mrs. Van Noort held baby Molly tightly as the vicar said his final words. John—or Jack, as Dody knew him now—stood pressed against her side, twisting his fingers through the folds of her black coat.

A police van pulled up outside the cemetery gate and out stepped Pike, hurrying over as fast as his limp would allow. He joined the small gathering just as the coffin was being lowered.

"Are you all right?" he whispered to Dody.

She nodded, wondering how he was faring. It couldn't have been easy watching Archibald Van Noort dive from the third-floor window to his death. As she'd faded in and out of consciousness, she'd caught more of the men's conversation than she would ever let Pike know.

The men had exchanged the most private of memories; memories even Mrs. Van Noort, she suspected, had not been privy to. Listening to them talk, Dody was no longer lying wracked with pain in a bloody room above the fishmonger's, but transported to the war-torn conditions of the veldt, conditions which the newspapers at home had grossly underreported. Though she now knew something of Pike's experience in that hospital tent, she hoped that one day he would be able to tell her the full story himself.

When the service was over and the minister had left, Mrs. Van Noort spoke to the small assembly. "Thank you all for coming. The vicar knew Archie well, knew that he was of unsound mind and how much he battled the Beast, and that was why he permitted him to be buried in consecrated ground."

No one knew how to reply. Dody dropped her head. All was silent save for the thump of earth on wood as the gravediggers went about their business.

Pike held Mrs. Van Noort's arm and escorted her towards the church hall, where they took tea. Jack grabbed a sticky bun in each hand and ran back to the graveyard to play.

"Go quietly now, Jack," Mrs. Van Noort admonished. "Show some respect. He means well," she said apologetically to Pike and Dody, "but how can he know what he has never been taught?"

Outside the open church door Jack handed a smaller boy, who had appeared from nowhere, one of the buns. A pal from the street, Dody supposed. She heard Jack shout, "I'll be the German spy and you have to hunt me down!" The resilience of children.

"How are you getting on with the paperwork, ma'am?" Pike asked Mrs. Van Noort.

"Very well. It looks like there will be no obstacles to me adopting all the younger Kent children, including the toddler still with her mother. The two eldest children wish to remain in Whitechapel. One has obtained a job as a carpenter's apprentice and things are at last looking up for the family. I can only thank you, Chief Inspector, for all your assistance in the matter."

"Mrs. Kent was delighted when I told her that the legal process was under way for the adoptions—and the cash payment of course," Pike said to Dody.

"Then seeing as you're getting on with Mrs. Kent so well, Chief Inspector, you'd better send her to one of my classes at the Clinic so she can learn how not to have any more children," Dody said.

"I can see you're better," Florence said with a frown.

"Much better, thank you."

Florence urged Dody away from the group. "Did you finally bring yourself to read that note from Henry Everard?"

Dody smiled. "No need to look so worried—it wasn't a poison pen letter."

"Well, that's a relief. I think you've had enough poison, don't you? I was of two minds as to whether to give it to you or not."

"I'm glad you did. Strangely enough, it was an apology of sorts. When he finishes his sentence, he plans on moving his family to Australia."

"Good riddance. Did he admit to his plagiarism?"

"No, he didn't mention it. I imagine he thought it was of little consequence compared with what followed—and in that he'd be correct, I suppose."

"Wretched fool of a man," Florence said, loud enough to attract the attention of Pike, who was still talking to Mrs. Van Noort. "Will you be all right on your own tonight?" Florence asked. "I have a meeting to attend."

Dody caught Pike's eye without meaning to, and self-consciously drew her gaze away from his. "Of course, Florence," she said. "I am not an invalid."

Dody heard the ring of the doorbell, the murmur of voices, and the familiar footsteps in the hall, and she realised then that she had been waiting for Pike since her return from the funeral. Annie showed the man she loved into the morning room.

Dody told Annie she could go to bed and felt suddenly nervous. She poured them both a sherry and downed hers in one swallow. Pike took hold of her hand as she reached again for the decanter, and shook his head.

"You don't need that," he said softly, and led her up the stairs to her bedroom.

Epilogue

Dody directed Annie and Fletcher as they turned the dining room into an operating theatre, her textbook on performing operations in the civilian home open in her hands. Carpets were rolled and removed along with framed pictures and upholstered chairs. Annie and Fletcher brushed the ceiling and walls down with a towel saturated in bichloride and then draped white sheets over the pieces of dining room furniture too heavy to be moved. The mahogany table was left in the centre of the room, sheeted and topped with a thin, rubber-clad mattress Dody had borrowed from the Clinic.

She scrubbed her hands and nails over a porcelain bowl of water sitting on their sheeted sideboard. Much had changed since the first operation she had witnessed as a medical student, before antiseptic notions had been replaced by aseptic techniques. It was now not only a question of getting rid of any germs present; the aim of asepsis was to start off with fewer germs in the first place. Thus the sheets had been boiled, the instruments had been boiled, and Dody wore a sterilised gown over her apron.

Pike had agreed to the operation only on the condition that it not be performed in a hospital and that Dody would see to the procedure. It had taken all her powers of persuasion to convince him how unethical that would be now they were lovers.

Lovers.

The memory of their first and only lovemaking still left her with a honey-warm glow and a deep desire for more. But it was a desire that strengthened her rather than weakened her with pointless worry about the future. How they could carry off further trysts, she had no idea; all that mattered was the present and the love she had found in it. They would sort something out—they had to.

It had taken almost as much effort to persuade Pike to have the operation as it had Barker to perform it. At first the surgeon had refused—for reasons of professional pride, he announced. Whether by that he referred to the insult of Pike's flight from the hospital or to distance himself from the scandal of Dody's accusation of criminal abortion, she had no idea. Dody had cajoled and flattered, finally winning him over by saying what an interesting episode this procedure would make for his memoirs, given that home operations would surely soon be a thing of the past.

Nurse Daphne Hamilton helped Barker into his sterile gown, but the surgeon turned down her offer of rubber gloves. "Never used 'em before and don't intend using 'em now," he said curtly as he scrubbed his hands with carbolic soap.

Dody arranged the anaesthetic equipment on a card table that had been brought in from the drawing room. Bottles clinked as she removed their glass stoppers and prepared a mixture of ether alcohol, plain ether, and chloroform, then took the anaesthetic mask from its small wooden case. Now all they needed was their patient.

On cue, Florence tapped on the door and entered with Pike. They stood at the door without moving for a moment and stared open-mouthed at the shrouded dining room.

Florence gave Pike a nudge. "There you go, Pike, up you get," she said with the enthusiasm of a jolly-hockey-sticks games mistress.

Pike looked anything but jolly as he shuffled over to the table, wearing a dressing gown over a striped nightshirt, and nodded to Barker. Florence relieved Pike of the gown, helped him onto the table, and then hurried from the room.

Daphne straightened the pillow under the patient's head and moved to the carbolic spray machine positioned on a planter near the window. The steam-powered contraption chugged into action and soon the room's occupants were covered in a fine mist of antiseptic spray.

"Are you ready, Chief Inspector?" Dody asked, mindful of what had happened the last time someone had attempted to operate on Pike's knee. Fortunately, she could see no sign of a pistol tucked in the folds of his nightshirt.

Pike nodded, his body shivering uncontrollably despite her earlier administration of calming bromide. Dody's hand lingered on his forehead as she remembered the stories she had heard above the fishmonger's. Well, why wouldn't he be anxious after what he had seen in that hospital tent? Van Noort had told him that if he had attended, he would not have amputated, but left his knee in a much better state than it was now. He had strongly advised Pike to have the operation that Barker was about to perform.

Dody smoothed away Pike's hair and lowered the mask.

If only Van Noort's own problems had been this easy to treat.

Author's Note

The inspiration behind this work of fiction was my examination of Dr. Bernard Spilsbury's handwritten autopsy notes at the Wellcome Library, London. The poignancy of each death recorded solely on a single, yellowing palm card struck me deeply, with many attributed to causes rarely seen today, especially death by criminal abortion.

My Bernard Spilsbury was fictionalised, though his personality was gleaned from several biographies. I experienced his chain smoking for myself when I examined his palm cards. After all these years, they still reeked of cigarette smoke.

I have been unable to find evidence of a female autopsy surgeon as early as 1910, but Bernard Spilsbury did have a female assistant, Hilda Bainbridge, by 1920. I hope the reader can forgive this ten-year discrepancy.

Dody McCleland's background is that of my grandmother, at the time one of only a handful of female graduates of Trinity College, Dublin. Much of the Fabian colour was inspired by her memoirs.